Book Design

# LOVESICK LITTLE

Based on Hans Christian Andersen's

*The Little Mermaid* (1837)

## LESLIE PHELAN

*verba volant* / *scripta manent*

VV - SM / PUBLISHING

TORONTO

cover art: Jocelyn Teng, WALL9 - *watercolor*

Copyright © 2014 by:

VV- SM PUBLISHING


Published by:

VV- SM PUBLISHING

TORONTO, ONTARIO, CANADA

www.vv-sm.com


*For additional information write to:*

**info@vv-sm.com**


FIRST EDITION published 2012

ISBN: 978-0988059245


Printed in Canada

*For Erica*

*my little siren sister,*

*the only other mermaid in my bathtub.*

# Lovesick Little

F ar out at sea, in the heart of the vast aqueous expanse that lends its blue to the lush, living planet, water is as clear as pristine crystal and deeper than most minds can fathom. Out past the breakers where the shallows drop off and chasms, massive and immeasurable, spread far and wide and deep, the most extraordinary creatures exist in a realm of saline brilliance.

Down in the deep, there is no wind or snow or rain, just a wash of perfect topaz that glimmers upon all it holds. Here make the homes of fish of every size and design, that dart between leaves and petals just like birds do in the sky. From the bottom, long vines reach upward to bow with undulation, and dance with the stirring of the tide.

The ocean is a gift; there is life-giving magic in every drop, and when the tides turn, the will of quintillions of tons shift our planet. But although the ocean is the very womb of all life for all earthlings, we as humans know more about stars in distant galaxies than we do about its deepest depths. Where the waters are most staggeringly abysmal, we've no means to tread. And so it comes as no surprise that very little is known of the Sea King and his subjects.

# one

Blue Kingdom

Once upon a time at the bottom of the Atlantic, there was a king who ruled over all the waters. He lived with his family in a grand sunken city that was gifted to him by the people of a civilization long past. He covered its ceilings with shiny shells and its walls with pinkest corals and in it, far beneath the surface, he kept his family safe.

The kindly merman had six lovely daughters, and they were the pride and joy of the kingdom. His beloved queen had died many years earlier, leaving him to raise the girls with the help of his aged mother, a wise and vibrant lady who loved her granddaughters above all things. Sometimes, she would tell them exciting stories about the world above and of the people who dwell upon it, and the animals they sometimes ride upon and the way they try to swim with their arms and two funny pillars. All of the princesses loved their grandmother's tales, but none so much as the youngest.

The youngest daughter was special, and was adored most by all who knew her. All six sisters had pretty manes of flaxen blond but the youngest had hair that grew so long and so soft, it was like a silk veil that danced alongside her slender body as she swam. All of the sisters sang like angels, but the youngest possessed a voice so ethereal that it charmed every ear it fell upon. Each princess was celebrated for her stunning beauty, but the youngest was so fair, so graceful and so lovely, she represented the very paradigm of beauty in their world. Her eyes were a shade of piercing indigo to match her powerful tail, a color valued more by her people than any other hue in creation. Yes, the littlest had everything a young mermaid could want or need, and her future was a thing that gleamed. But she lived her life with a yearning; for what, she could not say.

As the eldest of the sisters approached her fifteenth year, the entire kingdom buzzed with anticipation to learn what news the bright and sensitive princess would bring back with her on her birthday. You see, when a princess of the seas turns fifteen, she is allowed to make her very first trip to the upper limit of her dominion to observe the world of the humans for the first time. In the kingdom of the fish-people, only members of the royal family may visit the surface, for with great privilege comes great responsibility, and diligent care must be taken by anyone who would venture so far up. It is a most important law under the sea that all must endeavor never to be seen, for any reason, or under any circumstance. It had been a long time since anyone had gone to the top and as legend went, a pleasant trip and a positive report would mean a strong and prosperous life under the sea for many years to come, safe from the reaches of the human race.

The royal daughters spent their days singing and reveling while joyfully tending to their flowerbeds. They lived very comfortable, very sheltered lives in the palace, and so rarely had reasons to venture very far since anything in any ocean, river, or sea could be sent for. Their existences were very leisurely, and their very favorite pastime was to beautify the palace grounds.

Each princess had her own plot in the royal garden, where she could grow anything her heart desired. One sister dug her plot in the shape of a whale; another thought it nicer to shape hers like a seahorse. The youngest, though, made hers perfectly round, and only filled it with flowers that shone bright yellow and red. And when she lay in it, on her back and staring up at the ceiling of her big, watery world, she daydreamed about what it would feel like to be warm under the radiant sun.

All of the sisters decorated their plots with wondrous artifacts they found on sunken ships, but the youngest decorated hers with only one thing: a white marble statue of a handsome human prince. She kept it right in the center of her flower bed, beneath the shade of a fiery willow whose red leaves cast a glow upon him that blushed his stone cheeks. She could sit for hours admiring the handsome statue, allowing herself to get lost in her imagination while dreaming of the wonders she'd find on her own first trip to the surface:

> *When I see sky it will thrill my soul*
> *And the air will hit my lungs*
> *And I will thirst for it no more*
>
> *When the sun sees me she will flicker in the sky*
> *And I will be forever warm*
> *Under her loving, watchful eye*

The littlest mermaid was always filled with many curious questions, for she had an insatiable thirst for knowledge, especially about the world above. But this morning, there was one question in particular that tugged at her while she and her grandmother roamed the maze-like courtyards of the grand palace.

"How long shall I live?" the princess asked. Her grandmother smiled knowingly. Most mer-souls don't consider such things, but simply live their lives in such a way that has no concern for age or time. In their world, the only sensible attitude is one of deep appreciation for the moment of now. The far-reaching curiosity of the youngest's was just one more thing that made her special.

"Those of our kind can expect a life span of about three hundred years," said the old queen, straightening her gilded crown that still shone as brilliantly as it did on her wedding day. Born a commoner and having married into royalty, she was exceedingly proud of her royal status and always adorned herself with luxurious finery.

"What about humans?" asked the princess. "How long can humans expect to live?"

"Humans can expect to live about one hundred years, and that is only if they take excellent care of their bodies," answered the queen. "But they are given many chances to get it right because their souls have an eternity to live and a whole universe to explore!"

The young mermaid's eyes widened at the thought. "May our souls live on forever too, just like the humans?" she asked, anxious to understand.

"But of course!" answered the queen knowingly. "Just like the humans, we have bodies that do expire,but our souls shall live eternally with the divine energies that never die." This excited the little mermaid very much, and she began to imagine the sorts of things she would see and feel in the span of an eternity. "This is a very exciting time for us!" continued the queen. "As the youngest and very last of our kind, it will be your duty to bid the Earth farewell so that life here may go on without us. And once we are all gathered in Heaven, you will be the one to lead us to our next place among the cosmos."

The princess furrowed her blond brow while she considered what was being explained to her. "So, if I understand you correctly," she asked, "it's meant to be *me* who leads our kind to our next life?"

"Precisely. You are the chosen one!" answered her grandmother.

She thought about it some more. "Well if the choice is up to me," she said, "then I shall choose to lead us back to Earth to live as humans!"

"You certainly could," said the queen. "But I'm not sure you'd want to." The princess stared at her with a look that begged to know why. Grandmother continued. "Well, life among the humans would be a bit of a regression for us. Certainly, there is much beauty and adventure to be found, and there are many people up there who live consciously and with an understanding of their own divinity. But there are still many who are not quite so evolved, and their fear infects them and those around them. To many, the world is a hostile place and they bring this belief into their entire experience."

None of it made any sense to the princess. "But it all sounds so wonderful up there! What have they to fear?"

Her grandmother paused. She knew her stories were the reason the littlest was so interested in humanity, but realized that while she'd done a fine job of highlighting its brightest aspects, she had perhaps failed at preparing her granddaughter for the truth about what really separates the human race from their own. "Each other," she answered. "They are most afraid of each other." It was the oddest and most backward thing the young one had ever heard.

"Humans beings still kill each other, cheat each other and exploit each other. They are still growing, and at this stage of their development, hate and fear are still part of the experience. Ours is a more enlightened race; we have already experienced the shadows, and now we only want to know light. And you, the chosen one, will have to make the choice that will best serve your people."

The princess understood her grandmother, and knew that she would take her duty to heart and choose well for her kind. But there was still something about the upper world that enticed her so incredibly, and made her feel like she was missing out on the more exciting world above the waters.

"We really have it better down here, Princess," offered Grandmother. "Be happy and grateful for your three hundred years under the sea. Soon you'll be grown and you'll truly appreciate that there is nothing you should want that can't be attained through the bountiful providence of these seas."

The mermaid kissed her beloved old matriarch on the forehead and swam away to think about all she had just learned. One of her favorite secret spots was the sunken remnants of an old wooden sailboat that had gone down in a spring storm decades earlier. Most of the ship's contents were scattered and broken across the reef but the black and white photos that decorated its walls were still as clear as ever, preserved perfectly under layers of sand and dust.

The pictures told the story of a young couple in love and the life they had built together. In one photo they were bright-eyed teenagers being photographed on a picnic. In another, the pair smiled surrounded by family in front of a grand stone church. The lady wore a big white dress.

Next photos pictured them with friends, holding babies and children in front of large, square-shaped dwellings. There were photos of them riding on the backs of tall four-legged animals, sitting atop bizarre-looking wheeled contraptions, and leaning over big, round cakes and blowing at the little sticks of fire that poked out of them. Their lives appeared to be lovely adventures, full of beautiful milestones and travel. She decided to herself that while the world above might be the stomping grounds of a less-evolved species, it was still a wondrous and magical place. When it came her turn to venture up, she decided, she would drink it all in until every curiosity was quenched.

two

# Garbage Island

On the day of the eldest princess's fifteenth birthday, she was gifted a crown of the ocean's finest pearls to celebrate her coming-of-age. A party was held in her honor, and everyone in the kingdom came to eat, drink, and dance merrily while she prepared for her royal send-off. When it was time to go, her sisters formed a circle around her, clasped on to each other's wrists and spun up through the courtyard with her, singing songs of good wishes for a beautiful journey until the shimmering orange of her scales disappeared into the blue water, high above the palace.

As her sisters sang for her, she closed her eyes and let her heartbeat ring out into the courtyard. Freshly fifteen and every inch a royal maiden, she crossed her arms over her chest and floated up blindly through the deep blue sea, allowing the currents to take her into the far upper beyond until she felt her head break the surface for the very first time.

The air was chilly and put goose bumps on her skin, but the feeling of the cold air in her lungs was euphoric. The night atmosphere was brightened by a full harvest moon, and all around, tiny stars speckled the sky. The princess had never seen the moon or the constellations before, but likened them to bits of glowing plankton once disturbed. Off in the distance, she could see the lights of the city, and if she listened hard without splashing, she could also hear its sounds. Intrigued, she swam in closer to lie on a sandbar from where she could make out the voices of people boisterously shouting, laughing and making music in the streets. She could even hear dogs barking and car horns honking, but she couldn't imagine what sorts of creatures or machines could make such sounds. It was all so wonderfully busy; a glorious cacophony of noises that seemed to echo into the evening just for her. She sat on that sandbar for hours, allowing the sounds to delight her ears and watching the city lights flicker.

Once the streets were quiet, she left the sandbar to swim out to the middle to greet the sun as it rose from the other side of the world. Mer-people can swim amazingly fast, for with just a few flicks of a strong, shiny tail, they can propel themselves for miles through even the mightiest currents. Effortlessly and in no time at all, the mermaid reached a cluster of palm-covered islands that speckled the middle of the Pacific.

Joyfully she swam, savoring every second of her newfound freedom. She swam as fast as she could, leaping and diving like a dolphin, amazed at how high and far through the air she could hurl herself before gravity pulled her down to graze the surface of the water and pop back up again. Butterflying herself across miles and miles of ocean, she closed her eyes and just allowed herself to fly...

Until WHACK! Something smacked her in the face. Or rather, her face made contact with something hard and sharp, and it smashed her crown of pearls, sending it flying off her head. She knew it hadn't been a reef or a rock, because if it had been, her neck would have broken and she would be dead. No, what she had hit was an old, broken, yellow hardhat that had been bobbing in the water amid a nest of dead seaweed and melted blobs of sun-baked plastic. Of course, she didn't know what any of it was, but she could see the thick soup of it all around her in the water, and the sight and smell of it made her feel ill. Her brow bone throbbed and stung from the injury and all she could taste was the toxic slop she had just swallowed. She gagged then threw it up at the sight of a dead bird floating in a mess of busted pieces of buoyant trash.

She sunk lower into the water, deep down beneath the bits she could see from the top but found no end to the colorful grossness. There were things big and little, so obviously unnatural to the sea, but there seemed to be more of it than fish. They were human things, but not like the human things that decorated the palace gardens. She could tell they weren't lost treasures or anything of value, but a massive, poisonous collection of unwanted cast-offs. A flock of gulls fed on little red and orange pieces, mistaking them for food; an albatross ingested a red plastic lighter.

In the water she saw squid and jellyfish trying to navigate themselves around jugs and bottles, doll parts and discarded nets. It might all have been more interesting, maybe even beautiful if the mounds, lumps and scatterings didn't so obviously represent the by-products of a wasteful civilization. All around her they floated, like the confetti inside a snow dome she once found, churning, circulating and heading nowhere but back around. Whatever they were, they were everywhere and in everything. Disgusted, frightened and feeling sicker by the minute, she bolted from the awful mess and fled back to the palace.

When she returned to the grand hall, everyone was still feasting and dancing. As she swam in, they stopped the music to cheer at her return, but then gasped at the sight of the giant laceration that marred her otherwise perfect, milky complexion. "Father, I went to the most awful place," she said. "It was a giant, slow-moving island of debris. Unnatural things floated everywhere, choking the life out of the space it occupied."

The princess held her palm over her cut until the little one, the known healer, came forward to make her better. Since the youngest had been a baby, her touch could heal anything, and when she planted a kiss on her sister's forehead, it immediately began to heal up. Within seconds, her wound had completely dissolved, revealing skin that was even softer and brighter than before.

"You've been to the gyre of the North Pacific," said the king to his daughter. "The scraps and debris you described are of a substance the humans call 'plastic'. Even though it is filled with toxins, they manufacture it to contain their foods and fluids. They intend for units of it to be recycled, but still so much of it gets dumped and forgotten about, left to float for thousands of miles until it all gathers at the gyre."

Everyone present was confused. "But don't they want those things?" asked the birthday girl. "Why, father, would anyone make something just to throw it away?"

The king sighed; there were many things about human kind that were backward and made no sense to him. "They have discovered inexpensive ways of manufacturing it, and often it is more profitable to make more of it than it is to reuse what's already made. What the humans fail to understand is that every piece of plastic that has ever been made is still on the planet, and has nowhere else to go."

After hearing such a disappointing report, no one felt much like reveling anymore and the birthday girl allowed her sisters to carry her to her bed to spend the rest of her birthday in solitude. Once the hall had cleared out, the youngest swam over to her father and took a seat at the foot of his throne. He wore a troubled look while he pondered the state of the planet, but brightened up at the sight of his most darling child. "I wish I could give you a world free from wastefulness" he said tenderly.

# three

Black Spill

The following year, it was the second sister's turn to venture up. To adorn her with embellishments fit for royalty, her grandmother clamped eight exceptionally shiny, perfect oysters onto her beautiful emerald tail.

She broke the surface just as the sun was preparing to set, while the sky looked like a pastel smattering of pink and violet. She swam into shallower waters, found a big, algae-covered rock and, once situated comfortably, untied an old antique letter-opener from the strands of her hair. Mermaids, since they never have any pockets and so seldom carry handbags or rucksacks, love to tie their favorite tools, instruments and treasures into their long tresses so they're always handy. She swore she could hear the big sun sizzle as it dipped behind the horizon, and took the letter opener to her tail to pop an oyster off. It hurt and it took a few of her shiny green scales with it, but still she jimmied it open at its hinge and scraped it from its shell.

The princess puckered her lips and slurped back the wonderfully gelatinous mollusc inside. This oyster tasted like a juicy, ripe strawberry to her, and even though these particular ones were the finest, roundest oysters in the world, she popped the next one right off and shucked it, same as the last. Casually flicking off the perfect pearl contained in each, she ate all the oysters that were clamped to her tail while white swans bowed and danced off in the distance as if putting on a sunset ballet.

Suddenly, the distressed quacking of a flock of ducks interrupted the evening's peace. When she swam over to them, she noticed that all their wings were coated in an oily, black sheen and they were struggling to free themselves from it. All around, there were dead fish floating upside-down inside nasty swirls of black goo, surrounded by tangled bits of dead plant life. She tried to gently brush their wings clean with her hands, but all she could seem to do was spread the greasy stuff around and it made her hands as black as them. The giant blob was thick, dark as caviar and seemed to be slowly torturing everything in its path.

She followed the trails of surface residue for miles, watching it become thicker the deeper she ventured. Soon, she reached the source of the whole mess: it was a well in the ocean floor that pumped out black ooze like a bullet hole oozes blood from a racing heart. The mouth it poured from was large and wide, and there was nothing she could do to stop it from hemorrhaging. As she held herself back, watching it gush out and fill the blue space, she noticed a tiny yellow seahorse feebly swimming from it. She cupped her hands around him and saw the splotches that dappled his gills and snout. Not wanting to stay while the mean clouds billowed, she clutched the seahorse and high-tailed it back home.

When she returned, everyone was still up singing and dancing but as soon as they saw her frightened face and the black smudges across her, they knew something was amiss.

"Father, there is a leak, and it gushes blackness from the floor beneath us!" she said. "The darkness reaches and spreads, swallowing everything. You must stop it before it spreads across all the oceans!" Failing to display the kind of shock and fury his daughter was expecting, the mighty king just sighed, hung his head low and said, "You've paid a visit to an oil well."

She said she wasn't sure, but went on to describe the hole she found that pumped out the thick black veil. Then she opened her hands and showed him the tiny oil-covered seahorse that hadn't made it back alive. "Have you known about all of this, Father?" she asked, "Just like you knew about the gyres?"

The king had known about the oil spills of the world, and about the humans who would stop at nothing to drill for more. As king, he had chosen to carry such worrisome burdens alone. "The humans have made their modern society very dependent on this oil, and they have taken to drilling for it in every sea, even though drilling seabed has proven disastrous time and again. They suck it from the ground like vampires, then burn through millions of gallons a day. The price they can trade it at knows no conceivable limit, and yet they never seem to stop needing more."

The five elder sisters took the little seahorse out to the gardens to bury him inside a little clamshell. The youngest stayed inside with her father while he sat deep in thought on his throne. "I wish I could give you a world free from carelessness," he said.

# four

## Red Cove

The next year it was the third sister's turn. In order to make her tail luxuriously shiny, her grandmother drew a bath filled with the finest sea slugs and snails so that their hungry suction might polish her red scales to spotless perfection. This sister was the most daring of all, and she decided her day would be most fun if she spent it frolicking at the surface with a family of bottlenose dolphins, the baby of which was her most cherished pet at court. While they all played, chased and dove around under the warm coastal sun, they were sublimely unaware of the peril about to befall them.

While the elders of the family fed along the shallow bay, the mermaid and the pup allowed the current to carry them out a bit.

She lay on her back while her friend floated alongside her, drifting along without a care in the world.

Suddenly, a loud tapping noise filled the waters, assailing their ears with its harsh clamor and destroying the peace they'd been enjoying. It was so loud that she could barely think, and she wondered what on earth could be so audibly offensive. The dolphins instinctively darted away from the noise and soon found themselves corralled into a cove while a row of boats dragging long nets rapidly closed in on them.

The mermaid ducked under and bravely swam toward the boats to investigate. She soon discovered that the noise echoing through the bay was the result of men clanging hammers and metal sticks off long lead pipes that dipped several feet into the water off the sides of their vessels. They sounded like a thousand deafening gongs being banged upon all at once, reverberating and multiplying to discombobulate the sonar of the dolphins.

By the time the noise ended, the cove had been sealed off with a wall of heavy netting spanning from the surface to the sandy bottom. The dolphin family was trapped in there, along with a bunch of others who had been dragged in by the nets. Once all the nets were secured, the boats pulled out of the bay and left.

The hour of chaos and panic was followed by several hours of quiet evening. Once the sky was darker and it appeared safe to do so, the mermaid and the pup swam in to make sure everyone was okay.

All of the family members were accounted for and no one seemed to have been hurt too badly, so eventually they all calmed down and began to search the perimeter of the netting for a hole or the possibility of a way out. By nightfall, they had found one frayed spot in the netting and began scouring for something sharp with which to widen the hole. The mermaid tried to grind a few sharp stones and a broken glass bottle against the net but it was very strong and nothing worked. She wanted to swim back to the palace to get her father but was afraid of what could happen if she left her friends trapped there so she stayed with them, keeping everyone calm throughout the night.

They awoke in the morning to the sound of a motorboat loudly approaching the bay from down the coast. Soon, a whole fleet of small tin boats were pulling in, and swarms of humans began gathering along the beach. Within minutes, they were wading into the shallow waters to handle the dolphins, sizing up and scrutinizing fins, tails, and beaks, and laying claim to the ones that best fit a certain criteria.

One burly-looking woman in a black wetsuit called some men over and they forcefully loaded a little gray one onto a large gurney while the rest of her family cried and wailed. But for all their weeping, no sympathy was inspired, and the humans simply ratcheted the straps around her smooth, rubbery body and lifted her onto the back of a truck. When she struggled to break free, they bound her even tighter until she was unable to move at all. The same happened all around, and everywhere there were confused dolphins who could find no escape from the clutches of the upright monsters who continued to pick from them until less than half remained in the water.

After the last desirable dolphin had been bid upon and loaded up, the only people waiting around were the ones inside the boats. The mermaid tried to get the pup to swim to safety with her, but the baby would not abandon her family. When the people on the shore were out of sight and the big trucks had cleared out, an unimaginable massacre began.

A man steadying himself inside a little boat delivered the first blow with a long, sharp spear. He drove straight into the smooth, grey flesh of the dolphin nearest him like he had done it a hundred times before. The dolphin cried out in agony and terror as he ripped the wound open wider with his violent withdrawal, then brought his spear down again, this time harder, faster. The men stabbed those dolphins repeatedly until their blood spilled from a multitude of wounds. They continued their killing until the crystal-blue cove was awash in crimson blood.

As the last of their friends bled to their deaths in agonizing convulsions, the fishermen pulled them up onto their boats using large metal gaffs that they hooked into their sides. Once all the bodies had been collected, the only cries that could still be heard across the cove were from the pup that had refused to flee while the rest of her family was being butchered and stolen.

She was easy prey, in fact the very definition. Most of the boats were already filled, stacked high with dolphin bodies but there was one who still had room, and he wasted no time moving in for the kill. For a brief moment he admired her smooth, unblemished skin and contemplated how much more she might be worth alive. After just a moment's consideration, he decided it would be easier to just kill her. The mermaid swam beneath her friend and begged her to dive low and out of sight but she wouldn't budge an inch, too distraught to even think of escaping. With no other options, the mermaid bravely swam up, grabbed the side of tin boat and rocked it hard enough that the little man lost his balance and fell into the water.

While he was under and struggling to go up for air, she grabbed him by the shirt and dragged him lower, down to the floor. His eyes widened fearfully at the sight of her, but she felt wild with rage and didn't let him go. She grabbed the spear out of his hands and, in hard retribution for all her friends killed that day, she aimed it at his heart and drove it straight through him.

Blood spilled from the man just the way it did from all the dolphins killed that day but she felt no pity for him. Spellbound by the hurt and anger she felt and tasting all the metallic blood between her teeth, she jiggled the spear and watched him bleed out into the water. After watching the last bit of life escape him, she grabbed her friend, so weak with grief, and swam her back down to the palace.

When they arrived, everyone knew right away that something terrible had happened. The princess's hair and skin were stained red with blood.

"You've been to the coves of slaughter," said the king in a sad, knowing voice. He was aware of the terrible things that go on in that corner of the sea but, just as with everything else, was morally unable to interfere. It pained him to sit idly while human destruction extended deeper into his world but his hands were tied; to interfere would be to interact, and to do that would be to breach the cardinal rule of his kingdom, which is to let nature find its own order and balance. "Were they all taken?" he asked, his eyes low. In the sea, there is nothing sadder than to hear of dolphins being killed, for they are the most well-intentioned and pure creatures of all. The devastated princess nodded. Yes, they had all been taken.

The king explained to his daughters the great profit-driven enterprise of stealing dolphins and submitting them to lives of captivity. Then he explained the fishery industry and how people willing to pay the high price for whale meat are often sold dolphin meat that's been knowingly mislabeled. Sadly, the great king knew all too well that if humans could find a way to profit from something, they'd bleed it 'til it's dry, even if they had to kill over and over.

"I wish I could give you a world free from violence," he said mournfully.

# five

## Shark Water

For the fourth sister's birthday, the old queen covered her body in a wrap of seaweed and minerals to nourish her beautiful skin so that it would glow milky and bright on the day of her first surfacing. Rubies adorned the scales of her lavender-colored tail, and a tiara of sapphires glittered against the platinum and gold of her hair. This princess was very ladylike and not quite as adventurous as her sisters, and instead of getting in close to see the people in the towns and cities, she wished to stay far out at sea to observe the upper world from a safer distance.

She could see for miles in every direction, and the clouds in the bright blue sky passed over her head the way giant whales did when she'd lie on her back and stare up from the ocean floor. She closed her eyes and basked, just leisurely wading, enjoying the new and thrilling experience of sun and air. She was so relaxed that she didn't even notice a boat slowly passing behind her.

After a while of sunning, her face began to feel hot so she ducked under to cool her skin, opening her eyes to see a shark about twenty feet below her struggling against a fishing line that was tearing up his gills. She swam over and tried to pull the hook free but its sharp barb was stuck deep and every time she wiggled it, he bled profusely from the cut. She looked around her and saw several other sharks and fish caught on lines, fighting and swimming hard against them or submitting and floating lifelessly behind them. Just as she began to wonder how so many sharks and fish got fooled and caught by the same line, she noticed something small and shiny as it came flying at her face and just as she went to turn away, it stabbed into the corner of her eye and hooked itself into her socket, yanking her forward and lodging its sharp barb into her skull from the inside.

It was the most painful thing she'd ever experienced and she screamed in agony as her eyes clouded over in red. As it pulled her quickly through the water by her head, she realized there was only one way to free herself, and that would be to out-swim the drag of the line and use the slack to unhook it with her fingers.

She was fearful of losing an eye, but grateful for the benefits of having fingers and thumbs once she was able to carefully remove the hook from her head without noticeably severing any nerves. In disbelief of what had just happened to her, she covered the eye with her palm and began to back away from the long lines. When she looked up at the horrible boat to curse it, a huge shark carcass plummeted straight down at her from above and as it collided with her, its rows of sharp teeth sliced into the tender flesh of her shoulder.

After it hit her, the shark tumbled away into the depths and she understood that it hadn't meant to hit her. As it drifted downward, she could see that it had no fins, and in fact was bleeding from where its fins once were. Another lifeless shark body came plummeting down from above and she saw that its fins had been cut from its body, too. With her eye gushing blood and her shoulder raked and raw, she decided it was far too dangerous at the surface and swam away as fast as she could until she was back at the palace and safe again at last.

When the princess returned, everyone was still waiting up for her and when she entered the grand hall, her sisters gasped in horror and swam to her aid, for the poor girl looked a fright.

"What's happened to you, child?" asked her grandmother, getting up from her throne to inspect the fresh and painful-looking wounds.

"I surfaced in the open water. There were so many sharks . . . a hook meant for one of them tore into my eye and dragged me behind a boat. The humans are monsters; they kill them for their fins and toss the rest overboard. I wish to never visit the surface again."

The king nodded, in agreement that it was far safer at the bottom where the humans couldn't find them. "You've witnessed shark finning in the 21st century," he said.

"Father, it was barbaric," she whimpered. "What uses have they for so many fins?"

The king explained to his daughters that there were people in the world who believed consuming shark fins guaranteed lifelong health, based on the notion that sharks aren't usually known to get sick. He described the massive industry that sprung up from the concept, and how sharks are now systematically murdered around the world, simply for the price of their fins.

"I wish I could give you a world free from greed," he said to all his sad girls, while his youngest healed the cuts and scrapes of the year's sorrowful birthday girl.

# six

*Massacre on Ice*

The fifth sister celebrated her birthday in the winter, so in preparation for her first journey to the top, her grandmother ordered for thousands of white crystals from deep-sea caves to be mined and ground into a sparkling powder. Then, as is customary for any princesses born while the snows cover the land above, her grandmother had her golden yellow tail, her fair skin, and her long hair covered with it so she'd shine like a diamond on her special day and camouflage easily in the snowy, icy waters.

When she broke the surface, she found the ground above to be topped in a blanket of white, exactly like her grandmother had promised. All the boats in the harbor were lifted out until spring and in the bay, people glided around the frozen water swiftly in shoes that had metal blades stuck to the bottom of them. From the cold water she watched, exhilarated. She decided to venture north up the coast to see just how cold and icy it could get.

When she finally popped her head out of the water, she found herself surrounded by broken sheets of ice that covered the surface like jagged white tiles. Excited to climb out of the water for the very first time, she spotted a smaller iceberg and scaled its side, pulling her slippery tail up so she could sit. Snowflakes gently fell from the sky and she glistened with them under the diffused sunlight of the winter afternoon. She felt she had found a cold paradise.

Sprawled out comfortably, she sat and watched a huge family of seals as they played and fed, nestled cozily in a snowy sun pocket of a valley where they were shielded from high winds and harsh snow. She enjoyed watching the white cubs at play and laughed about how those creatures, much like herself, could be so graceful under the water but clumsy and awkward when they moved about on land.

At the edge of the valley, the mermaid saw a young boy appear, creeping in close behind the furry cluster of shiny coats and beady eyes. Her heart jumped at the sight of a real, live human! Intently, she spied on him spying on them from the iceberg she was perched upon, safely hidden in her camouflage of white. At first she wished him to just go away but the more she watched him, the more she was able to relax. The boy lay on his belly in the snow with only his pink face exposed, the fur lining of his hood rustling softly. He watched the seals with wonderment in his eyes, giggling at the sight of the fluffy white babies as they slid across the ice, bumping into each other and yawning.

Shortly thereafter, a group of large men appeared, each carrying a long stick in his hand. There was something odious about how the men moved and held their sticks so steadily, as if carrying weapons and about to wage war. She wondered who their enemies could be as they crouched down where the boy lie, staying low as they observed the seals, appearing to be counting cubs while they fed, played and let their mothers bathe them.

The men spread out until they had the seals mostly surrounded, leaving their only hope of escape reliant on their ability to make it back to the water's edge, at least fifty feet from where they were huddled. The mermaid kept watching, hoping nothing scary would happen, praying that her dark imaginings were just a bit of panicked terror playing tricks on her mind. She thought about screaming and calling them to safety, but just as she was about to act, she froze. Suddenly she became deathly afraid of what would happen to her if she was spotted, for she knew they would have nets and spears and sticks and guns and for all she knew, they might like to do to a mermaid what they do to sharks and dolphins.

So she stayed frozen, sure that her father would have wanted her to just stay safe, and keep herself hidden from them.

The mermaid's eyes went blurry as the men made their attack. It was a frightening, bloody tableau upon a frozen stage as they wound up their sticks and clubs, delivering hard blows aimed at little seal heads. Their methods were savage and inconsistent; sometimes they missed their marks and smashed the poor seals across their backs, breaking bones instead of knocking them unconscious, and causing blood-curdling cries to ring out. Mothers scrambled to help their pups to the water but were more often intercepted, bashed and left to bleed out while their pups were killed right in front of them.

Before long, the snow was littered with blood-soaked bodies lying face-down in their own puddles of garnet. Some of the men kept on killing, while others kneeled beside the motionless bodies and used sharp knives to skin the fur right off their still-warm corpses for reasons the mermaid could not understand. In the ocean, a creature only kills to eat but these humans were not taking any meat or bones, just skinning and leaving furless bodies behind to rot. It broke her heart into a million pieces, and she sang somber melodies for all the lives lost. The hunters heard her song but just thought it was the arctic wind through the barren trees and snow drifts.

Once it was all over, a lake of blood remained where once there was a pristinely icy vista. The men's boots left red tracks in the snow on their way out. Feeling frozen and empty, she slipped off her iceberg and back into the icy waters. With pain in her soul and anger in her heart, she swam back to the palace and vowed never to visit the surface again for the remainder of her three hundred years.

When she returned, she told everyone at court about the violent killings she'd witnessed.

"You've been to the Arctic," said the king knowingly. "And you've witnessed the seal hunt."

"I did, Father," responded the princess. "Why would the humans do such a thing? What did they want with so many skins?"

The king explained to his daughters the economics of the fur trade, and how, even though there are quality substitutes available, some people still insist on real fur even if it came at the cost of the innocent lives of several furry animals. He explained about catch-and-kill fur acquisitions, and also about raise-for-slaughter. None of his daughters could understand it. None could conceive of making such frivolous killings.

That night, all of the sisters went to bed early except for the youngest, who stayed up in the rotting crow's nest of an old wooden ship to watch boats as they passed overhead. Her outstretched arms reached up at them, and in spite of everything she learned about the crueler facets of humanity, she was still dying for her turn to see the top. She stayed out until the sea was black and the ships above cast no more moon shadows, then went to sleep dreaming of the things she would see on her turn.

That night, the sea king didn't get a wink of sleep, nor did he even retire to his bedchamber that evening. Instead, he sat awake on his throne in the dark and thought about his six darling daughters. He wished he could protect them from everything sad in the world but even the powerful monarch had to concede that there were some things simply beyond his control.

But the king worried most for his youngest daughter, who would be fifteen in the coming year. He knew the year would go by in a blink and it would soon be time to watch her venture up. He had always known her curiosity was a powerful, compelling force, and that sooner or later it would lead her to destinies that could be as dangerous as they could be enticing and beautiful. So the loving father stayed up all night hoping danger never finds her, and wishing nothing but beautiful things for his littlest girl.

seven

*Surfacing*

---

When the little mermaid woke up on the morning of her fifteenth birthday, she rolled over inside the giant clam that was her bed and it opened up for her so she could look out and see what kind of day it was. She looked up to see the sun's bright streams light up the palace like a ballroom chandelier. On the sunniest days, when light poured in, it always made her happy to wonder how the land people would be spending a sunny day. She felt her heart swell; this would be the day she would see it all for herself!

She got up and swam out to the courtyard to find a massive celebration in her honor that was more opulent and lavish than any party the ocean world had ever seen. Everyone in the kingdom was there to celebrate, for everyone knew how excited she was and if there was one princess who'd surely bring back good news, it was the youngest without a doubt.

The old queen presented a beautiful necklace to her granddaughter; its chain was made of woven necklaces of gold and silver, and from it gems, trinkets, and priceless treasures hung. At the very centre, a huge slice of blue-green ammonite stone fossil dangled heavily. The necklace was a work of art, the result of a decade-and-a-half's worth of sending for only the finest shipwreck jewels. It was stunning, although it felt like an incredible burden hanging from her thin white neck. Her sisters assembled around her for the big send-off, each in turn giving her pieces of advice on things like areas to avoid and situations to stay away from but mostly, not to be seen by any humans. She kissed each of her big sisters and thanked them all for their well-meant advice.

"I'll send a storm when it's time for you to come home," said the king. "When you feel it approaching, let it carry you safely back to us."

The youngest princess smiled and nodded at her loving father, and blew kisses to everyone who had come to see her off. She waved sweetly to her proud old grandmother, then closed her eyes and let her heart take over to drag her where it willed. Once she was high above the palace, she lent herself to the strong current rolling through and let it pull her for hours until it spit her out somewhere in the Pacific Northwest.

As she broke the surface, a gust of wind filled her nose and mouth and she coughed at the strange, dry sensation in her lungs. She could not believe that she was finally there, at the surface, free to explore anything she wanted to. A great warmth touched down upon her back and she turned to face the setting sun, which painted the late-summer sky a reddish orange. As she absorbed its beautiful warm rays into her cheeks for the very first time, she wondered how she had spent the last fifteen years without it.

It wasn't long before the last beams extinguished and the big burning ball disappeared from view. She swam in towards land, skipping across the surface, loving the feeling of the brisk wind through her hair. Off in the distance, she noticed a big white ship decorated in festive lights and sailing her way. She knew her father wouldn't approve but she couldn't resist! This was her day of exploration and her heart yanked her towards it like a moth drawn to a flame. A set of fireworks went off and brightly decorated the darkened sky, lighting up the world around her and exploding into the heavens.

Carefully, she watched the ship sail towards her and as it approached, its music got louder and she could hear the joyful sounds of the party. Maintaining a safe distance, she peeked in the windows and saw scores of smiling people dressed fancily and dancing merrily. The yacht was exquisitely decorated to celebrate a birthday, and the princess couldn't have been more excited because after all, it was her birthday as well, and it thrilled her to be attending a real human celebration.

As she scanned the room for whoever it was with whom she shared her birthdate, it didn't take her long to single out a boy that seemed to be receiving more smiles and attention than anyone else on board. They all seemed to be calling him Gabriel.

The sight of his face made her heart flutter in a way it never had before. What a beautiful creature he was! Though she had never seen a live human before this day, she was certain he represented the ideal specimen. The longer she watched him, the more she felt herself being drawn in by his deep brown eyes, his warm olive skin and his perfect white teeth. Everything around his face began to blur and she started to feel dizzy and light-headed. All at once, images of love shuffled through her head like a montage, tumbling over her like a waterfall of girlish and romantic expectations. Everything around him was just a mess of light and colors.

She bobbed upon the waves, not taking her eyes off him for a second as he walked around the boat enjoying his own party. He was beautiful, with a head of thick black hair, a long, lean body and a strong yet gentle composure that seemed to draw people toward him like a magnet. He was handsome in all the ways a young man should be, she thought. He looked just like the statue in her garden.

There didn't seem to be a person on board that was immune to his wit and charm, for as he strolled through the crowds collecting best wishes, he left his friends smiling and laughing. The girls on board eyed him dreamily and spoke of him kindly, and the guys remarked on what a good guy and genuine friend he was. The more she overheard people shower him with accolades, the surer she was that she too was falling for him right then and there.

The mermaid swam in closer until she was right up against the shiny white side of the boat, close enough to hear Gabriel talking to one of his friends as he leaned on a railing.

"Let me just start by saying that I am never disappointed your birthday falls on Labor Day weekend," said the arrogant-looking young man to Gabriel's left. This boy was tall and lanky, and wore a pinstripe blazer on top of a dangerously deep v-neck tee shirt. As he spoke to Gabriel, it was like he was posing, peacocking for the group of attractive girls dancing just a few feet in front of them. "It's the last weekend of the summer, the last chance to hit the late-summer swells, and one final weekend to select some trim from your always-impressive bevy of cottage girls."

"Oh here we go," said Gabriel, rolling his eyes.

"The Skyler triplets are seventeen now," added Rourke, nudging him with his elbow. Rourke said 'Skyler' funny, and he hoped Gabriel didn't notice but he did. Whenever he drank, the lisp that took him four years of speech therapy to shake came out ever so slightly. Gabriel enjoyed an inward giggle on account of it.

"You know," he started, "my mom will stop letting me have you over if she finds out that you just run around collecting v-cards up here."

"It's always consensual!" Rourke fired back.

"I'm just saying, we have a responsibility to our neighbors," said Gabriel. "We can't be a hostel for sexual deviants on the prowl for their teenage daughters."

"Clearly, that is somewhat understandable but I've been lucky, as the young lassies I tap usually just creep home quietly and never mention it again!"

"What do you mean, creep home?" inquired Gabriel gingerly. "Where do you take them?"

"Bushes, mainly," responded Rourke shamelessly. "Right around dusk, it's always amazing how the sheer convenience of a beach bush passes for romantic spontaneity to a chick. I get one in, then scurry home for suppertime." He knocked back the rest of the beer in his hand.

"And of course by 'suppertime' you mean dinner with MY family, right?" said Gabriel. "I'm just going to stop you right there," he said, shaking his head.

The mermaid listened to their conversation with eyes wide, for she had never heard words and phrases like theirs before. It was more than a new language; she felt like one of the aliens her grandmother once told her about, who lived on other planets but traveled through space to observe and be baffled by the earthlings.

"Well, Gabriel, it just so happens my tastes have matured in recent months," replied Rourke, unbuttoning his top button to let just a bit of his chest show. "I no longer have a taste for virgins, and I definitely don't want to waste my time with any more novices. What I'm after is an older woman, a seasoned vet. An O.G. in the game of love." Thunder cracked loudly off in the distance. Gabriel laughed out loud.

Rourke had been Gabriel's closest friend since the earliest sandbox days, their history being the sole reason he maintained a friendship with him, even though it was blatantly clear they shared less and less in common as the years pressed on. "So which of my mother's friends have you set your sights on, then?" asked Gabriel. Rourke gestured to a forty-something woman standing in the corner wearing stilettos and ripped jeans with a tight black leather tank top. Her top showcased her huge, firm, obviously fake breasts, a neckline that was cut just low enough to let her butterfly tattoo peek out on the left side. "Mrs. Britt? Really?" asked Gabriel incredulously.

Mrs. Britt was a glamorous cougar of a trophy wife whose latest enhancement was enjoying its grand debut surrounded by gawking young men. The mermaid observed the woman they were observing and compared her own modest breasts to the jumbo flesh pods that adorned the woman. "It's Ms. Radford now," corrected Rourke. "She and Mr. Britt split." The gold chain she wore had a stone pendant that hung deep in her cleavage, and a handful of guys pretending to be interested in geodes leaned in closer to get a better look. "And I always knew she'd keep the summer home," he said, transfixed, with his eyes trained on her freckled cleavage.

"Yep it's always nice when a woman's rack inflates along with her net worth," chuckled Gabriel. "At least she won't take up a lifejacket if this ship goes down!" Just then, another thunderclap echoed through the evening sky, followed by a bright lightning bolt that seemed to scrape through the sky like a live wire across a tin roof. Everyone on the boat cheered, for the lightning lit up the dance floor like strobes.

The little mermaid ignored the coming storm, opting instead to continue observing all of the fancy people dancing and socializing in their elegant clothing. As she clung to a porthole, her body half out of the water, she felt the wind upon her wet skin and began to understand why the people cover up their bodies in pretty fabrics. What a celebration it was! All around the boat, tables were beautifully decorated with white tablecloths and shiny silverware, and the bar was stocked high with pretty bottles. The dance floor was covered in shimmering lights and everyone in attendance seemed to be having a wonderful time drinking and enjoying the party. No one aboard even noticed the winds as they began to pick up severely.

As the mermaid watched the way Gabriel easily navigated the party for which he was the cause célèbre, it was hard not to notice an intensely beautiful girl with long cascades of golden hair and a prettily painted face eyeing him aggressively as he stood chatting up a short-haired girl in a blue dress. He pretended not to notice the hole she was burning into the back of his head, and kept his eyes averted. The mermaid overheard a few girls call her Arabella.

Arabella was a pop star of international fame. Spoiled since birth, Arabella always got everything she wanted. The only child of a pair of ridiculously wealthy and overindulgent Aristocratic Europeans, she was used to getting her way and threw a stink if ever she didn't. When she was seventeen, she told her parents, the Behrensens, she wanted to be a singer. The following weekend, they had a state-of-the-art recording studio built on their property, purchased a few sets of solid lyrics from certified hit-makers, and hired some big names in the music industry to produce her debut album. Once street credibility was effectively purchased, Arabella became an overnight sensation with fans around the world.

Of all the girls with whom Gabriel was acquainted, Arabella was easily the prettiest, the loveliest singer and the very best dancer. She was famous, accomplished, and always looked picture perfect. Unfortunately for her, those qualities did her no good when it came to catching his attention. She might have been all of those things, but Gabriel found her to be vapid, superficial, insincere and a little bit insane. And she wasn't particularly nice, either. Sure, she was nice to him and anyone in his direct proximity, but he knew deep down she was just an immature diva who was simply mistaking her unrequited childhood crush for love's undying devotion.

"Don't worry, Arabella," said the girl on her right, wearing little white nautical shorts with ultra-high red platforms. "You're the hottest dimepiece on this boat. He'd have to be an absolute crack-star not to invite you over tonight."

"Yeah, Arabella," said the girl to her left, wearing a tight, black bandage dress that was a size too small and required constant adjustment. "Gabriel is as good as yours; there's definitely no one hotter than you," she said perfunctorily before blotting her lips in the reflection of a shiny butter knife.

Arabella sighed. "Well I know all *that*," she responded coldly. "What I cannot understand is why he hasn't yet asked me to marry him when I've been throwing myself at him since the fourth grade!" It was true; she had been chasing him since the fourth grade. She made him a gingerbread house that Christmas. He ate it and thanked her. Unbeknownst to him at the time, a tradition was being born in her brain and every year since then, she had sent him another gingerbread house in the spirit of desperately clinging to the one thing she thought they shared.

As the years went by, her home-crafted gingerbread houses became more and more detailed. They began simply enough as icing- and candy-covered single room cookie shacks but recent years saw them morph into increasingly large, multiple-story gingerbread dream homes. He always thanked her politely, told her she didn't have to do that, reciprocated with a last-minute box of chocolates he'd fetch out of the stockpile his mom kept in the pantry. He had always managed to circumvent her advances . . . until tonight, it had been decided. She was touring in Japan when her assistant called to tell her she'd received an invitation to his birthday party, and so she cancelled her next two shows and a photo shoot for a Korean soft drink to be on the next flight home to be there. Looking stunning in a perfect red satin gown, she was easily the belle of the ball and had the attention of just about every set of eyes on board, except for the only ones she wanted on her. She had convinced herself that this would be the night she'd make him fall in love with her, and they could finally stop with all of their coy silliness and just get married like she always imagined they would. In her mind, he was already hers, but just didn't know it yet.

Her green eyes flickered bitterly as she watched a pretty redhead hug and kiss him a bunch of birthday wishes. She fixated on them so intently that she didn't even notice Rourke secretly taking pictures of her angry, jealous face on his camera phone to sell to the Hollywood gossip rags.

"Jealous gorgeous pop star, six o'clock," said Rourke as he dropped his phone back into his pocket, grabbed a champagne flute off a passing tray and downed its contents like it was Gatorade.

"I know, I can feel her eyes grilling me," Gabriel replied. "It's so awkward; I only invited her because my parents are friends with the Behrensens and I wanted to be polite! I didn't actually think she'd take time off her sold-out Asian tour just to be here."

Rourke looked at him like he was a foolish, naïve person. "Come on, man, of course she'd be here! She's obsessed with you and that will never stop until you finally give it up to her so she can see that you aren't actually as wonderful as she's built you up to be. Until you give in, she'll never leave you alone. You might as well prepare for a life of being stalked."

Gabriel shivered at the thought of getting intimate with her. "I had hoped to hear she was happily married to a foreign monarch or former Backstreet Boy by now. But no, she's here scaring girls away from talking to me at my own birthday party."

Rourke shot his friend an envious, disgusted look. "Well haven't you got just the direst of problems? Pfft. A sexy international songbird wants you for her boy toy and it distresses you that she refuses to give up on your stubborn ass!" The mermaid glanced back at Arabella through the port hole. She fully understood why Arabella wanted him, but could not at all understand his apparent aversion to her.

"That's what's creepy about the whole thing!" remarked Gabriel. "Arabella could have anyone! And I mean anyone --"

"BUT SHE WANTS YOU!" howled Rourke passionately. "So hit that! Take that down! God knows why she wants you so bad but she does... love is a strange and messed-up thing!"

Gabriel shook his head. "It isn't love; it's relentless infatuation. I'm about the only thing she ever wanted that her parents couldn't buy for her."

"So let her have you! What have you got to lose?"

Gabriel looked back over his shoulder to see if she was still watching him and accidentally locked eyes with her for a moment. She smiled casually and waved as if she had just noticed him over there, and hadn't been planted strategically under the light of a lamp, seductively flipping her hair over her shoulder every time she thought he might look over. She was silly, obsessed and terribly unbalanced, in ways that only pretty girls ever seem to get away with. And she really was very, very pretty. He thought for a moment about what he would really have to lose by just hooking up with her and getting it overwith. Their would-be romance played out in his mind a lot like the plot of *Vanilla Sky*. He shuddered.

When he realized his gap-out moment had been spent staring right in her direction, he glanced away awkwardly. She was convinced he was star-struck by her beauty that evening and was just playing shy out of intimidation. He was positive beyond positive that he would never, ever be with her.

Unfortunately, Arabella never got the picture, for she had a one-track mind and it was set on him. In honour of his birthday, she had rehearsed a song and dance number with the as-yet unreleased and highly anticipated first single off her third album. This collection of tracks promised to showcase her edgier, more artistic side after a four-year career of peddling bubble gum pop hits. She was sure that after he saw what she had planned for him, he would finally fall for her and they could live happily ever after.

With Gabriel's back unacceptably turned to her once again, she decided it was time to go on the offensive. She whispered something into the ears of her minions and, as if they had rehearsed it, the two girls beelined over to Rourke and began flirting with him, sparing no leg or breast in his face to get him over to the dance floor, leaving Gabriel conveniently alone. And vulnerable.

By the time he realized he was being cornered, it was too late and she was already gliding over to him. She strutted seductively, her voluminous tresses bouncing beautifully as she walked, framing her body from the small of her back up to the top of her face that launched a thousand billboards.

"I got you something, Gabe," she said in her sexiest voice, winking at him. His stomach turned.

"Oh hey there Arabella," he said, looking around for whomever might save him from her clutches. "A present? For me? You really shouldn't have. I'm just grateful you could make it; I thought there was no way you could. . ."

Arabella smiled and flicked her hair again, batting her thick, mascara-clad eyelashes twice. "Well, it's not exactly that kind of gift," she began, stepping in closer. "What I have for you is something much more . . . *experiential,*" she said breathily. He gulped. "*Experiential?*"

Smiling brightly, she looked up at him with her big green eyes and then looked away, trying to be intriguing. Then she began to giggle in a way she hoped he'd find to be sexy, cute, mysterious. Her provocative shtick might have proven effective on most other guys in the world, but Gabriel was decidedly immune to her feminine wiles. "Oh, here goes," he muttered to himself.

Arabella reached out and brushed his hair out of his eyes. "I don't want to ruin the surprise, so that's all I'm telling you for now," she said in her flirtiest voice, certain she'd planted a seed of mystery. "That said, you better like it or I'll totally die and then kill your whole family!" He gulped again. Then she clinked her champagne glass with his, kissed his stunned face on the cheek, then turned and walked a few steps. Like she'd been planning to, she walked just far enough in front of him that his eyes would be uncontrollably drawn to her flawless, round booty, for she was sure it would seal the deal. "See you later, birthday boy," she cooed as she blew him a kiss and sailed inside. Gabriel briefly considered jumping ship and swimming to shore.

Better sense prevailed and as he stood by the railing going over his gentle rejection speech, he glanced down at the glittery ocean surface and for a second, he could've sworn he saw a white shoulder wading in the dark water. He stood up and narrowed his eyes to better see what it was.

The mermaid, frightened of being seen, ducked under and hid herself in the shadows. He leaned down and saw nothing out of the ordinary, so he shrugged it off and went back inside to rejoin the party. The mermaid breathed a sigh of relief at having not been seen, and then turned to watch him walk back through his crowds of adoring friends.

Once Gabriel reached the middle of the dance floor, all of the lights blew out all at once, and everyone froze in silence. When the spotlight switched on and shone down, Arabella stepped up onto the stage and everyone began to clap their hands. She looked demure and theatrical, and was wearing an entirely different outfit than the one she'd been in just moments prior.

She began to sing her new song. It began slowly,

*"It was you I hunted, and it was you I claimed,*
*Then you slipped between my fingers, never to be seen again.*
*And the storms within my soul started shaking my foundation*
*I know I said I would love again, but this time with trepidation..."*

As everyone stood still, watching their free performance, winds began to blow harder until two loud thunder claps interrupted her song. Everyone looked out to see that rain was starting to fall, and three lightning bolts touched down around them in a span of six seconds. Big waves began to roll in, and rocked the boat so hard that all the DJ's equipment slid off the table and went crashing to the floor, causing all sound on the boat to come to an abrupt halt. Everyone looked around startled, then felt the yacht tip beneath their feet even deeper to the side, causing several people on the dance floor to lose their footing and fall. Just then, massive rain clouds seemed to appear out of nowhere and burst all over them, blotting out the bright moon and lashing down with rain. Bigger, scarier waves began smacking wildly against the hull, rocking the respectably sized party yacht as if it was little more than a plastic dinghy.

The decks were flooded with torrential rain, while lightning bolts put on a pyrotechnics show. Their vessel tried in vain to stay afloat but even over the thunder, the creaking and groaning of the beautiful boat could be heard threatening to bust from the pressure.

Gabriel and a crewmember went to work untying the life boats and the mermaid followed and watched him, dazzled and confused by the sudden change in the general mood of everyone aboard. Amid the excitement, she completely forgot that the storm had been sent to fetch her, and couldn't understand why everyone appeared to be so stressed out by the rain, thunder, lightning and high winds when she found them to be such great fun! The little mermaid watched with fascination as everyone hustled around with frightened looks on their faces, scrambling to put puffy orange vests on and fighting for spots on the mini boats. She began to sing her most soothing songs, about the delights to be found at the bottom. She sang sweetly about what would await them if they would just allow the waves to take them under.

Gabriel was on the other side of the boat now, reaching inside a bench to pull out more life vests when the boat rocked again and knocked a heavy magnum bottle of vodka off the bar shelf. When the bottle dropped, it fell straight down at his head and its blunt base thumped him on the left temple, knocking him backwards. In what felt like slow motion, he fell down the side of the yacht and into the crashing waves. On his way down to the water in the very second before he blacked out, the last things he saw were his friends dressed in their finest, drenched and flailing in gowns and suits, with hair all matted and mascara running down girls' faces. Between the heavy claps of thunder, terrified screams rang out into the night as everyone abandoned ship in any way they could. The people in lifeboats rowed vigorously through the choppy water and the people in the water kicked and paddled, clinging to their life vests. Everyone was so busy trying not to drown that no one even noticed the little mermaid as she swam between pieces of debris, oblivious to their danger. Gabriel was now under water, sinking lower into the darkness while blood billowed from his forehead.

As she swam towards him, she continued to sing about the beautiful life that awaited him if he would stay with her in her underwater paradise. How delighted she was! She could not believe her wish was coming true; that the statue of a boy that she'd adored for years was real, and would be coming with her down to her father's kingdom.

Then suddenly, she remembered how her grandmother had taught her that humans get their oxygen from the air, and the only way she could bring a human to her father's kingdom was as a dead man. Refusing to let him die, she swam over to him, grabbed him under his arms, and swam him straight up to the surface so he could breathe. Then she held him tight and swam him far, far away from the wreckage, just as rescue helicopters swooped in to lift his friends to safety.

# eight

_Him._

She brought him to rest in the sand where they wouldn't be seen, where a small bush sheltered them from the cool evening wind. The storm had died down, and the once-grand vessel was now reduced to little more than bits of wood and floating furniture scattered on the water. He was there, right there in her arms, and wishes really do come true.

She put her ear to his mouth; he exhaled and it smelled sweet. With every exhalation, he put goose bumps all over her and she closed her eyes to experience him as the thumping of his heartbeat made her own heart race. She smoothed his dark hair away from his face and inspected the crack on his forehead. Already it was beginning to bruise morbidly; blood was still seeping out, and the red skin around the cut was soggy and torn up.

She laid herself down beside him with her arm under his neck, letting his heavy, sleeping head rest upon her vernal bosom. Very gently she stroked his rosy cheeks with her fingers and watched his dark eyelashes flutter when the wind blew over him, calm and resting like a child in the arms of a woman he trusts. As much as she wanted him to be alive and well and to eventually wake up, the moment she was sharing with his still, warm body was so precious. With her free hand, she took a lock of her own damp hair and wiped it like a cloth across his face, brushing him clean, turning her pale yellow hair a shade of pink. Then she began to kiss his wound softly but thoroughly until it began to seal up perfectly as if it never was.

She kissed heartily his eyelids and brow, for the smell of his skin was intoxicating and she surrendered to it. She held her prince closely with her little white arms wrapped protectively around his body, and in this moment, he was her prince, all hers and no one else's. For as long as she watched over him and they were alone in the night, he belonged to her and she belonged to him and none of the silly details that divided their worlds counted for anything while they lay there in the sand. Her lips quivered as his breath warmed her chest and her chest warmed his face, and she ran her fingers through his raven-colored hair. For a brief second he opened his eyes and they met hers with a surge of electricity, as if they'd retained a bit of fire from the lightning storm. Her cheeks flushed red as she absorbed his brief but warm glance. In that second, she felt all the light and love in all the world flow into her, as if her entire life had been leading up to this. From somewhere deep inside, she felt herself begin to vibrate on a whole new frequency, an awakening that had her heart fluttering like a hummingbird's wings. He drifted off again, closing his eyes and slipping back to whatever beautiful place his mind was taking him. While she lay beside him, adoring everything about him she could see, she struggled to breathe quietly while her heart pumped so violently.

She stayed there with him all through the night, cradling him as he slept, feeling his chest rise and fall with every breath and praying that her time with him would never end. The dark night was their canopy and she wished it would shield them forever. But as it often does, dawn came all too fast with its sudden dose of reality; it would soon be time for goodbye, and time to slip away into her own world.

Oh, how she wanted him to see her! As the morning's first rays glimmered upon her milky white skin for the first time, she wished for nothing more than for him to see her. What good, she wondered, were all her charms and beauties if the only one she wanted couldn't appreciate them? She looked down and compared their lower halves; he was born to walk on land and she was born to roam the seas. As long as he had legs and she had a tail, love between them would be impossible. Suddenly, the notion dawned on her that perhaps her lifelong, previously inexplicable infatuation with the world above actually made perfect sense: had she been searching for Gabriel all along?

As the morning warmed up, she felt the pull of her underwater home tugging at her, knowing that soon he might wake and not understand what she was. Beginning to miss him already, she leaned in to kiss him one last time when suddenly, she felt a thundering rumble approaching from down the beach. Terrified, she pulled away from him and slid back into the water, jumping behind some big rocks to hide.

When she looked up, she saw a white horse galloping down the beach towards Gabriel's motionless body. He looked quite dead as he lay there in the sand, allowing shallow waves to push up over him in his tattered suit. The little mermaid was amazed at the sight of the swift and muscular white beast, realizing she had seen one just like it before, carved into the old walls of her father's palace.

How elegant the creature was . . . and there was a girl riding up on its back!

The thundering she had heard before was just the beast's hooves as they pounded the wet sand, gallivanting forward. The girl looked savagely beautiful, with her dark hair blowing wildly in the wind as she rode the brown leather saddle in denim shorts and a ripped t-shirt, her worn-out leather boots gripping the stirrups. She clutched the reins tightly and absorbed every gallop in perfect unison with the pace of her mare, recklessly speeding together down the beach, as if making an epic getaway. When she spotted Gabriel lying in the sand, she pulled back on the reins and her mare reared at the sight of him, coming to an abrupt halt. Startled and unsure, the girl jumped down and tiptoed toward the body, praying with all her might that she hadn't just stumbled upon a corpse. She had never stumbled upon a corpse before, but she was pretty sure something like that could easily ruin her day.

"Oh my God, gross if you're dead but please don't be . . . " she mumbled to herself as she got closer and leaned in, not knowing what to do. She tried shouting for help but there was no one around to hear her, except for the mermaid who was hiding from her. She knelt at his side and put her ear to his mouth like the princess had done. She had taken a CPR course once, but all she could really remember learning was that if a baby is choking, you're supposed to use your pinkie to check its mouth for lodged food. Once she felt his breath on her face and was sure he was alive, she gripped his collar with her left hand and pulled him up to sitting. As his head drooped to the side, she could tell that he was probably cute when he was conscious. So she wound up her right hand and slapped him, open-palm, hard across the face.

"JESUS!!!" he exclaimed as his dark eyes flew open, startled to death (or, in this case, to life.) As the girl backed away, she began to laugh nervously as the guy scrambled to his feet and then dizzily fell back down, discombobulated and confused by his surroundings. "Where am I?" he asked the girl whose palm was still throbbing from the slap. Her cheeks were rosy from the coastal winds and her hair was an unholy mess, but she was beautiful and full of life and such a sight for sore, waking eyes. She was like an angel. "Who are you?" he asked, scratching his head.

"Just glad you're not dead!" she replied excitedly, jumping to her knees to hug him. "I do apologize for slapping you, but I didn't know how else to wake you up! What are you doing sleeping on the beach so close to the water, anyway? What if that rip tide dragged you out?"

Gabriel looked around, puzzled. "I have no idea how I got here; I think the tide might have dragged me in. Unless … did you bring me here?" he asked her. She shook her head no, and so groggily, he attempted to piece together the events of the night. She giggled as she watched him because the concentration he wore on his face made him look like a slow kid doing math homework. "I was on the boat partying with all of my friends . . ." He squinted his eyes to the bright sun as he struggled to recollect. " . . . And then suddenly, a massive storm hit."

"I'll say!" the girl remarked. "The damn thing came out of nowhere, too; I swore it was going to blow the roof off the barn!" She took the reins of her mare and pat her on her big, dappled nose. "It sure scared the crap out of poor Savannah!"

"Well it was even scarier out in the water, let me tell you," said Gabriel. "I was untying one of the lifeboats when something big fell from a high shelf and cracked me on the head ..."

"Where?" she asked, coming closer to inspect his face for injuries. His eyebrows were manly yet pretty. "I don't see anything," she said, not entirely believing him.

"Right here on my temple!" he said, stretching out the skin of his face to show her. The one thing he definitely did recollect in his final lucid moment was being smashed on the temple by a giant vodka bottle. She stepped in to look closely, but found hardly a blemish across his evenly-tanned forehead. "There are no fresh wounds or bruises here," she said.

"That's impossible!" he said, tilting his head so she could see it better. "I saw it fall towards me and felt its blunt crack on my skull, and I remember it all fading to black as I fell head-first into stormy waters."

The girl shrugged her shoulders. "Well that's weird," she said, "'cause all I see is a tiny old scar that looks like it healed over some time in the nineties. And it looks more like a chicken pock anyway."

"Weird," he concurred, running his fingers over it and beginning to wonder if he had dreamt the whole thing. "So was there a lot of storm damage? Clearly I napped through the worst of it!"

"Not really," she said, thinking about the beaches she just rode by. "A few lawn chairs were upturned and some guy lost a kayak but that's about it for this area. Although, I did hear on the barn radio that there was a big party yacht that got tossed 'til it busted and some of the people on board had to be airlifted to shore!"

Gabriel started panicking. "Did they get everyone in okay? Did you hear if anyone was badly hurt?" Suddenly he became very worried about all his party guests.

"Yeah, they got everyone," she replied reassuringly. "Except ... they did say the search was still out for the birthday boy who fell overboard and disappeared..." she looked him up and down, noting how his ripped, tattered clothes had probably looked really fresh and crisp when he first put them on. She realized then what she had found. "Wait... the birthday boy was YOU, wasn't it?" she asked, almost laughing at the rare and unexpected situation.

He nodded gravely. "My family must be throwing conniptions right now!"

She shook her head in disbelief. "As if you're the guy they've been searching for all night!" she said incredulously. "They've had divers combing the reefs for your waterlogged corpse since midnight and all the while, you were right here, napping peacefully in the sand." Her eyes blurred as she recollected the tempestuous night he had survived. "That was the most hectic summer storm I've ever seen . . . but that still doesn't explain how you ended up all the way over here when they pulled all of your friends out of the waters just South of Chesterman Beach," she said, amazed and confused at the same time.

Gabriel stood dumbfounded. "Where is here?" he asked.

"More than halfway to Effingham Inlet! Probably like twenty miles down the coast."

Gabriel looked down at his body. He checked out his arms and was mildly happy to see the garish Audemars Piguet watch his aunt had given him was still on his wrist. He wondered how it could be possible that he could have swum that far with no recollection of it. He shuddered at a flashback of his terrified friends jumping from the rocking, busting ship.

"Are you going to be okay?" she asked with concern.

"I think so. But I have to get home now!" he answered. "What time is it?"

"Almost five a.m." she answered.

"What are *you* even doing awake?" he asked, looking at her funny.

"Well I went out to the barn to hang with Savannah last night 'cause she trips out during storms. I could hear her bucking and rearing from my room; she's a savage!

"Eventually she chilled out and the next thing I know, it's morning and I'm waking up to her nudging me with those massive, steamy nostrils aimed at my sleepy face. So we went for a ride to assess the local damage and spend our raucous exuberance. And then we found you!" she said ardently, clapping her hands. "I can tell this is going to make a lot of people very happy!"

"Thank you," said Gabriel, humbly but appreciatively.

"Happy birthday," she replied sweetly. "So did all your wishes come true?" she asked facetiously, reaching into her pocket and pulling out a handful of oats to feed her horse. Gabriel thought about that for a second and then smiled to himself.

"Pretty much!" he said, looking her up and down and noticing how pretty she was. "Except when I pictured this whole scenario, I didn't look like a shabby beach derelict and you hadn't just woken up in a barn."

"Well I try not to make a habit of it!" said the girl, mock-defensively. "But Savvy was freaking out, and I couldn't exactly bring her into *my* bed!"

Gabriel laughed. "Fierce equestrian loyalty; I respect that. So where do you live?"

"Right now, my residence is the Genevieve Meredith Ranch," she said.

"I've heard of that place. Isn't that an orphanage?" he asked, confused.

"Kind of," she answered. "I went to live there after my parents died and now I just spend my summers there. It's more of a sleep-away camp than anything."

"I'm sorry," he said.

"Yeah, me too," she said softly. "My parents were really cool. But, I've had a great life; I've never needed for anything, and in just a few days, I'll be taking off to go explore a chunk of this big, beautiful world!"

"That's wicked!" he said. They caught themselves gazing into each other's eyes, and both shyly looked away.

"Anyway, I should help you get home!" she said. "We can borrow a Sea-Doo from the marina and I could zip you home so they can call off the search party…"

"Uh, that won't be necessary," he said. "After the aquatic adventure I just had, I'd rather just keep this show on solid ground, at least for today."

"Fair enough," she said in agreement. "But it'll be a long walk!"

"Yeah really," he said, looking down at his feet with one shoe missing and the other filled with water, sand, and seaweed. "Crap."

"Savannah could get us there in under an hour, though!" she said, climbing onto her horse and motioning for Gabriel to climb on behind her. "Jump on, we'll take you!" Gabriel gave her an unsure look. "She's a good girl, I promise," she said, offering her hand and moving her foot out of the stirrup so he could step up and climb on. As he jumped on behind her, he steadied his arms around her waist and off they dashed down the beach towards his family's place. "Hold on tight, she's a spirited one!" she said as they took off, kicking up sand in their wake.

The little mermaid, still watching, was glad that someone had found Gabriel and that he was alive and well. However, it saddened her that he had no idea that she was the one who'd saved his life and kept him safe through the night. She followed them from the water all the way.

They arrived at his home after about an hour of riding, just like the girl had promised. They would have had him there in even better time, she swore, if only he hadn't needed to stop for a pee on five separate occasions along the way.

"This is it," he said as they approached the edge of his family's property. "Thanks so much for the ride, and the slap. How can I ever thank you?"

"I guess you could always slap me back," the girl said with a naughty wink, followed by a giggle. Again they held a stare for a moment, connecting in an indescribable way. "I should get back, though, and you should get inside! My people will be wondering where I've run off to with the horse, and your people are probably dying to know you're alive!"

Gabriel laughed a little and rubbed some sand out of his eyes. "Thanks a million; I mean it," he said.

"I'm really glad you're okay, and it was really nice meeting you," she replied.

Gabriel extended his hand to meet hers. "I don't think we technically did meet yet; I'm Gabriel."

"Erica," she said as she fit her hand into his. He squeezed her hand tightly and it sent shivers up her arm. For a second her imagination went wild and she pictured ripping off his torn shirt and taking him down in a passionate embrace.

"Well, Erica, it's not every day my birthday boat gets shipwrecked and I'm rescued by a mystery woman on horseback!" he said.

"Well, Gabriel, aren't we fortunate that the storm spit you out right onto my path?" She grinned at him as she lifted herself back into the saddle, having trouble holding back a huge, goofy smile.

"It was a bit of good fortune, all things considered!" he agreed. "Now I'd like the opportunity to show you my gratitude, both for the slap and for the ride home . . . "

The girl turned away from him and inwardly rejoiced while pretending to be adjusting something on the other side of the saddle. Then, impulsively, she pulled her foot out of the stirrup and hopped off to stand facing Gabriel. "Come here then," she said, pointing to her cheek and motioning for him to kiss her there.

"Love to," he said quietly to himself as he stepped forward to kiss his heroine on the cheek. As his lips made contact with her soft skin, she swiftly turned her head so that her lips met his. This caught him by surprise and he opened his eyes but held the kiss. Her warm breath on his face made him tingle, and after a long moment locking lips with this beautiful stranger, Gabriel pulled away and smirked. "You smell like barn," he said.

Instead of being shy and embarrassed about it, Erica pinched her shirt and held it to her nose, taking in a big whiff of her smelly clothes. "Yes, yes I do," she said with a laugh. "Well, good luck to you, Gabriel. Hopefully we'll catch each other on the flipside," she said as she jumped back onto her horse.

"When?" he asked, quite obviously intrigued by her.

"I don't know," she said with a smile as she turned her horse back the way they came. "I really have to go now, though."

"Why the rush?" he asked, confused.

"Because you have to get back inside to your family," she answered. "Remember that right now, they probably think you're dead. And Savvy and I have to get back to our smelly barn!"

"Can't they all just wait a minute?" he asked. "At least give me a number or an email address so we can stay in touch!"

Ericas sighed. "To tell you the truth, Gabriel, I know we just met, but I think I might like you. So what I need to do right now is get out of here now before I'm sure I do."

Gabriel shook his head. "But that makes no sense! At least let me call you so I can take you to dinner," he insisted. She shook her head. "Lunch then?" he asked. She shook her head again. "Coffee?!"

Erica smiled, flattered. "I'm sorry. You are so incredibly handsome, but going on a date with you would be against my plan!" she said. "I'm on this tip where I'm not trying to like anyone right now. I have a big year of traveling ahead of me and I promised myself that I wouldn't get involved with anyone that could potentially slow me down."

Gabriel waved that comment off. "I'm not looking to slow you down; I'm just trying to thank the girl who saved my life by taking her out for a nice meal. Won't you let me?" he asked as he stared hopefully into her eyes. She smiled.

"You're very sweet but here's the thing: I know that my next great love is already on its way to me. I've felt it coming for quite some time and I'll be ready for it very soon, just not *yet*. I don't want to meet the right guy at the wrong time, you see. I hope you understand."

"Then let me be the wrong guy at the right time!" he pleaded, feeling like a desperate man whose dream girl was about to take off on horseback. He looked and felt disheveled and kind of crazy in his torn clothing while he begged her for a date. He had never begged for anything before in his life.

While she considered his tempting offer, she looked over his shoulder at the house behind him. Then suddenly, her face dropped and she looked like she had seen a ghost. She realized she recognized it, like it was a place she had once known very well, long ago. Then she looked down at Gabriel and in spite of the rough shape he was in, she began to realize she recognized him too. "Wait—you're not—Gabriel *O'Faolain*?" she asked in disbelief. He nodded, wearing an unsure look upon his face. "Ok, now I really have to go," she said with a stunned laugh. "Very nice to see you Gabriel, it is so good that you're alive, I'm so glad I could be a part of that, good day to you sir!" With that, she clicked her tongue a couple times and her horse gladly took off into a spirited canter before he could even begin to ask her how she knew his last name. "Wear a lifejacket!" she yelled back to him while he stood in her dust with a dumbfounded face.

Gabriel, still stunned by the impromptu kiss, put his fingers to his lips as he watched her ride away. Once she had disappeared around the sandy bend, he adjusted his boxers, as they still felt a bit tight in the crotch since their kiss, and there was a lot of sand in there, chafing him. He waited a few moments, vainly hoping she might reconsider and come back around but when she didn't, he turned to walk up the steps to his family.

As he wearily walked up to the house, the little mermaid pulled herself up onto the rock she had been hiding behind. She imagined how wonderful it would be to walk up those steps beside him.

As he approached the front door and reached for its handle, it flew open wide and his petite mother, Lucia, jumped up into his arms and administered the most suffocating hug she could muster, shellacking his face with the plasma of a hundred teary kisses and holding her son like she planned to never let him go again. Her dark hair and her usually pretty middle-aged face looked puffy and tired, like that of a mother who had been up all night worrying about her baby. Pulling him gregariously into the house, she let the screen door fall shut behind them and just like that, the mermaid was left out all on her lonesome. His home had wood and stone steps from the front terrace all the way down into the sea, as if the ocean was merely the south-west wing of the family's lovely home. She felt a cool breeze blow over her, so she slid back off the rock and sunk herself low into the shallow waters. She was chilled to the bone; it was as if even the air itself was taunting her, letting her know just how out-of-her-element she was in loving a human. With her heart feeling strangely heavy, she slumped herself into the soft mud in quiet contemplation of her day's events, and of the new soul she had just found to love.

# nine

## What News of the Upper World?

"Gabriel's home! Everybody, he's here!" His mom screamed as they stepped into the living room where the family was gathered. His youngest sister Demetra jumped up and ran to her beloved only brother.

"You're alive! You're alive!" she shouted gleefully, jumping up into his arms. He held his sister close as she sniffled. "We thought we lost you, too," she whispered.

Gabriel looked around at the tired, worried faces of his loved ones that all looked relieved but amazed to see him standing right in front of them. His dad, mom, and two sisters looked like they had just spent the night camped out on the living room couches, as they were all still wearing the clothes he last saw them in and there were crumpled tissues, pillows and throw blankets in piles around them. He tried to lighten the mood by laughing. "No one lost me; I'm here and I'm fine! Don't tell me you were actually worried ..."

Ava, his eldest sister, stood with her back turned to the family in front of the large living room window that faced the beach. "Actually, Gabriel, no one got a wink of sleep in this house because we were actually worried." Her unimpressed tone was obvious.

"Well, I'm terribly sorry, dear family, but the boat got wrecked and I washed up on shore somewhere near Effingham." He said, kissing his little sister on the forehead. "I woke up to a hard slap from a girl who happened upon my unconscious body while she was out on her horse!"

"Someone slapped you?" asked Demetra.

"That is correct," he answered. "Before anyone asks, I have no idea how I got there but I remember the freak storm and the waves busting the boat up." He turned to his father, a kindly man named Cliff. "Dad, I'm so sorry."

"Don't even worry; we have insurance for that!" said Cliff, stepping forward to hug his boy. "We're all just thanking our lucky stars you're okay!"

Lucia shoved the Kleenex she had been dabbing her runny nose with into her pocket, then wiped her teary hands on her jeans before putting them to Gabriel's cheeks. "What took you so long to come back?" she asked.

"I came back as fast as I could," he began.

Ava snorted. "But not before you were done kissing that girl, right?" She had seen Gabriel and the girl through the window, and was offended that he would leave his family worrying for even a second more than necessary just to chat up a girl on the beach. "Was that the same bitch who slapped you?" she asked him.

Gabriel couldn't hold back his grin. "She gave me a ride back. And she's not a bitch, she's a nice girl. Like I said, I washed up really far down the beach. . ."

"How is that even possible?" demanded Ava. "The current couldn't take you that far in that much time."

"I don't quite understand it myself," he replied.

"I saw you go under water, knocked out with your head all bloody!"

"I remember that too!" he said as he felt the skin of his forehead. "But somehow I've miraculously healed . . . it doesn't make any sense."

"I dove in after you," she said bitterly. "But you had disappeared. We all thought you were dead! So thanks for taking your sweet-ass time getting back to us; it's been lots of fun."

"Ava, please!" interjected Lucia. "Can't we just be grateful he's back now?"

"So no one got hurt?" asked Gabriel anxiously.

Cliff stepped forward. "But for a few scrapes and bruises, everyone is fine. It seems all your friends are really strong swimmers! The only things that didn't make it out were a few designer purses and a lot of deck wood."

Lucia, starting to choke up again, grabbed a hold of her son and began to sob. "Gabriel, I don't know what we would have done if we lost you too," she said, peering up at him through teary eyes.

"Hey now! Come on, Mom, I'm fine! And everyone else is fine! Didn't you hear Dad? All we lost were the boat and some purses!" He hugged his mom close and pulled Demetra in, too. Cliff wrapped his arms around their group hug and the only one left was Ava. "You too, big sis!" he said as he waved her over. But Ava refused to budge, choosing instead to stand away from them with her arms crossed.

"I'm sorry I made you worry," said Gabriel. "Now please get over here; you're in this hug too!" But she just wiped her teary eyes nonchalantly and started across the room towards the kitchen, eyeing her brother coldly. "When you're done down here, I suggest you run upstairs before your playmate Rourke finishes his forgery of your last will and takes with him anything he thinks you won't need in the afterlife. I'm going to let the coast guard know they can call off the search party now." And with that, she pulled her cell phone out of her pocket and dialed, walking out of the room.

Gabriel, Dagmara, their mother Lucia, and their father Cliff all caught each other's eyes and, in silent agreement, grabbed each other by the hands and swiftly followed her into the next room. As soon as she was in their sightline again, they all hollered like beasts and ran at her, attacking her with the group hug she had declined. She protested but they tickled her into submission and her pouty face opened up into a smile, at long last.

After a good long hug, they all let go of each other and stepped away. "Can I get you anything? You must be parched," asked Lucia, noticing how red the whites of her son's eyes were.

"Yes, Mum, water would be awesome. My throat feels all gross and salty."

"Okay, baby," she replied, fetching him a glass. "Well, now that you're home and all is well, I see no reason to change our plans! Are you almost done packing? Think you'll be ready to leave by tomorrow?"

"Yep, almost done!" he replied, then kissed his mom on the cheek one more time before dashing up the stairs to his bedroom. Lucia stared lovingly at her son as he went, admiring the polite and handsome young man he had grown into. She congratulated herself on a job well done and said a quiet prayer of thanks that the storm hadn't taken him away.

Gabriel sent his friend Rourke away with a backpack full of DVDs and after a few hours of dragging bags out and organizing, the O'Faolain family sat down to their last cottage dinner until the next year. The beach was strangely quiet, in the lonely way it always felt after Labor Day weekend was over and the town was noticeably less populous. Mentally preparing themselves for their return to the bustling city, they were already beginning to miss the wonderful sounds and smells of summertime at the beach.

As the sun went down that evening, it cast a blood-orange glow through the wide windows of Gabriel's bedroom while he sat up in bed reading the last few pages of *Anna Karenina*. He was eager to finish so he could leave the five-pound leather-bound edition on the cottage bookcase instead of lugging it back to his condo where his bookshelves were already jammed. For reasons even he didn't quite comprehend, he was only ever drawn to reading old books with soft, worn covers that looked (and smelled) like they once lined the walls of some brandy room or eighteenth-century library. To Gabriel, there really was something about an old book that felt to his hands like it had been held and read about a thousand times, and experienced over and over.

By the time he turned the last page, it was already getting dark outside. He felt strangely comfortable up there in his room, taking in Tolstoy with after-dinner tea and biscotti just like he had so many other nights that summer. Except that this time, he truly appreciated every second of his quiet indulgence, knowing that he could have very easily perished in the storm, never to know the chilled-out joy of reading classic literature in his room ever again. Beginning to feel sticky-hot under the light of his lamp, he walked out to his balcony for some fresh air.

As he sat in his lounger quietly recollecting, he believed he was very much alone under the moonlight with the breezy gusts that filled his nose with the scent of rain-soaked cedars. He pulled his grandfather's old harmonica off the windowsill and began to play a tune that complemented the whistling of the winds. Then he noticed something splashing around in the moon's reflection on the water.

Curiously, he stood up and squinted to see what it was. From where he stood, it looked like it must have been a creature of nimble grace, like a dolphin out there twirling among the shiny speckles that dappled the surface. He kept his eyes on the creature, appreciating its dance, surprised to see how close it was to the shore. He never imagined that whatever it was, it was dancing on the water just for him.

"Maybe it's a mermaid," whispered a voice from right behind him. Startled, he dropped his harmonica and it fell off his balcony and into the sand. He jumped and turned to see it was just his little sister Demetra, who had no trouble sneaking up on him while he watched the water, entranced.

Gabriel laughed her suggestion off while he pulled her up to the railing beside him. Sometimes she could be pretty unrealistic but her dreaminess and blatant disregard for popular belief was his favourite thing about her. "What did I say about sneaking up on me, you little monkey?" he said as he caught her in a headlock and began tickling her sides.

She began to giggle hysterically. "You . . . said . . . you . . . would . . . tickle . . . the . . . sneaky . . . right . . . outta me!" she squealed between laughs. "Okay, okay . . . enough, Gabe!"

"Well I hope you've learned your lesson this time, because next time, I'm going straight for the armpits!" he said playfully, smoothing out her hair that he had just made a mess of. "Check it out," he said, pointing to the water. "It's my dolphin!"

Demetra stepped up onto the railing and leaned into her big brother. She was only nine and very petite, but she was a formidable personality, and wise beyond her years. She squinted to see. "How can you tell it's a dolphin from here? It could just as easily be a mermaid."

Gabriel laughed at her suggestion once again; his little sister always seemed to look for reasons to believe that things generally accepted as mere make-believe could actually exist. In her eyes, the world was far more magical a place than most people allowed themselves to imagine.

"Good point, little D; perhaps it is a mermaid," he said, looking out at the graceful creature as it danced. The more he watched, the less ridiculous her assertion sounded, for there was something unmistakably feminine in the way it moved across the water.

"Maybe it's the same mermaid that swam you to shore," she said, her eyes lighting up. "Maybe she's just hanging out to make sure you're okay."

Gabriel thought about that suggestion for a moment. Sure, he sometimes found it amusing to play into her whimsical ideas, but now that she was getting older he wondered if he was doing her any favors by continuing to be a party to such silliness. He agreed there was some merit to being imaginative, but mermaids? He decided to kibosh the notion, lest his baby sister grow up maladjusted and spacey.

"You should write some more storybooks," he said, patting her on the head.

"Yeah? Why's that?" she asked.

"Because you're always coming up with fresh, cute story ideas!" he answered. "And because mermaids and the like belong in fairy tales, not in the waters around our beach house."

Demetra thought about what her brother said and was just the slightest bit offended. "Fine," she said, crossing her arms over her chest. "I'll save my theories for someone who can appreciate the logic behind them."

Gabriel laughed. "Logic?" he said gently yet mockingly. "Meaty, are you trying to tell me that all of this mermaid talk of yours stems from logical, sound reasoning?" She shrugged but then nodded. "Demetra," said Gabriel, putting his hand on her shoulder, "you're the smartest kid I know . . . but let's not confuse fairy tales with reality. Mermaids are folklore; the stuff of Disney cartoons. Try not to get 'em too twisted, or people might start thinking you're a whack job!"

Demetra just smiled patiently and gave him a knowing look, as if to say *you poor, insipid thing*. "Indeed, that is the predilection most widely accepted so at that, I acquiesce and bid you good-night, dear brother." Then she yawned, stretched and gave him a big hug, whispering in his ear, "I'm just glad you came back to us. You're my only brother . . . who would protect me from mean boys?" Gabriel was touched, so glad to be back as well. As she stepped through the doorway into the house, she glanced back over her shoulder at him, still leaning on the railing. "Oh and Gabe," she started, "do let me know when you come up with a more reasonable explanation for how you ended up safely on shore twenty miles from the wreck, all magically healed from your bottle wound and with no recollection of how you got there." Then she winked, and scampered off to her room.

Alone in the night again, he thought about what his sister said and looked back out at sea. The dolphin or mermaid or whatever it was, was gone off to wherever it is they go and after the day he'd had, it was time for him to go to bed too. So he waved good night to the moon and went inside, blithely unaware that his mermaid had swum in closer to eavesdrop on his conversation with his sister. Still too far to hear their words, she daringly pulled herself out of the water and crawled across the sand until she was sitting just beneath his balcony. There, she found the harmonica he had dropped and tied it into her long hair while staring up at the light in his window, hoping for another glimpse.

Lying on his bed, his thoughts turned to Erica. He wondered if she would come around to drop in on him the next summer, or if she would fall in love somewhere along her travels and forget all about ever meeting him. He turned onto his side, pulled the cord of his lamp, and closed his eyes. It had been a crazy twenty-four hours for him, and it was high time that he finally went to sleep.

When the little mermaid saw the last light in the house extinguish, she crawled back to the water and began to wade out with her lips on his harmonica just the way he had been playing it. One day that will be my home, she said to herself as she looked back one last time, and, with a huge grin from ear-to-ear, she dove under and began making her way back to her father's castle. When she arrived, everyone was still up waiting for her, almost as worried for her as Gabriel's loved ones had been for him.

"What news of the upper world, child?" asked her grandmother as she entered, relieved to see her safe. All was silent on the ocean floor as everyone in the kingdom gathered close to hear what she had to say.

The princess took a deep breath. She knew she couldn't tell anyone that she had rescued a human from drowning, because no one would understand and it would get her in a great deal of trouble. So she simply spoke about the beauty she'd seen. "It was the most wonderful place," she began. "I saw the smoldering sunset and just knew I couldn't leave without seeing the sunrise on the other side. I'm sorry if I made anyone worry." Everyone was so happy to see that she was safe that they all forgave her tardiness and continued with their revels. As soon as she was sure no one would notice, she snuck away from the courtyard and swam to her garden to daydream about Gabriel all by herself.

# ten

## *Fandom*

---

The next morning, Gabriel woke up bright and early to take advantage of the neat swell that was rolling through on his last day at the beach house. He pulled his damp wetsuit off the balcony railing and slipped into it, tucking in his board shorts so they wouldn't catch the zipper. It was cold as always but as always, totally worth it because North Pacific water can be freezing on bare skin. He grabbed his board from the toy shed and walked down to the water. The waves were perfect and it surprised him that there were no other surfers out. So he strapped his leash onto his ankle and paddled out alone.

Between rides, he kept his eyes trained on the beach for signs of Erica, but she never showed. Slightly disappointed but not entirely surprised, he came in after a couple hours, unstrapped himself and took to packing the last of his things. The O'Faolains enjoyed one last lunch on the patio and then loaded up the cars, secured the storm windows and took off for the ferries, excited to get back to their normal lives but already looking forward to the summer that would follow after the next three colder seasons.

About half an hour after they locked up the house and left, Erica came galloping down the beach. She'd spent the entire day considering whether it was a good idea, and had only decided that afternoon that she would just go for it. The truth was, she had been thinking of him non-stop and was unable to get his warm brown eyes out of her head since she dropped him off and they parted ways the day before.

When she arrived at the edge of the property, she climbed off Savannah's back and tied her reins into a loose knot so she wouldn't trip on them while grazing on the grassy lawn. She pulled her ponytail out and finger-combed her hair, smoothed her t-shirt and pulled her jeans down so they sat seductively upon her hipbones. She had gone through a few different outfits before riding over but had decided on this white tee and jeans, because she knew she looked hot in them without appearing to be trying to be hot. As she walked up the steps, she noticed the storm windows were closed and all the lawn furniture had been taken in. The closer she got to the house, the more she arrived at the sinking realization that there was no one home. She knocked on the door anyway but when she put her ear to it, heard nothing from inside. *Shit. D a m n. Oh, well . . .* she thought, and gave up.

She walked back down the stairs slowly, berating herself for waiting too long and thereby, missing her chance. She thought about leaving a note for him, but decided that by the time he got it, likely in the spring, he would have by then forgotten all about meeting her. So she climbed back onto her horse and began to ride away. She was disappointed, but decided it was all for the better, anyway.

The little mermaid went back to visit Gabriel that day too but like Erica, she came too late to see him. Cloaked in darkness, she hid behind the rocks and sang her most beautiful songs, hoping to coax him out of the house somehow. Sadly, for all her efforts, there was nothing she could do about the fact that he was gone. In his absence, all she had was the vivid memory of his face, the steely taste of his harmonica in her mouth, and a view from the water of his cold, dark and empty summer home.

# eleven

# Visits

---

Autumn came quickly with a chill across the water and still, he never returned. Fall foliage gave way to winter flurries, and still, every day without fail, she came back and sang, hoping he would show. Springtime saw fresh green grass push up from the damp dirt but still there was no sign of him. But she thought about him every minute of every day, and couldn't get his face out of her mind.

At home in the palace, she became very withdrawn. Her family saw less and less of her and she fell deeper and deeper into her own little world. One night, upon returning from yet another fruitless visit feeling bored and despondent, she decided to visit her garden for the first time in a very long time. She had long since given up caring for it, and vines and weeds now overran her once thriving flowerbed. At the foot of her beloved statue, she lay down on her belly and stared up, admiring its noble brow and languishing without the company of its flesh-and-blood doppelganger. Though the statue was made of cold stone and in no way compared to the warmth of Gabriel's sleeping body, it was still the closest thing she had to him, and so she cherished it. Bringing her head to rest at the statue's feet, she wrapped her arms lovingly around its ankles and fell asleep dreaming of her love.

The next day, she woke up feeling even emptier and lonelier than she had before. After a silent breakfast by herself in the courtyard, she swam very slowly out of the palace and up through the water. Like she had been doing all autumn, winter and spring, she made the long trek to the North Pacific and began to rise to the surface in front of Gabriel's place. After ample thought and consideration, the princess decided that after this day she would never again visit, for as much as she missed him with all her heart, she thought it best not to waste her life pining for someone who may or may not even exist anymore.

When she reached the top, the day was warm and sunny and the fragrance of a thousand flower blossoms filled the air. She swam in a little closer and as she approached the breaker, noticed that she was sharing the water with scores of surfers out there bobbing on their boards or standing up riding the waves. Curiously, she moved in closer, even though she knew she was in great danger of being seen. Then, only a few feet behind the surfer farthest out, the unmistakable scent of him carried out upon the wind. Instantly, she knew it was him right there in front of her!

She ducked back under and let out an elated scream of joy while she spun in hoops and marveled at her unbelievably good fortune. It seemed unlikely and impossible that after all that waiting, he was there, right in front of her, with nothing between them but a bit of churning water. She swam under his feet as he let them dangle off the sides of his board, and when she reached out a finger to touch one, she giddily watched him flinch away. As a wave rolled toward him and he paddled in to catch it, she let herself tumble along the sand beneath him, looking up as he balanced on his board right above her. He had no idea that there was a little mermaid right under him, watching him enthusiastically and applauding his impressive skills.

Her cheeks were pink with exhilaration as she secretly played with him, never more than a few feet away but invisible so long as she stayed beneath the surface, obscured by weeds and dark slimy things. After each ride, she watched him slide belly-first back onto his board and paddle back out, propelled by his strong arms and cupped hands. After a while, she began to get bolder, swimming even closer to him, running her fingers along the board's smooth resin and investigating its four plastic rudders that seemed to mimic her own pelvic fins. As he paddled out, she was careful not to let his arms and hands hit her, but allowed his fingers to run unknowingly through her long hair, letting him think he was just touching a bit of sea vine.

Growing bored of hiding from him and desperately wanting him to see her, she threw caution to the wind and popped her head up out of the water, allowing her face and milky white shoulders to sit in plain view. Her tail was hidden beneath the surface but even still, allowing herself to be seen at all went against the most important rule her father had ever given her. Today, though, her father and his rigid law seemed far beneath her so she did what her heart told her and surfaced just a few yards ahead of him, smiling like the happiest girl on land or sea.

When the bright sun reflected off of her ornate necklace, the shimmer caught his eye and he steered away from her just in time to avoid letting his board strike her in the face. He lost his balance and fell backwards into the water and when he came back up, he looked for her but she was nowhere to be found. Meanwhile, the mischievous little mermaid giggled uncontrollably to herself under the water, intoxicated and dizzy after their close encounter and feeling as though her ribs could burst open from the pressure of her pounding heart. Gabriel kept his eyes trained on the water, thinking that whoever it was he saw in the water would eventually have to come up for air. He waited several minutes for her, but she never did come back up.

Gabriel's perplexity was interrupted by the sound of his friend Rourke's unimpressed voice. "Dude, what are you looking for?" he asked, sitting back on his board and watching for the next set of waves. "Saw your bail; that was embarrassing. Good thing there are no girls out here today."

"Did you see that girl that was just here?" asked Gabriel, pointing to the water and looking confused. Rourke shook his head and spoke like he was talking to a three-year-old.

"No. Like I just said, there are no girls out here today."
Gabriel scratched his head. "But there was a girl, and she was right here in the water a minute ago. I almost hit her with my board - that's why I bailed!"

Rourke rolled his eyes. "Don't tell me you're lame enough to blame your bail on a chick that's not even here, Gabe."

"Seriously!" Gabriel insisted. "She popped up right in front of me, I tried to pivot around her and then fell. Now I don't see her anywhere."

"That's because there are no girls out here today," reiterated Rourke.

"I wouldn't make this up," said Gabriel. "I swear I saw a girl in the water."

"What did she look like?" asked Rourke, interested as always.

"I only saw her for a brief second," Gabriel responded, thinking.

Rourke furrowed his brows. "If you can't even describe one girly characteristic, how can you presume it was a girl?"

"Because she had long hair and a girly face," offered Gabriel.

"What color?" asked Rourke.

"White," said Gabriel

"Her hair was white?!" Rourke threw his hands up in the air.

"No, she was white. Very white. Her hair was, I dunno, blonde. Honey blonde. But also kinda white. Really light honey-white blond."

"Hot?" asked Rourke.

"Like I said, only saw her for a second," said Gabriel.

"HOT?!" repeated Rourke, growing impatient.

"She was pretty," answered Gabriel.

A sly smile of disbelief crept across Rourke's face. "If there were girls out today, I'd be flexing mad nuts, perfecting my dirty layback. I certainly would NOT be sitting here with you discussing the possibility that there might be girls in the water that I didn't see come out. After all these years you've known me, don't you think my peripherals are conditioned to spot a pretty blond if she swam out?!"

Gabriel paused for a moment then acquiesced like he often did, not because Rourke was necessarily right, but because it was so rarely worth arguing over. "You're right," he said sarcastically. "There could not have been a girl out here 'cause you'd have definitely seen her first."

Rourke nodded and scanned the beach with his beady eyes. "I would've smelled her approaching," he said slimily, grinning like a hungry crocodile.

"I have no doubts," said Gabriel in mock solemnity. "She must have just been another vision."

"Wait a sec ..." said Rourke, grappling to pull up a memory that had gone fuzzy after years of regular pot smoking. Suddenly his tone was one of concern and he asked his friend, "Are you having visions of Dagmara again?"

This was not the first time Gabriel had thought he saw a girl in the water that just wasn't there. On several occasions while out on his board, he thought he'd seen the face of his long-lost twin sister appear to him in the water's wavy reflections.

Dagmara had gone missing after a solo surf one evening several years earlier. Gabriel had been out with friends that night or he would have been in the water with her, a fact that never ceased to make him feel somewhat responsible when he thought about it. The friends she had been surfing with had long since packed it in for the day but she stayed out, alone like she usually preferred it, to be the only dark silhouette against the deep red horizon. Dagmara was an inspired surfer who was always searching, always pushing herself to improve which often meant staying out in the water longer than anyone. When the skies had turned dark that night and her daughter had not yet come in, Lucia went out to find her but by then she'd already vanished. Only her board was left behind sitting neatly in the sand, and there was a set of footprints from it going straight down to the water. She called a search party and they scoured the water, coast, and forests, but could find her nowhere. Dagmara was never seen or heard from again.

"Come to think of it," said Gabriel thoughtfully, "she did look a bit like Dagmara, except with that light white blonde hair I mentioned." It had been a long time since she disappeared, but there was something in the air that day that reminded him of the old days when he still had his twin by his side. He shrugged it off, thinking it must really have been just another hallucination of her. Meanwhile, the mermaid stayed below, deciding not to pop up again, at least for today. While Gabriel sat up on his board waiting for another break, she took the opportunity to observe his feet up close. Such funny-looking things they were! They were long and flat and had little digits growing off them, escalating in size from the outside toe to the big one. For reasons unbeknown to her, she suddenly felt the compelling urge to bite one. She wasn't thinking about biting hard, but something about the sight of his twinkling toes in the cold water made her just want to take a little nibble. Perhaps it was instinctive, due to the fact that she was technically half-fish. In any event, she put her mouth around his big toe and gently sucked on it. Gabriel felt it but thought nothing of it, for fish had definitely nibbled at his dangling toes before.

After a few more hours of paddling hard and perfecting tricks, the guys finally tired themselves out and went in for dinner. With a strange and wonderful lightness in her soul, she sang her most joyous songs all the way back to the palace. The fruitless months she had spent looking for him now seemed like dark and distant memories compared with the unreal beauty of being as close to him as she had been that day.

When she arrived at the palace, songs that dripped with the sweet honey of young love still fell from her lips, permeating the quiet stillness of the halls. Her father, having grown increasingly suspicious of where it was she kept swimming off to, had ordered her to be followed that day. By the time she returned that evening, her whole family had already been given a detailed account of everything she'd been up to at the surface. Upon her arrival, she was met by two of her father's guards who ushered her to the grand hall where they were all waiting for her. As soon as she entered the room, she knew she had been caught.

All five of her sisters looked up at her with sad, worried eyes while her father wore the arduous expression he always wore when he was about to make the kinds of difficult decisions that only a king and a father could be charged with. As her sisters got up to leave the room, each in turn gave her a kiss as they filed past her, wishing her luck. She hung her head low, bracing herself for a reprimanding. Taking a deep breath, she looked up at her grandmother whom she could usually count on to lighten up the situation. This day, the old queen's face was stoic and austere as she sat on her throne with her hands folded in her lap. The little mermaid knew right away that she was in deep, unavoidable trouble.

"Are you aware, daughter, that your actions today have put everyone in this kingdom in grave danger?" The king's stern voice bellowed out through the grand hall, making all the walls rumble with the serious nature of his words.

The mermaid closed her eyes and nodded. "But I only let him see me for a moment. I swam away fast; he did not see my tail!" After she admitted to her actions, she looked up at her father's face expecting it to be angry but was surprised to find it had already faded some. Usually he was a hard man when it came to addressing important security matters but right now as he sat before his incorrigible teenage daughter, he simply wore the face of a concerned and loving parent.

"I'm sorry, Father," she said. "I know I acted recklessly, and I shall never go in so close again. You have my word." But even as the words escaped her lips, she knew there was nothing that could stop her from seeing him again.

Her father, the wise, all-knowing king of the seas, could see right through her bold-faced lie. "Daughter, you must understand my position," he said in a voice that was far less stern than she was expecting. "For the safety of all of our kind, I cannot allow you to visit the surface ever again."

The mermaid looked up at her father disbelievingly. She even smiled for a second in hopes that he was joking, because the idea of being forbidden from the surface was an idea far too bleak to wrap her head around. But the king was serious, and his word was law.

"Father, my soul has carried me to his and I've been powerless to pull away. My heart beats for his, Father. I must be allowed to see him, or strike me dead right here and now for there will be no life for me without him."

The king was taken aback; he had underestimated just how afflicted his youngest daughter was. His face softened up even more. "Daughter, you are so young. I remember first infatuation, and though it has all the symptoms of love, it is not the same thing."

The princess shook her head, and would hear of nothing that suggested this was anything less than true love. "He is my match, Father," she insisted. "I feel it in my bones when I am near him. When I am not near him, I feel nothing but emptiness."

"You are well aware of the situation," he said. "We are different from the humans. You heard your sisters' reports! We must keep our existence a secret from them for the rest of our time here, and that is final."

She scowled. "He is not like the rest of them!" she exclaimed desperately. "He loves the ocean and today I saw him dance upon it more beautifully than anything I've ever seen! I love the human world so much, and I love him with my whole heart. I know that I will not lead our kind back to this planet, even though I would love to. So I want to see the world above while I live here in the blue! I want to experience it all so that when it is time for me to go, I will have seen it all and will be satisfied."

The queen cast her eyes down to the eight beautiful oysters clamped to her tail. The oysters served as both a symbol of her royal status as well as a reminder of the immense responsibility that went along with it. It was royal duty to put the welfare of the kingdom before all else and today, her young progeny would learn the hard way that no mer-person who makes themself known to a human would be free to ever do it again.

"You will not love a human, Princess," she said sternly but softly. "As a daughter of the seas, your place is here."

The littlest mermaid shook her head in frustration. "But I have chosen him! And he will choose me, I know he will!" she said passionately. "I have already fallen in love with him; it's already too late to turn back!"

The king looked his daughter up and down with his slate grey eyes, in disbelief of what she was saying. "If he learns of our world," he said, "his kind will find us eventually, and when they do, their crusade of exploitation will not end until they have destroyed our whole world for profit."

The mermaid lowered her head. She knew that she could not argue, because everything he was saying about humans had already been proven. But she didn't care, for something inside her had awakened the day she saved him and she was addicted to the feeling of being close to him. Now fiercely dependent on being in his proximity, the princess was helpless to pull away.

"Father, I realize it makes no sense to you, but there is nothing you can do to stop me from loving him, for I must follow my own heart." Then she bowed to her mighty father and turned to swim away to her room, hoping he wouldn't challenge it, at least for the night. But behind her, the king sighed regretfully and then spoke, his deep voice echoing out into the courtyard.

"I am sorry, daughter, but I am afraid it has already been done." As the words hit her ears, they sent chills up her spine and an aching to her chest. Suddenly, it all became clear to her and she knew exactly what he meant. Without a second's hesitation, she flapped her tail wildly and took off like a shot, propelling herself straight up towards the surface. The closer she got, the harder she pushed her strong, pretty tail to carry her even faster to where the water would end and the sky would begin. She braced herself, then, as she went to jump through the threshold, slammed into it so hard, she swore she felt her bones crack. Just as she had feared, her father had ordered the gateway to the upper world closed off to her as a security measure for the benefit of their entire race. It was as if a shiny pane of thick glass enrobed the ocean's surface, creating a ceiling that was hard and impenetrable. Frantically, she backed up and hurled her body into it again, trying desperately to break it, throwing all her weight at it in a vain effort to make just one little crack, but to no avail. She pounded her fists against it like she was being buried alive and screamed so loud one would've expected it to shatter but it held strong as solid stone and her every painful attempt was quashed.

Defeated, she resigned from her futile endeavor and let her limp, sore body sink back down to the palace where her father and grandmother still sat on their thrones, wearing pitying expressions for she whose dreams had just been dashed. It saddened them both deeply to cage her in but they did not know what else they could do when she was such a liability.

The princess stood before them, staring them both down from behind her sad, tired eyes that carried a fury in them that flickered intermittently between moments of understanding and regret. She knew she had left them no choice. So the sad little mermaid bowed her head and turned and swam out to her garden to be alone. When she was quite sure that no one had followed her, she wrapped her arms around her marble statue and wept, sobbing bitterly until she fell asleep curled up at its feet. And just like all the other mermaids, she was unable to shed a single tear, and so the unreleased, exquisite pain of her heartbreak just kept recycling itself throughout her body, mind and soul, hollowing out her heart and torturing the poor girl all through the cold night.

When the princess awoke the next day, she felt hopelessly lost. Her face ached from weeping and she felt like she had aged a thousand years. She lay on her back and stared up at the surface, a sight that used to bring her so much joy but on this day, only served to remind her of the warmth she would never again feel, and the door that was once so open that now locked her in. The ocean, her prison, had never felt so small.

She closed her eyes as she lay, flattening the weeds and flowers of her wilted garden. She began wishing her three hundred years were up already so she could begin fresh in a galaxy far away. Still groggy and filled with a deep, heavy sorrow, she got up and began to swim briskly away from the palace. On her way, she passed friends and family but did not wave or say hello. All by herself, she passed through the gates and out into the jungles, where sea weeds grow even taller than the castle's highest towers. When she passed them she continued outward, swimming as fast as she could to leave the palace and her father's laws as far behind her as possible. She wasn't sure where she was headed but she did not slow down, for anywhere would be better than there. She kept swimming until she reached the roaring maelstroms, a place all mer-people know better than to cross because if they catch you in their cyclones, there is no hope of swimming out. Bravely, she darted through them.

Once safely on the other side, the little mermaid swam deep; deeper into the dark, cavernous pits that not even the bravest of her kind dare ever trespass, for it is known throughout all the oceans that the Sea Witch dwells at the very bottom, in her cave of all things lost.

# twelve

A Trade

---

The little mermaid didn't fear the witch; the only thing on her mind was finding a way to break her father's spell so that she could return to the surface again. The further she went, the more frightening the variety of sea creatures swimming about her, sniffing her out, testing her resolve to go further. As she swam past the black polyps that lined the cave walls, they reached out and wrapped themselves tightly around her fins, arms and hair but she managed to wiggle out of their grip. Unstoppable in her quest, she proceeded further down until she was hovering at the edge of a wretched garden of worms.

She had heard about the garden before, where row upon row of slimy, slithering worms dwelled in a bed of green muck that was like a horrid welcome mat at the witch's doorway. Each worm in the garden was a poor soul who had made a deal with the old hag and lost, now doomed to spend their remaining sea years as one of her muculent little pets. The mermaid knew the massive risk she was taking just by being there, but, in spite of it, she crossed the garden to knock upon the heavy stone door.

The door groaned as it opened, dragging like a moving barricade, stirring up dirt and dust as if it hadn't been opened in years. It allowed her a second to swim inside before it slammed shut behind her, almost pinching her tail fins. Once inside, she found herself in a frighteningly black tunnel, thinking seriously about turning back and swimming home to safety. But her strength was renewed when she reminded herself how badly she wanted her freedom. Bravery restored, she proceeded head-first into the darkness.

As she swam blindly through the aphotic crevasse, she was relieved when she finally noticed a tiny speck of light deep down below her. She followed it until the crevasse narrowed into a tunnel with squishy, slimy walls that seemed to expand and contract around her as if she was being digested. Finally, the bottleneck opened up into in a huge, wide chamber. Once inside, she was blinded.

A century's worth of shimmering crystals and precious treasures were strewn by the barrel across the floor, glistening brightly against the eerie cave walls. And there, draped in jewels and sitting amid piles of gilded riches sat the witch, her bony back turned, with the pointy peak of her twisted spine pointing straight at the door. The skeletal hag was admiring herself in a large, golden mirror.

Her scarily, freakishly thin body was decorated with strands and strands of pearls, gold chains, and beaded necklaces. Her fingers were long and spindly, with rubbery webbing between them and an ornate bauble or three on each one. Her hair was long, stringy and white, littered with worms and black snakes that weaved themselves in and out of her brittle locks. Her tail was like that of a sea serpent, covered in black scales that held a slight tinge of purple. Her face was pale and long with flapping gills in her cheeks that resembled deep red wounds, and row upon row of sharp black and yellow spikes for teeth crowded her mouth. She had a forked tongue that pushed hungrily through her thin white lips. From every angle, the witch was more frightening than a creature from a paralyzing nightmare. But then, for a brief second as she turned her pointy head, the mermaid thought she saw another facet. For just a split second, the witch showed the face of a beautiful young maiden with a shy smile. But just as soon as it happened, the moment of beauty was gone again and the witch's hollow, horrifying face reappeared.

The sea hag rose from her seat quickly and slithered towards the princess until their faces were almost touching. She spun around the princess swiftly and smoothly as a hungry snake, inspecting the young beauty as if taking inventory of what she could gain. The witch was well aware that no one ever comes down to see her unless there is something they desperately need, and in her experience, anyone that has made it that far has always agreed to her terms, even if it would cost them everything. She licked her thin lips then extended her bony hand, removing the lid from her volcanic cauldron that had sailors' skulls lining its base. She tossed the remains of an eel carcass into it, several sharks' teeth, a handful of rotten fish eggs, and finally, the peeled-off face of a human man that she pulled out from inside a fishing bait jar.

"I have been saving this for you," said the witch as she stirred her cauldron with a pirate's sword. Menacing swirls of smoke rose from the pot.

"I have been watching you, Princess," she said in her slow, creepy tone. "I know you love that boy. . ." The princess nodded at the witch. Slowly, a revoltingly evil smile crossed the witch's face, so that her long, sharp mess of teeth was bared. "But your father won't hear of it, will he? Closed the surface to you, hasn't he?" The princess nodded again, and the old witch laughed wickedly. "Well it's a good thing you came, for I am the only one who possesses the power to defy the Sea King's will."

The witch's haggard voice gave her goose bumps but she choked back her fear and asked the witch what she came to ask.

"You can make it so that I may rise to see my prince again?" she asked hopefully.

"But of course! I can do *anything*," the witch said as she licked her thin lips.

The little mermaid gulped. "Then will you open up the surface to me?"

"I can do better than that," the witch said as she untied a bejeweled dagger from her hair and cut herself across the top of her long, sagging breast and squeezed it, allowing her black, oily blood to ooze out between her fingers and drip into the cauldron, sizzling as they splashed. She licked her fingers as she stirred the cauldron with her other hand, rapturously letting blood to drip from her lips down her long, pointy chin. It was a sight so horrifying, the princess gagged. The witch giggled out of her mangled mouth and then began to recite a spell:

*Into this cauldron go a witch's intentions,*
*which are hardly conducive to broken-heart prevention;*

*I craft a potion that will grant you the only thing you wish*

*A life on land among the humans, the end of life amongst the fish*


*You're an ungrateful mermaid; all your blessings aren't enough*

*I've heard your tearless weeping, Princess, haven't you got it so rough?*

*Wouldn't I like to be beautiful and have the kingdom obey my whims?*

*Shouldn't I prefer your shimmering tail to my eel-like, eerie fins?*


*Your sisters sing their days away and never have so much as a care*

*But you pine for something more; here isn't it, you long for there*

*But we can't all have what we'd like; some of us just accept our fate,*

*But some of us want for something more, and by Poseidon, it cannot wait-*


"Wait?" asked the mermaid. "Perhaps it can wait," she said. "Perhaps, if I could explain it all better to my father, I could make him understand . . ." The witch erupted into a loud, cackling fit of laughter, mocking the naive, lovesick girl.


*You think that this can wait, that it will all be yours when you're ready;*

*That your love is yours for the taking, that it's all just rocking steady . . .*

*But while you fetishize his likeness here in stone down in the water,*

*Kings from rich and foreign lands parade for him their lovely daughters*

*And while they may lack your mystery, your beauty and those eyes,*

*They are lovely ladies; you'll be no more than a fish in disguise*

*And they are pretty too, and they have so much more to offer . . .*

*Their bodies are flesh and blood; you're little more than salt and water.*


The little mermaid frowned deeply and stared sadly down at her tail. The witch, for a brief second, felt almost sorry for the ambitious little thing. "Are you sure this is what you want?" she asked her. "There is no turning back once you've taken the potion."

Without a second thought, the little mermaid replied assuredly. "This love is the only thing I want from this life. I want to go up and never come back down to the wretched sea." The witch flashed her teeth again.


*Renouncing water, I must warn you, could exact a bitter toll*

*For now you must learn to fear it, or it shall sabotage your goal*

*For even so much as a drop, where it hits your skin shall sprout a scale*

*More than a drop shall turn those legs into the same old flapping tail!*

*And if ever he saw that tail, you'd be a monster in his eyes*

*And no happiness will ever find you; you would forfeit the ultimate prize . . .*


*If you never get near your love you'll be distraught and hopelessly lost*

*But you've still yet to inquire, darling, about the grave and exorbitant cost!*

The mermaid swallowed hard. "Cost? I'm sorry, Witch, but I have nothing to offer you; my hands are empty."

*You didn't presume I'd work for free? A stupid and entitled person!*
*Don't insult me with your ignorance; the high cost could only worsen!*

She panicked. "What could I possibly offer a wise and powerful witch?"

*I want the magic in your tongue that makes the ocean breeze sound sweet*
*I want your voice that warms the chilly nights and makes rain clouds retreat*
*I admit, it is a heavy price so that sea life you may transcend*
*But do you understand? It'll cost you your voice, so you'll never sing again!*

Quite literally dumbfounded, the mermaid pondered the witch's demands. "My voice? If I cannot sing to him, how shall I win his heart? If I cannot speak to him, how will I tell him it was I that saved his life and that I love him more than anything in the world?"

*Don't act like you've got nothing but that whistling in your throat*
*The pretty sounds you make are not the only ticket onto his boat*
*Don't forget about your dainty frame and those expressive eyes,*
*It won't take much to turn a gentleman's head, once you're in your grand*
*disguise . . .*

*Of course, the legs will come with feet, and the feet shall come with pain-*
*An evil, bloody, hateful hurt that could drive any soul insane!*
*Every step you take will feel as though you walk on knives*
*But don't shy away from agony, darling, it lets you know you're alive!*
*I admit the pain's a mean and strange and odious effect*
*But I promise you it'll stop hurting about the same time you stop noticing*
*it!*

The mermaid nodded. The witch continued ...

*There's an upside to every down and a silver lining on every cloud;*
*Your legs will be so graceful that your dancing shall draw crowds*
*And all the humans will wonder where you learned to dance so sweet,*
*The legs will bring you so much joy you'll forget your wretched feet.*

*But you'll have to move that body; catch and hold your soul mate's eye,*

*Don't think it will come easy, you'll need to dance and smile and try!*

*Or this will all have been for nothing, and you'll be heartbroken and with*
*no voice*

*And so I'm obligated to offer you one last chance to consider your choice!*

The mermaid thought to herself silently for a moment, then answered with a strength and bravery that surprised even herself. "I can take the pain, Witch. Take what you need from me, I am ready."

The witch narrowed her eyes at her. "Listen carefully, princess, for I am about to hand you the gravest caveat of this deal. Know that once you go to the land above to seek love, you must find it. Or on the morning after your love pledges himself to another, your body and your soul will both expire to remain simply as sea foam until the end of days on Earth."

The little mermaid closed her eyes and thought hard about what that would mean for her. The harsh reality of it all began to sink in; she'd be putting her soul's chance to experience eternity on the line. But it was already settled for her in her mind and in her heart; she was prepared to agree to anything that would get her up with the one she adored. She looked the witch dead in the eyes, and, with a cadence of absolute sincerity, nodded her head. With that, the witch lifted the heavy black cauldron onto the fire.

She moved towards the haggard old matron, closed her eyes and braced herself. She didn't know how the witch was going to go about taking her voice from her, but she braced for unimaginable pain. The witch opened her mouth, displaying her sharp, spiky teeth, and then puckered her lips and put them to the princess's lips. The princess was horrified, and kept her eyes closed while she winced. Then, the witch sucked the voice right out of her. As her beautiful voice flowed out of her throat for the last time, her very favourite song rang out perfectly, but all backwards. Once there was no song left, the witch bit the mermaid's tongue right out.

She wanted to scream from the pain, but no sound escaped her and she clutched her throat, choking on her own blood while her tongue healed itself, growing back a new one in the bitten one's place. After the witch feasted messily on the little tongue, she licked her lips in gruesome satisfaction. Then she turned to her cauldron and wafted its strong, offensive fumes into her face. It smelled like rotten flesh. It smelled just right.

Then she dipped a long yellow fingernail into the pot and brought it to her lips to taste. She grinned, satisfied with her work. Then, just to be sure of its potency, she snorted a drop of it up her nostril.

"It's ready," she said proudly, and reached for a whale bone ladle to scoop up just enough to fill a tiny glass bottle. The potion glowed a bright, eerie green but once it was sealed inside its bottle, it glowed like a bright, white star. Without delay, the mermaid took it from the witch's hand and fled the horrid cave, making all the eels and polyps shrink back in terror as she passed them with the bottle clutched in her little hands.

On her way up, she went by her father's palace for one last look at her home. All the lights that had brightly lit the palace were now extinguished, and all was silent at the bottom of the sea. She knew how devastated her family would be to discover she was gone, but she knew that this was meant to be her big adventure. She blew many kisses towards the underwater castle for her beloved family, then swam up through the dark blue waters to reach the surface just as dawn was breaking over her love's beachside dwelling.

# thirteen

## Straight Up

At so early an hour, all that could be heard were the waves on the shore and a few gulls overhead. She swam slowly and carefully, sweeping her tail smoothly without splashing so as not to disturb the peaceful calm of the dawn. Only her eyes peeked out of the water as she swam keeping low, imitating the slow-floating drift of a beach-bound log. After much inching, she finally let the waves drop her on the sands in front of Gabriel's house.

When she reached the sea's edge, she shimmied herself up to where the sand was dry and stretched out her beautiful fins. The people would be waking soon, and she knew it was now or never. She held the bottle up to the light to inspect it and saw that it no longer glowed, but just looked like a bit of water inside a simple glass bottle. It was hard to believe that this potion was all that stood between her and the life she'd been wishing for. *Just drink it*, she said to herself, and pulled out the little brown cork.

Without a second thought, she swallowed the entire contents of the bottle and once it was empty, tossed it back into the sea. Then she sat still and waited.

The waves spit out three jellyfish right in front of her, then five urchins rolled up behind them. She began to wonder if the potion was going to work. After a few more moments, she was already tiring of waiting and began to curse the witch for cheating her with a useless potion. Then, all of a sudden, the most incredible pain she'd ever felt shot through her whole body like a bolt of hot lightning.

Propped up on her elbows, she winced and writhed as what felt like an invisible sword sliced through the center of her beautiful blue tail. Every scale felt like it was being torn from her like fingernails from their nail beds, and her bottom half ripped and split open at the seam. How excruciating to watch her own tail halving right before her eyes! Again she went to scream, but once again, no sound escaped her but a deep, hollow exhale through her voiceless throat. The pain was fierce and it shook her to the core, and as the potion worked its way through her, she squirmed and convulsed until she spewed the contents of her aching stomach, black and green all over the sand.

In an instant, the pain was over, and the glare of the rising sun blinded her as it beamed into her sweaty face. She looked down at where once was her tail, and even though she had dreamt of nothing else, it still shocked her to see the dainty white pillars that now sprouted from her hips. Disbelievingly, she lifted one leg up slowly, almost afraid of it, inspecting the strange, skin-covered appendage through squinted, cringing eyes. Staring very intently, she wiggled her baby toe for the first time. Weak from the violent metamorphosis, she became woozy at the sight and fainted back onto the sand.

Hours passed and she came to as the piercing sound of squawking shore birds rang out into the morning. Overhead, a flock of gulls hovered, taking turns swooping down to snap at the abnormally large school of baitfish that was collecting in the shallows. She went to pull her arm up to shield her eyes from the glare, but a heavy starfish pinned her lethargic arm down as she saw several more roll in with the waves, reaching just beyond her toes. They encircled her new feet, curiously checking them out for themselves. The sea creatures, it seemed, were following their princess into shore.

She pulled her new feet in closer so they wouldn't get hit by waves. All the loud noises of the air seemed to amplify under the hot sun, and they made her feel sick again. Out of the corner of her eye, she noticed a tall figure walking towards her, with several little furry things surrounding it on the ground, all being drawn her way by the commotion of the feeding frenzy. The furry monsters began barking wildly and running towards her with their tongues hanging out. Terrified, she struggled to stand up but her new legs were weak and she clumsily fell back down, hitting her temple against a stone. In that moment of kaleidoscopic clouds, barking dogs and spinning suns, she felt so nauseous she thought she might spray her insides out through her nose. Her eyes rolled back and she blacked out once again, collapsing in a tangled heap of hair and seaweed.

# fourteen

*Dry & New*

A while later, she awoke in a big, sunny room all alone, lying across a soft leather couch with a damp cloth resting on her forehead. The room was all painted yellow and on the wall above her head, pictures of smiling faces hung scattered in pretty, mismatched frames. Her eyes were blurry and her skin felt tight and dry as she stared groggily up at the ceiling fan, likening it to the propellers that would push the boats she used to watch from below. She reached her hands out to it the way she always used to, back in the days when she never thought she'd get to see the inside of a real human home. On her arms, she noticed the soft, plaid sleeve of the flannel shirt she was wearing, and had no recollection of how she came to acquire it. She sniffed it; it smelled just like

Gabriel! She knew she must be in his home, and began to pant with the anticipation of seeing him. When she heard footsteps in the hallway getting louder as they got closer, she began to pant so hard she thought she might faint once again.

In a sudden panic, she scrambled to free her legs from the blanket they were under and went to stand once again but just stumbled to the floor with a thud. The footsteps in the hall started running towards her and in a last-ditch effort to appear composed and lovely, she pulled her legs in and arranged her long hair to fall prettily over one shoulder.

Expecting her prince to dash into the room, she was let down when she caught sight of the short, round and bespectacled man who rushed in to check on her. "Oh good, you're awake!" he said while crouching down to press the back of his chubby hand to her hot forehead. "Caught a bit of sun stroke, didn't we?" The man spoke with a scruffy voice and his breath smelled like cherry chewing tobacco, but the little mermaid didn't know what that was, and just thought he smelled sweet and fruity.

Right behind him, Gabriel's mom sashayed in with a mug of coffee in one hand and a glass of water in the other. "What a relief!" she said with a smile, passing the water to her. Gingerly, the mermaid accepted the glass but was very careful not to spill on her lap. "Are you feeling okay, dear? It looks like you bumped your head." The little mermaid smiled back at the nice woman, who was most definitely Gabriel's mother because she had the same dark brown eyes and perfect white teeth as he. She began to wonder where her love could be hiding.

"I'm Lucia O'Faolain and this is Doctor Twiddy," said the nice lady. "What's your name, dear?" The little mermaid opened her mouth to speak but when no sound came out, she remembered and lamented her new voiceless condition. Her face saddened and she pointed to her throat, shaking her head. She cringed at the memory of the witch's nasty lips against hers, sucking the wind out of her pipes.

"Can you not speak, child?" asked the doctor. "You gave us all quite a scare, out there passed out with no sunscreen on!" he said authoritatively. "And, I know how you young people deplore tan lines . . . but unabashed nakedness might give the local boys the wrong idea!" The mermaid couldn't understand what he meant by that, when she was pretty sure being naked in front of Gabriel would give him an idea that was exactly right. She smiled shyly at the doctor but kept looking past him and over his shoulder, praying her love would soon appear. "Let's get you up slowly, shall we?" The old doctor offered his hands to her but when she tried to stand, her legs felt like dead weight and she flopped right back down to where she was sitting. She picked up her sore feet with her hands and rubbed them down, trying to massage the pain away.

"What's the matter with her legs, doctor?" asked Lucia. "Do you think they're just exhausted from the swim she must've had?" The doctor patted down her legs gently to feel for injuries but she didn't flinch once. He picked up her bare foot and checked it out but nothing seemed out of the ordinary there. "Well, it appears her legs are just fine. However, I highly doubt she could have swum from very far, take a look at those legs! I've seen better musculature on coma patients! Brand new babies, even."

"What?" asked Lucia disbelievingly, inspecting the girl's legs for herself.

"They're so soft and weak, they look like they've never been used before," noted the doctor. For a brief second the mermaid was fearful of being found out. "Well they're very pretty, anyway!" he said kindly, and the topic was dropped.

Doctor Twiddy sat down next to her and put his stethoscope to her chest. Her heart rang out steadily; *tha-thump. Tha-thump. Tha-thump.* "Besides those baby-legs of hers," he said, "she seems quite healthy to me!"

Just then, Gabriel walked into the room with a full breakfast tray in hands. *Tha-thump! Tha-THUMP!! THA-THUMP!!! THA-*

*THUMP!!!!* Her young heart sped up like a champion racehorse. *There he was! He was there!*

"Oh my, now your heart's racing!" teased the doctor, pulling the stethoscope from his chest. "Well, young lady, you'd be well-advised not to get too taken by Gabriel here, you'll have to get in line behind every other young lady on this coast," he said, snickering as he packed his things back into his house-call bag. The mermaid looked up excitedly into Gabriel's eyes, hoping that some part of him remembered her from the night she saved him.

"Stop it, Doc. If it were that easy, I wouldn't still be single, would I?" said Gabriel as he winked at the pale and pretty stranger he had carried into his family room that morning.

"Well, son, you can't shoot the fish in the barrel if you won't even take out your gun!" said the doctor, half-joking and half-serious.

"Yes, so I've been told," replied Gabriel, rolling his eyes. He was used to getting teased for choosing to abstain in spite of his apparent sex appeal, but he could never quite understand why everyone and their uncle seemed to be so interested in his love life.
"Thank you, doctor, I will keep that in mind," he replied respectfully, with a gentle backhand of sarcasm. He turned back to the girl on the sofa, and apologized for the family's five rescue pugs

having scared her when they came out and found her. "They really are the most harmless monsters you'll ever meet," he assured her.

The mermaid sat still on the couch, intoxicated. She could not believe she was there, in his house, less than a few feet away from where he stood carrying a tray of something that smelled strange yet so delicious it made her mouth water. And, the cherry on the cake was, he appeared to be bringing it just for her. It was all too wonderful to wrap her little head around. She tried to imagine what was under that serving lid.

Gabriel cleared his throat, and she gapped back in from her delectable daydream. "I didn't know what you'd want to eat so I grabbed you a bit of everything," he said. Without a second thought, she jumped up onto her feet and dashed towards him until she was standing right in front of him, her chest pressed against the tray of food, breathing in the euphoric scent combination of food/him. "Okay, good! Glad you're hungry. I'm Gabriel," he said. Her heart jumped. She knew his name. Oh, how she knew his name. "What's your name?" he asked. Her bright smile faded back to a frown.

"Gabe, honey," explained Lucia, "I don't think she can speak."

"Oh really?" he asked. He had never known a mute person before. "Whatever, I'm not really that great at it either," he said with a smile. "Talking is overrated anyway." She melted, understanding he was being kind and fell even more in love with his easy nature. Feeling her temperature rise from deep inside her hungry, empty belly, she wondered how many other human girls were so lucky to have such a gentleman as her soul mate. An overjoyed smile crept across her face.

"At least we know she can walk now, which is good!" remarked the doctor.

Gabriel looked down at her white and dainty little legs. It was true; they did look brand new, without so much as a single scar, freckle or blemish on them. It was as if they'd been kept in glass casing her entire life and she had only just chosen to break out the pure, white legs that morning.

The little mermaid remembered that the witch had promised that her new legs would be the most graceful pair in the world, so she decided to get them working for her right away because every second spent in his presence was another chance to make him fall for her. Pain shot up from her toes to her brain but she endured the sensation bravely, not wanting to ever lose points for poise.

"Are you hungry?" Gabriel asked, lifting the lid from the plate. She smiled at him and cautiously poked at the different foods, all so new and foreign to her. She picked up a piece of bacon with two fingers and brought it close to inspect it. Steam rose from the crispy strip and it smelled so delightful, she just had to lick it. The saltiness of it made her salivate for more.

"Well, that's one way to eat it, but most of us just bite into it," he said, making biting gestures to show her what he meant. She stuffed the whole piece into her mouth and looked up to him for approval. "Yes, you got it! And now, chew…" he said, encouraging her to chomp down on it. Its dripping, warm fat seemed to romance each and every one of her taste buds. She closed her eyes while she stood there, just savoring, wondering if everything in the upper world tasted so lovely. Once it was swallowed, she opened her eyes and scanned the plate for the next delectable item to try. "I've set you a place out on the patio; come with me!" he said, glad she was interested in the breakfast he had fixed for her.

"Good idea, darling; get this poor girl fed!" said Lucia. "I'll run upstairs and find her something to wear."

"Well I think my work here is done," said the old doctor, yawning. "Lucia, a pleasure as always; Gabriel, all the best; and lil' miss, best of luck to you . . . I think you landed in the right place for now," he said as he tipped his hat and headed outside to his car, a loud little brown vintage hatchback.

When they got to the porch, Gabriel showed her to her seat and she ran her hands over the top of the clean white tablecloth. Humans have such grand decorations, she thought to herself as he set her plate down in front of her. There was cutlery next to her plate but she ignored them, opting instead to go straight for another piece of greasy bacon with her fingers. She picked up a chunk of hash browned potato and inspected it closely and from all angles before popping it into her mouth, tasting it with her eyes open, then with her eyes closed. Next she went for a slice of buttered toast, biting only the corner of it off then inexplicably setting the remainder of it down on the seat next to her. Everything was so tasty and warm and felt so nice in her mouth while she chewed. Gabriel watched her enjoy every single bite with complete fascination, observing from across the table while she ate as if she had never enjoyed a cooked breakfast before. While she was concentrating on the meal in front of her, he let his imagination run wild as he speculated about where she could have come from. Perhaps she had just escaped from a slave ship where they didn't feed her, or perhaps she had been lost at sea, surviving on canned bait. He gapped back in again when he noticed she had stopped eating, and instead was staring down at her plate in wide-eyed wonderment. She had discovered the most beautiful surprise hidden for her under the second slice of toast: a beautiful, miniature yellow sun!

She beamed at him with her sweetest, most appreciative smile. There was bacon and spinach in her teeth and he considered telling her, but she looked like she was having way too much fun so he decided not to bother. The wonderful sun she admired was simply an egg fried sunny-side up but to someone who had never seen such a thing before, it represented everything magical in the world. She glanced out over the balcony railing to the sun over the water and closed one eye while she traced the perfect circle with her finger, and then did the same to the little sun on her plate. She leaned forward to smell it and felt its warmth rise up to her nose and cheeks. She touched it right in the center and under the weight of her finger, the yellow sac burst. She watched as the pale orange yolk streamed out over the whites like hot lava and as she licked her yolk-covered finger, she decided that mornings taste far better on the dry Earth than they ever did under the sea.

Once she had all but licked her plate clean, Lucia came outside to fetch her. "I found you some clothes to put on, dear. Not that you aren't stunning in Gabriel's old flannel; I just thought you might like something prettier and in your size."

The mermaid grinned. She wanted to be as pretty as could be! So she stood up to follow Lucia inside. Her feet still killed her when she stood upon them, but somewhere between her first few failed attempts at standing and the present, she had discovered the lovely, graceful strut the witch had promised her. She began to feel wonderfully feminine as she mastered the art of gliding, maneuvering light as air upon her tiny, lady-like feet. She could feel Gabriel's eyes on her as she disappeared into the doorway, and that alone made the steps worth their pain.

Lucia led her back into the living room, where she had awoken from her blackout less than an hour prior. Sitting on the sofa was a yellow sundress; beside it was a cotton bra and panty set. The little mermaid picked them all up and inspected each piece curiously. "They're fresh, I promise! See? The tags are still on." The mermaid looked at her with a blank, clueless expression as she dropped them back onto the sofa. "And if I had to guess, I would say that they are your exact size!" said Lucia as she picked them up and put them back in her hands. "Go ahead, try them on!"

The mermaid still stared back at her blankly. "What, have you never worn a bra and panties before?" she asked incredulously. When her mild laughter was met with yet another clueless expression, she realized that the girl must really have no idea of the function those garments were meant to perform. Lucia was dumbfounded but considered that the strange mute girl could perhaps still be in shock from whatever circumstance had left her on the beach naked and alone in the first place, and decided not to make a big deal out of it and just help the girl into the clothes.

When the panty set was on, the girl stood in front of the large mirror that hung on the wall behind the sofa, taking in the new sight of her new body. With the bra on, her modest breasts sat higher and looked fuller than they had before. Curiously, she cupped them with her hands and turned to check them out from the side. Then her gaze moved downwards and she checked her legs out in the mirror. She stood to one side, then to the other, watching every muscle flex and contract. It still hurt so much to stand, but she bore every second of it with grace. She leaned forward and reached down to feel her leg from the highest point on her thigh to the lowest part of her ankle. She could not believe how soft her legs felt; a pleasant, smooth expanse of skin where her shiny scales once were. Her bottom half felt strangely naked and she wondered if perhaps this is what her tail actually looked like when it wasn't bound tightly in scales; perhaps she had had legs all along, two white pillars just waiting to be freed. She wanted to show Gabriel how pretty she looked in the bra and panties, so she began to skip towards the door…

"Darling!" called Lucia, sensing that the girl was about to run out in her underwear. "You're only half-dressed! Let's get this sun dress on you." She motioned for the girl to raise her arms so she could slip the dress over her head. The mermaid complied. "There! Just as I suspected, a perfect fit."

Just then, Gabriel knocked on the door. "Are you decent?" he asked. The little mermaid perked up enthusiastically at the sound of his voice.

"Come in, Gabe, she's dressed now," replied Lucia, and in he came, stopping dead in his tracks when he saw her.

"You look gorgeous," he said as he looked her up and down. She looked lovely in a way that he'd been missing but hadn't realized. There was something incredibly comforting about seeing new life breathed into his sister's long-forgotten clothes, and his happiness at the sight was written all over his face. The little mermaid never felt so good.

Lucia turned to her. "I have a few things to take care of today; our youngest returns from boarding school this aft and we're throwing a soiree in her honour. Everyone will be here and I have a million things to do today so now that you are fed, dressed, and lucid, I must excuse myself and get back at it!" Lucia jumped and began to dash back to the kitchen when she heard the oven timer go off. "Come find me if you need anything!" she called from the hallway.

Once again testing out the grace in her new feet, she rocked back and forth upon them before rolling up onto the tips of her toes as effortlessly as a principal ballerina who had spent her entire life practicing. Gabriel clapped for her, amazed at her incredibly surprising talent. Then he reached into his pocket to pull out his cell phone to hand to her.

"Go ahead and dial your family, and I'll let them know you're safe here," he said. She took the gadget in her hands and just cradled it in her open palms, staring down at the baffling piece of technology with sad eyes. "Is there no one you can call?" he asked. She looked him deep in the eyes and shook her head. No, no there wasn't.

Gabriel felt for her in a way that felt very new and peculiar; part of him was suspicious about the girl who couldn't say where she was from and had no family to call but at the same time, he could not remember the last time he wanted so much to care for another living thing. The stranger in front of him appeared spirited and strong-willed but still vulnerable in a way that made her dearer to him already than most girls he'd known his whole life. He took the phone back from her hands and slid it back into his pocket.

"Well, we can figure it all out later," he said. "Would you like to stay for the party this evening?" In an instant, her face went from pitifully lost to bursting with joy. *A real human party!* She nodded a very enthusiastic *Yes! Yes! Yes!*, and bit her lower lip, not in a trying-to-be-sexy way, but to keep her mouth from smiling so big that it could swallow her entire face. Happily, she spun and twirled in the yellow dress, dancing before the mirror, dying with excitement for the party. She felt like the loveliest girl to ever walk upon two legs. Just then, they heard a big crash and clamor just outside the living room window and they all ran out to see what happened.

Cliff O'Faolain, along with his bike, tackle box, fishing rod and a basket full of live seafood, had just crashed into a wheelbarrow full of garden weeds. Cliff was the patriarch of this family, a sincere and kindly man, who was an avid fisherman and lived for his wife and his kids. As he scrambled to his feet, his wheels still spun and the now-loose crabs were making a play for the ocean. When he stood up, he found his wife Lucia choking back her laughter. "Are you alright, honey? How many times have I warned you to be careful when flying around this corner?" she asked him. "Even the kids know better!"

He smiled, embarrassed but not hurt, and dusted himself off. "I know I know honey. But as I passed the window, I swore I saw Dagmara in there with Gabe." He propped his bike up on its kickstand and began collecting all of the oysters that had tumbled out across the grass.

"I thought that too!" replied his wife, beckoning the young girl to step forward. "This morning, Gabriel was walking the pugs on the beach and found this poor girl lying out there unconscious! She was a little dehydrated and we had Dr. Twiddy over to see her and thankfully, she seems to be just fine. She's mute, though, and so far we haven't had any luck figuring out where she came from."

The mermaid curtsied and bowed for Cliff, who appeared to be the king of this fine home. Amused, he bowed back with flare. "Well it's very nice having you over, but won't your family be wondering where you are?"

A frown crept across her porcelain face. Her family would be worrying about her by now, and her father would be sending search parties to every corner of the ocean. She worried he would blame the humans for her disappearance and wreak stormy vengeance upon the coasts.

"Well perhaps you can stay for the night and we can figure everything out in the morning?" suggested Cliff.

"A lovely idea," said Lucia. "I've got to get back to the kitchen. Gabriel-- perhaps you could take her for a walk?" she said as she gestured towards the far end of the beach. "You never know; a few more clues may have washed up with the flotsam."

Gabriel turned to the girl. "Do you want to go for a walk with me?" he asked. She nodded; there was nothing she wanted more than to be alone with him again.

Lucia waited until her son and his mystery girl were out of earshot before filling Cliff in on the rest of the story. "The poor thing was naked when he found her. She had suffered a bit of sunstroke, so he carried her into the house and we fed and clothed her, and now she appears to be in perfect health!"

"Naked? This beach is becoming a real commune..." said Cliff as his neck noodled his head back to face the beach.

"No, no, it wasn't like she was out there sunbathing; it was like she had washed up. Didn't you see the tangles of pearls and seaweed in her hair?"

"Yes and what about that necklace she's wearing! It looks like pirate treasure!" said Cliff excitedly like a kid describing a fieldtrip. Cliff had had a lifelong obsession with pirates. (Buccaneers, specifically, for he wasn't fond of all pirates - for instance, the ones currently terrifying seafarers off the coast of Somalia.) He had a pirate hat that he wore around the house sometimes when no one else was around and sometimes he called his wife 'wench', but only ever in the bedroom. And he really liked spiced rum.

"Anyway, much too much to do!" said Lucia, running back into the house leaving Cliff to park his bike.

# fifteen

## Fish out of Water

---

Ava woke up that morning from a dream in which she was a warrior princess defending her dark castle. The skies were black over her medieval yet space-age kingdom, and her knuckles were white as she gripped the silver reins of her armored rhinoceros. The sword hanging from her belt was heavy and pulled her down its right side, and with every step they took, the scales of her metallic sheath clinked together loudly. The enemy was closing in on her army from all angles, and she could see that they were gaining in numbers as they assembled on the horizon, their intergalactic gunships flying in slowly from behind them, blotting out what slivers were left of the evening sun. As her archers took their places and set their aim upon the enemy, she could see that her war was already lost. The words of defiance she had spit against the new world emperor had brought herself and her army of mere mortals up against him and his mighty machines. The gunships closed in and as she screamed her final *CHARGE!*, she pulled out her heavy sword and pointed it at the dark sky. Her rhino bellowed and reared, and she tumbled in slow motion off its back and down to the ground as the enemy infantry rode in to finish her and claim her throne . . .

*THUD.* She fell out of bed. Again. Ava, Gabriel's eldest sister, was a very deep sleeper, and the most active dreamer in the family. It was not at all uncommon for her to fall out of bed and that is why before she went to sleep, (having learned a hard lesson after spraining her wrist one time) she was in the habit of scattering her impressive collection of throw pillows on the floor beside her bed to break her fall. Annoyed at having woken up in this unpleasant fashion once again, she climbed back into bed, congratulated herself on having been prepared for the fall and rolled over to look out to the ocean through the small gap between her heavy white drapes. Scanning the horizon for invaders, she saw nothing but blue sky and water. Her first night back in the Tofino house every year was always a very heavy sleep; her dad had always insisted it had something to do with the pure ocean air. Still in warrior mode but groggy, she smelled the bacon steam wafting up the stairs and got up to go down for breakfast.

As she walked down the stairs sleepily tying on her silk robe, she was surprised to see a strange, pretty girl dancing in front of the living room mirror while her mother, father and brother watched, spellbound. Her guard immediately went back up and she was as prepared as ever to defend her kingdom against invaders. "Who is this?" she asked in her signature bitchy, deadpan voice. As she looked the little mermaid up and down, a twinge of jealousy flowed through her. She was never a good dancer, so she always hated when people pranced about, boasting their grace when she didn't seem to have a rhythmic bone in her body.

"Gabriel found her on the beach this morning, the poor thing," answered Lucia, getting up to greet her daughter. "She was unconscious and wasn't wearing any clothes--"

"--And that is our problem how?" interrupted Ava, unimpressed. The girl turned to her and smiled, then dipped into a low curtsy for her. Ava never trusted anyone that seemed happy for no reason. She sneered at her.

"Well of course we had to bring her in out of the sun and get her some medical attention; she was passed out!" answered Lucia. "And did I mention she was naked?!" Suspiciously, Ava eyed the strange girl in her living room as she bounced around perusing the family's picture collection, stopping to take close looks at all of them, balancing from one foot to the other, effortlessly standing on her tippy toes.

Ava narrowed her eyes defensively. "Where did you come from and why were you naked on our beach, you dirty hippy?" she spat.

"Ava, heel!" hissed her mother. "Anyway, she can't speak; we've already asked her all those questions."

"Well what are we supposed to do with her?" asked Ava, even bitchier than before. "We can't just adopt every naked mute that washes up on our beach, you know."

Cliff, a gentle mediator, interjected. "I think the ideal everyone here is shooting for is that we should endeavor to help people who appear to be in need, Ava." Ava rolled her eyes. The girl was now standing in front of the window, running her curious little fingers up and down the smooth window pane, then pressing her face to the shiny glass.

"What do we even know about her?" asked Ava with unwarranted suspicion. "How do we know she's not a shady pirate hooker looking to rob us?"

"You're ridiculous," said Gabriel, shaking his head at his paranoid sister.

"What's with the pearls and the weeds in her hair? Is she some kind of sea-nymph or something?" The mermaid was now looking at a vase on the side table, admiring its colors and the way light reflected through it, definitely not paying any mind to the hostility being directed at her. "Look!" exclaimed Ava angrily. "She's casing the joint right now, and she's doing it in Dagmara's favorite sundress! Who gave her that?" she demanded.

"Well I did, of course," said Lucia. "What's the problem? Did you call dibs on it?"

Ava huffed. "I didn't know our sister's things were up for grabs to complete strangers."

"Ava, she had nothing to wear," said Gabriel, trying to incite some sympathy in his hard sister.

"Riiight," hissed Ava. "Great plan, actually . . . just show up at people's houses naked and they're sure to offer you their dead sister's most treasured things. And all for free!" She glared at the stranger in her house. "It' genius; I applaud you."

"Yeah, you're right," remarked Gabriel sarcastically. "This was probably all just an elaborate scheme to get her hands on a used sundress."

"Don't sass me, Gay-briel!" shot Ava.

"From zero to Rottweiler in 2.3 seconds," said Gabriel with a chuckle. "I don't know why I am ever surprised by your hostility."

"Pull it back, kids . . ." interjected Cliff, feeling the argument reaching new heights.

"Well you all are so dumb and welcoming," she countered, "I wouldn't be the least bit surprised if you invited a total psycho to come bunk with Demetra."

Gabriel sighed. "Ava, are you actually taking aim at the fact that we took in a naked, possible shipwreck survivor, or did you just wake up from yet another bad dream?"

The family all knew about Ava's active dreaming because she had been jarring the house with bloodcurdling screams ever since she was little, and was famous for waking up on the wrong side of the bed after having fallen out of it. "Gabriel, shut your face," she replied. "Why don't you go trolling for more vagabonds, and take that little stray out with you."

"Okay sis, and while I'm out 'vagabond trolling,'" he replied with a smirk, "why don't you go smoke something and chill out? It's too early to act like a steroid freak in traffic." But before Ava could counter with another venomous statement, everyone's attention shifted to the aquarium in the middle of the room. Their little houseguest had ceased dancing and was standing perfectly still in front of it with the palms of her hands pressed firmly against the glass. Her eyes looked far away and blurry as if she was concentrating on something none of them had the slightest idea about.

Feeling the rhythm of the water and the way the little plastic pump mimicked the ocean's undulation inside the tiny glass box, the girl, unbeknownst to all present, was communicating with the octopuses who lived inside. One was orange and one was black, and they had been silently watching over the family for years. It was curious how they had never tried to escape, even though it would have been easy since there wasn't even a lid on their tank. They told her they liked the family, and that they had no desire to return to the ocean. "Me too," she told them. "And me neither."

With her palms still pressed to the glass, the little mermaid turned and locked her eyes boldly into Ava's mean stare. Her glaring face was so hateful it felt like it could burn a pinhole straight through her retinas and out the back of her head, but she didn't flinch or look away. The mermaid was defiant, yet at the same time, sweet and unassuming, and when she pulled her hands away from the tank seconds later, everyone could see that both of the little octopuses in the tank had affixed their bodies to the glass, stretching and contorting to mirror the very shape of her hands. Ava's eyes widened as her stare shifted from mean to bewildered, and the strange girl in her living room just smiled at her sweetly, and, with barely a sound, took Gabriel gently by the hand and led him towards the door to go for their walk.

Once they had disappeared through it, Ava turned and without another word, walked quietly upstairs to her room and closed her door gently behind her. Cliff and Lucia, now alone in the living room, stared at the aquarium and then at each other, trying to make sense of the odd exchange that had just taken place. Boggled, they both just shrugged their shoulders and went back into the kitchen to return to their party prep.

Walking down to the beach with his new little friend on his arm, Gabriel stopped dead in his tracks and gasped. "What is that?" he asked, squinting his eyes towards the rows of starfish that had washed onto the sands in front of their place. There had to be at least a hundred of them, scattered across the beach, piling up as each wave carried in a few more. When he got closer, he noticed that the shallow waters were chock-a-block with small fish and the bigger fish that were feeding on them, and a few gulls still picked at the water but most were fat full from the rich meal they'd just enjoyed. "That's incredible," he remarked, scratching his head. "I've never seen so many fish in there! I wonder what's brought them all in so close." He never would have imagined they were pulled in by the gravity of the girl standing next to him, who began kneeling down to pick them up, being very careful not to let her toes get too close to the water. She was flinging them back in, lest they dry out in the sun like she nearly did. Seeing what she was doing, Gabriel lent a hand tossing them back in as well.

Once they'd finished, they resumed their beach walk and brought along the family's five pugs, Brutus, Isabel, Mabel, Olive and Honeybutter. As the dogs weaved through their feet and each other sniffing and peeing on stuff along the way, Gabriel noticed how remarkably the family pets all seemed to love and accept her right away. Then again, he remembered, pugs, by nature, do have a tendency to like pretty much everyone.

Every time he glanced at the girl, her deep blue eyes readily met his, as if she was willing his to meet hers, always one step ahead. At first, he found the one-sided conversing with the pretty little mute to be a bit awkward so he overcompensated with his own rambling, but by the time they were back from their stroll, all was well and a bit of silence was oddly comfortable. He half-expected to see rescue boats and patrollers out in the water searching for her, but there were none, and she didn't seem to be in any rush to be anywhere else but there with him. He didn't know anything about her yet, but he could tell she was very different kind of creature than anyone he'd ever met.

# sixteen

## Soirée

---

"So she was just lying unconscious out in the sun with no clothes on?" asked Demetra, who had just arrived home from boarding school. She sat out on the balcony with her big sister Ava, who was helping her to remove the chipped glittery nail polish from her fingers, and the ridiculous temporary tattoos that littered her arms. After last class on the last day of school every year, it was a tradition for Demetra and her little dorm friends to wild out and wear the make-up, accessories and civvies clothing  that were otherwise forbidden all year at Maeve Primrose while they packed up their things for the summer.

"That is correct," answered Ava, "which isn't entirely out of the ordinary out here, considering some our neighbors and their penchant for day-drunkenness coupled with nude tanning."

"Yeah really!" concurred Demetra. "They just bake out there half-dead, clutching their bloody Caesars!" Both sisters laughed at the all-too common image. "So Gabe is out walking with her now?"

"Yep, he is," answered Ava. "And I really don't know about her . . . she's a weird one, Meaty. It's like she's from another planet; she can't talk but she seems to somehow understand us, and I swear she was having a silent conversation with Druid and Poodle."

Demetra giggled. "Dad's aptly-named pet octopi?"

"Yup. They were communicating through the glass; don't ask. Suffice it to say, it was incredibly bizarre. I don't know what to make of her just yet, but I definitely don't trust her."

Demetra thought for a moment. "Imagine she's just a chick from town that Gabe doesn't know, but who knows Gabe and wants his body . . ."

" . . . Like every other sad local girl . . ." said Ava.

"Right! And maybe she just ditched her clothes and sprawled herself out on our beach to get his attention!" Both girls contemplated the probability. Both sisters bore the very same expression while pondering mysterious matters.

"I've never liked a guy that much." said Ava.

"Nor I," said Demetra, "and I hope I never do." But as soon as the words escaped her lips, she reconsidered them. "Actually, on second thought," she said, "I hope so much that I do someday!"

Ava grinned at her dreamy young sibling. "Yeah well, as your older sister, it'll be my duty to ensure you don't look like an exhibitionistic hussy while you hatch your desperate schemes!"

"Thanks Ava you're a pal." Just then, they spotted their brother and the girl in question heading towards them from down the beach. Demetra stood up to get a closer look and was taken aback to see that there was something strangely familiar about her. As they came closer, she was better able to make out the girl's face, and gasped in disbelief. "Weird, but from here, the hussy kind of looks like Dagmara!"

Ava darkened. "Please don't ever say that again," she muttered as her sister jumped up and ran out to greet them.

Demetra didn't stop running until she was jumping up into her brother's arms, letting him lift her up over his head. "Getting meatier, Meaty!" he said with a huff as he set his baby sister back down on her feet. "What are they feeding you out there? You're like a foot taller than you were at Christmas!"

"That's impossible, Gabey," said Demetra, matter-of-factly. "My major growth spurt isn't even due for another two point five years or so. But enough about my impending pubescence, who's your friend?"

"This is . . . actually, I don't really know!" he said as he pat the mermaid on the head. "We haven't been able to figure out her name yet but I found her on the beach, she's staying with us for the night, and she can cut a rug like no dancer I've ever seen!" Then he turned to her and said, "This is my sister Demetra." The mermaid excitedly kissed the lovely child on the cheek.

Demetra blushed. "I love your necklace," she said, noticing the veritable wreath of trinkets around the girl's tiny neck, and marveling at the big, smooth fossil that dangled heavily from it. She noticed that tied into the girl's hair was an ivory caviar spoon hanging right next to an aluminum soda can tab, which hung next to a giant antique emerald ring. "Where did you find all of these amazing treasures?" she asked. "Some of this stuff has got to be worth a fortune!" The mermaid smiled at her and wondered what 'a fortune' meant to humans. She wished so much that she could tell them about the hundreds of sunken ships she'd scoured and all the reefs she'd combed to find all of these wonderful sparkly things and of her dear old grandmother, who gave her the necklace. "Oh yeah, you can't talk. I'm sorry, that must be rough," said Demetra. "'Suppose, it could be worse, though!" she offered sweetly. "Not being able to talk is definitely better than being one who talks too much!" The mermaid bowed in gratitude for the kind comment, and Demetra, never shy or bashful, even in the presence of complete strangers, reached out and traced her index finger along the round edges of the large fossil stone. "That's an ammonite; I learned about them in school. They're, like, millions of years old!" The fossil dangled between her modest breasts and laid flat under them across her stomach. The shell pendant was the only thing on the necklace that saw its origins in the ocean, for the rest of the treasures on it were pieces of human jewelry and so they never imagined that most of it was procured from grand shipwrecks at the bottom of the seas.

Gabriel held the pendant in his hand and remarked at how heavy it must be around her delicate neck. And it was even heavier, she noticed, than when she wore it under water, for the gravity of the upper world made it a burden she never used to notice. Right now, though, as they stood close enough that she could smell his sweet breath, the only gravity that concerned her was the one pulling her towards him like he was the very center of the Earth. She closed her eyes and went back to the day she saved him, when she felt his breath on her cheek as she held his head to her chest. Every inch of her thin, lithesome body was braced in anticipation of his touch, for she wanted him to touch her so badly. She opened her eyes as she fell forward and right into him, and he caught her easily, reflexively. "Watch yourself!" he said as he set her back on her feet. "You aren't still dizzy, are you?" Indeed she was dizzy, but not for the reasons he thought.

"I'm going to go in and finish unpacking before people start showing up," said Demetra as she spun to head to the house. "I'll see you guys in a bit!" And with that, she skipped back to the house, leaving the mermaid alone once again with her prince. He turned to her with a suggestion.

"So I'm thinking I should take you into town for a bit and stop by the police station, just to make sure that no one's looking for you," he said. "How would you feel about that?" She gave him an unsure look. "We can take the drop top!" he added. She didn't know what that meant but it sounded fantastic, so off they went in his convertible Jeep to drive swiftly down tree-lined roads, where gusts of warm wind all woody and fresh made her feel like she was finally home.

They pulled into the quiet police station in the middle of town and she could sense right away that they were at a place filled with the sort of uniformed men and women who could be your salvation or foil your plans completely, depending on what you're up to. Gabriel asked if there were any runaway alerts or missing persons' reports, but the officers on duty said there hadn't been any in months. It became apparent that there was nobody looking for this girl, at least, if there was, they didn't know where to search for her. The police said they'd be in touch if they heard anything so with no apparent urgency to reunite her with her familiars, they drove back to the house to help set up for the party.

When they returned, they found the Von der Klaasen family's Hummer parked in Gabriel's spot. In classic Von der Klaasen style, they were unfashionably early by about two hours, and right behind them a huge white delivery truck blocked the driveway so Gabriel had to park out on the road. The two skinny deliverymen began wheeling out a large ice sculpture centerpiece carved into an orca whale, dramatically breaching. "Where do you want it?" the first one asked, wiping sweat from his forehead with a sports wristband. It was quite sweltering out that day; there was no way an ice sculpture would survive for long.

"Do you like it?!" asked a very self-pleased Veronica in a sing-song voice to her friend Lucia who was walking out to greet her. Veronica stepped out of her yellow Hummer like a pageant queen, her orangey hair and pale ginger complexion clashing hilariously with the bright crayon-coloured truck. Her husband Martin, a furry little hedgehog of a man, had jumped out the passenger side door before the truck had even stopped rolling, headed for the beach like an overly-excited child. His greyish-red hair was combed and oiled back aristocratically, and he wore a paisley ascot tied around his fat neck in colours that matched the lining of his black velvet blazer. It was painfully obvious that his wife had styled him, and that it would have been an arduous process but still he ran, off to wreck his look like a hyper kid on picture day. Waddling swiftly with his toy helicopter and its remote clutched in his sweaty hands, it was like he was a mildly retarded adult. Which wasn't completely untrue. And their relationship was quite inexplicable, until you found out that Martin was an incredibly wealthy accidental jackpot winner.

Veronica had been the clerk on duty the day he went in to redeem the possible winnings from a ticket he found stuck to a sewer grate. Twenty-four million and change, it was. She was excited, for she had never checked a winning ticket before. Feeling lucky, he asked her to marry him on the spot and she decided to let the fact that he now had mountains of money overrule the fact that he was an odd, childish and generally useless-seeming man. This was back in '82.

"I commissioned this sculpture with Andre LeGould," said Veronica, ignoring him as he ran off, and ignoring their thirty-something son Reginald who snored deeply with his mouth wide open in the back seat. "Mr. LeGould, as I'm sure you know, is the local sculptor-slash-Reiki masseur. The piece cost about a thousand dollars but you really can't put a price on divinity!"

Lucia got a closer look at it. "Yes, it certainly is handsome, Veronica," she said as she admired the piece of art. "And this is very thoughtful, but I wish you didn't spend a thousand bucks on something that will be little more than a wet spot on the tablecloth by midnight. . . "

"Oh poppycock!" said Veronica, for whom money was no object. "A thing of beauty is a joy forever! Even if it does melt."

"Well it was a lovely gesture and it will fill the empty spot on the salad table nicely!" said Lucia as she gestured the deliverymen towards the table on the end.

"Oh no, darling. No, no, no!" countered Veronica. "A piece like this absolutely must be on the middle table. Why do you think they call it a centerpiece?" she said smugly, ushering the delivery guys toward the middle table.

Ava interjected from where she sat in the corner of the patio in the shade. "A centrepiece is so-called because it's meant to sit at the center of a table. Any table, really, and definitely not necessarily the very epicenter of the most central table, Mrs. Von der Klaasen." Ava spoke even more smugly than Veronica ever could, and, as per usual, a hint of venom could be detected in her voice. Veronica narrowed her eyes at the brazen, outspoken girl. It bothered her very much that her arch-nemesis was less than a third her age, but Ava had made sure to rub her the wrong way every chance she could ever since, at the tender age of six, she dropped a handful of mud onto the seat of Veronica's camping chair the day she wore bright white culottes to the Canada Day picnic. When she stood up to sing the national anthem in front of everyone, laughter erupted in the crowd and she had no idea why until her own son, eleven years old at the time, started everyone chanting *Diarrhea mudslide! Diarrhea mudslide!*, until she noticed the brown stains across her butt that looked convincingly enough like she had soiled herself. Absolutely mortified, she knew it was all Ava's doing when she looked up to see the tempestuous brat waving at her with muddy hands, grinning proudly and cruelly. Ever since then, Veronica knew to keep her eye on Ava, who loved so much to make enemies, and for whom bullying adults brought a satisfaction rarely felt from bullying her peers.

Gabriel came out onto the patio with a tray full of martinis. "For the ladies!" he said as his mother, sister and Veronica gratefully received their frosted glasses full of shaken vodka and dragon fruit nectar. Lucia tasted hers, and a euphoric look crossed her face. "Mmm," she cooed. "Son, you are officially exempt from dish duty this evening!" Lucia was kidding, of course; they had hired people for the after-party cleanup that evening. She winked at Veronica, who had just guzzled her martini in one gulp across the table. Veronica smiled politely and thanked him but behind her oversized sunglasses she scowled, for she'd always been envious of Lucia's relationship with her charming son. Her own son Reginald, still snoring out in the truck, had been a screaming, colicky baby who grew into a whiny, spoiled child who grew up to be a lazy, fat and entitled young man. She, his own mother and a woman very aware of the fact that her husband was an imbecile, could still never understand how her own son could have turned out so awful. Reginald was about a decade older than Gabriel but even someone as young as Demetra found him to be petty and immature.

Veronica, beginning to fear that her dud of a son might never give her grandchildren or worse, never move out of her home, had recently made it her mission to find him a suitable bride. She knew it would not be easy, was prepared to lower her standards and was willing to make offers too good to refuse. It was her mandate to get a girl to agree to mate with Reginald. So when she caught sight of the lovely, waifish blond that had followed Gabriel out onto the patio, she jumped up to meet her. Veronica was not a woman to let a prospective daughter-in-law slip by, un-propositioned.

"Well hello darling, it's an absolute pleasure to meet you! I'm Veronica Von der Klaasen but you can just call me Mrs. Von der Klaasen." Veronica wore her married name with the pride of an heiress, but the truth was, the Von der Klaasen clan her husband belonged to were blue collar through and through. It had been widely speculated that Martin was the peculiar way he was because of the factory fumes both of his parents were exposed to around the time of his conception, and the prescription pain-killers his mother gratuitously took for a sprained toe while she was breast-feeding him.

Veronica looked the girl up and down. She knew that whoever would agree to the lackluster honor of marrying her awkward, socially inept son would have to be someone with a dire few options, and the mute, albino-esque and seemingly family-less girl Lucia had just filled her in on was sounding like a viable candidate. Gabriel sat her down in a patio chair next to Ava and ran inside to grab some more wine glasses. Ava stared at her silently and coldly from behind blacked-out sunglasses.

"Aren't you serene looking," said Veronica, her voice dripping with saccharine. "You're like a little porcelain doll. You must meet my son Reginald, he'd simply adore you!"

"I'm sure nothing would thrill her more . . ." snickered Ava coldly. The mermaid smiled kindly but unsurely at Veronica, then, out of the corner of her eye, she noticed something poke out from behind a trellis, shaking the vines. When she turned to look, it retreated, and then slowly a pair of eyes and a shock of unruly red hair poked back out again, only to once again retreat. Several seconds later, a ginger-colored, chunky freckled man in a pink polo shirt and white linen shorts sashayed out from behind the house with one hand casually in his pocket while the other held his flashy, high-tech gadget of a cell phone to his ear. Pretending not to notice her sitting there at the table, Reginald proceeded to feign an entire conversation in which he acted the role of a sort of power player, calling shots and running his non-existent empire like a baller CEO.

In his contrived exchange that went on for a solid eight minutes of bull crap and tragically exaggerated bravado, he had his imaginary secretary/manager/bookie character throw down eighty-five grand on a Blue Jays game, move thirty per cent of his net worth into a Russian ballistics company and, a second after looking up and catching eyes with the mermaid, had the assisting figment cancel all of the fictitious "dates" he had lined up for that week (all with "eager" and "attractive" women, as he made sure to mention loudly.) He also had his investments pulled out of a Helsinki deal, sent a private jet to Switzerland for a case of his favourite artisanal chocolates and scheduled a racetrack test drive in a new McLaren GT. It can only be speculated that Reginald carried on like this because he thought he was being impressive, but his act was so painfully transparent and unfeasible that if he actually thought he was fooling anyone, there was legitimate cause for concern. So much about Reginald was legitimate cause for concern.

Once he'd 'hung up' the phone, he wiped his breath from the shiny chrome receiver and, going for the gusto, threw a big wink at the pretty blond stranger on the porch who, with even her limited knowledge of human communication and its tools, could quite easily tell that there had been no one on the line with him. Everyone on the patio was his captive audience, observing his performance like an amusing train wreck they just couldn't look away from. While he attempted to peacock, walking a very rehearsed, very pathetic strut over to the wooden armchair at the head of the patio table, Ava made a long, slow, digusting fart noise in the background. The sound effect was meant, of course, to illustrate and draw attention to the sheer, lame, and all-around malodorous presence of Reginald, on the whole. It was effective. Ignoring her, he slowly pulled his orange Wayfarers out of the pocket that sat above his left man-breast's permanent nipple erection and slipped them onto his chubby face, where they sat awkwardly on the bridge of his upturned piggy nose. Realizing everyone was looking at him and that they were all on the brink of uproarious laughter, he attempted to change the subject and take the attention off himself "Look at that swamp cow!" he said crudely, pointing to a larger lady in a pink muumuu walking her dog down the beach.

"Please don't make fun of Mrs. Hufton," said Demetra, unimpressed. "She's a very active lady, but suffers from a lazy thyroid."

"Well she looks like a slothful swamp cow," he chuckled, looking to the mermaid for agreement. She smiled politely at him, at a loss for how else to respond. He looked her up and down before asking her in a deepened voice, "So . . . they say you're a mute, how's that treatin' ya?" She frowned and looked away, praying Gabriel would come out and rescue her from this abrasive and ridiculous person. "No, no . . . don't be offended," he said with a snicker, "In all honesty, I'd be dazzled if I never had to hear the high-pitched, nasally voice of the weaker sex ever again!" All the females at the table looked at each other amusedly and then burst out laughing at his ignorant comment. The mermaid sat with her eyebrows raised, confused as to why all the girls thought his inappropriate comment was funny. "No, that came out wrong," he continued. "What I meant to say is that, while a woman's voice can be, on rare occasion, quite pleasing, a woman has nothing of interest to speak of. Just a lot of bikini waxes, tampon troubles and *The Bachelorette*, ha ha. But you, you rare beauty, pale as a white rose . . ." he said, eyeing her up and down creepily, "YOU have got life all sorted." Wink.

Veronica, mortified as she was to admit this creature lived inside of her for nine hellish months, decided to attempt damage control, or some version of it. She stood up beside her son and with her hands on his wide, low shoulders, made his introduction:

"Dear, this is my son, Reginald. I know he doesn't look or sound like much but I promise that if you marry him, we'll build you a very large house; so massive and so luxurious that you'd hardly have to run into each other, ever! Unless, of course, you wanted to . . ."

"Okay, easy does it, Ronnie!" interrupted Lucia, smiling and shaking her head at her pushy friend. "The big introduction should really be more of a soft sale..."

"Your bedrooms could be on separate wings," Veronica continued unabashedly. "We could install a grand partition! You'd only have to visit his side when you're ready to impregnate--"

"Alright, Von der Klaasen! Give the girl a minute to mull it all over!" said Lucia, amazed at the boldness of her friend. The mermaid was hardly able to compute the things she was being told.

"Of course, this is the age of in-vitro!" Veronica continued, persisting. Lucia gave up, and just let her friend get it all out. "No one will blame you if the sight of my son makes you want to dry-heave. I just want a grandchild; it cannot stop with Reginald, it simply cannot!" With a panicked look on her face, she grabbed and slurped back the rest of Lucia's martini and then sat down.

"Mom, you're psychotic," Reginald droned, then invited Demetra to play a game of Bocce in the sand with him. (She really didn't want to, but, like a good host, she obliged him.) Sheepishly, Veronica grinned. She knew she was being intensely gregarious but found it difficult to help herself when it came to such matters. The little mermaid was wide-eyed and taken aback by her aggressive, obsessive energy. Once the silence had gone on long enough and the table started chatting about other things, Veronica leaned in toward her and whispered one last thing:

"If you were to bear my grandchildren, darling, I promise you, you would never, ever want for anything again until the day you die, which I'm sure we could even extend if need be . . . you'd be amazed at the things the Von der Klaasen wealth could afford you." Just as she thought the girl was beginning to consider her generous offer, Gabriel came walking back out to the patio and Veronica, whose eyes were still trained on the girl's face, witnessed the young thing's psyched, enamored expression and gave up immediately. Oh well, Veronica thought, she's a bit pale anyway. She had been hoping to liven up the gene pool a bit by throwing it a racial curve ball that might hope to dominate the freckles. She had heard that the Johnsons might be bringing their South American au pair to the party that evening. She made a mental note to accost Consuela then.

Half an hour later, Demetra returned to the patio proudly brandishing Reginald's Rolex. Reginald, now watchless and wearing the sullen expression of a poor sportsman, followed. "Reggie!" exclaimed Gabriel, "Looks like Meaty disgraced you with the Bocce balls once again . . . I told you never to bet your Rolexes, she's a shark!" he said as he uncorked a bottle of wine.

"I assure you, it's fine, I have dozens," said Reginald as he glanced slyly at the mermaid, hoping she heard his bragging. "And it's 'Reginald'," said Reginald. "Not 'Reggie'."

"My bad," said Gabriel with mock prudence. When the cork was out, he poured three glasses of wine and passed one to the mermaid, who took the glass in both hands and breathed the scent in. He offered the second one to Reginald but was met with a sneer and the wine was dismissed with a sweeping hand gesture. "Mom, did you pack the Lagavulin 18 like I told you to?"

Veronica replied that she had and that it was in the car. "Oh great," he replied. "It's probably piss-warm by now . . . way to drop the ball!" He sniveled at her seethingly but she just rolled her eyes and went back to her conversation with Lucia. "Real men drink scotch," he said to Gabriel as he stood up to go retrieve the bottle from the Hummer. Gabriel took a sip of his wine and turned to the girl he found that morning to see how she would react to the taste of the wine. She took a sip and didn't love the Chardonnay's bitter taste, but kept sipping happily not because she was growing used to it, but because she loved that she was drinking the same thing he was, from the very same bottle. A few moments later, Demetra came outside and climbed right up onto her big brother's lap, which made the mermaid suddenly envious. Of course, it dissipated quickly when she remembered it was just his baby sister, who was in no way a threat to her ultimate happiness.

"And there is the girl who stole my heart and my watch," said Reginald as he re-emerged with his Lagavulin gift box in hand. "It's okay, I'll win it back next time. Or I'll just wait 'til you're eighteen and marry you so it'll become our communal property . . ."

Demetra giggled innocently as a baby but replied sharp as a tack. "Reginald, by the time I'm even old enough that the creepy things you say cease to make you sound like a total molestor, I sincerely hope you'll have taken a victim, er, bride by then." Everyone laughed except his mother, who pretended not to be listening.

Reginald's orange neander-brow lowered as he addressed her brash comment. "For your information, Lizzie McGuire, I have beautiful women jockeying for pole position as we speak! I'm just taking my time deciding which, if either, is worthy of the Von der Klaasen name."

Demetra giggled even harder, for she found almost everything he ever said to be infectiously funny in its fatheaded pomposity, for Reginald was like a caricature of himself. "First of all, you can't marry someone that's made in CGI," she chirped. "Secondly, and I mean no offense, but maybe it's time you gave yourself and your *'Von der Klaasen* name' a break. I mean, I know it sounds cool and Dutch and stuff but your dad won the lottery; that doesn't make you a duke."

Reginald's face went bright red as he sneered at her as well. He, like his mother, couldn't stand being mocked by his juniors. "I'll have you know these ladies I'm speaking of are bright, athletic olympians who competed in the last winter games. One is a cross-country skiing sensation from Mongolia, the other, a slalom goddess from Liechtenstein!" He had a way of making his nasal voice boom at the end of sentences whenever he was angry. Fumbling awkwardly and unskillfully, he cracked open the gift box and poured six fingers of the warm scotch into the promo glass it came with.

Demetra watched Reginald as he poured, spilling on his hand as he tipped the bottle back up. "Is this for real, or is it like the time you tried to tell us the concept for *The Matrix* was all your idea, stolen from your diary while you napped on the airplane?" she spoke dryly and her question irked him, but Reginald just ignored her. He picked up his scotch, stirred it with his middle finger then took a sip, trying hard to hide the face he was making in order to appear to be enjoying it. He didn't like scotch; he liked Shirley Temples. But no one was ever to know that. He offered his glass to Gabriel.

"No, no buddy; it's all you," replied Gabriel. "Can I get you some ice?"

"Hmpf," muttered Reginald. "Real men drink scotch."


Within an hour, the patio was filled with people toasting, laughing and eating from iced seafood towers, cheese platters and fondue pots. When it came to throwing parties, one could always count on the O'Faolains to put out an impressive spread. All of their neighbors and friends were present, young mingling with old, just about everyone indulging in moderate to heavy drinking. Gabriel was with some friends by the bar when he noticed Mr. and Mrs. Behrensen walk into the party. He didn't see Arabella with them but knew that she would most definitely be there if they were. He sighed. A freak storm helped him dodge the bullet last time, but what would save him this time? He ducked a bit and looked around, hoping to avoid her as long as he could when suddenly, he heard a familiar voice over the loudspeakers.

"Good evening, Tofino!" said Arabella as the party guests cheered and stepped back so that she and her two back-up dancers would have room. "Last year at Gabriel's birthday," she said in her sexiest pop star voice, "a late-summer storm put the party on hold and I never got to give him his present." She made a pouty face, and everyone, reflexively, went *awwwww*. "Well it's a beautiful night out, and I have his present right here with me so happy belated, Gabriel!" Everyone cheered again, and with that, she put the microphone on its stand and signaled for the lights to lower before she began her song:

*It was you I hunted, and it was you I claimed . . .*
*I've kept you in my cross-hairs, and I've been practicing my aim . . .*

As she sang, everyone froze where they stood. Her song and her voice were, surprisingly, stirring; it was a sweet lament about the exquisite pain of unrequited love. It gave everyone unexpected goose bumps, for it was a drastic change from the upbeat pop tunes she was famous for. The shift in her style surprised no one more than Gabriel, who, upon hearing her croon with such depth and feeling, decided that perhaps he had been wrong about her. The buzz was that she had been training rigorously with a top-tier vocal coach to take her career in a new direction, and even though she had very much enjoyed her time at the top of the charts, she longed deeply to be taken more seriously as an artist. Mostly, Arabella wanted to be taken more seriously by Gabriel.

Her plan was working; she was delivering her song beautifully, and had the whole party entranced. Gabriel watched her with eyes that told of awe and wonderment, for she sounded as sweet as a siren and he was only noticing now even though she had spent so many years trying desperately to get his attention. Maybe it was the low glow of the patio lanterns, or the gentle melody of the song she was sharing but Arabella looked more beautiful to him than ever before.

It filled the mermaid with deep sorrow to be standing next to him as he watched her, for she knew that she herself had once sung far more beautifully. If only he knew that she had given her voice away forever, just to be there at his side while he delighted in the song of another.

Just then, the mermaid looked down to notice a couple of little crabs crawling around the floor at her feet. They stopped for a moment right in front of her and seemed to look right up at her until they both took off in straight lines towards the performers. As Arabella began to dance the routine she had been rehearsing for months, her two dancers held their positions a pace behind and on either side of her, swaying gracefully to the music. All of a sudden, just as they were preparing to all spin in unison, the dancer to Arabella's left spotted the crabs down at her feet and, thrown off balance, rolled her ankle and fell down hard, smashing her hip. The whole crowd gasped as the dancer hit the floor and the crabs quickly scurried away but in that strange and unexpected instant, the little mermaid felt her body being taken over from the tops of her fingers to the tips of her toes. Almost involuntarily, she raised her arms in the air and lifted herself up on her new toes and over to the show to fall perfectly in line with the dance choreography. The fallen dancer sat on the floor gripping her sore ankle, and stared up in disbelief at the girl who was so quick to take her place. The little mermaid followed the steps as if she knew them by heart, and as she swayed, her eyes spoke more deeply to the heart than any girl's pretty song ever could. Arabella and the dancers had shoes on but the little mermaid's feet were bare, and as she rose to her tiptoes, she seemed to glide upon them weightlessly and effortlessly, looking lovelier with every step.

Arabella continued to sing her song, confused about how this girl knew all her moves but glad her performance didn't have to miss a beat. Soon, though, she began to fill with anger and jealousy as she watched Gabriel, her target audience, clap and cheer and stare in amazement at the little mute girl instead of her.

Everyone was captivated, and the little mermaid who was so new upon her feet felt absolute exhilaration as her body floated to the music as if it knew every note intimately. Every movement of hers was so perfect, she looked as natural dancing this complicated routine as she did simply walking. Gabriel's smile was now exclusively for her, and she relished the feeling like it was the only bit of joy there would ever be. She promised herself then and there that she would always be the one winning in his smiles.

When the song was over, Gabriel gave Arabella a quick hug and thanked her for the song, then turned to the little mermaid and hoisted her in the air like she was the pride of his life. He told her she was amazing, and that he had never seen a person move so beautifully in all his life. She soaked his praise up, and had never felt so happy. He told her he had something to give her, then put his arm around her shoulder and walked with her towards the house, so excited about the little dancer that he completely forgot that it had been Arabella who had put on the performance for him in the first place. It was all very wonderful for the mermaid, but it did not sit well with Arabella.

After a few seconds of gaping at her microphone, dumbfounded, the salt in her fresh wound began to sting fiercely and she was unable to maintain her composure any longer. She grabbed the wrist of the fallen dancer and dragged her swiftly over to Gabriel and the mermaid just as they were about to step inside. She shouted at them dramatically, "What the eff? She pushed my dancer!"

Gabriel rolled his eyes, for it was an outrageous accusation. "Arabella, that's not true and you know it. We all saw it happen; she didn't push her at all. You should be glad she saved the show!"

"STOLE the show!" whined Arabella indignantly. She hated herself for how petty she was being in front of all those people but she was a falling woman reaching for a branch. "She stole my show and my choreography! You should throw her out of this party!"

Gabriel smiled and attempted to calm her down by resting his hand on her shoulder. "There's no need to be dramatic, Arabella," he said. "She didn't mean any harm. And she's really sorry for stealing your thunder, aren't you?" he asked, turning to the mermaid and nudging her. Baring all her pearly teeth with a huge felicitous smile, the mermaid nodded "yes."

"So there you have it," he said. "Great new track though, Arabella. Seriously, you'll be able to shake off that cheesy pop persona in no time with tracks like that! Good work, buddy." He patted her on the back and with his unintentionally backhanded compliment still lingering in the air, he went inside with his tiny dancer, having finally shaken Arabella loose and now free to enjoy the party without her eyes on him everywhere he went. As they walked up the stairs to Dagmara's old room, they heard the Behrensen's SUV limo screech out of the driveway and knock down a cast iron flower urn. Unless she was coming back to torch the place, she wasn't going to come back and that was a great comfort to him. He turned to his little mermaid and said, "You might possibly be the greatest thing I've ever found on that beach! You must never, ever leave me." He uttered the sweet words so casually as they walked together down the hall, having no idea whatsoever that that was already her plan, and it had been all she thought about since long before she knew he'd return her feelings. I would never leave you, she seemed to say with her piercing blue eyes.

The party was a great success and saw the wines and liquors flowing until the very end. From every huddle and corner could be heard riotous belly laughs and warm acclamations for the O'Faolains, who were famous for their memorable fetes and soirees. (They were now also famous for Gabriel's infamous birthday shipwreck, but that wasn't enough to deter their friends. In fact, since everyone from his birthday had survived and were already laughing about the shared near-death experience, it had made invites to the family's jams that much more coveted.) After the last party guests had cleared out, the family and their mermaid sank into their patio chairs, finishing off their drinks and winding down.

"Well!" started Lucia, exhausted but hyper from the rush. "You sure made a splash tonight, didn't you, little mystery lady! I think the Behrensen limo took down my peonies on their way out . . ."

"Yeah!" exclaimed Demetra. "Where did you learn to dance like that?"

"Remember, Meaty," said Ava, "It's pointless to ask her any questions that can't be answered with a nod or a head shake." The mermaid, cool and unfazed, just smiled and shrugged her shoulders. She was almost glad to be dumb in this situation because she wouldn't have wanted to lie to them, but she also didn't have an answer they'd understand or even believe.

"People kept asking what your name is tonight," said Gabriel to his little friend. "It was weird having to say I didn't know. So I was thinking . . . I know you can't tell us what your real name is, but if it's alright with you, maybe we can come up with something to call you in the meantime. I mean, we have to call you something, right?!"

The little mermaid smiled and nodded, even though she wasn't sure she agreed. She was never given a name, just a number and a superlative: the sixth born princess, the littlest. It did, however, seem a novel idea to her that a person be given a name not based on rank, but simply because of the way it sounded rolling off the tongue.

"Should we just call out names and judge your liking based on facial expression?" he asked. She nodded happily -- it sounded like fun.

"How about 'Kelsey'; that's a hot girl name!" offered Gabriel. The mermaid pondered it.

"Pass. Conjures up images of Kelsey Grammer and his giant kneecap of a forehead." said Ava. "We wouldn't want to invite the comparison," she added coolly. The mermaid arranged her fringe to obscure the top half of her face.

Gabriel thought for a moment. "How about 'Katrina'? That's pretty!" he said. The mermaid smiled then looked to Ava.

"Pass," she said. "Makes me think of hurricanes, and also of strippers. Next."

"Well then how about Chloe? She kind of looks like a Chloe," said Gabriel.

"French hooker," said Ava. "Next."

"How many sex industry workers are you personally acquainted with?" he jocosely asked.

"I'm just trying to make sure we don't give our mute squatter an intolerable whore name, that's all," she snapped back.

Cliff piped up. "Well, I had hoped to name one of my daughters Gertrude Gladys, after my two aunties," he said. "But that's already been vetoed three times in this family, I don't know why I bother suggesting it now . . ."

Lucia patted her husband on the back patronizingly. "Neither do I, darling. Neither do I."

"How about Anne?" offered Gabriel. "It's simple, not whorish, but pretty."

"I always thought if I had another daughter, I'd call her Octavia," suggested Lucia.

"That's really pretty, Mom," said Demetra. "But I think we should call her Ariel."

Gabriel laughed out loud. "Ariel?" he asked. "Like that Disney mermaid?"

Ava rolled her eyes at the suggestion. "Pass-- cheesy and juvenile."

"Ava, are you actually going to contribute anything or are you just going to sit there and rip on our suggestions?" asked Gabriel, tiring of her negative comments.

"I don't actually care what we do with her, but I'll be damned if I don't make sure we're at least calling her by something decent while she's freeloading in our home."

"Hear me out before you dismiss me," demanded Demetra in the most polite way possible. She stood up to speak. "Check it out: she's given us nothing to go on regarding her origins, can't speak or write any languages but can somehow understand everything we say. Look at that necklace and her impossibly long, pearl-woven siren hair! AND let's not forget, Gabriel found her naked out on the beach, just as the prince so famously does in the fairy tale." She knew she had made her point. "Ariel, I think," she said triumphantly, and sat back down. Gabriel couldn't argue, neither could Lucia. Cliff glanced at the girl they were taking the liberty of naming, and felt himself getting a little emotional. "It's remarkable how much the young lady looks like our Dagmara." Everyone turned to look at her.

"Well before anyone suggests it, we are NOT calling her Dagmara!" said Ava defensively, with a look on her face that said she was ready to scrap with anyone who'd disagree.

"Ava, relax. No one wants to call her Dagmara. We just think she bears a striking resemblance, that's all," said Lucia.

"Well she sure looks comfy in her clothes!" Ava shot back.

Lucia smiled patiently at her combative daughter. "She showed up wearing nothing, Ava. And since Dagmara doesn't need it these days-"

"You know I hate when you say things like that!" barked Ava angrily.

"I'm sorry, you're right," said her mother apologetically. "I'm just saying that the Dagmara we knew would have wanted us to share her things with someone who had nothing."

"And it's not like we'd dare ask YOU to share with the down-and-out," said Gabriel under his breath. Ava sneered at him.

"Yeah, that's the part I'm having trouble with," she said. Why is everyone so quick to believe she's actually 'down and out'? How do we know she's not lying to us, when she says absolutely nothing at all? Am I seriously the only one here that thinks this whole situation is messed up? I don't even mess with Dagmara's stuff and I'm her sister!"

"Dagmara really wouldn't have minded, Ava," said Demetra knowingly and affectionately.

Ava's face reddened with fury. "What the hell do you know?" she asked, rebuking her harshly. "You weren't even old enough to have had a conversation with her! Don't presume to know my sister, since you were still in diapers when she disappeared!"

Tears welled up in Demetra's eyes while her only remaining sister berated her. She had a high threshold for other people's nonsense, but this actually hurt her feelings. "Well she was my sister too and I miss her as much as any of you do!" she said in protest, standing up and sprinting away from the table and down to the beach.

The whole family shot Ava a disapproving look. "Happy now?" asked Gabriel as he got up to go after Demetra. "You know, it's interesting how you'd rather protect our lost sister's old clothes than our baby sister's feelings." Then he ran down the steps and chased her down the beach. The tides were high and he didn't like the idea of her walking out there alone.

Ava sunk lower in her seat and crossed her arms across her chest, mad at herself for having said such things and even madder still that she was far too stubborn to admit it.

"Well I think this is as good a time as any to conclude this meeting," said Lucia, getting up and collecting the last glasses from the table. "Are we happy to just go with Ariel, then?" she asked the little stranger. "Do you like it?"

The little mermaid nodded *Yes*. Yes, she certainly did.

"Conjures up images of 'front-side ten-eighty inverted aerials," said Cliff enthusiastically. "Are we going to spell it the same way?"

"Hmmm, perhaps a slight alteration," said Lucia. "Arielle, maybe?"

The little mermaid nodded, satisfied with what the family had come up with for her.

"Arielle sounds nice," said Ava softly, watching as her brother and little sister walked away down the moonlit beach.

"Well, Arielle, I'm sure you're dying for a warm bath after the day you've had!" said Lucia. "Let me show you to the bathroom so you can get all washed up before bed."

Arielle stood up and curtsied to the table before stepping away. She gave Ava a warm smile, after having gotten just the briefest glimpse of her softer side. She nodded a sweet goodnight to Cliff, glanced out to the beach at Gabriel, and then followed Lucia into the house.

Upstairs, the halls were wide and inviting, and the wind chime that hung in the open window at the south end played melodiously upon the night breeze, drawing her towards a doorway spilling dim flickering light into the hallway. "This is my favorite room in the house," said Lucia as they walked into the big, airy bathroom. The tiles and the marble countertops were an earthy pink coral; the walls, sinks and tub were a perfect pearly white. "It's where I come to be alone," she said as she turned the faucet to make warm water pour out. She reached for her frangipani bubble bath and poured it into the running water, making tufts of bubbles spread out across the surface until the whole bath was covered with the white, spongy froth. Arielle poked her fingers into the floral-scented foam then brought it to her lips to taste it. Lucia giggled as the strange girl made a face and spit the bubbles back into the tub. "If only everything tasted as good as it smelled," she rued.

When the tub was filled almost to the brim, the newly-dubbed Arielle watched with amazement at how Lucia could stop the water from pouring out by just simply turning the tap. A miniature sea on demand it was, and from it, lovely, sweet-smelling steam rose. She had never seen a little pool look so warm and inviting.

"Alright darling, go ahead and jump in. I'm just down the hall if you need anything," said Lucia as she pulled two fresh white towels out of the closet and set them down by the sink. Then she walked out, pulled the door closed behind her, and Arielle was left by herself for the first time since she regained consciousness in the family's living room that morning.

Arielle dipped her hand in; she had never felt water this hot before, and its warmth put goose bumps all over her body. Without taking her eyes off the steaming bath, she stepped out of her sundress and kicked her flip-flops off to the side, leaving her in her bra and panties. Sitting down on the ledge, she wiggled out of her bra and then trickled a bit of the sweet water onto her thighs and watched as her white skin gave way to the pearly blue scales she was used to seeing her whole life before this day. She picked up her right foot and massaged it, wincing as her hands moved over the tips of her toes, whose bottoms were covered in dried blood from her earlier exertions during Arabella's song. While she was dancing, the enjoyment she felt upon her graceful new feet coupled with the sheer adrenaline of performing in front of all those people helped to numb the pain but now that she was alone, she could no longer ignore their aching. She braced herself on the ledge of the tub and swung both feet around until all ten toes were hovering an inch above the water, wiggling blissfully in the steam. She dipped them in and watched as the dark blue tips of her tail fin pushed out from under her toenails and spread open into the bathwater. The pain that had burdened her all day began to quickly dissipate as the soft white skin of her ankles tightened up into rows of shiny, round scales, spreading all the way up to her thighs and when they finally reached her hips, the panties she wore stretched and ripped off her body as soon as there ceased to be any space along the middle of her lower half. Propping herself up on her arms, she slowly dipped her entire lower half into the warm tub and let her dry tail saturate with the scented water. The transformation from girl to mermaid washed over her body like a blanket of soothing relief, and her day's suffering lifted out of her like a woman's feet freed from shoes that have looked lovely all day but are two sizes too small.

She slunk herself low until she was lying in the water, letting the warmth flow into her ears and nostrils, sending shivers up her spine. She opened her eyes but they stung in the bubble bath so she kept them closed underwater, enjoying the feeling of her slippery tail sliding around across the smooth tub that cradled her. Suddenly, she heard a knock at the door and sat up panicking, frantically hiding her tail under the bubbles.

"Arielle, I just remembered the shampoo in there is empty, so I'm coming in with a fresh bottle, okay?" Lucia came in with the shampoo and Arielle sat perfectly still, careful not to disturb the water and reveal her deep blue tail. "It's from this handmade soap shop the girls and I love, have you ever tried it?" From the puzzled look on Arielle's face, it was clear to Lucia that the girl had no idea what it was she was holding. "Shall I wash your hair for you?" she offered.

Before Arielle was able to come up with a way to politely decline, Lucia took a seat in the chair behind the tub and began to lather up her long strands. Anxiously but inconspicuously, Arielle arranged the bubbles so they covered the whole surface of the water evenly.

"You have so many knots and tangles in here," she said as she ran her fingers across Arielle's scalp with the gentle finesse of a mother who had raised three long-haired daughters. "I had super-long hair in college, but your locks look like they've never been cut before!" Lucia reached her hands under Arielle's head and behind her neck, and felt something hard tied into her thick locks. She squeezed some conditioner into her hands and untangled the hair around it until she pulled out a silver key that was etched in an intricate design. "What's this key for?" Lucia asked curiously.

Arielle remembered the day she braided it into her hair; it was the day after a big storm that had moved mountains of sand around, uncovering an 18th-century shipwreck that had been buried since it went down. She had found the key dangling from a silver chain around the neck of a skeleton whose clothing had long since rotted off. Beside him sat a big wooden trunk filled with gold coins and rubies but she liked the pretty little key the best so it was the only thing she had taken with her that day.

In response to Lucia's query, Arielle just shrugged. She learned quickly that shrugs often go unchallenged, not that she could give her any more information if she wanted to.

Lucia continued to wash Arielle's hair, running her fingers through and finding all sorts of random treasures tied in. After pulling out a caviar spoon, a few soda can tabs and a wing nut, she found a harmonica that looked strangely familiar.

"Dear, where did you get this?" she asked in amazement as she untangled it too from her locks. "This was my father's; he gave it to Gabriel." Upon inspecting it closer, she saw that it surely enough had her father's initials engraved into the mouthpiece. Arielle froze; she remembered the night she crawled across the sand to scoop it up after he dropped it from the balcony. But they couldn't know that! So she just sat perfectly still and waited for Lucia to change the subject. "Well, anyway, he'll be grateful you found it for him!"

By the time Lucia was done combing out Arielle's head full of small treasures, she had a table's worth of artifacts. Once all the pearls, knots, weeds and braids were combed out, she could see that the hair was longer than the girl was tall. After combing lots more conditioner through it, she used a water jug to rinse the sugary-smelling lather from her hair. Arielle had never felt anything so luxurious. To her, it felt like heaven, and it would have been only slightly more enjoyable if she didn't have to worry about keeping her tail hidden under the bubbles the whole time.

"Alright, all clean," said Lucia, standing up. "I left a fresh toothbrush by the sink for you and when you're done in here, you can sleep in the blue room tonight, through this door," she said, motioning to the room off the bathroom. "Tomorrow we can see about finding your family for you; they must be worried sick! Good night, dear."

The little mermaid sat still in the tub, graciously smiling, waiting for Lucia to close the door so that she could spread out comfortably again. Once the door was shut and Lucia's footsteps were all the way down the hall, she breathed a big sigh of relief and allowed her fins to dangle once again over the edge of the tub. Once back in her space of solace, she began to think seriously about her family, and the consequences of her decision. She thought about the worried face her grandmother would be wearing, and how her father would be harshly blaming himself for her disappearance. She felt very badly but her decision was made in the name of true love, and she was determined to have it. She only wished it didn't have to come at such high costs.

When her warm bathwater had cooled to lukewarm, she quietly lifted her body out of the tub and sat herself down on the bath mat, allowing the fluffy shag to soak up some of the water on her tail. Quickly and quietly, she used the towels to pat her tail dry until her blue scales evaporated to reveal soft, white legs again. Standing beside the tub, she let the water drain and went to the room she would be spending the night in.

When she stepped inside, she was amazed to see that she was surrounded by mermaid things! There was a mermaid lamp, seashell decorations everywhere and the shelves were lined with books on mermaid sightings and folklore. Surrounded by things that reminded her of home, she switched off the lamp and put herself to bed, happy to know that the girl who had lived in the room before her must have loved her without ever knowing her, just the way she loved the world of the humans before ever seeing it for herself.

She woke up a few hours later in the middle of the night. Everything was quiet but for the crickets and the crashing waves. Being alone in the dark made her feel deeply homesick and she began to long very much for the company of her sisters so she could tell them all about her day with Gabriel. Feeling lonely, she got up and gently opened the big wooden door to peek out into the hallway and see if anyone else was awake. All of the bedroom doors were closed, and the whole house appeared to be fast asleep. Quietly, she tiptoed down the long hallway barefoot and, without making a sound, pressed her ear to Gabriel's door. She could hear him breathing, and smell the sweet scent of him wafting out from under his door. She didn't dare open it, but sat down on the floor and leaned her cheek against it, settling at the door, happy to be as close to him as she possibly could be without disturbing the quiet. After only a few minutes of imagining where his dreams were taking him that night, she fell fast asleep right there in his doorway.

## seventeen

## _Firsts_

Arielle awoke to a sliver of bright morning sun burning a hole into her eyelid. Her cheek was on the floor and the light hit her from the gap between Gabriel's door and the hardwood floor. Sleepily, she stood up and began to tiptoe back to her bed but as she approached Ava's door, she began to smell something funny in the air. As she crept closer, she noticed little swirls of smoke coming out the open door and as she went to peek in, Ava, sitting by her window, turned to the door with her keen ears perked. Arielle froze in her steps.

Ava exhaled deeply and smoke billowed out of her mouth and nose. "Come in, come in my child. We mustn't lurk in doorways; it's rude." She spun around to face her and Arielle noticed she was sitting in a strange chair that had big wheels on it where its legs should be. Shyly, Arielle took a few steps into Ava's big red room and curtsied for her. Ava laughed wickedly.

"I don't know where you come from, but no one here curtsies anymore. I think that custom was actually abolished along with slavery." Arielle looked around in bewilderment at Ava's beautiful room with the crimson walls and the ivory and gold window frames. As the breeze came in, it ruffled her long, white linen drapes and with the early morning sun pouring through them, they looked like the sails of a grand ship against a red sky. Ava inhaled again off the joint she was smoking and wheeled herself forward to pass it to Arielle. Not wanting to be rude, Arielle put her lips to it as Ava had and breathed in. The smoke tickled her throat and at once she began to cough.

Gabriel's dark sister giggled as she took her joint back and put it out in the armrest ashtray of her vintage wheelchair. When Arielle was finally done coughing and hacking up the last bit of smoke from her lungs, a little sneeze came out of her nostrils. Her head felt dizzy.

"Haha just as I suspected . . . baby lungs!" laughed Ava. "You're like what, fifteen?" Arielle, now feeling somewhat high and playing with the wheels of the chair by rolling it forward and back, was amazed by how the wheels could turn but the chair stayed upright and parallel with the ground.

"Okay, okay; enough already, this thing is an antique!" Ava ran her fingers along the soft leather armrest. "People keep telling me it's bad luck to roll around in a wheelchair. They say I'll probably break a leg or something, like I'm tempting fate. I say phooey! It's all voodoo and horse shit. Bad luck? Seriously? People who believe in that stuff are all so dense and preoccupied with superstition that they can't even see the bright side, which is, if and when I ever do end up breaking a leg, I'd already have this pimp roller-chair worked in nicely, and I'll already be very skilled at driving it! Plus, it was my grandpa's. It still smells like him."

Ava looked Arielle up and down from her chair. She decided that while she'd concede that the squatter standing before her was pretty, there was something strange about her that seemed odd and otherworldly. Ava would have sooner shaved her own head than admit out loud that Arielle looked anything like her beloved lost sister, but from some angles, there were undeniable similarities - the fact of which made her uneasy. She spun around in her wheelchair and faced her vanity mirror, away from Arielle but holding her face in its reflection over her shoulder. She took the half- joint that sat in her ashtray and re-lit it, taking a deep inhale to stoke it, then releasing a long, slow exhale. "Run along now,

Arielle; I'm sure you've got a thousand more firsts to experience today." Arielle, sensing she was no longer welcome in Ava's room, left promptly to go back to her own room to wait for Gabriel to wake up.

Two hours passed and still she lay awake, waiting with bated breath to hear Gabriel's door open. Alas, she heard nothing and, finally tired of waiting, decided to walk out to the beach to greet the morning. As she emerged from the shaded front doorway of the house, the glow of the already hot sun warmed her cheeks and she basked in it. She began to wonder seriously how most of her kind can go an entire three hundred year lifetime without ever having felt it for themselves.

She squinted out to sea and, shielding her eyes from the glare with her hands, scanned the horizon and was surprised to see several sets of white arms waving at her from past the breaker. It was her sisters; all five of them! She beckoned them but none would dare swim in past a jagged rock pile that hid them from the shore. So she ran to them, climbing across the sharp rocks barefoot while they sliced her delicate soles wide open, not even noticing the pain because it was no worse than what she felt when walking on soft sand or carpet, even as they bled and stung. Overjoyed to see her sisters again, she greeted them all with warm smiles but as she came closer to them, she saw that none of them had smiles for her.

"You have made the entire kingdom dark and unhappy," her eldest sister said.

"Why did you leave us?" asked the next sister. "You didn't even say good-bye."

"How could you disobey father?" asked the third sister. "How could you act so selfishly?" Everyone paused to hear her answers, but Arielle could only look at them with sad eyes and right away, they knew what she had given up in order to be standing before them right there.

"The sea-witch took your voice for those legs, didn't she?" asked the eldest. The littlest mermaid, who had once sung more beautifully than any creature on land or sea, nodded in silent remorse. All the years she had her pretty voice to enjoy and to enchant, it had never dawned on her that one day it might be taken from her and she would have to learn to live without it.

"Well?" asked the fourth. "Is your prince falling in love with you?" Arielle stared back at her sister with eyes that told of love and hope, but also of uncertainty. All of the sisters joined hands, closed their eyes, and wished love on their youngest sister, while a passing pod of whales swam in close behind them, wanting to get a better look at the sea princess who was dressed like a human girl.

All of a sudden, Gabriel's voice could be heard from the beach, and her sisters witnessed the way her face lit up at the sound.

"ARIELLE!" he called with a tone of warning in his voice as he spotted her on the rocks. "Be careful on that slippery-sharp rock heap! You'll cut your feet!" Arielle turned around and waved to him sweetly, then crouched back down to kiss her sisters goodbye. "Seriously, those barnacles are heinous!" he yelled. "One time I lost a Frisbee on there and in its heroic retrieval, mangled my feet so bad, I was a cripple for days!"

Her sisters lowered themselves into the water and disappeared into the deep blue, while Gabriel continued to implore her to be careful.

"First came the blood, then came the INFECTED GREEN PUS!" he shouted, shuddering at the memory. She jumped to her feet and, light as air, skipped across the jagged rocks and ran to him until she leapt up into his arms.

"Aww shucks," he said as he twirled her around then set her back down on her feet. "I had you at 'green pus' didn't I?" He chuckled but she, for obvious reasons, didn't catch the Jerry Maguire reference. "Didn't that hurt? Let me see your feet," he said, reaching for her ankle to see her soles. There was a bit of blood, but the cuts it had sprung from were already healed up and her feet looked good as new. Gabriel was amazed; he'd seen what those rocks could do. But he just assumed her delicate balance, light body weight and thin limbs were to thank for her unmarred feet. That, or she had the regenerative healing powers of Wolverine.

"I have an idea!" he said to her enthusiastically. "Go put on a bathing suit and grab a wetsuit from the mud room - we're surfing today!" Expecting her to be thrilled, he was surprised when his idea was met with apprehension. "Come with me," he said, and then led her to the toy shed where all the surfboards were kept.

As soon as she saw what he meant, she backed away, shaking her head. "What's the matter?" he asked. "Surfing is the ultimate; it'll change your life!" He pulled out a smooth yellow board for her to use but still she shook her head and backed even further away, refusing to even take it in her hands. "What's the matter?" he asked her again.

She looked him in the eyes. His dark grown-out hair sat messily on his forehead, and she felt a wave of lust come over her, or maybe it was just a heat spell. It was such a warm morning, and she knew how nice it would be to feel the cool water on her skin. She appreciated very much how her love wanted to share his favorite pastimes with her and desperately she wanted to partake in them, but, alas, this was the very paradox of her new dry existence, and she could not risk revealing herself to him. So she took another step back.

"So you're out, then?" he asked with disappointment in his voice. "You just outright refuse to try surfing?" He couldn't understand why a girl as adventurous and seemingly fearless as she would opt out of the chance to surf. She smiled apologetically and nodded. He set the yellow board back down and reached for his own. "'Your loss, babe," he said as he shrugged and darted down to the waves.

Once he began paddling out, she took a seat in the sand where she could watch from a safe distance. How he danced and glided upon the surface, one with the water but also riding high upon it. She wished she could have joined him. After a few hours went by feeling like mere minutes, he came back out of the water, undid his velcro ankle strap and ran toward her with a big smile on his face.

"Did you see that, Arielle? I finally mastered my three-sixty; the waves were perfect for it!" Exhaustedly, he dropped his board in the sand and fell down onto his knees next to it, smacking his palms together as if in prayer, and sent a kiss up to the heavens in gratitude. Arielle clapped her hands enthusiastically and dropped to her knees in front of him, also kissing the sky, happy that he was so happy. They stayed on their knees for a few moments, sharing in a mutual gratefulness for the beautiful day they were enjoying. Gabriel took a deep breath followed by a satisfyingly large exhale, then grabbed her hand and said "Come with me, I have a wicked idea you won't be able to pass up!"

Gabriel threw on a pair of jeans and a t-shirt and, at his insistence, she also went inside and put on pants and they both jumped into the Jeep and went for a drive. The road was winding and it took them up the side of a big, steep hill. The higher they got, the better their view of the ocean from the road. Cliffs dropped off not three feet from the outer stripes of road paint but still they ascended past curves and bends, some boasting guardrails, some only having the odd tree at its edge to separate their car from the vast sky that stretched out to their right. They weren't quite in the heavens but they were higher than some low-sitting clouds. She closed her eyes and let the breeze kiss her face, and let her fluttering eyelashes kiss it right back.

They reached a small parking lot and pulled over. Behind them, a small, carpeted runway stretched all the way to the edge of the cliff. "Have you ever been hang gliding?" he asked her. Her eyes widened as she looked over the edge at the wide-open sky in front of them. "For some reason, I hadn't thought so," he said, while behind him, a man in a reflective vest laid out their wings and harnesses.

She gasped in disbelief. While she had never seen a contraption quite like this, she did recognize how it seemed to mimic the wingspan of a bird, proportionate to the size of their bodies. It was marvelous. This was the day she would spread her wings and fly.

Before long, they were both strapped into their harnesses, helmets and goggles. As she discovered, Gabriel was in fact a seasoned hang-gliding pro who had many successful glides under his belt already. The breeze was stiff at the top of the cliff, and it gave her chills of excitement because it was so unreal. How she had dreamt of this day.

With a One - Two - Three, he aimed their wings and they launched off the cliff tandem and into the air. It was frightening at first, thrilling but scary as they rode upon the winds with the land so far below. From way up where they were, the earth actually looked round, like they were up on the highest point of the arch that was the skull-cap of the spherical Earth. "Isn't this the best?" he asked her over his shoulder while she clung to his back, looking down at the world from behind him. She had come up from the ocean to be with him, never imagining he would take her to the skies.

The early days of summer went by in a blink and the family became more and more fond of their little foundling, and the longer she stayed with them, the harder it was for them to remember a time before she came. They received no word from the police, and never heard anything about any missing girls matching her description. And Arielle appeared to be quite happy with them, and showed no signs of wanting to leave or having anywhere else to be, so they kept her. She and Gabriel became inseparable, and he took her with him everywhere he went as his constant companion and favourite friend. There was something so refreshing to him about being around someone who always seemed to be seeing and experiencing things for the first time. Her wonderment was infectious and Gabriel very much enjoyed having her as his quiet, talented and beautiful sidekick.

# eighteen

# No Rain

One morning, the sky was a thick, foggy gray. The atmosphere was so dark and heavy, the sun could find no holes to peek through from behind such thick clouds. Arielle sat on the living room sofa with her knees up and staring out to sea, watching steam rise from the water as little raindrops began to speckle it. She began to wonder about the world above the world above; that is, the next tier up from the world of the people, even higher than the skies she danced upon with Gabriel and his hang-glider. She wondered if there had been other mer-people before herself who had won their place with the humans by capturing the heart of one. As raindrops trickled down the windowpane, she wondered if maybe the rain itself was just the ocean returning to the earth as it fell from the hearts of water-bound souls that had crossed over into the heavens. She snapped out of her daydream when she heard Gabriel calling her. She stood up and spotted him down on the beach, his hair all wet and matted and his unbuttoned shirt soaked and clinging to his arms and chest. "Arielle come out here, it's gorgeous!"

She smiled, ran for the door and fumbled with it giddily. But then, just as soon as she got it open and was about to step outside, she remembered. No getting wet, lest her tail should grow back. Disappointed, she pulled the door closed in front of herself and stared out at him longingly.

"Come on, I've got the monkey pod!" he yelled happily as all five of the family's pugs circled his feet and rolled around in the wet sand. Safely but lamentably inside while he was out, she glanced down at her little feet and dried off on the welcome mat a raindrop that had landed on her big toe. Gabriel called to her again, watching curiously as she stood still in the doorway. "Arielle, what's the hold up? Come dance with us!" he said as he spun in a circle with his arms wide out, letting the cool rain soak him more. "There's really nothing like it!" he called across the yard.

But she stood there frozen, her heart pulling her outside but her head soberly aware of the consequence that would ruin her. Her heart sank as she resisted the tempting siren's song of one more thing she couldn't enjoy with him. More rain splashed on the deck and the doorframe, and she took another step further back into the house.

"Aww come on, really? No rain dancing for you either?" he was even more disappointed than when she refused to surf with him. Sadly, she shook her head 'no.' His smile faded to a frown and for a moment she thought seriously about what would happen if she just ran out into the wetness and presented him with her truth. For a second, it seemed like a better option than allowing him to think for one second that she was willingly refusing him, when there was nothing she would rather do than dance out in the rain with him.

Gabriel, giving up, shrugged his shoulders and waved her off as he turned towards the beaches to the south and dashed through the sand with the soaking wet dogs. Arielle returned to the sofa and sat with her knees up again, somberly staring out the window, watching all the fun she was missing. Of all the things she knew she'd miss, she hadn't counted on missing the feeling of cool water so incredibly.

When the sun came back out that afternoon and drank up most of the puddles, she emerged from the dry safety of the home. When she found Gabriel, he taught her how to ride a bicycle. When he thought she had advanced her bike skills enough, he took her for a spin on his motorcycle, and even let her steer for a few blocks.

When they returned home and went to park the bike in the garage, they noticed a group of about twelve snails moving across the garage floor and towards the door to the house. Since Arielle had arrived, more and more sea wildlife had been coming in close to the house. It didn't make any sense to him, given her apparent aversion to the ocean itself but like everything else, he just shrugged it off as odd and unexplainable. Together, they both gently picked up the snails by their shells and carried them to a dark, moist spot under a spruce tree, lest they be stepped on or driven over.

That night, as Arielle climbed into bed after another fun, fulfilling day, she heard a tapping at her door and saw it was Lucia peeking in. The woman who had come to be her friend and also something of a mother figure came in and sat at the foot of her bed with a mug of tea in her hands. "I just wanted to make sure you're comfortable here," she said, taking a sip. The mermaid sat up and nodded gratefully, for she had been very happy and very comfortable in their home. "Cliff and I love having you here, the whole family does! Well, except for maybe Ava, but she's a hard sell." Lucia winked, and Arielle winked back knowingly. "The point I'm trying to make is, we don't know where you came from or really, anything about you. We don't know if you have a family somewhere, or what you were running away from that landed you on our beach but perhaps most troubling of all is the fact that we don't care about any of that. We already feel like you're part of this family, and nothing else matters to us at all." Arielle smiled at her warmly. "Do you feel like part of this family?" Lucia asked her.

Arielle smiled and nodded happily as if to say *Oh, yes!* She knew in her heart that ultimately, she had to become a part of this family for real, because doing so meant her very survival. Lucia watched Arielle's eyes gaze around the room appreciatively.

"I painted that for my daughter," said Lucia, gesturing proudly towards the piece hanging above the bed. "Dagmara was obsessed with all things to do with mermaids." The painting was pretty and colorful, and depicted a young mermaid with the tail of a goldfish sitting on a giant lily pad in a pond. There was a ceramic mermaid with golden fins sitting on the dresser, and an Inuit soapstone carving of Sedna on the night table. Lucia's eyes glanced over to a framed snapshot of her daughter wearing the mermaid costume she had sewn for her fifth-grade Halloween dance.

"I wish you could have met her; you two would have really liked each other. This summer home was her favorite place on earth. Dags was a natural at pretty much everything, but she lived for surfing. Always first in the water and always last out, I can hardly remember a time I saw her without her hair all salty and sopping wet, just like a daughter of the sea." When Lucia spoke of her lost daughter, there was a sparkle in her eyes but a heaviness in her heart. "Then, one summer evening," she continued, "she went out surfing by herself at sunset, and we never saw her again." Lucia had a faraway look on her face, as if she was partly blaming herself. "Normally our house rule is that we employ the buddy system when playing in or around the ocean but everyone was busy that night, and it was one of those perfect, pink apple blossom sunsets where the waves were nice and clean. She didn't want to wait for Gabriel to come home, so I let her go while I fixed dinner."

Lucia looked out over the beach fondly but with pain in her eyes. "We found her surf board sitting upside down, its leash strap neatly coiled around the tail fins, the way she always left them. We searched all around these waters for her, but never found anything. And no one has seen her since.

"Police wrote it off as the story of another runaway, because there was never any evidence to suggest foul play. As her family, we were given the option of either believing she drowned, or ran away." Lucia choked back a tear, and gazed at Dagmara's picture lovingly. "I like to think she swam off to join the mermaids."

Lucia sat there for a second and let her emotional heart release a few quiet sobs, then sat up and dried her eyes on a corner of Dagmara's bed sheet. "Look at me, tearing up when all I wanted to do was come in here to let you know how happy you make us! It is so very nice to have someone breathe a bit of life into this room again." Arielle smiled, wishing there was more she could say and do to express her gratitude and gladness. But like every day since she got there, all she could do was smile, and so she did. "Sleep well, Arielle," said Lucia, getting up and kissing her on the cheek. "Please stay with us just as long as you'd like."

# nineteen

## The Orphan Erica

The next morning, Arielle woke up and selected an emerald terrycloth dress from Dagmara's wardrobe. She slipped it over her head and tied the strings up on her shoulders, then admired herself in the mirror. Her hair was so long and smooth now; she was beginning to forget what it felt like with pearls and ornaments all tied up in it. Its color seemed to be changing too; she had never noticed so many streaks and variations through it before. Her skin was changing as well! Little brown flecks now dotted her nose and cheeks in tiny constellations.

As Lucia flipped omelets downstairs, Cliff sorted through a large stack of mail. "Oh good morning, Arielle!" he greeted her as she came into the kitchen. "Can you believe how much snail mail stacks up in just one week? I think I'm personally responsible for the slaughter of about ten trees right here." Arielle nodded and went to the fridge to pour herself a glass of orange juice. Lucia and Cliff always insisted she help herself to anything she wanted to eat or drink, and she was getting quite comfortable doing so.

Cliff picked up a small red envelope and read the return address. "We got a letter from Erica!" he exclaimed excitedly.

"Wonderful! Read it aloud, honey!" said Lucia. "How long do you think it's been since we last heard from her?"

"Who is *Erica*?" asked Demetra as she bounced cheerfully into the kitchen and poured herself some coffee.

"Erica is the daughter of my very best friend. Besides your mom, of course," said Cliff lovingly, winking at his wife. "Ben and I were buddies since kindergarten, cohorts in Cub Scouts, roommates in college and the best man at each other's weddings."

Lucia swiped the coffee mug from Demetra's hands and replaced it with a glass of milk. She rolled her eyes, then sipped her milk. "How come this Ben never comes around then?" she asked curiously.

Cliff paused to remember his friend and how close they had always been. "Ben and his wife Darlene died in a car crash many years ago," he answered. "It was their tenth anniversary, and they were on their way home from dinner when a speeding drunk driver rear-ended them at a red light and knocked them into the busy intersection," he said matter-of-factly and with sorrow in his voice. "Darlene died instantly, Ben died in the ambulance."

Demetra put her arms around her father's shoulders and pressed her soft cheek to his. "I'm sorry, Dad, that must have been so sad."

"Yes, it was a sad time," said Cliff, "but it was most tragic for their daughter Erica, who was no older than you are right now when it happened."

"Read us the letter, Cliffy; I'm dying to hear how Erica's doing," said Lucia.

"Alright, then," he said, and began to read the letter aloud:

*Dear Uncle Cliff,*

*I hope this letter finds you and your family well, for I have had an amazing year seeing the world! I spent my twentieth birthday in Nicaragua for a school-building volunteer mission. There, I met a crew of Italians who then invited me to their family 'podere' in Umbria where I spent last autumn picking olives and developing a taste for fine wines. After that, I backpacked Vietnam with some Germans I met two years ago in Whistler and when that was done, I came to Australia to spend time on a cattle ranch with three of my cousins. Life has been sweet, and I have been so blessed. I have met so many wonderful people, but I have never forgotten my dear O'Faolains.*

*Exactly three weeks from today, I will be on a plane headed for Vancouver. I write you now to remind you of an invitation you extended to me all those years ago at my parents' funeral. You told me that any time I wanted to come spend time with you guys on the Island, I would be welcome. One month from now, I plan to finally take you up on it!*

*I hope there is still room for me, because I have thought of you, Lucia, Ava and Gabriel often, and have been looking forward to seeing you all for quite some time. Lucia was pregnant with Demetra when I last saw you all, and I cannot wait to meet her at long last. I have thought of Dagmara too; she has visited me once or twice in my dreams, and has never failed to remind me of the beauty to be found in this life as well as the next.*

*I will call you once I've arrived at my aunt Julie's place in Horseshoe Bay, and hopefully then we can make some arrangements. Until then, I will be looking forward to my visit, and to catching up with all of you. I know it will be great times, and I can hardly wait.*

*Love, Erica. Xoxo*


Cliff paused for a moment and wiped the still-forming tears from his eyes. "Well it seems young Erica will be visiting us in a month!" he said happily.

"Does Gabriel remember her?" asked Demetra.

"I'm sure he does," answered Lucia. "She, Gabe and Dagmara used to play together, before you were even a twinkle in your daddy's bright blue eyes.

"She was a portly little tomboy, but still cute as ever. I think she had a bit of a crush on Gabe back then, too . . . Oh, I hope she stays for a while, there is so much catching up to do!"

"There certainly is," said Cliff, standing up. "And what a brave little thing she was, so strong and independent, even after losing both of her parents on the same night."

"I know, darling," concurred his wife. "Even as a child, she was an inspiration to us all."

"I'm going to dig up all our old photo albums to show her, there are some good ones of all of us from back in the day!" And with that, Cliff ran upstairs to the hutch where they kept all their old pictures and keepsakes, and embarked on his stroll down memory lane.

# twenty

## The Talented Miss Arielle

Right before waking up, Ava dreamt she was in McDonalds ordering a meal. It had been a while since she had last polluted herself with the sinfully delicious trans-fatty processed puck they call a Big Mac, and the thought of its dirty indulgence coupled with the salty steam of the fry pit made her mouth water. She set her plastic tray down on a plastic tabletop inside a plastic booth (fitting, she thought, upon which to enjoy her plastic meal) and sat herself down. She opened the cardboard box containing her burger and picked it up with both hands, the way they do in the commercials, shaking a side salad's worth of shredded lettuce free. Mac sauce squeezed out the sides but she didn't care; she knew it was always worth the mess. She brought it to her mouth, inhaled its scientifically engineered fumes, and bit into it deeply.

As soon as she chomped her teeth down, she felt the roof of her mouth tear open as something sharp hooked itself into her soft palate and yanked her out of her seat by her mouth. She looked up to see the roof of the restaurant had opened up, and she was being pulled up into the air by a hook attached to a line. She squirmed and writhed but quickly realized that the more she struggled against it, the deeper the hook set itself into her skull. She couldn't help herself from wriggling though; she was in survival mode now and everything inside her said to fight for her life. The higher it took her, the more she felt its barb rip into her tongue and cheeks.

Finally after an ascent that seemed to take forever, she was picked up and the hook was torn roughly from her mouth by a giant set of pliers. Dizzy, gasping for air and bleeding from her mouth, she was handled, weighed, and had her photo taken with the proud angler that hooked her. He laid her comparatively small body down on the rocks and as she squirmed between them in a semi-lucid state, she groggily looked up to see two hands holding a boulder over her head. As it came down on her, blotting out all light on its descent, she remembered in vivid detail her favorite seafood dinner of all time: lobster and fried ling cod with buttery béarnaise. Lights out.

*Thud.* She woke up on the floor again. Lying perfectly still on her throw pillows and staring wide-eyed at the ceiling, she ran her tongue across the roof of her mouth carefully. Still swearing she could taste her own metallic blood spilling, she rolled over to glance at her alarm clock. It was 2:32 pm; she was the only one in the family who ever slept in so late and so often, and if ever she was awake early in the morning, it was only because she hadn't yet gone to bed. She sat up, reached for her robe and walked out to her balcony to find it was just another perfect day on the coast. There were a few fishing boats out in the water, and she shuddered to imagine what they were doing to their catch. Still in a daze, she headed downstairs because she was starving and whatever her mother was cooking smelled fresh and fantastic.

"Well, good afternoon, sleeping beauty," said Lucia. "How is my big girl?" Lucia was, as per usual, in a chipper mood and cooking in her bathing suit. Breezes flowed liberally through the open windows on either side of the kitchen, wafting its intoxicating smells at Ava's face as she took a seat at the breakfast bar. Lucia dropped a plate with two fish tacos on it in front of her. Usually, they were Ava's favorite, but today she wasn't quite in the mood for them. She pushed the plate away.

"Not feeling it today, Mom," she said flatly. "What else are we working with?"

Lucia looked at her strangely. "What do you mean? Since when are you not *feeling* my fish tacos?"

"I had a weird dream," she said, rubbing her temples with her thumbs. "Any other options?"

"My shrimp and scallop ceviche," answered Lucia brightly. "I put grapefruit chunks in it the way you like!"

Ava slid off her stool and walked to the pantry. "I'm in more of a cereal mood today. Thanks anyway, Mom."

"Suit yourself," said Lucia, gladly digging in while Ava poured almond milk over her Honey Nut Cheerios.


Outside on the patio, Gabriel and Arielle enjoyed their personal bowls of ceviche, and between sweet and tangy bites, he brought up the proposed next day's activities. "So our neighbors and good friends the Von Der Klaasens have just bought a huge crazy sick yacht and they've invited us to join them on its maiden voyage tomorrow!"

The little mermaid shot her love an unsure look. She knew that being on a boat would mean having to be dangerously close to the water, and that all it would take would be one good splash to make her tail burst out in all its flapping, scaly glory. The O'Faolains and the Von der Klaasens would all shriek in horror while she slithered to the edge of the boat to leap into the water and disappear forever, a monster shamed and disgraced. She shook her head *'no.'*

"What do you mean *no*?" he asked her incredulously. "Who says 'no' to a ride on a brand new luxury yacht?" He thought for a second. "Is it that you can't swim?"

She made a face at his silly suggestion, then remembered that she had never actually allowed him to see her wet, let alone swimming. He laughed. "Well, what then? Are you afraid of sharks?" She made another face. Of course she wasn't afraid of sharks; to be eaten by one would be the best death there is.

"See, I don't get you," he started. "Everything about you suggests you come from the sea; that necklace you wear, the way you washed up on our shore, all those pearls and stuff you had tied into your hair. But ever since the day I found you out there, I haven't been able to get you anywhere near the water 'cause you run screaming from it! Well, perhaps not so much *screaming*, as silently protesting while clawing at doorframes. You are a mystery, woman!"

Arielle frowned and wondered if, once they were married, she would be able to show him her tail. She wondered if it would still matter that she was different if he had already pledged his love to her, for better or for worse.

"Well, whatever your problem with boats is, I would still love it if you came. It's not some rickety little ocean jalopy, it's the newest, shiniest Von der Klaasen cottage toy. We're going to the mainland to pick up a friend, and all of us are going so if you exempt yourself from this outing, you'll be left at the house all alone. Bored. Lonely. Withering away in solitude . . ."

She thought about it more. Would it really be the worst thing ever if he saw her tail? What about the rest of the family? The very room they gave her to sleep in was a veritable shrine to her kind. Would he think her tail was hideous, or would he find it beautiful and special? She shrugged.

"So it's settled then! You're going to love the view of Van City from the water." She didn't disagree; she had loved absolutely everything he had shown her. "Anyway, I told my buddy in Amsterdam that we'd Skype this morning, so I better go in and log on . . . you can entertain yourself for a bit, right?" Arielle smiled, and turned to walk around the house over to the sunroom.

When she got there, she spotted some kind of large instrument in the corner of the room, covered with a brown sheet. Curiously, she pulled the sheet off to find an antique wooden harp. The discovery pleased her greatly, because mermaids are not only beautiful singers, they are musically inclined on all levels and are exceptionally talented at picking up instruments incredibly fast. She pulled the harp out from the wall and pulled a chair up beside it. She strummed slowly at first, acquainting herself with the notes, adjusting the strings by ear. Inside each mermaid is, at any given time, a song just waiting to burst forth from her heart. When the sea witch took her voice, the songs in Arielle's heart began to pile up, dying for release. She couldn't believe she hadn't thought of finding an instrument sooner!

When she began to strum and pluck at the grand old harp, she filled the room with the most angelic notes. The tunes just came to her, and she played as if she had been practicing her whole life, even though she had never before played upon one that wasn't rotting in the brandy room of an old sunken ship.

She sang along, if only in her head. How beautifully her voice would have accompanied the notes from the twanging strings, and how melodiously those sounds would blend and float out to sea, carried upon the breeze to where they'd pierce the tossing waves and find her father, and let him know that she was happy and well. Through song, she would have explained her pursuit of happiness and why it stole her away, and why there was no one on this planet for her but this human. She played a song that was both happy and sad, for while she delighted in all that she was experiencing, she missed her family dearly.

When she was finished losing herself in her beautiful melody, she opened her eyes and heard Lucia clapping behind her.

"That was beautiful, Arielle!" said Lucia, astounded by the amazing closet harp prodigy that was currently staying in her home. Lucia stared at her wide-eyed, still clapping, wondering where and how the girl learned to play so flawlessly.

"That was my mother's harp," she said. "She played like an angel, but my clumsy fingers were never much good at it. It's a shame, really; I don't want to get rid of it but no one in this house plays so it just sits there collecting dust." Lucia paused, reflecting. "Dagmara could play. My mom used to come over on the weekends to give her lessons and she would practice a bit every day. I didn't realize how much I've missed the way it makes the whole house come alive with its vibrations. She made my mom feel like the best teacher in the world." She smiled as she sat down, remembering. Arielle could see how much she was enjoying the music, so she played another song, making it up as she went along, creating pretty sounds that brought tears to Lucia's eyes while she listened and reminisced. "Our house has felt so quiet," she said.

Gabriel logged off with his friend and, halfway down the stairs, found himself spellbound and following the music into the sunroom. He walked in just as she was wrapping up her tune.

"Don't tell me she just learned to play that this afternoon!" Gabriel was positively awestruck by her surprising talent. "Seriously, that sounded amazing! Where'd you learn to play like that?"

Arielle shrugged her shoulders. Technically, she had just learned that day, but there would be no way of explaining that to him. Gabriel's face softened when he looked over at his mother sitting on the wicker lounge chair, smiling hopefully from behind tear-soaked cheeks. He sat down and held his mom close, motioning to Arielle to play one more gorgeous song. Gladly, she brought her fingers to the strings and began to play song that opened up like a fragrant bouquet of fond memories, taking them back to times long past and to moments spent with souls sorely missed. But while the music stirred up old pain and dormant longing, it also filled them with gladness for the memories they got to take with them, as well as an appreciation for their beautiful life and the loved ones who still remained.

Lucia sniffled. "That's what I've been missing!" she said as she stood up.

"Yeah, this is so nice!" her son concurred. But the sounds of the harp had reminded her of something, and brought to her nose (the way fond memories often do) the memory of an old smell she hadn't experienced in years. "Your grandma's famous olive-stuffed cheesy focaccia!" she said excitedly.

"Oh yeah, you haven't made those in about a decade!" said Gabriel, rubbing his hands.

"I think I forgot about them until now!" she said. "But now that it's in my head, it's gotta happen! Arielle, you'll love 'em!"

Arielle wasn't sure what she was talking about, but figured anything that could make a crying woman instantly pep up has got to be pretty tasty. So they sent Gabriel out to the garden for some fresh tomatoes and hustled into the kitchen.

"I don't know how I forgot about this recipe," said Lucia, using a paring knife to pit a handful of black olives. "When I was listening to you play just then, I closed my eyes and all I could smell was a salty, cheesy, toasty loaf baking. It took me right back to snack time in my parents' home, smelling it in the oven, hearing my mother play."

Arielle smiled while she crushed the garlic, happy to be a part of their human family tradition. Then all of a sudden she jumped at the sound of Lucia's sudden painful shriek and turned to see what happened.

"Shit! I'm so clumsy!" she said as she gripped the finger she had sliced open with her knife. "Owww! Ewww, I hate blood!" she said, wincing as blood spilled onto the white cutting board. Calmly and slowly, Arielle set her garlic crusher down on the counter and took Lucia's cut hand in hers, looking her deep in the eyes as she brought her lips to the gaping wound.

"What are you doing?" asked Lucia. "That's, um, yuck, no--" but before she could protest anymore, Arielle let go of her hand, pulled away and went quietly back to her garlic crushing. Lucia, unsure of what just happened, looked down at the finger that had only moments ago throbbed in stinging pain, and could feel nothing out of the ordinary. She inspected the wound, and found nothing but perfect, normal skin on her perfect, unsliced finger. This confused her greatly, as there was still a small pool of blood on the cutting board, but the wound no longer existed on her hand. She began to ask Arielle "How did you-" but she stopped short and abandoned the query. Arielle, who just smiled at her sweetly and unassumingly from the island counter, would not have been able to answer her anyway.

That evening, the whole family gathered in the sunroom to hear Arielle breathe more life back into the long-forgotten strings of the harp. Demetra was thrilled; she wasn't old enough to remember Dagmara and her grandmother ever playing but the harp had been in the home even longer than she had. Cliff vibed along, Ava smiled a very reserved smile and sat still, fighting tears from welling up. Lucia closed her eyes and lost herself in the melodies, feeling happier than she had in a long time, feeling like somehow, her family was complete again in a way it hadn't been in many years. Gabriel looked around the room and his heart warmed at the old, familiar scene. In this light and to this tune, he finally realized how much Arielle really did resemble the twin sister he missed so much.

After three songs and an encore, they all took to the beach for a game of three-on-three ultimate Frisbee. Now that there were six of them, games like this were possible.

"Now Arielle, before I teach you the finer points of disc throwing, it's important that you know Meaty and I have been practicing pretty much since she could walk so don't feel bad if you're our weakest link at first," said Gabriel as he flicked the red Frisbee from his wrist towards his sister.

"Yeah, and tossing a few wobblers is par for the course;" said Demetra as she leapt into its path and caught it between her legs. "So don't feel sucky and unskilled if your tosses don't slice as gorgeously as ours." Demetra sent it neatly back towards her brother, who waited 'til it was past him to pluck it from the air, then spun around to toss it at Arielle.

Arielle watched the disc spin towards her, casually, and with her arms at her side. Gabriel and Demetra started shouting "Catch it! Catch it!" all the while thinking there was no way she was going to catch it . . . until it whizzed by her head and she turned to catch it in her teeth!

"Oh my God!" laughed Demetra in disbelief as Arielle turned and spun, sending it perfectly back into Gabriel's hands. "That was stellar! She's ready to play!"

The game was intense but the three of them beat Lucia, Cliff and Ava by a long shot, although no one really bothered to keep track of the score. Throughout it, Arielle threw the disc perfectly and with style, effortlessly mastering backhand tosses, low-throws and routinely leaping several feet into the air to catch high tosses on the spin. She was so good at it that the family had to presume that there were Frisbees wherever it was she came from but of course, there was no way to know for sure. In any event, they could all agree that she was the best Frisbee player they had ever seen.

"Alright family, I'm kind of wiped after my exertions here; I'm off to bed," yawned Gabriel, kissing his mom on the cheek. He looked out to the horizon before heading inside and kept his gaze fixed on it for a moment, as if taking a mental snapshot to see him through the many days of greyness and rain that were routine to the Western coast. Arielle had been noticing how everyone always seemed to do that before walking away from the picturesque shoreline; it was nice how a pretty sunset never seemed to get old to anyone. "Red sky at night, sailor's delight!" he said as he walked towards the house.

# twenty-one

## Yachting In

The next morning, the O'Faolains sat down to a quick breakfast before driving to meet the Von der Klaasens at their boat slip. They all dressed in shorts and t-shirts, Lucia in her big straw sun hat and Ava in her black bikini and oversize sunglasses that showed her off but hid her at the very same time. It was a warm, bright morning; Gabriel's sailor's almanac prognosis had been bang-on.

"Has anyone seen Arielle yet this morning?" asked Lucia as she dished out portions of scrambled egg onto six plates.

"She's awake, I heard her rustling around her room as I walked by," said Demetra. "Shall I fetch her?"

"If she's not down in five," answered Lucia, halving and sectioning three large grapefruits. "You know Martin will be raring to go and will not want to wait!"

"Aaaaaaariiieeelllllllle!" called Demetra in a singsong voice, doing her best siren impression as she buttered a stack of toast points. She rolled her tongue operatically as she called "It's time for brrrrreaakfast!" The family giggled when they heard a mild thump from upstairs, followed by more frantic shuffling. After ten more minutes had gone by and everyone else was almost finished their breakfast, Arielle came down the stairs.

They all looked at her strangely. "Ummm, I don't think you'll be needing your rain gear today," said Gabriel as he took in the sight of her, amused by the inappropriateness of her dressing for the sunny, bluebird weather. Oddly, she wore head-to-toe rubber, from the big blue gumboots on her feet to the yellow rain coat to the waterproof bucket hat on her head.

"We're going on a yacht ride to the mainland," said Ava through her lenses, big as black saucers. "Why are you dressed for the Maid of the Mist?"

Arielle shrugged and sat down to her breakfast, her jacket and boots squeaking as she moved. She knew she looked ridiculous but cared not, for she would be on a boat this day, and the boat would be in the water, and she couldn't allow a single splash hit her legs.

No one could see it under her pants, but she had secretly covered her legs in clear plastic wrap for added protection from potential splashes.

Once everyone was done eating, they left their dishes in the sink and headed out to the driveway. "Last chance for anyone who might want to put on something more practical," said Ava, pausing a second before punching the house's security code into the pin pad. Arielle just smiled at her and curtsied in her raincoat as she passed her on her way out the door. "No takers? How embarrassing."

Ava and Demetra rode with the parents and Arielle sat shotgun in Gabriel's Jeep. She loved riding in the car next to him; she always felt like his woman when she sat to his right, like his wife sitting beside him, first mate to his captain. Also, she had come to love how sometimes, when he reached for the gearshift, his hand sometimes accidentally brushed her thigh. She now lived for such moments.

When they pulled into the marina, they parked their cars in the lot and boarded the pristine new yacht. Everything sparkled, and every surface on the vessel was perfect, smooth, unblemished. How different it looked from the only other boats Arielle had ever been inside of, half-buried at the bottom of the sea like the skeletons of boats past, scattered in pieces across a sandy floor.

After about three smooth hours of touring, they arrived at the pick-up spot by the ferry docks. They were still just tying off when they felt the wooden docks bounce the way they do when someone is running across them. When Gabriel looked up from his knot, he had to blink to make sure he wasn't seeing things; at first glance, he thought he saw the girl from the beach standing in front of him. Then he realized all at once, that Erica IS Erica!

"NO WAY," he said, shocked and elated. "It's you!"

"It's me!" she said knowingly, equally elated, thrilled to see that he was still as handsome as she remembered him from the previous summer.

"You knew?!" he said, so excited that he was finding it difficult to formulate sentences using more than two words at a time.

"Sorry I didn't say anything last summer, but I didn't want to ruin the surprise!" she said.

"You knew!" he said incredulously, yet in the affirmative. "And you're here!"

Ava, coming down from her spot on the bow where she had been lying out catching rays, stepped in to interrupt as she was finding their hyper-flirtatious banter quite unbearable. "Yes, Gabriel, this is your old friend Erica," she said, "the little girl I caught you playing 'cats' with under the kitchen table when you both were five, eating liver pate and lapping up milk from a bowl on the floor."

"Ava! So nice to see you again, you grew up lovely!" said Erica happily.

"You as well, Erica, looking swell!" she replied in a quasi-mocking tone. Ava never believed in laying it on thick with compliments and so she never gave any, and was always uncomfortable when someone paid her one. "It's nice to see you grew out of that baby fat, and into those tree trunks," she said, glancing down at Erica's legs. Erica and Gabriel glanced into each other's eyes then burst out laughing together, the way they always did when they were younger and Ava tried to get their goats. They, as a team, had learned quickly that responding to her tongue-in-cheek jabs with nothing but good humor was the only way to disarm her. After about a minute of reciprocal chuckling, Gabriel came up for air and said, "No seriously, that was Ava's idea of a compliment and you should really take it as such." Finally, Ava cracked a smile and said genuinely to Erica, "I'm glad to see you're well; it's been too long." Then she hugged her tightly, but only for a second.

"Thank you, you too," responded Erica without averting her eyes from Gabriel's gaze; the way the sun reflected off the gold dots in his dark irises seemed to make time stand still and all the world quiet. They seemed to be sparkling just for her.

Gabriel looked at her glossy, bee-stung lips and remembered how soft and warm they had been when she pressed them to his. Memories of play dates with her when they were kids began to blend with the memories of that day on the beach. How sneakily she had surprised him with that kiss, how craftily she had ambushed his mouth with hers. He knew that he had never surrendered like that before in his life. He hadn't forgotten about her, even for a day. And she had been counting the minutes until she would see him again.

Lucia came up from below laughing at something Veronica said about her husband, carrying a vodka martini that was dirty and wet and wearing a briny wet spot on her white one-piece swimsuit. "Erica! Darling! How wonderful to see you again!" she said, wrapping the girl up in a gregarious tipsy hug, smelling heavily of manzanilla olives. When she pulled back for a second to get a good look at her, she blinked hard and opened her eyes wide. "You're stunning!" she exclaimed.

Erica blushed, grinned and looked down at her feet. No matter how many times she heard it, she never really believed it; she was more down-to-earth than vain as a result of her chubby youth and Gabriel already loved that about her. "She really is," said Gabriel, concurring with his mother. Erica believed it when he said it, and it made her heart flutter.

Veronica appeared at the top of the cabin steps, posing like Venus on the half shell and sporting a completely different outfit than the one she'd been in all morning but for the peach and gold Hermes scarf that stayed tied at the side of her neck. "Hi there, I'm Veronica," she purred. "Welcome aboard The Seaward Empress."

"Hi, Mrs. Von der Klaasen! Thank you very much for taking your amazing new boat to come to pick me up, I'm so honored!" Erica reached out both hands to take hers.

"Call me Veronica, and it's nothing at all!" replied the wannabe doyenne with all the poise of a late Kennedy. "We'd have needed a reason to open this bitch up anyway," she said as she patted the perfectly polished gold knob at the top of the wood-grain railing with one hand, and sloppily toasted her glass into the air with the other.

"I actually saw people taking pictures as you guys cruised in; I think they were expecting the Beckhams or something. I'm so excited to be going to Tofino! I haven't been back since last summer, and I miss it dearly after, like, a week away!"

"A year? My, my . . ." said Veronica. "I'm sure you'll find it's changed considerably since then. Perhaps my son Reginald could show you around to where all the young people congregate.

Couldn't you, Reginald?" she said over her shoulder down to the cabin below where her son was playing Halo, wired in with his headset on, yelling at a kid somewhere in Mongolia. Reginald, in his infinite unimpressiveness, grunted without even looking up. Veronica smiled sheepishly and made a mental note to 'accidentally' spill sangria on his game console.

"Erica, this is my baby sister, Meaty," said Gabriel, eager to get Erica acquainted and get all the introductions out of the way.

"Yes, Demetra! I remember Lucia telling me what your name would be when you were just a bump on her stomach. Why do you let them call you 'Meaty'?"

Demetra laughed. "Everyone loves to tease me, saying I was the meatiest baby ever. You know, the other, *other* white meat. The name just stuck. It doesn't distress me."

"Yeah, I was a meaty one too at one point . . ." started Erica, but trailed off when she noticed the pretty fair-haired girl in the raincoat walk up daintily behind Gabriel, lacing her little white fingers around the crook of his elbow. She caught a glimpse of the girl's face before she buried it childishly into his arm. Her heart sank; she was sure it was his girlfriend, and that she had come too late.

"Hi, I'm Erica," she said, trying her best to sound happy to meet her. The little mermaid just looked up sweetly with her piercing blue eyes, and dropped into a curtsy without letting go of Gabriel.

"Erica, this is Arielle. She stays with us," he said, like it was the most natural thing in the world. Erica acknowledged her with a nod and said she was pleased to make her acquaintance just as Cliff came up from tying off and signing in The Seaward Empress with the harbour master.

"Uncle Cliff!" she said as she jumped up into his arms, inhaling a big breath of him, "You still smell exactly the same!"

"I get the same after shave every Christmas!" he responded excitedly. "You're even lovelier than I remember you, Erica. Your parents would be so proud."

"Thanks, Clifford!" she said, tears welling up in her eyes. Her reunion with the O'Faolains was so perfect, and going exactly the way she had been imagining it would. Except for that blonde girl who appeared to be very into her own lifelong crush . . .

She decided to waste no time finding out who and what she was, so she reached her hand out to shake Arielle's in order to finish legitimately meeting her. But the girl just stared at her outstretched hand without stirring, then once again buried her face into Gabriel's arm like a shy child.

"Okay then! Leave me hanging; we don't have to shake," she said, shrinking and feeling a little snubbed.

"You'll have to excuse our Arielle, she hasn't been acquainted with such uncommon and esoteric customs as hand-shaking," said Ava sarcastically.

"*Ariel*? Like *The Little Mermaid*?" said Erica, realizing after a second that perhaps the tone she had just then taken could've been seen as mocking by the quiet, diminutive girl in front of her. "I mean, it's just that I don't know anyone else named Ariel," she went on. "It's pretty though," she offered. Smiling generously, she looked into Arielle's eyes for any sign that she understood and accepted what she was saying, but her dreamy expression was so otherworldly, it seemed impossible that anyone could ever pin her focus down long enough to have a conversation with her. She stammered. "And . . . and this is your girlfriend, Gabriel?" she asked cautiously, bracing herself as if she was about to take a bullet.

"No, no!" he said, much to her relief. "This is my . . . she's my . . . this is Arielle!"

Demetra cleared her throat. "OUR Arielle!" she said.

"Yes," he continued. "She is mute, and she stays with us. She's not my girlfriend, she's my extra special buddy." Demetra cleared her throat again, this time elbowing her brother in the hip. "ONE of my most extra special buddies!" he said, correcting himself to include his baby sister.

"Amazing!" said Erica, unable now to contain her relief. "So how do we know her name is Arielle if she can't speak to tell us so?" Gabriel suggested they grab a table at the dockside restaurant and they could fill her in on everything over lunch. Everyone agreed it was the best idea.

Once everyone was seated comfortably with a drink in front of them, Gabriel began to explain. "Arielle is just a nickname we gave her on account of the fact that we have no idea where she came from except that it must've been by way of the Pacific. Right Arielle?"

Arielle just smiled at Gabriel and batted her eyelashes. She had gotten really good at non-committal smiles, saying neither yes nor no with her vague yet cheerful expressions.

Ava piped in, "Tell her the whole story, Gabe! 'Arielle' as she is so-called, was found by my brother one morning passed out naked in the sand with nothing to cover her nips n' box but her abnormally large mass of white-yellow hair, seaweed, and that jumbo prehistoric fossil necklace."

Erica smiled cheekily. "Did you have to slap her to wake her up?"

"No!" replied Gabriel, mock-defensively. "I gave her my shirt, picked her up carefully and carried her inside so we could send for a doctor!"

Erica giggled. "I guess everyone's got their own way!" she said. "So you named her 'Arielle' because she washed up in front of your place like a beached mermaid?"

"Ascended from the bluest depths, she was," said Gabriel. "Yes, that is the working theory, at least according to young Meaty."

"Damn skippy," responded Demetra with a nod. "And of course, as always, you're all invited to formulate your own hypotheses regarding the origins of our mute and mysterious houseguest."

Erica laughed, tickled by the clever nine-year old sitting in front of her. "Your theory works for me!" she said. "There are certainly worse things to be called than Arielle."

"Slut," said Ava.

"Excuse me?" said Erica, caught off guard.

"I wasn't calling *you* a slut; I'm sharing with everyone the worst thing I've been called."

"Ava!" blurted Lucia, shocked. Her daughter never seemed to have much of a sense of propriety.

"Oh," said Erica, relieved. "Do I dare ask why they called you a slut?"

"A silly high school rumor gone awry. When I refused to dignify it with a response, the high school bitch tabloids had a field day fabricating all kinds of stories about my supposedly lewd exploits. Lies spread the way herpes do in incestuous mountain towns where there's nothing to do but snowboard, huff gasoline, and bang each other raw."

"Ava! Yuck," said Cliff in his most authoritative, fatherly tone.

"Ugh, take this away," said Reginald loudly over his shoulder to the passing waiter, not even waiting to be asked if the rare, sixty-five dollar filet mignon was to his liking before giving Ava the hairy eyeball, muttering "Wait 'til I bring up yeast infections just as they drop your creme brulee."

"Well I'm sorry I'm so distasteful and inappropriate to you all." said Ava, sneering.

"So are we!" said Reginald without looking up, pulling his PSP game out of his breast pocket.

"That sucks. I don't ever want to go to high school," said Demetra. "Girls are bitches."

"Not to worry, little sis - I got even with that gossip mill of a hen party."

"What did you do?" asked Erica, Demetra, Lucia and Veronica, all in unison. Women love stories about social revenge. Lucia cringed a little.

"I banged all their boyfriends purple," she answered. Everyone's jaws dropped. All was silent.

"Ava!" muttered Lucia, more shocked than ever.

"I did, mom! I banged them all. And I'd do it again," she said, crossing her arms proudly over her chest. All fell silent once more.

"Well that was a tad gauche," said Veronica, pulling a small tube of antibacterial gel from her purse and squeezing some into her hands. "I hope you stopped in at a clinic after your rampage."

"Here, here," said Gabriel, intervening before Ava took the conversation to new depths of depravity, just to offend Veronica further. He wasn't sure about his sister's methods, but nonetheless respected her style of swift, non-violent retribution.

Erica had a question. "So, [and this is just for my own clarification,]" she began, "In order to get even with the girls who called you a slut, you went on a slutting spree, and with their boyfriends?" Everyone at the table chuckled, except Ava's parents, who glanced at each other nervously.

"Precisely," she replied coolly. "If those bitches didn't think I'd find a way to have the last laugh, then they obviously didn't know who they were screwing with," she said triumphantly.

"Well at least their boyfriends got to," said Veronica, smirking, taking the only chance she'd ever gotten to bag on Ava the way she does her. Ava's eyes flickered mischievously as she glanced up at her old adversary.

"Nicknames are a funny thing," began Ava. "Some are kind, some are cruel . . . Veronica, what did you get called when you were a young lady?" she asked smarmily.

Veronica, taken aback, responded casually. "Nothing quite comes to mind," she said, hoping to dodge the subject.

"Oh come on, Ronnie. There's hardly a ginger alive that hasn't been dubbed some kind of nickname, perhaps in reference to that sizeable mop of *fiery* red hair?" Ava smirked. "I could've sworn I read your nickname in your old year book . . ." Veronica narrowed her eyes but was so steaming on the inside, she could think of nothing to say back.

"Ava, stop bullying Mrs. Von der Klaasen," instructed her father sternly. Veronica turned away with crossed arms, looking to see where her husband had run off to. There he was, at the far window standing with his binoculars pressed against the glass like an embarrassingly unabashed travel nerd. Except he wasn't watching otters or island coastlines, he was checking out his new yacht from all angles. Veronica hated the way he insisted on wearing that captain's hat everywhere he went since purchasing that boat. She wouldn't have minded so much if he actually committed himself to the captain look and wore lots of white and gold, but that was definitely not the case. He wore pastel purple shorts with beige socks pulled halfway up to his knees. There was hardly a thing about her husband that didn't irritate her.

"Anyway, I'm dying to hear more about Erica's trip!" continued Cliff. "How did you love Roma and Umbria?"

"Those places were beyond stellar!" she exclaimed with eyes sparkling. *"L'Italia è conosciuta come un paese dall'eccezionale bellezza sia architettonica che natural."*

The table all stared at her, gaping. "Well I wish I had something clever like that to throw back at you!" said Cliff. "Unfortunately, we were only out in the countryside for a Thursday night wine tour. We saw the coliseum, but only from the outside because the line-ups were outrageous. Back at our hostel, our German roommates kept stealing pages from our Lonely Planet to use as rolling papers, so we missed a few key landmarks. And our shower water source was right next to a sulphur deposit so we pretty much smelled like poo the whole time. But it is the magical place where Lucia and I met!"

"That is so romantic!" gushed Erica. "How did you two hook up, initially?"

"Well . . . it was muggy and blistering hot, that summer in Rome. Gelato melted down the wrists of every man, woman and child . . ." started Cliff.

"He was popping wheelies uphill on a rented scooter, I was hopelessly lost trying to find the gateway to Vatican City," added Lucia.

"I spotted her there, struggling with her tourist map. I watched her for half an hour before I finally worked up the courage to ask her if she needed a lift somewhere," said Cliff.

"Once I trusted him enough not to take me someplace ghetto and sell me into white slavery, I jumped on," added Lucia.

"And as it turned out, we were staying at the same hostel. Even weirder still, we were booked into the same room!"

"No way!" said Erica incredulously. "Is that total serendipity or what?"

"Complete and utter serendipity," said Cliff with a serious nod. "Things like that make you know, if you didn't already know, that there are forces at work we have no idea about."

"I never heard that story before," said Gabriel curiously.

"You never asked how we met before," answered Cliff. "If you had, I'd have told you all about our blistering hot Roman holiday."

Lucia smiled flirtatiously, still giggling for her husband the way a happy girl giggles at a clever joke on a first date with a beautiful boy. "Perhaps it was just the teensiest bit presumptuous of us," she said, "but we made a pact that summer to spend every summer together for the rest of our lives."

"And how is that working out for you?" Erica asked.

"Spotless record!" she answered, winking at her husband. Ava rolled her eyes.

"And then of course when the kids came, we jumped them in on the pact as well!" said Cliff.

"I doubt you had to twist any arms," said Erica. "But now that everyone's growing up, it's a bit harder to maintain a pact like that, no?"

"Not really. See, we told them years ago they won't inherit a dime from us unless they are present and accounted for every summer," said Lucia. "The rest of the year is fair game for travel and other pursuits, but every summer we expect them here. And while they're here, we expect them to be active, creative, and to be busying themselves with whatever it is they love. That way, family time doesn't have to end just because everyone eventually grows up."

"But what if someone gets a job that doesn't let them take summers off?" asked Erica, not challenging the arrangement but genuinely wanting to know more about how they make it work.

"Well you've been gone a long time so I guess you haven't been filled in, but the kids are already doing quite well for themselves without ever having had to take a job!" said Cliff proudly.

"That's fantastic!" said Erica, surprised and excited by the idea. Of course, she didn't have to work either because the life insurance policy her parents had taken out combined with her banked inheritance was more than enough for her to live on quite comfortably, but she was still very interested in how these her old playmates with two live parents were accomplishing the same, at such young ages. "Pray tell! How?"

"Well, it's quite simple, actually," began Lucia. "We just encouraged them all to do what they love every day until they got so good at their respective hobbies, they could begin to capitalize on them and support themselves."

"I'm just a surf bum that gets paid to do it." said Gabriel.

"Don't be so modest!" his proud mother urged, and went on to tell his story for him. "When Gabriel was sixteen, he had his eye on this tricked-out, thousand-dollar mountain bike so he began teaching surf lessons to tourists to save up for it. As it turned out, he had a knack for teaching and before long, he was signing up full classes and doing private clinics all up the coast! Eventually he got so busy, he had to hire an entire staff of instructors."

"That's so great!" said Erica, for whom Gabriel just got even sexier. "You just get paid to splash around all day. Sweet!"

"Yeah but I haven't been teaching a lot lately 'cause the team has got it covered. I've just been honing my own skills…"

"Gabey is a sponsored rider!" said his proud little sister. "He has shots and spreads in surf mags around the world. He takes home mad awards, wins comps with his eyes closed, and gets all his clothes, shoes, and watches for free. He's famous within the neoprene mafia."

Erica was so impressed. She told him how she remembered going out on foam boards with him when they were little, never guessing he'd make a career out of it. She felt proud of her old childhood friend, but at the same time, felt exceedingly attracted to the handsome surfer/entrepreneur sitting across from her, whom she'd always known would grow up to do special things. His pecs looked strong and cut under his white shirt, and he was the most scrumptious boy she had ever seen up close and in real life. "So where have you surfed?" she asked him, trying to play it cool.

"Everywhere," said Gabriel. "So far this year I've been to the Maldives and Grenada. Last year I surfed Indo, Nica, the Gold Cost of Australia. It's been a pretty swell gig!"

"I'll say!" said Erica. Arielle's jaw dropped as she realized all the days she wasted waiting for him at his home when she should have been out combing the waves in exotic equatorial locales around the globe. "So what about you, Ava?" she asked. "What is it that you are successfully offering to the world?"

"I started a fashion blog a few years ago as a platform from which to protest saggy jodhpurs."

"You mean like, riding pants?" Erica asked curiously. "Because I wear those sometimes . . ."

"Yes, but no. I mean, jodhpurs as fashion. The saggy kind. Those pants that were for a brief time inexplicably trendy among the dirty hipster set."

"I think I know the ones," she offered. "Loose and diapery around the butt, but tapered in the leg?"

". . . and make women look like they've just shat themselves, yes!" Ava answered, nodding. "My work began as a crusade against such atrocities, as a forum from which to oppugn anything I found to be equally objectionable and upsetting in the world of fashion. As it turned out, a lot of people shared my views and before I knew it, I had a huge user-submitted pic gallery and was getting, like, a thousand hits a day. Before long, people started offering me lots of money to fly ad banners on my page."

"That's hilarious! So you're like peopleofwalmart.com, then? You collect pictures of people wearing ridiculous things and post comments on them?"

"Kind of. We're set up pretty much the same way but while they're simply about the entertainment value of mocking motley Wal-creatures, the goal of my site is to proactively shame style offenders into thinking twice before stepping out looking like an aging Thai fisherman who couldn't find a butt rag he hadn't already soiled."

"Here, here!" said Erica, definitely agreeing but also making an effort to be agreeable with the ever-mercurial Ava. "It's like I once read, 'Style is optimism made visible. It presumes that you are a person of interest, that the world is a place of interest, and that life is worth making an effort for.' I don't know who originally said that, but it's stuck with me."

"Exactly. People who don't bother with themselves drag down the average for all of us."

"Ava's blasts have all the effect of a modern-day stoning," explained Gabriel. "It's like 'comply with my idea of style or your blundering faux-pas may be immortalized on the intraweb.'"

Veronica, who had been biting her lip while Ava was speaking, said shyly, "Of course, there is more than one definition of style, Ava . . ." But Ava just waved her off, muttering, "She's just disgruntled cause she's positively famous on idsoonerdie.org."

"We made you take those photos down!" said Lucia, sticking up for her friend.

"Gone but not forgotten," said Ava solemnly.

Erica turned to little Demetra and asked her if she'd given any thought to what she would end up doing with herself. "I'm already doing it!" was her chipper reply.

"Even you?" asked Erica in disbelief.

"Especially Demetra!" said Gabriel, who then explained how three summers ago, Demetra started writing and making illustrations for her own series of children's books that were currently selling like hot cakes at elementary school book fairs across the country.

"Very impressive!" said Erica. "I can't wait to see them! What are they about?"

"Pugs, mostly," she replied, then explained how she had started painting the family's five smoosh-faced, curly-tailed pets and then started writing storylines to go with them until they were books. "I made so much dough last year, I was able to donate a huge stack to the pug rescue network. It's all been very fulfilling, both creatively and charitably. "

Erica was speechless; she had been expecting to find a little girl not yet even ten, and here sitting beside her was a published and paid young author and philanthropist. "You guys are all blowing me away!"

"So what else have you been up to, Erica?" asked Lucia. "Besides traveling, of course. What are your greatest loves and interests?"

"Well, lots. For one thing, I got this ink done a few months ago," she said, rolling up her sleeve to reveal a big silver-grey moon tattoo on the inside of her forearm.

"La lune!" exclaimed Veronica, always trying to sound exotic. "Whatever inspired this?"

"After my parents died, I received incredible amounts of support from everyone I knew. I appreciated it, but it got kind of exhausting to feel like everyone was trying desperately to distract me so I'd forget I was an orphan. Every day was an endless parade of fun activities, gentle therapy, home-cooked meals and fresh-baked treats. They were trying to create 'normalcy,' whatever that is. I appreciated it all very much, but found myself on most days looking forward to the nighttime, when I could finally be left alone with my thoughts and memories. And no matter where I was, I would curl up beside a window and stare out at the moon, looking for my mom and dad in its face. Over the years, the moon has come to represent them for me, and the precious, fleeting hours of dark night when I'm free to miss them and remember them," she said while running her fingers along the design on her skin.

"I'd never get a tattoo," said Ava, snobbishly. "It'd be like throwing a bumper sticker up on a Mercedes. Fail."

"That's one way to look at it!" said Erica, laughing. "But I think of tattoos more like hanging a picture in a nice house with bare walls. Kind of like, something pretty to complement the architecture."

Arielle was transfixed; she had not noticed the pretty moon picture on Erica's forearm but thought it was magnificent, for she had never seen a drawing so vivid on a person's skin before.

It was almost sundown by the time they got back to their side of the island, riding fast and smooth in the shiny new but now-deflowered yacht. Just like the night before, the skies were awash in a berry red. Gabriel carried Erica's bags from the yacht and set them down in the trunk of his Jeep. When he hopped into the driver's seat, he found Arielle already buckled in sitting shotgun, smiling happily with her hands folded in her lap. Seeing Erica walking up close behind, Gabriel thought to make one minor seating adjustment.

"Actually Arielle, what do you think about letting Erica be co-pilot this time? Would that be okay?" He asked it like a question, but it was a question for which there was only one answer, lest she appear difficult. Erica grinned; she thought he might do that for her, but Arielle did not appreciate her demotion to the back seat. Deflated and not quite sure how to take it, she crawled over the console and into the back, fastening her seat belt while Erica thanked her breezily and occupied the spot next to Gabriel, who was fiddling with his iPod for an appropriate playlist.

On the way home, Arielle kept her eyes fixed on Gabriel's right hand as he shifted gears. As he kicked it into fifth, the back of his hand brushed Erica's thigh. Erica felt it, brisk and gentle, and in dwelling on it, her cheeks blushed to mauve. Bitter and beginning to experience what it is to be envious, Arielle couldn't help but feel robbed. That's my seat, she silently pouted to herself. And my HIM.

When they arrived at the house, Gabriel grabbed Erica's bags and, chatting engagingly and excitedly with her while they caught up after so many years, carried them up the stairs to the cosy room above the boathouse that Lucia and Cliff had set up for her, since all the bedrooms were taken.

"I still can't believe it's you," he said as he set her bags down of the floor inside. She spun around to face him and giggled. "I know!"

"You knew and didn't tell me," he said.

"I refused to ruin the surprise!" she said unapologetically.

"That was positively wicked of you," he said, taking a step closer.

"And it was worth it just to see the look on your face today!" She couldn't hide how thrilled she was at how perfectly it all seemed to be working out.

On a more serious note and in the spirit of getting everything out of the way, Gabriel sat down on the end of her bed and asked her why she never came to live with his family after her parents died, since, after all, his parents were her godparents and the ones charged with caring for her if anything tragic ever happened. "It was tempting," she answered. "Cliff and Lucia are the greatest. But I knew if I came to live here, I probably never would've left."

"And would that have been the worst thing?" he asked.

"It would definitely not have been the worst thing," she said. "It's just that something inside me compelled me towards adventure and wouldn't even hear about settling in, anywhere. I ran with it. But I always knew I would end up back here one day."

The two continued to catch up, feeling themselves flit between adoring each other as old friends and feeling attracted to each other as hot-blooded adults whose worlds were echoing with a resounding click. Their minds kept returning to the sweet kiss they shared on the beach that morning, and both wanted to have that kiss again. But neither wanted to move too fast because to rush would be to fail to stop and savour.

"You know, after your parents' accident, Dagmara and I were really shaken. Like, up-all-night frightened nine-year-olds, thinking our parents were going to die in some freak accident too. We were terrorized. We could barely wrap our tender heads around the situation... but you should know that we were humbled by your bravery. I continue to be humbled by the girl who fearlessly took on the world, all by herself."

"That's sweet," she said. She paused for a moment, and the corners of her lips curved up as he watched her. "Did you know I liked you when we were little?"

A smile crept across Gabriel's face as he remembered his chubby childhood playmate. "Maybe a little," he said, "but I was never sure. Boys are dumb at that age and girls are vague; I don't think it ever occurred to me to wonder."

She laughed. Arielle's ears perked up from outside the window as she listened in. "Do you want to know the real reason I didn't come to live with you guys?" she asked while Arielle strained to hear her. Gabriel shot her a confused look, nodding. "Because I didn't want to become a sister to you . . . I was too in love with you for that."

They held a gaze for a moment while he searched her face for any signs she was pulling his leg. She wasn't.

"Seriously?" he asked, seriously. "You didn't come because of me?"

"You were the only boy I'd ever liked," she said. "And to this day, you're still the sweetest boy I've ever met. There was no way to be sure we'd ever get the chance to be together, or if you'd even ever want to . . . but I knew any semblance of a chance would be dashed if I moved in with your family and became one of your sisters. So I didn't."

Gabriel was speechless. He had no idea she had felt that way, but he was very moved by her honesty, and impressed by her foresight as a nine-year-old.

"It's so nice to be back here with your family again, though. It's the last place that feels like home to me. You've all done so much for yourselves and yet, you all seem exactly the same as I remember you . . . except for the little 'Meaty' prodigy that didn't exist yet the last time I came around!"

"I guess Lucia and Cliff like to pump out all winners" he said with a wink. "So, how long do we have you for? And what sorts of things do you want to get up to while you're here?"

"Thank you very much for asking," she replied. "Because I am just dying to go visit Savannah! I keep having dreams about her, I miss her so much! Feel like coming for a ride?"

Gabriel respectfully declined, explaining in the most polite way possible how he didn't like how riding felt on his balls and that he would prefer to sit it out. But offered his car to her as he planned to spend most of the next day in the water since the forecast was so peachy. She thanked him sweetly; he really was as darling as she remembered.

"Anyway I'll get out of your way so you can unpack," he said as he stood up to hug her good-night, which was Arielle's cue to make herself scarce because he would be emerging soon. "See you at breakfast," said Erica, wrapping her arms around his neck and shoulders while he wrapped his arms around her back and waist. "It's really nice to have you back."

"Nice to be back," she replied, and he left her to it.

Arielle ran upstairs and stood at the bathroom vanity fumbling with the toothpaste. When Gabriel came in, she heard the screen door open and shut. With her foamy toothbrush dangling from her mouth, she tiptoed to the top of the stairs and looked down to see him with a huge, goofy grin on his face as he stood in silence reflecting on the exchange that had just taken place. Arielle saw him smiling, and his smile was definitely not for her.

Crouching at the top of the stairs and staring down, she brushed her teeth passively and absently, going almost cross-eyed with lust for him as he stood staring off into space. She watched him intently, praying he wasn't thinking thoughts of love for that Erica.

When he flicked off the lights, she snapped out of it and dashed back into the bathroom. She threw her toothbrush in the sink, swallowed all the minty paste in her mouth and wiped her chin on a hand towel before running into her room and diving onto the bed to sprawl out in her most siren-like seductress pose, waiting for him to pass by her doorway.

He came whistling down the hallway and stopped in front of her open door. "That was fun today, right?" he asked her cheerily. Arielle smiled and nodded. It had been a nice day . . . up until they picked up Erica. "What a day," he said to her but mostly to himself while he stared off through her window. His gentle joy made her uneasy, because she was aware of where it was coming from.

"Well, good-night!" he said with a wink before pulling her bedroom door shut. She melted down into her bed and turned out the lamp, lying still in the darkness and feeling the beginning of the end creep over her. She thought about Erica's wild, dark hair and golden skin, and how much they contrasted with her own fair white coloring. Enviously she imagined Erica's round cheeks and big, white smile, and the way her hips curved so womanly and nubile. Mostly, though, she thought about the sound of Erica's voice: sweet, dynamic and somewhat raspy, and the way her words made Gabriel light up. She missed her own voice desperately, for she knew she could touch him more deeply with her song than any other girl's pretty words ever could.

Hours later, unable to get comfortable in her bed or think of anything except her desire to be close to him, Arielle sat up in the dark. Quietly, she wrapped the fluffy duvet from her bed around her shoulders, opened her door carefully, and tiptoed down the hall to Gabriel's doorway. It was closed, but when she pressed her ear to it, she could hear him inside shuffling about and whistling softly. Sleepily, she dropped her blanket on the floor and sat down in his doorway. There was something strangely satisfying about being there, even without his knowledge, to guard him from the other side of his door. Imagining the immense and unbelievable joy she would feel if only she could be inside curled up next to him, she lay her body down upon the soft blanket and drifted off to sleep

# twenty-two

## Jericho

---

The next morning, Arielle awoke to magnified sunlight in her face, heated up through the dome of the hall skylight. Clammy and hot under the heavy blanket, she wriggled free from it, stood up and stretched, then moseyed back to her room, dragging it behind her. The more she thought about the events of the previous day, the sadder she became and she stopped at her window to stare out at the boathouse. Painfully curious about Erica and upon detecting some movement from behind the blinds, Arielle stepped into her big rain boots and ran out in her nightie to spy.

She crept up the stairs stealthily, and hid under the window of the door, pressing her ear to it. She listened for a moment but couldn't hear anything inside, and just as she was about to go and spy from another angle, the door flew wide open and smacked her hard in the face, cracking her nose.

"Arielle! What are you doing?" said Erica as she jumped back, startled. The mermaid, crouching at the door, gripped her nose with both hands and sneezed blood all over the welcome mat. "Oh no, did I break your nose?" gasped Erica nervously, feeling awful and panicking that she might have really injured her. But then just a second later, Arielle stood up, let go of her still-perfect, unmarred nose and walked into her room without invitation. The bleeding had stopped and it was as if it never happened, except for the blood still splattered all over the doorway and the bit that still stained the rims of her nostrils. "Come on in," said Erica, following her in. "Is there something I can help you with?"

Arielle just ignored her, and began gently rifling through the products, accessories and random belongings that Erica had strewn across her dresser. She wasn't sure what she was looking to find, but she'd have been damned if she didn't at least take a peek at her rival's arsenal. Erica had tubes and bottles of things that either smelled nice or were a nice colour. She had kits and cases of tools and brushes, and clothing by the pile. She had everything with her that a girl might ever need in just about any situation or occasion, because she liked to be prepared for anything. Arielle suddenly realized how ill-equipped she herself had been when she arrived.

"Actually, I'm glad you're up," said Erica, watching Arielle curiously as she inspected all her things. "Gabriel said I could borrow the Jeep today to go visit my pony, Savannah. Feel like coming with me? We could go for a ride! Do you like horses?"

Arielle gave her a puzzled look, but then noticed a picture of Erica with her big white horse on the night table and knew what she was talking about. How exciting it was! Since the morning the mermaid saw her riding on the beach, she had badly wanted to meet such a beast. "Would you like to come with me, then?" When her question was met with a very enthusiastic nod, Erica tossed her a pair of stretchy beige riding pants that definitely did not sag in the butt. "Okay! Go put these on with a tee-shirt and meet me at the Jeep in five!" Five minutes later, Arielle came skipping out to the driveway and off they went.

They pulled up and parked behind a small farmhouse with a huge flower garden, and walked up to a big red barn that smelled of dust and hay. The door was open, and there were two young girls inside brushing a white mare.

"Kara and Jane and Savannah! How are my girls?" asked Erica happily, giving hugs to her friends and a kiss on the nose of her horsie.

"Mary said you were coming by for a ride today so we were getting her all pretty for you," said Kara, the older one wearing overalls and outback boots. Jane, the little one, just smiled shyly as she picked a burr out of the mare's white tail with her pink fingernails.

"Thanks so much ladies; she looks great! We'll also need to get another pony ready for my friend Arielle here."

Arielle looked around the barn as if she had wandered into the cave of wonders. The smell of the place was so strange, and the little bits that floated around in the air tickled her nostrils 'til she sneezed again, this time with no blood spray. Almost all of the stalls held a pretty horse inside, but a loud whinnying from the other end of the barn caught her ear and so she started walking towards it, anxious to meet whomever seemed to be calling to her so anxiously.

"Arielle, the horses you'll want to choose from are out in the paddock; come out here!" called Erica, but Arielle kept straight, following the noise. In the very last stable, she found the fiery roan stallion that had been kicking up such a racket. He was tall and muscular and his hooves were the color of beluga caviar. He was most definitely the one she would be riding that day.

Erica walked up beside her as she stood in awe of the valiant beast. "That's Jericho," she said. "He's beautiful . . . but you'd be crazy to ride him until he's been well-broken." Jericho threw back his head and whinnied even louder, stamping his big, heavy hooves, demonstrating his power and zeal. Arielle stepped in closer so that she could smell the hair of his cheek, smooth and skin-thin across muscle and vein, smelling of summer's hot dust and grass. She was enamored.

"Seriously, come take your pick of the geldings. I've seen Jericho throw grown men off his back and if I let you get hurt, the O'Faolains will never forgive me!" But Arielle locked eyes with the mighty beast and he nuzzled her face with his big, soft nose. "Please be careful around him," implored Erica, but Arielle and the horse were in their own little world, making each other's acquaintance through scent and touch but communicating on an entirely different level. Arielle breathed up his big nostrils and held her hair to his nose so he could sniff her. She scratched under his chin and down his neck and kissed gently the end of his soft snout. Erica was impressed and taken aback by her apparent animal magnetism, for no one had ever been able to get that close to him. "Old Frances bought him at auction about a year ago, very cheap because he was impossible," said Erica with a sigh. "Like most devastatingly gorgeous creatures, he's extremely difficult, hard to get close to, and kind of insane!"

When Arielle put her hands on his big, chiseled cheeks and stared him in the eyes, she could feel his intense energy beckoning her, drawing her in, begging her to set him free. Understanding completely what he was asking of her, she stepped away from his stall and looked up at Erica.

"Alright, let's go get Liberty or maybe Lightning tacked up for you, okay?" said Erica, turning to lead Arielle towards the tack room. "I think I have an extra pair of riding boots here somewhere, if not there are spare Blunnys by the door." Thinking Arielle was following right behind her, she was already halfway back down the long hall when she heard a latch open and stopped dead in her tracks. She turned around and saw that Arielle had disappeared. "Arielle?" she called, squinting her eyes into the dusty dark of the corridor.

Suddenly, Jericho's stable door burst open and out he flew like a racehorse through his starting gate. He galloped past a stunned Erica with Arielle riding on his back and clutching a shock of auburn mane in her bare fists. They were gaining speed, making a break for the daylight and heading for the forest quicker than Erica could react.

"OH MY GOD, HEEEELLLLLLLPPP!!" she screamed as she ran towards her own horse and, in leap-frog fashion, vaulted herself into the saddle from behind. It was a move she had once seen in a Western film and had been practicing for years, awaiting an emergency just like this one. In spite of the crisis on her hands, she took a second to congratulate herself on her form. Then she tapped Savannah's bum with her crop and kicked the chase into high gear. Jericho bounded full-tilt through the forest with Arielle up on his strong back. She felt like she was flying while the tall boughs brushed her shoulders and the birds in the trees orbited around her head. Erica braced herself for the worst as she rode around a corner, expecting to find Arielle's little body in a mangled heap. Certain she would discover the girl bucked off of the rambunctious horse, she was shocked to find Arielle holding on tightly and absorbing the canter in her legs like derby-winning jockey.

"Come back and tack him up!" yelled Erica, but they were now deep in the forest, galloping down the dirt path and rounding past trees like a barrel racer heading for the beach. She and Savannah chased them as quickly as they could, and almost lost their footing in such hot pursuit. She began to worry about what she would say to the O'Faolains when it came time to explain why she let Arielle jump on the back of an unbroken stallion without a saddle, reins or even a helmet on. At the edge of the shaded wood, Arielle and Jericho disappeared into the sunny brightness and by the time Erica and Savannah reached the clearing, the renegades were already way down the beach, but had slowed down and were now trotting easily along the water's edge.

"You can't just jump on an untrained horse like that, you could fall off and break your neck!" said Erica between breaths once she'd finally caught up. "It would be a quick thud-crunch-tumble to your untimely death and I really can't be responsible for that!," she piqued. But even as she gave her sort-of-angry-but-mostly-concerned safety speech, she knew could already eat her words for it was plain to see she needn't worry about Arielle, who handled the stallion with grace and control.

"I take it you've spent some time around horses then?" she asked. Arielle just smiled at her shyly. She made bareback look so natural and so easy, that when Erica looked down to observe her own gloved hands as they held her shiny leather reins, all of her riding essentials suddenly felt superfluous and extravagant.

Just then, as if she was already bored with the convention and ease of staying seated on a horse's back, Arielle kicked the blue sandals off her feet and stood up on Jericho's back. Erica nervously asked her to please sit down, but Arielle just pretended not to hear her and instead stood up all the way, holding her balance as skillfully as a tightrope-walker. Once steady, she stood on one foot and held her arms out at her sides, flying along the shore just like the seagulls she used to envy. Jericho's mighty hooves thundered through the foamy, shallow surf, and together they traced the very line dividing blue ocean from sandy shore and her new life from her old one. In that moment of sheer joy, she realized that she had never felt so free.

That night after dinner, the little mermaid retired early. Actually, she fell asleep at the dinner table before dessert was even served, so Gabriel carried her upstairs and tucked her into bed.

"She had a big day," said Erica, standing in the hallway with two mugs of B-52 coffees while he closed Arielle's doors behind him. The two of them went out to Gabriel's balcony for their nightcap.

"Was she any good at riding?" he asked.

"I'll say!" she answered. "I turned my back to her for one second and the next thing I knew, she was taking off bareback on a wild, untrained and massively powerful stallion!"

A look of concern washed over his smiling face. "Oh my God! Did she get thrown off?"

"I was so sure she would, Gabe. I was already thinking about what I was going to tell you and your parents . . . I was definitely crapping my pants. But, as it turns out, that girl can ride like an act from some crazy rodeo circus! She was standing up, balancing on one foot, spinning around and riding backwards . . . all that was missing was an apple on my head, and a bow and arrow in her hands. Or feet, for that matter, 'cause I'm sure she could have done that too."

Gabriel lit up. "Did you get any pictures?" he asked excitedly.

"There was no time to grab a camera! Luckily the girls had Savannah all tacked up or else I would never have caught up to them!"

"That's hilarious," he observed. "She just took off on a savage horse?"

"It was the wildest thing I've ever seen. You know, she may not breathe a word to any of us, but when she was with that horse, it became clear to me that she speaks languages that neither you nor I could ever touch." Erica's tone was one of admiration, but also of incertitude and incredulity.

"Like a little horse whisperer or something?" he asked.

"Yes, but even deeper than that. From the second their eyes met, they had a connection. He immediately trusted her, and she had not a drop of fear for the huge, strong animal. She's kind of my hero." They both stared thoughtfully out to sea. "It was just like in Avatar when Jake Sully makes 'the bond' with his dinosaur-looking equestrianoid. Except, without actually plugging a braided ponytail into his ear antenna."

"Their connection was wireless," said Gabriel cheesily as he gazed up into the foggy sky. Only a few very bright stars could be seen through the damp haze, but where he noticed a twinkling up there, he could imagine it was a parallel world like Pandora where people ride dragons and are pretty much always naked. When he came back down to earth, he noticed Erica was chewing on something that smelled fruity and sweet. "Is that a Sour Patch Kid?" he asked, squinting into her sugary hand. She answered that yes, there were Sour Patch Kids in her purse, along with jujubes and gummy worms from a bulk candy purchase that had spilled out into the main compartment a few weeks prior. "They're all over the place in here," she said as she scraped her hand along the bottom of her bag, fishing out candy, cookie crumbs, random beads, gum wrappers and even a petrified French fry.

"You've had candy this whole time?" he asked suspiciously, joking but partially offended that he hadn't been offered any.

"Yeah, sorry," she said with a giggle. "I didn't think you'd be interested in these ones; they've been bouncing around in there for weeks. It's gross of me to be eating them; I wasn't about to offer them to you!"

"Well it might have been nice to have been given the option," he asserted. "The Erica I knew would never hold out on me! I thought we were pals . . . this changes everything."

She laughed. "You're right, I should have at least offered you a few of my rancid candies." Then she pulled out another handful of purse-bottom debris, picked out a red jujube and handed it to him, and picked out an orange one for herself. "Of course, we could always just go get some fresh ones," she said, but Gabriel just wiped it on his jeans and popped it into his mouth. "Are you kidding?" he said. "The things I've dusted off candy before eating it! I'm pretty sure I invented the two-second rule."

"Oh please!" she said, slapping his knee. "I've been fostering the TEN second rule for longer than I'd care to admit! Dusting off is child's play . . . the things I've *rinsed* off my candy before eating it!"

"Bang!" he said, "That's disgusting! And I think I might be in love . . ." He was exaggerating of course, but was feeling very glad to have found a kindred spirit where it pertained to candy. "Favourite flavours?" he asked.

"Same as most, I'd expect," she responded casually, pretending not to be thunderstruck by his last comment. "Reds, pinks, purples, and, depending on the variety, blues, whites, clear ones. The usual suspects. I favour the sweet ones."

"And what of the inferior colours?" he asked her. "And by 'inferior' I mean the greens, oranges and lemon-yellows. And of course, black. It takes a special palate to appreciate black licorice candy, and I don't have it."

"Well, I eat 'em all," said Erica, taking down a lemon yellow and passing another red one to Gabriel. "I like to think of the less-favourable ones as palate cleansers," she explained, "ginger slices to my sashimis." Gabriel found her outlook amusing, and couldn't help but be touched that she'd given him the last two reds in a row.

"You're giving me all your sashimis," he said.

"I guess that means I like you," she replied. And under the dim patio light in the stillness of the foggy evening, they both chewed their old candies and thought about each other.

"You're beautiful," he blurted out. "More beautiful than I could've imagined you'd turn out."

She smiled, blushed, and cast her eyes down into her coffee. "And you're smooth!" she shot back. "You know just what to say to take a girl's breath away!"

He shook his head earnestly. "Actually, if you get to know me (again), you'll see that there is nothing smooth about me."

She raised an eyebrow disbelievingly. "Well, with a face like that, I guess you never needed to be!"

"Now who's smooth?!" he said, reaching out and tickling her sides. She jumped and screeched, almost spilling her mug, then came back at him with tickling fingers until she was sitting on him, her face hovering just above his. They both paused in truce and caught their breath, their foreheads just an inch from touching. "You know, I spent the whole next day hoping you'd come by again," he said softly, pulling her onto his lap comfortably (and smoothly). "I thought you definitely might," he said. "And I felt only slightly dissed when you didn't."

"Well how do you think I felt?" she asked him, catching him off guard. "Because I did come, I must've just missed you, and I got to spend all winter kicking myself for not getting here in time." He argued that at least she knew where to find him, and she argued that with no guarantee he'd be single when she returned, that fact was of little comfort.

"I hope you didn't worry too much about that," he said with a chuckle. "I pretty much gave up on love when the only girl I ever liked rode away on a white mare last Labour Day." She could hardly believe he was saying such things to her. Every word was so sweet, it had to be a line. And he was so beautiful, he couldn't be real. But he was, and when she peered into his dark eyes, all she could see was genuine interest, attraction, and blooming adoration. He was real. She was so taken, she thought she might cry, so she spoke to break the spell.

"I'm so glad you stayed cute," she said flirtingly, but also with a tone of relief.

"Oh yeah?" he asked, noticing her tone. "Was there a big chance I might not have?"

"Just sayin'," she continued, running her fingers through his thick black hair as if he belonged to her and always had. "I'm just incredibly grateful for you that your boyish good looks didn't go the way of, say, Macaulay Culkin's or Ralph Macchio's, leaving you awkward and troll-like in adulthood."

He laughed, not used to receiving such wayward compliments. "Well Miss, I, too, am very glad there's nothing troll-like about the grown-up you. Except maybe for that jewel in your belly button," he said, pointing to the canary rhinestone pierced through her navel. She laughed out loud, not just at his joke, but because it was simply too much that he was this beautiful AND this clever.

"I'm glad you finally made it back," he said cheerfully but seriously. "And I'm very glad you didn't go off and marry some foreigner on your travels."

"Me too," she said sweetly as she wiggled in closer. "I thought of you all the time."

"I thought of you too," he said, placing his warm hand on the small of her back. "I thought of that kiss every day." Every part of her felt like it was surrendering to him. They could both feel that their next kiss was upon them but they let it linger, for the anticipation itself was its own brand of delicious.

Moments passed, and they didn't kiss. They got to talking, for there was still so much catching up to do. They spoke of likes and dislikes, of biggest fears and of wildest dreams. They told each other stories about their lives since losing touch, of her adventures in growing up without parents, and of the bewildering void he often felt carrying on without his twin sister. When she spoke, he watched her face, looking for clues that the beautiful woman in front of him was actually just a version of the little friend he used to know. When he spoke, she wondered, like she always used to, whether he was even aware of the charm and power he wielded with his almost insufferable champion's grin. Then, without another thought, she puckered up and kissed him right on it. This kiss was even better than the last.

# twenty-three

## The Ten-Party Throw-Down

The following day when the sun was high in the sky and it was a little too sweltering to be anywhere but in the shade, the young souls of the house sat in the breezy solarium under the fan, enjoying the afternoon from the air-conditioned indoors. Sprawled comfortably across sofas, ottomans and armchairs, Gabriel and Ava read, Erica added to her scrapbook, and Demetra painted watercolour onto origami sheets while Arielle strummed at the harp. Their peace was disturbed when they heard a vehicle pull into the driveway and a voice over a loudspeaker say "GABE O'FAOLAIN!" When they looked up, they saw a white van with a massive LCD screen hung across the side of it. Gabriel, Erica and Arielle ran out to see what was up. The writing on the screen read:

*On this the eve of July the thirty-first,*

    *Come lose your head and quench your thirst!*

    *It's time for the tenth annual*

    *TEN PARTY THROWDOWN!!*

*Kicking off at sundown @ Jy & Jaz's*

*23 Boundary Rd.*

    *Next venues to be revealed as the night progresses!*

*BE THERE!*


"Yessss!" cheered Gabriel excitedly as the van pulled out. "I totally forgot this jam was tonight!"

"I've heard about this before!" said Erica. "It's the big house party crawl, right?"

"Yup!" he replied. "We'll stay in one spot just long enough to dance a bit, take a few pics, and when all the supplies are depleted, it'll be on to the next one!"

"I'm so down!" said Erica ardently.

"It's going to be epic!" he assured her. "Arielle, 'you coming?" She nodded enthusiastically. "Ava?"

Ava set down her Vogue, pulled her shades down her nose and glared at him. "Well I am free tonight, but it just so happens I'd rather stay in and clip my toenails than drink from the same trough as all those unwashed island rats, thanks. I'll pass," she said coldly as her eyes went back down to her article. No one fought to convince her to join.

"What about me?" asked Demetra, slightly offended.

"Oh Meaty, I know you'd make a swell addition to any party but I think you might be a little young for this one," he replied in a big brother tone.

"How's that?" she asked, "because I've been the toast of parties where the average age was at least fifteen years older than that of this one, I'd suspect!"

"You make a good point," he conceded, "but as long as I'm your big brother, I'm not bringing you anywhere near the kinds of guys that will be out wheeling tonight."

"How old will I have to be before you bring me to parties with you?" she asked.

"At least nineteen," he answered. "At least then you'll be legal."

"Well why does Arielle get to go? We don't know for sure how old she is."

"Because she's definitely older than you."

"By how much, would you say?"

"At least five years, Meaty."

Making her what? Fourteen?"

Gabriel thought about it for a second. "She's got to be older than that."

"But there's no way to know for sure!"

"You're right about that. Okay you win! I guess you're coming, if Mom says it's okay."

Demetra relaxed down into her seat, satisfied. "Meh, it's alright. I never really wanted to go to that horny drunkfest anyway; I signed up for debate squad this fall and I just wanted to practice arguing." She smiled cheekily at her brother. "For the record, this one was mine."

"It's true, you're good!" he admitted.

"You'd be bringing me if I wanted," she teased.

"If Mom said it was okay," he corrected her with a wink.


That evening while the girls got ready for the party, Gabriel shaved in his bathroom mirror while his mom sat chatting with him, sipping a glass of pinot grigio.

"Well tonight sounds like fun," said Lucia, "but I was thinking . . . maybe you should just bring Erica."

"I already invited Arielle, Mom," he said. "I can't un-invite her now! She's up there shining her rain boots, all stoked to go!"

Lucia's motherly instincts tugged at her. "I just don't know how I feel about you taking her to the ten parties shindig; she's so little and naive, I fear even the ants could carry her off."

"No one's going to take her, mom. We're on an island, remember?"

"I'm just afraid you could lose her if you weren't watching her closely."

"Mom, it'll be fine. Erica and I will both watch her; she'd be heartbroken if we left her behind."

"Well, just make sure the guys there keep their groping hands off her. We don't know how old she is, but we know she's far too young for that," said Lucia with concern. "And don't let her drink, either. You're responsible for her tonight so I think you should know that I read somewhere something about how kids that drink before the age of sixteen are about a hundred times more likely to become raging, belligerent undignified alkies."

"I won't let her drink, mom," he reassured her. "And I won't let anyone touch her, and I'll bring them both home at a decent time."

"Okay, son. I trust you. Just sayin', she has the heart of a baby."

"I know," he said. "I know."


Arielle was particularly excited for the party, as she had been feeling like she was losing ground in the fight for Gabriel's heart ever since Erica showed up. She was dying to dance for him again, to use the only means of seductive expression she felt she had left. She tried on several things, but decided on a pair of white denim shorts, an army green t-shirt and, of course, the big yellow rain boots she loved so much. She figured they'd be going to the kind of place where people would be spilling and she couldn't be too careful. Demetra weaved her large mass of blond hair into one big side braid, and tied a few feathers into it, just for fun. She preferred the way Arielle's hair looked when she first arrived, with all the stuff she used to have dangling from it. She had never had any feathers before, though!

When they arrived at the first party, the yard was packed full of young adults drinking, smoking, dancing and mingling. It was definitely more relaxed and nowhere near as classy as the last human party she had attended, but there was something in the air at this one, at this un-catered but hip and rowdy fete. It was vibrant and full of people yet to reach their prime, where everyone bounced gleefully around just basking in the collective glow of youth.

"Ava wasn't exaggerating when she said there would be a few island rats," said Gabriel, gesturing towards a crowd of shirtless guys in backwards hats playing an aggressive game of beer pong.

"It takes all kinds to give a party flavour!" said Erica through her slick red lips, glad to be out among partiers their age. "Looks like we've got a lot of catching up to do," she said, pulling Gabriel and Arielle towards the keg and the stacks of red plastic cups.

"Gabriel, fancy a beer?" asked one of the girls pumping and pouring.

"Rachel! Yes thanks, one for me, and one for my girl." While he made chit chat and caught up with Rachel, Erica beamed. He called me *his girl*! Arielle pretended she didn't hear that.

"Anything for your other lady?" asked Rachel.

"Do you have any pop or juice?" he asked. Arielle furrowed her brows; she couldn't understand why she couldn't have the same drink as they.

"What's the matter, your friend can't handle a few pints?" she asked, reaching for another red cup and some iced tea.

"She could handle anything;" Gabriel said nobly. "But I wouldn't want her to pollute herself." Just as Arielle smiled at that, her heart sank when she saw him grab Erica by the waist. "You, we can pollute," he said softly into her ear, just as Arielle wedged herself between them and stood on her tippy toes to pop her head between their faces, grab each of them by the hand and lead them inside toward the lively music.

The home's sizeable dining room had become the dance floor and therefore, the centre of the party. From the giant speakers on either side of the DJ table, music boomed and bounced off the walls as a mix of melodious electro tunes set over hip hop beats had the crowd dancing. A group of attractive girls in the middle of the floor strutted sexy beat-triggered gyrations but the second Arielle hit the floor, all eyes moved to her.

The crowds parted around her as she took to the floor, giving her room to flow with the music and, with her arms, punctuate the rhythm of her hips. Not only was she the most graceful dancer on the floor but her moves were the most precise, even with her chunky rain boots on. Everyone watched her in awe like she was performing magic tricks with her little body, gliding and lifting as if she was hooked up to wires from the ceiling. Just like before during Arabella's song, she moved with the confidence of a dancer who had rehearsed the choreography a hundred times. While she danced, captivating every soul in the room, Gabriel and Erica stood side-by-side, watching her proudly. His eyes were on her, and that was all that was important. She had his attention now! And she smiled with every move, effortlessly winning hearts with every thrust and spin.

At the mercy of her cheering crowd, she jumped up onto the solid wood dining table that, for the night, was doubling as a stage.

From the sexy, almost interpretive jazz routine she had just thrown down, she went straight into a hard-core crunk routine to complement the hip hop track that was fading in. From up there, she soaked up applause and accolades while they watched and waited to see what she would pull next. She was the star of the party and she loved it but when she looked up to make sure Gabriel was still watching her as intently as everyone else, she was distraught not to see him or Erica anywhere. Her dancing slowed and she lost her rhythm as her eyes squinted against the strobe lights, scanning the room for their faces.

And then she spotted them across the room, embracing each other intimately, face to face amid the party lasers and dry ice smoke. She watched as they laughed together closely and, as if in slow motion, watched as their arms tightened around each other, hers around his neck and his around her waist, and she kissed him on the cheek with her glossy red lips. Arielle felt herself fall apart from the inside as she saw their faces meet, linger for a moment, then close their eyes and press their lips together. As they kissed, their passion was electric, and the sight of it felt like a punch to the stomach, causing her to double over in breathless agony.

Feeling queasy, she slumped down off the table and made a beeline for the bathroom. As soon as she got inside and slammed the door shut behind her, she threw up violently into the toilet before dropping down to the floor in despair. Suddenly, she heard coughing coming from inside the shower ring, and she pulled the curtain back to find three girls laughing, smoking and taking shots from a bottle of Baja Rosa.

"Well that almost killed my buzz!" said the girl on the far right who was wearing bejeweled sunglasses and had stacks of bangles up her arms. "Next time be sure to take a huge dump in front of us too!" The other two girls cackled deliriously. Arielle frowned and turned for the door.

"Oh don't be sad, she didn't mean it!" said the nice-looking blond girl in the middle who wore a white baby tee with a red sequined anchor on it.. "Hide out in here with us if you like; what's your name?" But Arielle could only pat herself on the neck to let them know she couldn't talk. The third girl in the tub, a little dread-locked redhead stood up excitedly and started using sign language. "I - have - been - looking - for - someone - to - test - my - new - skills - on!" she said with her hands, but Arielle just stared giggling at the funny hand dance  the girl was doing, fumbling to try and imitate the gestures with her own.

"Oh, I'm sorry," said the redhead, "I just assumed that since you couldn't talk, you probably knew sign language. My bad!"

The first girl suddenly realized she recognized her. "Ladies, this is the mute girl Gabe O'Faolain found almost dead on his beach a few months ago! They call her Arielle." Arielle nodded happily, glad to be recognized. "I'm Jacquie," said the blond. "This is Ella and this is Sophia," she said, gesturing to the dreadheaded girl and the girl with glasses on, respectively. They all heard a knock at the door. "We're in here!" they all yelled in unison.

"Not the Arielle that supposedly pushed Arabella's dancer?" asked Sophia scandalously, remembering the drama.

"According to Arabella, this one's a thunder-stealing sneak hussy!" said Jacquie. "But who really knows except Arielle here, who can't tell us either way?!"

All three girls laughed their drunken laughs, tumbling over in the bathtub over how fuming mad the attention-monger starlet was at being upstaged by some little unknown. "In any event, you're okay by me!" said Sophia. "Are you having a good time tonight?" Arielle wanted to nod that she was but her devastation of only moments ago was apparent on her face.

"Then stick with us, twinkle toes, things are about to get ridiculous!" Jacquie took a swig of the creamy pink tequila liqueur and passed it to Arielle, who, in her bleak melancholy, saw nothing wrong with polluting herself a bit if it meant she could feel even one-tenth as carefree and silly as the fun girls she had found. She put the bottle to her lips and tilted her head all the way back, drinking the entire contents of the bottle in one long chug.

"Pepto Bismol! Pepto Bismol!" chanted the girls, amazed at how the little dancer could drink. Arielle burped a strawberry-cream belch and the girls cheered wildly. "Let's go dance!" shouted Ella. They heard another knock at the bathroom door. "Occupado!" shouted Ella.

"Let's warm up in here first!" suggested Jacquie, standing up and reaching into her bag to reveal two small bottles of Moet & Chandon. "Courtesy of mother's secret wet bar!" she exclaimed as she carelessly popped one, sending the cork straight into the mirror and cracking it. All three girls laughed hysterically. More knocks were heard at the door.

"We're peeing! All of us . . . peeing!" yelled Sophia, falling over laughing and clumsily pouring champagne into her friends' mouths.

Meanwhile, out on the dance floor, Gabriel and Erica eventually came up from their steamy kiss and when they did, they saw that Arielle wasn't dancing up on the table anymore. They looked around the main floor then went upstairs to check the bedrooms but couldn't find her anywhere, so they went outside to search the grounds.

"Anyone fancy a love pill?" asked Sophia, using a shard of freshly cracked mirror to apply a coat of tangerine lipstick. "These ones feel really pretty," she said, winking and blotting her lips on a square of toilet paper. The other two replied with definite affirmation, and Arielle thought about it for a moment, unsure because she had never heard of love pills before.

"Have you ever been in love, Arielle?" asked Ella. Arielle nodded slowly, as if it pained her to admit it. "Well, judging by your face right now, I'd guess it didn't go so well. That's okay . . . this kind of love requires the co-operation of no one else!" Arielle perked up, but wondered how such a love could be possible.

"Let me tell you a little story," started Sophia. "Once upon a time in my life, I wasn't really sure I believed in love. My parents were divorcing, I never had a real boyfriend and any house pet I ever loved had either run away or gotten eaten by foxes. . . there were hungry foxes in the ravine behind my house, and there was a tar-black void where there should have been love in my life.

"But then, years later, I met a boy and he made my heart go upsie-daisy bang bang boom!" she said, emoting with her whole body to express the divinity that is new love. "Have you ever felt that?" she asked. "Have you ever felt so happy and so gorgeous, like the entire world was yours?!" Arielle, thoroughly engaged, nodded enthusiastically. "Well, it's always fun for a time, right? But eventually, life seems to get in the way and hearts grow cold, or grow hot in other directions . . . either way, it can't always stay the same way forever. But one time, while it was good and sweet and love coursed through me like a fatal injection, I remember thinking, 'Someone really ought to manufacture a pill that can do this to me, if only for a night at a time. . . '" She smiled deviously, and her friends smiled fiendishly back. She opened her hand to reveal four little pink caps that had tiny hearts stamped into them, and took one and placed it on the tip of her tongue.

"Ever tried 'em?" asked Jacquie as she took her pill and chased it with some champagne. Arielle shook her head curiously.

"Think of them as edible rainbows," said Ella as she put her pill in her mouth and swallowed it dry, then began chewing on a cubic chunk of purple gum.

"They're like rose-coloured goggles that come in pill form," added Jacquie, wiping her mouth on her sleeve. Arielle wasn't sure what she was getting herself into, but since her love couldn't seem to keep his hands off another girl, she decided she would take any love that was being offered to her. She nodded.

". . . then open wide," said Sophia as she stepped close so that her face was right in front of Arielle's. Arielle thought it strange, being so close with another girl, but allowed it because the tingling sensation she was feeling was better than the sadness she had been feeling just before. "Here comes original sin," said Sophie as she pressed her lips to Arielle's, unknowingly giving the mermaid her first real kiss. Arielle, floored by the tender feeling of being lip to lip with a warm-skinned, warm-blooded person, closed her eyes and allowed the pill to pass onto her tongue. Without a second thought she swallowed it, then swilled the entire remains of a champagne bottle after it.

The next few moments all blurred together. All was quiet, as if she was back under the ocean and the thick glimmer of the cool water dulled the sounds of the party and of the girls as they clapped and cheered.

"Welcome to the team!" said Sophia triumphantly, breaking the spell with her peppy, raspy voice. Another knock was heard at the door. "I'm . . . HAVING . . . a . . . FOOD . . . BABY!" she yelled in a constipated voice. Arielle smiled; her naughty yet nice new friends were making her feel like she was part of their group and momentarily, it helped to distract her from her peril. "By the way, the rain boots are a good look," said Sophia with a wink.

When all of their bottles were finished, the four of them burst out the door in a hyper-drunken explosion past the queue of people waiting for the bathroom. They took to the dance floor like an assault team, gripping each other's wrists as they jumped and danced around. Their bounciness commanded the attention of a group of guys standing by the dance floor pouring whiskey shots. As quickly as they could line them up, Arielle and the girls took them down and before they knew it, their three bottles of Jack were empty and all together they laughed out the door. At the end of the driveway a van cab awaited them, and, following her new friends, Arielle jumped in. Jacquie told the driver to take them to the nearest bar, since all the liquor stores were closed for the night and none of the girls felt like drinking keg beer. Arielle, beginning to feel the effects of the pill and definitely feeling the effects of the alcohol, began to feel the world spin around her. It was nauseating and exhilarating all at the same time, and she felt oddly comfortable in the company of her new friends, independent from Gabriel and his direct world for once. It felt nice. It gave her hope.

By the time they arrived at the bar, their eyes were like pies as they blissed out, feeling their ecstasy roll through them. Arielle felt her eyelids droop and her heart pulsate wildly, opening her up, unfolding her from the chest out as she slovenly followed her friends out of the cab. The bar, full of rough-looking and hard-partying people, seemed like a bright wonderland full of new friends she simply hadn't met yet. The drug's effects washed over her like a blanket of warmth as she drifted through the bar all the way to the back, where she found the most beautiful pieces of art hanging on the walls. When she looked closer, she realized that they were in fact photos of people, posing and showing off their bodies that were covered in sometimes colorful, often intricate and consistently beautiful stretches of art across their skin. She glanced over all the pictures, loving the pretty designs, wanting so much to decorate her own skin just like all these people had.

"First hit's free to tattoo virgins," said a raspy voice from the corner of the room. Arielle looked over to see a thin man with his nostrils pierced sitting beside a cushioned table. "It's a special we're running," he said with a crooked smile, and she noticed the artful, color-soaked designs that covered his arms from shoulders to wrists. "See anything you like?"

Arielle was thrilled! She had wanted a tattoo of her own ever since she heard Erica describe the meaning behind the moon tattooed to her wrist. While there were lots of ideas and pretty things to choose from, she could only really think of one thing that she would want to wear on her skin until the day she died: the bright, red sun that she had loved her whole life. The man gave her a pencil and some paper to sketch whatever she wanted so she drew for him a round ball of fire with rays that shone out from every angle. When she was done, she handed it to him and took a seat on his table. He prepped her skin, and went to work.

As the needle buzzed and her arm vibrated, she barely felt it when he pierced the thin skin of her white wrists and etched the design onto her. The sights and sounds of the bar moved around and through her, out then in, shrinking and expanding. She let it all go, allowing the world to spin around her while she sat still in the eye of the storm. When her new friends came around and found her getting inked, their wild laughter could be heard all across the bar. They were all so blissed, they pawed each other adoringly while they watched the tattoo artist make hot sunshine happen on her arm.

Meanwhile, back at the party, Gabriel and Erica frantically looked for her. Asking around did them no good because most people were too much in beast mode  to give straight answers, so they just searched. They searched the beach, combed the yard and checked every room in the house again but she appeared to have vanished without a trace.

"I should have kept a closer eye on her," said Gabriel, frustrated and blaming himself. "I should never have let her out of my sight." "I'm sure she's fine, and around somewhere," offered Erica, her eyes darting through the crowds for a little blonde head.

"I shouldn't have brought her to this party. I should've known tonight would be way too hectic. There are ten houses hosting parties in town tonight. Ten! I don't know why she would've left but I have a feeling she probably followed some people to one of the next parties."

"Okay so on to the next one, then?" suggested Erica. "We have nine other houses to hit; we'd better get started." And so they jumped into the Jeep and went to the next party.

After searching that house thoroughly and finding nothing, they continued on to the next. The people throwing the parties had printed off treasure map scorecards for everyone, so finding all the houses was easy. Finding Arielle, however, proved to be futile. After leaving not a couch cushion unturned or basement unexplored in all ten houses, they decided they should just wait for her at home.

The two of them sat up waiting for her in the family room all night. After three cups of tea and what felt like several hours, Erica passed out, slumbering peacefully on Gabriel's lap while he kept vigil, sitting up and willing Arielle to arrive home before his parents woke up. He too, in his exhausted state, was about to pass out as well when he heard the low rumbling of a truck pulling into the driveway. He jumped up and ran out to her just as she stumbled from the truck bed down to the driveway, and he caught her before she hit the ground. Before he could say or ask anything, the truck peeled out and took off down the road, leaving a cloud of dust around them and the bass of their loud sound system in their ears. As he held her light little body up, her groggy eyes looked adoringly into his, already feeling like it had been a lifetime since she last saw his face. She was wearing a hooded sweatshirt that belonged to a person unknown, and she was covered in sand and dirt and her hair was a sweaty mess. He wished he could ask her what he got up to but, alas, he couldn't. As he looked down at her with gladness, her heavy eyes stayed open just enough to observe his while he held her. He was inspecting her with care and concern; she was saturating herself with the sight and smell of him, and decided that the moment she'd been waiting for was upon her. Finally, they were alone, and he was holding her so close, and she could feel that this was her time to make a move and make him see her for more. In her head she heard the voices of her sisters; *KISS HIM! KISS HIM! KISS HIM!* They beckoned her to take the chance, so she dared herself and puckered up.

As she lifted her chin to square her face off with his, she was so close to his mouth, she could already taste him. She closed her eyes and licked her lips . . .

*Creak! Bang!* They both turned their heads to the house to see the screen door shut behind Erica, who had come out to the porch. Arielle glared at her; she had been ruined once again. But Erica, pleasantly oblivious, just yawned and rubbed her eyes. She looked beautiful, even dressed in pajama pants with a plaid throw blanket around her shoulders. "Oh good, you're home," she said with another big yawn. "Gabriel shat a chicken with worry; try not to disappear like that!"

Arielle, exhausted, burnt-out and horribly disappointed, collapsed into Gabriel's arms. As her tired little body went limp, he lifted her easily and carried her up to her room.

He laid her down gently and pulled off her boots. Erica peeled the dirty sweater off her and noticed a big, white bandage taped to her forearm. "Think she burned herself?" she whispered, pointing to it.

"Maybe she cut herself!" he said nervously, beginning to peel back the bandage to see what was under it.

"Leave it for now!" urged Erica, smacking his hand away. "Looks like whatever happened, it was cleaned for her; people who stock proper bandages and medical tape tend to also stock rubbing alcohol and Polysporin."

"Good point," he said as he tucked her in, pulling her blankets up to her chin and then tiptoeing to the door. Relieved she was home, Gabriel could finally just relax. "Well, now that I know she's safe, I am suddenly *starving*! How about you?"

"I could definitely eat," replied Erica gladly. "What did you have in mind?"

Gabriel led her to the kitchen and pulled five large potatoes out of the pantry. "Well, if there is one thing I consistently crave after an entire night of sleepless worrying, it is a big, dirty poutine!"

Erica's eyes widened with delight, as she had been craving something heavy, salty and warm all night. "I like the way you think, sir!" she said breathlessly. "I, too, have been known to find myself face-deep in curds and gravy. A grand idea!"

Gabriel laughed. "Honestly, I don't trust anyone who says they don't love a hot, steaming pile of the French-Canadian artery-clogger." He reached into the fridge and pulled out a gravy boat, emptying its contents into a small saucepan on the stove. "This will bend your head!" he said, switching on the deep fryer. Erica grinned hungrily; golden-fried junk food was her weakness. And now, it appeared, so was he.

The rising sun began to peer in through the kitchen windows, drying up the dew and playing upon the wicker ceiling fan blades. When the poutine was done, they grabbed forks and a bottle of red wine and headed down to the beach to enjoy them together.

Seated comfortably on an upside-down rowboat, Gabriel generously let Erica dig her fork in for the first bite. She savored the salty goodness like it was the finest snack in the world, and they both hummed with their eyes closed while they enjoyed each cheesy forkful. She barely noticed the errant gravy as it dribbled down her chin.

# twenty-four

# Rain Dance

Arielle woke up a few hours later to the sound of raindrops falling on her window pane. She sat up and looked outside to see misty showers, descending around the pockets of sunshine that burst from the clouds. She didn't remember going to bed, and when she looked down at herself, she saw the bandage that covered her wrist and had to think very hard for a moment to remember what had happened to her the night before. Carefully, she peeled it back to reveal her bright, yellow sun! There it was on her wrist, just like she had requested, covered in a clear, gelatinous lotion. She was thrilled! It was vibrant and pretty, and she loved it already. She wiped the lotion off to reveal a perfectly healed tattoo, as smooth as if it had always been there. As she admired her new flesh accessory in the mirror, she heard the sound of Gabriel's voice carry in from under her window. He was jovial; it sounded like he was laughing at something. When she peered out, she saw him with Erica, holding her in his arms. She felt her chest tighten at the sight.

They were laughing together, dancing barefoot in the sand as the rain came gently down on their heads and down their backs. Their hair and clothes were soaked and heavy, and the cuffs of Erica's pajama pants left brushstrokes across the wet sand. Their hands were clasped tightly, and their eyes only saw each other.

She watched them with envy as they enjoyed their romantic moment. She imagined how unforgettable a moment like that would be to share with another. The rain that fell around them was like an avalanche of glitter, making their dewy skin glow, smoothing their clothes to their bodies. Erica rested her head on Gabriel's wet chest as they swayed. Gabriel had found a girl to dance with him in the rain.


It was happening right before her eyes, and she felt powerless to stop it. He was falling in love with another, and drifting further away by the second. She knew she was losing him, but was suddenly not quite sure she ever had him in the first place. Such agony it was, for poor Arielle could not even go out into the rain to cut in. Defeated, she felt her hangover kick in and went to bed with the covers over her head. Still exhausted and still devastated, she fell back to sleep.

When she awoke several hours later, the rain had stopped and the sun had come out. Erica and Gabriel were no longer outside her window, and it appeared to be a brand new day. Then, just as she stood to stretch, she began to hear the unmistakable song of her sisters so she quickly threw on her scuffed rubber boots and ran out to the rock pile they had swum up to the last time.

She skipped across the rocks and crouched down to greet her sisters. They were all dying to know how it was all going.

"Has he asked you to be his wife yet?" asked her eldest sister. Sadly, the little one shook her head '*no.*'

"Has he kissed you on the lips yet?" the second one inquired, but that too was met with a disappointing '*no.*' It was clear that things had not been progressing in their sister's favor.

The third sister's eyes narrowed at Arielle's sad, defeated face. "So that's it?" she asked, unimpressed. "You gave your voice to the witch and left us all behind for one chance at real love, and already you've given up?" Arielle lowered her eyes in shame. She knew she stood to lose everything if she did not win his heart, but what could she do now? He was falling more in love with another girl with every heartbeat.

"You mustn't give up yet! Make him yours!" said the fourth. "Just be sure to always be prettier than her!"

The fifth chimed in. "You must be lovelier than her, too! You must capture his attention!"

"Shower him with affection!" said the fourth. "Make him crave your kiss!"

"It's all in your hands, sister," warned the third. "It is time to get in their way!" The little one considered the implications. She wondered how she'd get in their way . . .

"Be grateful the witch only took your voice," said the eldest, sternly. "Now, use the rest of your charms to win him! Make him know that you're the one for him!"

The two-legged mermaid stood up with a fresh resolve. She would not give up just yet! She decided she would do whatever it took, follow him anywhere she had to, and do anything at all to get closer to him and take him back from Erica.

"The eels said that your fins can grow back. Is that true?" asked the third sister. Arielle nodded. "Then won't you jump in? Come play with us!" Arielle took a step back and shook her head, for as much as she was tempted to jump in, she knew it would be far too risky to try and dry her tail off without being seen. "Come live for three hundred years under the sea with your family!" said the second, reaching for the ankles of her boots. But Arielle quickly stepped out of her reach and bid them all good-bye to run back up to the house. It was time to begin to hatch some love schemes.

## twenty-five

## The Best Laid Sardines

---

When she got back into the house, Arielle collected an armload of women's magazines from the coffee table and stole them away to her room. As she flipped through them, she ripped out pages of her favorite looks and laid them out across the rug, deciding that her first task would be to update and personalize her wardrobe because he'd never want her for his love so long as everything she wore reminded him of Dagmara. Once she'd collected enough ideas, she took a pair of scissors, a needle and some thread and she went to work altering and improving upon the pieces she'd been wearing. Having no money for new clothes and not wanting to be given anything more from the already generous family, the crafty girl commenced her re-vamping project and re-created some of the sexy styles she was seeing in all the magazines.

By the time she was finished wildly snipping, sewing, re-buttoning and tying knots in things, she had six new outfits, all hotter and more grown-up than anything she was working with before. Modeling them for herself and feeling satisfied with her work, she examined herself in a long mirror to see where else she could make improvements. All the women in the magazines seemed to have the same dark, lush eyelashes and next to the mascara ads, her own light blonde lashes looked nonexistent. Magazine girls had all sorts of colours painted onto their faces, so she decided her next step would be to try makeup.

In Lucia's bathroom drawers, Arielle discovered a wide array of lipsticks and eye shadows, so she began to experiment with looks and colours. Once her lips were a glossy fuchsia and her eyes were lined and smoky, she decided she looked ready for the great reacquisition. She knew she would have to be sneaky and would possibly have to be cruel, but desperate times, she felt, called for desperate measures, and she had never even heard of times as desperate as those of her current experience.

When she got downstairs in her new-old clothes, she found the kitchen floors covered in drop-sheets and the wall moldings lined with green masking tape. On the one end, Lucia was painting a big orca whale. On the other end, Cliff was painting a shark.

"Good morning, Arielle!" they said in unison before laughing at their old married folk synchronization. Arielle smiled brightly, liking very much the direction the kitchen decor was taking. "Do you want to help us paint?" asked Lucia as she dipped her brush into her colorful palette. "We're doing an underwater scene; paint any creature you like!" Having nothing better to do until Gabriel would finally re-emerge, Arielle picked up a paintbrush and helped herself to some paints from a big plastic tub full of colours. She sat for a moment in front of the bare space across the middle, then when she knew what she would be painting, went to work re-creating from memory the portrait of a sea-turtle she had once known. Lucia and Cliff were blown away by her amazingly detailed rendition.

A mere few hours later, the wall was almost done and looked just like a window to an undersea menagerie. When Gabriel finally got up and came downstairs, he was shocked and surprised to see the wall.

"What prompted this giant indoor mural?" he asked as he scratched his head and lumbered hungrily toward the fridge.

"Well, your mother and I were just thinking how sweet it would have been if we had a million-dollar view to the North as well as to the South. So we got the idea to paint one for us! And since we already get stunning sunsets out the front, we thought it would be sweet to look under water out the back!" said Cliff.

"How long have you guys been working on this?" asked Gabriel with a yawn. "It looks like you're almost done!"

"I did the orca, your father did the Great White, and the rest are by Arielle, painted as intricately as portraits of well-known friends. Look at the detail in the turtle, and the smile on that dolphin, and the impossibly perfect gelatinousness she captured in that jellyfish. Aren't they amazing?"

Gabriel smiled at Arielle proudly, ever amused by her little surprises. "Isn't our little foundling just the most talented little thing?" he said as he walked over to her and rested his strong hands on her shoulders, softly rubbing them as she kneeled in front of the school of herring she was painting around a reef. She closed her eyes and enjoyed the feeling of his touch; moments like these had become so few and far between since Erica's arrival. She needed his touch; it was the only thing she delighted in. Besides, of course, the surrealistically handsome sight of him and the gentle rasp of his voice. And the smell of him. *Oh, the sweet smell of him.* She breathed him in.

Just then, Erica walked in from outside, breaking the spell as she always did. "Good morning, all!" she said perkily as she finger-combed her messy hair into a low ponytail. "Wow, great work guys!" she said as she stepped toward the mural, causing Gabriel to step aside so she could get a better look. Arielle quietly fumed over the shoulder rub sabotage and while she wondered what her first retaliation would be, Erica's dewy face darkened to a shade of sickly green. "Eww, what's that smell?" she asked as she covered her mouth.

Lucia pointed at the wedge of blue cheese on the tray they had been snacking from. "No, not that," replied Erica through cupped lips, looking around. "Are there sardines in here?"

Gabriel bit down on a cracker. "There are! Mom put 'em on these crackers, you want?" At that very second, while the pungent smell of smoky canned fish filled her nostrils and the previous night's poutine began creeping back up her throat, Erica had no choice but to flee the room, gagging uncontrollably and gasping for fresh air.

Lucia and Cliff laughed and went back to their painting while Gabriel followed Erica out onto the patio. He closed the door behind him, lest the scent follow him out.

"That was a close one!" she said as she fanned herself with her hand. "I'm sorry you had to see that; I have this thing about sardines . . . I can't be within ten feet of them without puking my guts up."

"As you nearly just demonstrated!" he said. "That gag of yours could make a bulimic weep. What is it about sardines?"

"Freshman year in student rez, these kids pulled a prank where they filled a bucket with gross stuff and leaned it against a guy's door. Then they knocked on the door and ran away, leaving the bucket in such a way so that it spilled in when the guy opened it," she explained.

"They gave him a 'leaner,'" he offered.

"Yes!" she concurred. "Anyway it was filled with sour milk blended with canned sardines. You can imagine how that combo would reek. It took weeks before the odor even began to fade from the hallway. We had to plug our noses, hold our breath, and sprint through it to and from classes so we wouldn't all yak. But that first night, before the cleaning ladies had a chance to Lysol the shit out of the carpets, the stinky hallway proved itself an impassable gauntlet for a crew of kids coming home from the bars. Five people puked in that hallway that night. I had never been so disgusted, and I haven't been since. Ever since then, sardines equal puke for me. It's the cross I bear."

"That's hilarious!" he said, amused. "But since you're such a puker, I feel I should let you know right now that I personally cannot see or smell puke without needing to puke myself. It's a reflex, and so far, an infallible one. So I'll be sure to Food Bank the club pack of sardines we have in the pantry!"

"No, no," said Erica, embarrassed. "You guys eat what you want; just warn me and I'll stay away!"

"Nonsense," he replied. "We don't even like them all that much. I think they were on super sale and we just eat them because we have so many. I doubt we'd miss them terribly."

"Well thank you, sir," she said in her most seductive tone, "I still appreciate the sacrifice, however insignificant."

Unbeknownst to the two chatting and flirting on the porch, Arielle had been eavesdropping on them from inside an open window. Jealously watching the two, she began to wonder how she could use Erica's sardine aversion to keep her away from Gabriel. On her way out of the kitchen, she stealthily swiped three cans from the pantry stack. Carrying them up to her room, she was struck with a wonderful, awful idea. She decided she would smear them all around Erica's room so that she wouldn't be able to stay there anymore and would therefore have to leave because there were no more bedrooms. Excitedly she waited for night to fall and for everyone to go to sleep so that she could sneak out and kick off her smear campaign.

That night, the moon was fat and bright as she moved swiftly down to the boathouse. She peered in and could see that Erica was fast asleep, snoring with her mouth open, belly-down and lying like a starfish. Very carefully did the scheming little mermaid slip inside the door and close it gently behind her. It was time to be ruthless.

She reached into the pocket of her robe and pulled out the first can. Muffling it with a t-shirt she found on the floor, Arielle cracked it open and used her fingers to mash it into an oily brown paste. When it was ready, she began generously dabbing the mushy sardines onto inconspicuous surfaces around the room. She dabbed a bit behind the headboard and in the corners of Erica's pillowcases. She tucked a bit under the mattress and wiped her hands inside the duvet. She applied it under the tongues of all of Erica's sneakers and into the pockets of her jackets, tops, and jeans before moving on to purses and bags, smearing it into fabric lining and inside zippered pockets. She even went so far as to dab it into the padding of all the bikini tops hanging on the bathroom doorknob, so that when the sardine smell ripened to full potential, not even Erica's breasts would be safe from the stink. It would drive her crazy, then it would drive her away. Of this, young Arielle was sure.

When all three cans were empty, she slipped back out the door and into the night. Stopping only to bury the cans in the sand, she dashed back to her bed to dream about the rude awakening to greet her rival come morning. She felt underhanded and vicious, but at this point, she had to be willing to play dirty if she was to ever reclaim her prince.

When Erica awoke the next day, her room was bright and warm. She rolled over on her pillow, stretched and rubbed her eyes. It was a beautiful day outside and she looked forward to it. Then suddenly, in the middle of a great yawn, her face was assaulted with a repulsive smell. It was a fishy one she knew and hated . . . Sardines! But how?

The stink was all around her, in her pillow that she buried her face in, and in the clothes she reached for to shield her nose and mouth. She gagged and ran into her bathroom, shut the door and turned on the shower. The bathroom was the only area Arielle hadn't thought to attack, so Erica was able to stave off vomit urges by inhaling from her fragrant shampoo bottle. Once she was brave enough to emerge, she threw her robe on, plugged her nose, and ran for the door.

Minutes later, she was back with Gabriel. He had laughed at her the whole way down, insisting she was paranoid but when he smelled it for himself, he couldn't deny that something definitely smelled fishy in her room. Arielle watched mirthfully from her window while Gabriel went in and Erica stayed far back from the door with her hand over her mouth and nose.

A few minutes later, Gabriel emerged with Erica's bags in his hands. Arielle rejoiced, certain that he was helping her vacate her room and exit their lives. She began to prepare her fake-sad goodbye hug, until she noticed that he wasn't carrying her bags to the driveway, but was carrying them into the main house!

"Seriously, it's no problem!" she overheard him tell Erica as he led her up the stairs and into his room.

"But you don't have to give up your bed;" she replied, "I am more than happy to take the couch."

"You may have my bed, Miss Erica," he insisted like a perfect gentleman as he set her things down on his big wooden dresser. She picked up one of his pillows and sniffed it for fishy traces. Nothing but sweet-smelling Gabriel scent there.

"Thank you," she replied, graciously accepting. A jolt of excitement coursed through her and made the hair on her neck stand up. "I don't mean to displace you, but I appreciate your generosity."

"What kind of host would I be?" he asked, smiling. His demeanor oozed next-level chivalry, the kind she hadn't witnessed since her own late father. Arielle cringed, realizing as her plan backfired that she should have known better. She briefly considered doing to Gabriel's room what she did to Erica's but ultimately, she couldn't run the risk of driving them both out. So it was back to square one for her, and back to mentally concocting other ways by which to ruin their budding romance.

# twenty-six

## Like a Date

Gabriel's friend Rourke arrived early the next morning by way of the beach. He wore a tattered salmon Polo and ripped Bermuda shorts, the outfit he was last seen in the night of the ten parties, except torn up and covered in dirt from head to toe. Cliff, sitting on the patio with a mug of butter rum coffee, nudged his wife to look up from her magazine. It was Rourke all right, approaching with a dramatic hobble and looking like he had just crawled out of a grave. They both burst out laughing at the sight of him.

"What happened?" asked Lucia. "What gutter did you just wake up in?"

"Ya, which dirt mound had its way with you?" asked Cliff.

"Thank you, I am fine Mr. and Mrs. O'Faolain," he replied in his best brown-noser voice. "Might Gabriel be around today? I was hoping he wouldn't mind a couch surfer for the next few days."

"Gabriel is inside making breakfast," said Lucia, "but I'm afraid his couch might be spoken for at the moment." Rourke's face darkened; he had been laying claim to that couch for almost two decades, and had yet to meet a worthy challenger. "What do you mean?" he asked. "Gabriel said I could crash up there whenever!" "I'm afraid he has a lady friend staying with him right now," said Cliff, rubbing it in ever so slightly. "So it might be a little crowded up there."

Rourke grinned. "I knew that boy would eventually break down," he said as he pulled the cord to the outdoor shower and began to rinse himself off. Cliff and Lucia chuckled. "Yep, I've known all along that he'd give in to Arabella some day." They briefly considered setting him straight, but decided not to ruin the surprise.

As Rourke climbed the stairs, he could hear a girl's voice singing Crimson & Clover from inside Gabriel's room. It was a little off-key, but that's what audio techs were for, and anyway, she sounded pretty enough. As he approached, he could see white bed sheets being lifted and tucked through the crack in the door.

"Arabella, what a lovely surprise!" he said as he gallantly flung open the door. "I knew our Gabe would come . . . WHO ARE YOU?" he shrieked as he jumped back, shocked to find a brunette where he was expecting a blonde superstar. "Oh, excuse me, madam," he said, confused and somewhat annoyed. "Might Gabriel be around?"

Erica giggled at the stiff, try-hard mannerisms of the guy. "Certainly, good sir," she said, trying to keep a straight face. "I'm sure you'll find he hasn't ventured far." She gestured elegantly with her hands. "And who, pray tell, is Arabella?"

Rourke stuck his hands in his dirty, ripped pockets and swaggered into the room slowly. "Oh, she's just this huge starlet we know, no biggie," he began. "She's sold like a gazillion albums, is pretty much the most bangin' smokeshow on the planet and she's so aesthetically relevant, she has a staff member assigned to each and every aspect of her image."

"Which aspects specifically?" asked Erica, feigning star-struck wonderment.

"For example," he began, catching on to her subtle mockery and wanting to shut her down, "there is April, who makes sure all her clothes smell like cotton candy; Joanie, who follows her around with hair glossing mist and a teasing comb; and Pam, who makes sure there are no mutants or overly-blemished people in the crowd when Arabella gets photographed with fans."

Erica's eyes widened. "You must be speaking about Arabella Behrensen, chanteuse extraordinaire!" she said as if bowled right over. "But why on earth would she be here?"

Rourke grinned a weasly grin. He wanted to oust the girl more than Arielle did, determined to reclaim his crash spot. "She is kind of Gabriel's long-time love and girlfriend," he said casually. Just then, Gabriel walked in wearing nothing but a white towel that came up to about three inches below his board-short tan line. Erica silently swooned; she couldn't believe she wasn't bored of his perfection yet.

"Buddy you look like hell! Where have you been?" Gabriel asked, laughing at the sorry state his friend was in.

"Thanks buddy!" replied Rourke sarcastically. "I've been in hell, actually! I was hoping to get some rest on my trusty old couch here but it appears you already have a squatter," he said, looking Erica up and down.

"Erica, this is my old buddy Rourke," said Gabriel, almost apologetically.

"A pleasure to make your acquaintance," said Rourke before Erica had the chance to say anything. He turned to Gabriel and looked at him gravely. "May I have a word with you in private?"

"Umm, sure," said Gabriel as he tucked his towel tighter and stepped out onto the balcony, and Rourke shut the door behind them, leaving Erica to finish making the bed. "Okay so are you going to tell me what happened to you?" asked Gabriel.

"I WAS KIDNAPPED!" barked Rourke angrily. "This crazy cougar slipped something into my drink and the next thing I knew, I was in her dark basement zip-tied to a crushed velvet bed spread! She violated me, then left me in there, man; what day is it?"

"Wednesday," said Gabriel, cool and unsurprised. "What exactly did she do to you?"

"A more appropriate question would be, 'what *didn't* she do to me!' I was gagged and blindfolded . . . it was weird, man!"

Gabriel laughed. "Violated? You? Last time I checked, you were into that freaky stuff AND dying for, and I quote, 'the *taste* of the *coug*.'"

"I *was* kind of into it!" Rourke said, his voice cracking. ". . .Until she started putting swimming caps on me, gluing doll hair to it, making me use pacifiers and pinching my nipples with barbeque tongs!" Rourke, paranoid and broken, lifted his shirt to show Gabriel the nicks and bruises the tongs left behind. "My nipples ache. I just want to go to sleep and never wake up," he said dramatically.

"But she didn't rape you?" Gabriel asked him, confused.

"SHE RAPED MY WILL TO LIVE!" yelled Rourke, shuddering. "The last thing I remembered was cheetah print and dimpled cleavage . . . and then I woke up in that windowless dungeon! I begged for water but all she'd bring me was Tang, and I think there was Nyquil in it 'cause I was drowsy the whole time. She wouldn't stop tickling my feet . . . I *HATE* it when people touch my feet!" Rourke stopped to catch his breath. "But I escaped," he continued. "I ground the zip ties off on the bedpost and escaped through the window well. I came straight here; you must have been worried sick about me!"

Gabriel thought about his response for a moment. He wanted to tell Rourke he'd been worried, but he knew he was a terrible liar and it had honestly not occurred to him that Rourke could've been missing, since Rourke had never been in the habit of announcing his comings and goings anyway. He went on to describe more details of his stint in cougar captivity, but in the end, the fact remained that Gabriel's room was full up as long as Erica was staying.

"*WHY* is she even here?!" Rourke demanded angrily. Gabriel suddenly realized how grateful he was to be trading Rourke's company for Erica's. "She's an old friend of the family here visiting, and she's great; I'm pretty sure I'm falling in love with her!" Rourke made a disgusted face, and suddenly they heard rustling up on the roof.

"What was *that*?" whispered Rourke with fear in his eyes, stepping closer to Gabriel like a frightened child.

"Probably just raccoons," Gabriel answered, stepping away from his wet, dirty friend. But it wasn't raccoons up there, it was Arielle on the roof. She had climbed up the trellis from her bedroom window moments earlier and was perched up there, eavesdropping on their conversation. But the Pacific coast humidity had left some slick shingles and she slipped on one, sliding down to the eaves trough on her belly. But she held on for dear life, and, as quiet as could be, she pulled herself back up, perched herself low and continued to listen.

"Anyway," continued Gabriel thoughtfully, "I think I love her."

"I HEARD YOU THE FIRST TIME!" barked Rourke. "WHY?"

Gabriel laughed. There were so many reasons why. "First of all, she's sweeter, more interesting and more beautiful than any girl I've ever met." Arielle heard that, and for her it felt like taking a knife to the heart. "And on top of all that, she's cool," he continued. "It's like I'm hot for her in every single way I could be. I've waited for this. I'm going to make her my wife!"

Arielle's vision went black and she fainted, tumbling sideways down the roof. On her way down, she smashed her shin hard against the patio railing, breaking her tibia.

Rourke jumped at the sound of the tumble. "Seriously what the tits was that?"

"Fat raccoons," insisted Gabriel. "Anyway, bud, I'm gonna get dressed, then I'll drive you to the ferry, okay?"

"You're ridiculous," replied Rourke, sneering.

"Me? Why?" asked Gabriel, eyeing Rourke. "Because, between the two of us, it's *you* that looks like a strung-out, preppy, nuclear holocaust survivor."

Rourke grumbled. "You're ridiculous for letting your life's biggest opportunity slip away so you can propose to some nameless broad you've only known a week."

Gabriel rolled his eyes. "She isn't nameless; as I mentioned when I introduced you, her name is Erica and she's an angel." They both looked inside at Erica while she sashayed around the room in a white cotton dress, tidying and making room for her things. The sight of her made Gabriel genuinely happy. The sight of Gabriel in love made Rourke feel jealous, frustrated, annoyed, and a little bit gassy. He belched. Gabriel pretended it didn't happen. "I haven't only known her a week," he said, "I've known her my whole life, actually. But I haven't seen her in years until she arrived about a week ago. Except for the morning after my birthday when she found me washed ashore . . . in any case, if you haven't been picking up what I've been putting down, I'll tell you again: I don't want Arabella! I think she's kind of crazy – at least, too crazy for me. Some rock star or actor will love her 'cause they'll understand her type more, but if you think she's so amazing, YOU yourself should take a swing at 'er!"

Rourke was so angry, he ripped out a few strands of his own hair. "It's Arabella, you tit!" he shouted. "I can't just go for her, no one can . . . except YOU!" The fact that Gabriel had repeatedly turned her down was the stuff of legend in their circles. "For some asinine reason, the gods have smiled on you, giving you Arabella as an option! So do her- please just do her- so that the rest of us may live vicariously! Take one for the team, man, we're dying out here!" Gabriel tried to change the subject but Rourke wouldn't speak of anything else. "Tell me- how does one say 'no, thank you' to the body that launched a hundred million shower skeets?"

Gabriel pondered that for a moment. "A hundred million? Really?" he asked dryly.

"Her 'Hot n' Steamy' video saw over a hundred million YouTube hits, so YES, a hundred million," said Rourke not only matter-of-factly, but as if Gabriel was weird for not knowing. "And that's not even counting skeets made from MEMORY of her 'Hot n' Steamy' video, that would therefore not count as hits."

Gabriel sighed while he tightened his towel tuck. He realized he had no idea why he still bothered explaining anything to Rourke. "I don't know what to tell you," he said. "I'm off the market! Maybe forever."

Rourke put his fingers to his temples, as if Gabriel's insolence was giving him a migraine. "Arabella is richer, more famous, sexier, thinner, but with bigger breasts, blonder—"

Gabriel interrupted him. "Those are only pluses according to personal preference," he said.

"No way!" shouted Rourke in the passionate way he liked to assert his opinion when he knew he didn't have a leg to stand on. "Those are universal preferences! Everyone prefers blondes; gentlemen prefer blondes! Blondes break necks in ways brunettes can't touch."

"First of all," replied Gabriel, "you're not a gentleman - not even close. Secondly, necks only break because they're straining to see if the face matches the Barbie-doll hair. But often, it's just a lot of eye makeup and skin like orange peels. Or, trannies in wigs."

Rourke stood there dumbfounded, with nothing to rebut. Gabriel burst out laughing and told him he was only kidding, but that he was, regrettably, not kidding about the lack of space to accommodate another guest in his room. So he sent him out to the boathouse loft for some sardine aroma therapy. The stink was ripe in there, even with all the windows open to air it out and after only twenty minutes of bearing it, Rourke asked Gabriel to just take him to the bus station.

Erica came outside with a bag of grapes, a towel around her shoulders and a book under her arm. Headed for the beach with intentions of zoning out under the sun, she was shocked to find Arielle laying limp and lifeless on a bush beneath the deck.

"Arielle! Are you okay?" she shrieked. In a panic, she shook the girl's little white shoulders to wake her. She dropped what she was carrying and was winding up to try the old slap approach when Arielle's eyes flew open and she sat up. Arielle looked up at the roof and down at her broken leg, and realized that she must've fallen. She remembered the last thing she heard Gabriel say. She looked her enemy dead in the eyes.

Erica reached out and took her hands to lift her but when Arielle rose to standing, her shinbone made a loud *SNAP!* and she collapsed to the ground. Erica screamed, shuddered with her entire body and ran into the house for help, leaving Arielle on the ground with her bones jutting out of her skin.

Still groggy, Arielle reached her healing hands out and smoothed out the broken bone. She gently set it back in its place and massaged it until it was all better, leaving zero evidence behind that it was ever broken at all. Moments later, Erica came running out with Cliff and Lucia in tow. Expecting to find her in a mangled, broken heap, they were surprised and relieved to find Arielle sitting comfortably, looking perfectly fine.

"Did you hurt your leg, sweetie?" asked Lucia. Arielle smiled and shrugged, then her eyes turned to Erica.

"I definitely heard a snap!" Erica assured them. "Someone ought to check her legs– I would, but broken bones give me the heebie-jeebies."

"Cliffy, check her legs," urged Lucia. So he sat her up straight and picked up her left foot. She didn't even wince, nor did she when he picked up the other. Her feet carried only their usual sharp pain, (which she was pretty well used to by then) and her legs were smooth, unmarred and healthy as ever. He applied pressure all the way from her ankles past her knees but she was apparently injury-free so he pulled her up to her feet once again, this time to stand well as ever. The whole time, she didn't take her eyes off her adversary. Lucia asked her if she wanted anything like a glass of juice or something, but Arielle just barely shook her head in response, fixated. Her staring was starting to creep Erica out.

Since everyone appeared to be okay, Erica picked up her book and grapes and towel and continued out to the beach. She would've sworn she had just heard Arielle's leg break in a loud, bone-breaking crack, but she had just seen the leg with her own two eyes and it was certainly not broken . . . anymore. She wondered if she'd imagined it all or, if she wasn't crazy or hallucinating, that perhaps Arielle simply had special powers and could heal herself like Wolverine. She wondered what she would've seen if she didn't run off to get help . . .

Scouting out a nice, sheltered sun trap, she shook and laid her towel out and as soon as she did, Arielle flew past her to plant herself upon it. "Oh, hey Blondie," she said, surprised. Arielle said nothing like always, but sat there on Erica's towel continuing her one-sided stare-down. "Do I have a booger or something?" she asked, ". . . because you're creeping me hard and I'm startin' to think you're just a little lesbo!" Erica laughed and said that of course she was kidding. She pulled her dress off to reveal a mismatched bikini in orange and brown, made up of her last two pieces of swimwear that didn't smell like sardines.

Arielle's eyes swept across Erica's body, from her tanned toes with their bubble gum pink nails to her rounded hips, up to her full bosom. She envied the way Erica's breasts, mountains next to her own modest pair, filled out their bikini cups, overflowing amply yet still understatedly. In size, she was so much more than Arielle. In warmth and in voice and in meat on her bones, she had more and therefore was more. She was soft and natural, and Arielle could see why Gabriel wanted her. Her body looked cosy and strong. She looked her nemesis up and down, taking inventory of rival assets. On her face she wore a look of heightened concentration. She hated Erica, or at least would if she wasn't so kind and lovely.

Erica averted her eyes. She decided that openly staring must have been a commonplace and acceptable thing wherever Arielle was from, and thought nothing more of it. To her, Arielle was odd but harmless.

Arielle looked down at her wispy body and suddenly she felt small and insignificant. Wrapped in a nightie and hidden away, her humble frame left her much to be desired. Sighing mournfully, she laid herself down next to Erica. She felt sorry for herself, and despised the feeling.

When Gabriel returned home, he parked the Jeep and wasted no time running around the house and out to the beach where he knew he would find his woman. He acknowledged Arielle with a pat on the head, then sat down in the sand to face Erica. Wasting no time at all, he asked her if she'd like to have dinner with him the next night.

The question made her laugh. "I've eaten every single meal with you since I got here!" she replied. Arielle stared at her with jealous eyes.

"That's true," he said. "But I mean dinner, just you and me. Someplace other than home. Interested?"

She was so very interested, but played it cool just for fun. After all, she had been wishing for this moment for a while. "Would this be like a date?" she asked cheekily. She had to savour the moment. "I believe it would be, yes," he replied, smiling because he already knew the answer. Her keenness was written all over her face.

"That sounds swell," she said with a nod, popping a grape into her mouth. She feigned aloofness but deep down, she was very excited since she had a dress that she'd been looking for an excuse to wear.

"Perfect. I already made reservations," said Gabriel, pulling a pear out of his pocket and biting into it with his big white teeth. She called him a cocky bitch and tossed a grape at his head. He wrapped his arms around hers and with the weight of his body, pushed her down to her towel. Arielle looked away; it was too much to bear.

Then he leaned into her, like her face was a shiny new prize that had his eyes twinkling. He pressed his warm cheeks to hers, first one side, then the other. "Can you be ready by eight?" he asked, even though that very night they would definitely eat together, as well as breakfast and lunch the next day leading up to their date. She nodded, and kissed him on the tip of his nose.

## twenty-seven

## The Ring

---

That afternoon, Gabriel stayed back with his dad to wash and wax the family's fleet of cars while Lucia and the girls went into town to hit the salon. Arielle didn't really want to go but when they finally found her hiding up on the roof, they insisted she join them if for nothing more than to experience the girly rite of passage that would take care of her brittle cuticles.

When they arrived, Lucia sat down for her usual gloss treatment and blow-dry while Ava got a fill for her eyelash extensions. Demetra had her toes painted the same turquoise as her headphones, while Erica picked a hot fuchsia for hers. Arielle perused the polish rack and was deciding on a colour when she found herself in front of the airbrush design wall, marveling at all the colourful detail.

"You wan' to wear long?" asked the little Asian manicurist who had crept up to her, wearing long purple talons and tattooed-on eyebrows that were black with a faint hint of blue. She took Arielle's hand and inspected her nail beds. "Long look better," she said in her endearingly broken English while running her nails over Arielle's short, rough tips. All of the designs on the wall were colorful, vibrant and required at least three inches of acrylic on each finger just so the designs would fit. She pored over every nail glued to the board until at last, she found the perfect one! It had flames of magnificent orange, red and yellow, sitting upon a base of shimmering gold. It even had three black rhinestones across it! She had never seen anything so pretty adorn someone's digits. It was magical and badass, all at the same time. She pointed to it, nodded seriously, and prepared herself for a hot transformation.

The manicurist went to work on her nails using glues and files and tips and an airbrush. Arielle watched the manicurist's skilled little hands go as they created tiny pieces of art upon her fingertips. She loved the salon, the smell of the acrylic and how it made her a bit dizzy when she inhaled its fumes. Once the nails were finished and just about dry, Arielle ran over to present them to Lucia. "Goodness gracious!" remarked her adoptive mother as she began to laugh merrily, nudging Ava to check them out. Ava glanced up from her magazine and stared at Arielle's unstylishly long, square-tipped manicure puzzlingly. "Those look fast," she said in a tone of mock adulation. "You look like an eighties metal groupie," she laughed. "Seriously though, those nails are more vicious than a Puerto Rican drag queen." Arielle wasn't sure what any of those things meant, but she shrugged off the remarks because she knew her nails were mind-blowingly amazing and it didn't matter what Ava thought. But as embarrassed as Ava was to be seen with the clueless little urchin with the questionable fashion sense, she was beginning to appreciate Arielle's strangeness - if for nothing but comic relief.

"Well I think they're an excellent choice," said Lucia, holding back a giggle and speaking in the tone mothers use when praising their kids for things like macaroni jewelry. While Lucia settled up with the receptionist, Arielle wandered around the salon admiring her hands. Over by the retail racks, she noticed a life-size cut-out of a sun-kissed model next to a stand full of bronze bottles. The cut-out had skin like Erica's, all taut, dark and glowing, and the bottles seemed to promise the effect. Turning to glance at herself in a big mirror, all she could notice was her light white skin and ultra-fair hair. Appalled at how she literally paled in comparison, she swiped a bottle from the rack, dropped it casually down into her rain boot and backed away towards the door.

The whole way home she held back a devilish smile. She was excited to start working on her come-hither glow, planning to stop only when hers would finally rival that of Erica's. Once they got home, she wasted no time in dashing upstairs to be alone.

She popped open the bottle and spread the lotion across her face, carefully applying it in thin, even strokes. But after a thorough application and several minutes of waiting, her skin showed no change and it baffled her. So she squeezed a big dollop into her palms, slathered it thick across her little arms and again she waited. Still, no change.

Growing impatient, she rubbed handfuls of it up and down her legs but still it left nothing to show for itself but faint yellow streaks, and the lotion she slopped onto her forehead and cheeks just didn't seem to be working at all. Rattled, she threw herself across her bed. Cursing her pallid, ashen skin, Arielle fell angrily asleep.

Out in the driveway, Gabriel and his father applied final coats of wax on the cars they'd spent all day babying. It was something the two men enjoyed together, bonding as they buffed, and it was often during such bonding sessions that many of their clichéd father-son chats had found a natural stage. Sometimes Cliff shared pearls of wisdom that were sprung from his own initiative, and sometimes Gabriel had questions on his mind that a guy can really only ask his dad. Over the years, many topics had come up, from drugs to investments to pubic hair. Now that he was grown, his investments were solid. But for the odd marijuana fix, his life was pretty much drug-free, and it had been a long time since they last had to discuss pubic hair, although nothing would ever be gauche or taboo between the O'Faolain men.

On this day, this bright, sunny afternoon spent out in the driveway shining up the family's fleet, Gabriel brought up a topic he had never raised before: he wanted to talk about love. So he asked his father, "Dad, when did you know that mom was the one for you?"

Cliff's face lit up like a Christmas tree. "I had a feeling you'd be asking me this stuff soon!" he said gleefully. "And I've been thinking about how I'd answer that since long before you were so much as a twinkle in my zippered fly."

Gabriel laughed. "Nice one, Dad. Always reminding me I began down in your nuts . . ."

Cliff shrugged and said "I'm sorry, son. It just never seems to get old to me that my balls produced people. Anyway, back to your query . . . to give you an idea of how quickly she had my attention, I'll start by telling you how she made me laugh within the first two minutes of meeting her," he recalled happily. "And it wasn't just a mild, half-hearted tee-hee; she had me loudly and embarrassingly busting a gut over a joke she made about Roman 'vomitoriums' which are not, as it turned out, actually auditoriums full of people puking to make room for more spaghetti . . ."

"I know *that*," said Gabriel, looking sideways at his dad. "Did *you* think that's what vomitoriums were?"

"We digress," said Cliff, steering the conversation back. "Within the first ten minutes of talking to her, down in that tiny little cellar that was the only kitchen in our hostel, I could already appreciate how, even though she was so mellow and soft-spoken, she was such a passionate and commanding presence.

"By the end of our first date, I had already fallen in love with the way she seemed to walk and talk with such a gentle, well . . . *lightness*. She had this great kindness flowing through her, constantly showing itself in her cheerful observations and inspiring stories. And while we drank wine and ate pizza by drippy candle light, I saw an angel sitting across from me. She was so sweet and virtuous but at the same time, a real firecracker who was not afraid to tell it like it is, even if she had to be brutally honest. And I realized that night that there are two kinds of women in the world: ones who speak the truth, and ones who do not."

Gabriel listened intently while polishing the rims on Ava's coupe. Cliff continued:

"Mid-way through our second date, eating gelato under the stars and chatting easily about theories of creation and the reaches of infinity, I saw a side of her that made me finally understand why people pair off as they do. Suddenly, I understood the dream people are chasing when they decide to pledge themselves to another imperfect person. I barely knew Lucia, but already she seemed to bring out all that was best in me, but more importantly, she seemed to find all that was worst in me to be endearing and quirky. I can't explain it . . . but from the day I met her, I knew she had my back. And I realized that night that there are two kinds of women in the world: ones who want to be on your team, and ones who just play for themselves."

Gabriel nodded in thoughtful agreement, for his mother was undeniably awesome. Cliff continued: "By our third date, I knew something had definitely and irreversibly come over me. Suddenly, I couldn't remember any girl before her, and I couldn't imagine ever finding another who could even hold a candle. I *had* to have her, but even more, I had to be had *by* her. That night, I realized there are two kinds of women in the world: Your mother, and the wacky, clucking hen party that comprises all the rest of them."

Gabriel smiled in gratitude, so glad to have been blessed with such solid people for parents. He always admired the way they spoke of each other; proudly, respectfully, and in a way that left no room for doubt that true love really exists. Cliff eyed his son curiously as he collected the scattered polishing cloths and sponges around their work area. It had been obvious to Cliff and Lucia in recent days that for the first time ever, their boy was falling in love and they couldn't have been more proud of the girl he had chosen.

"Was any of that helpful?" he asked, rousing Gabriel from his daydream.

"More helpful than you'll ever know," answered Gabriel assuredly. And it had been.

"Was there anything else?" asked Cliff. Gabriel paused before answering, grappling for a moment with the reality of his next words before just blurting them out: "I'm proposing to Erica tomorrow!"

Both men stood in silence for several moments, absorbing his momentous announcement. Cliff knew that if his son said it, his son meant it, and he didn't have to ask him if he was sure or truly ready or if he should sleep on it another night. His boy was a man now, a gentleman of his own means who was grown enough to call his own shots. However, it still amazed Cliff to think his kid was about to ask a girl to be his wife.

"Have you picked out a ring?" he asked, finally breaking the silence.

"No need; I plan to give her Grandma Betts's ring," said Gabriel decisively. Cliff was charmed by the notion but asked his son whether he really thought the antique half-carat teardrop diamond flanked by mossy little emeralds would meet the bling expectations of the modern bride. "Erica isn't one of those girls," Gabriel assured him. "She doesn't want a massive, sparkly conflict diamond from some store so she can brag about how much I spent . . . she'll love Betts' for what it means to our family." So Cliff congratulated his son on a choice well made, and promised to have the ring polished by the following afternoon.

"Oh, and son," he continued, sounding choked up with emotion, "on the off-chance that Erica shoots you down, you have my blessing to pawn the ring and buy yourself a second-hand Japanese sports car, or some other moderately-priced consolation because, while the ring is indeed a handsome piece, I don't think it's worth all that much."

Gabriel was touched. "Thanks big guy!" he said while shaking his father's hand with genuine revere.

"Any time, son," replied Cliff, flicking a tear from the corner of his eye.

# twenty-eight

## Botched Application

Demetra crept down the hall on her tip-toes, approaching Ava's door quietly while it stood slightly ajar. She stopped to listen. Silence inside, followed by a bit of shuffling. When all fell silent again, she flung the door and jumped in with a "Hiiiiiii!"

Ava didn't even flinch from where she sat on a little footstool in the middle of her newsprint-covered floor. She had her pottery wheel out, and her hands were currently massaging a large chunk of moistened clay into a smooth column that was beginning to resemble a vase. "What's up?" she asked flatly.

"Do you have any candy?" asked her little sister, getting right to the point.

"Not usually." replied Ava.

"Today though?" asked Demetra.

"Negative. Why?" replied Ava.

Demetra sighed. "I saw your Facebook status. It says 'call me, I have candy'."

"So?" asked Ava.

"So why would you post that if you don't actually have any candy?" replied Demetra, growing impatient.

Ava didn't bother to look up from her clay as it rotated atop its spinning disc. "It was a social experiment," she answered.

Demetra raised an eyebrow. "Testing what theory?" she asked, annoyed with her sister's short answers but at the same time, interested.

"Well, two days ago," began Ava, "I posted 'as I lay here dying, screeching demons haunt my wretched soul'." She paused for a moment, allowing the dark, miserable depth of the statement to sink into her sister's young head. "One person private messaged me to make sure I wasn't feeling suicidal," she said. "And three people clicked 'Like'."

Demetra scrunched up her face. "Yeah I saw that, you Goth. Were you feeling fed up with life or something?"

"No more than usual," replied Ava casually. "But then, just for fun, and just to test my theory that people are inherently self-centered, I posted 'call me, I have candy' to see how many of my friends would respond then. And, just as I suspected, already today I've received thirteen text messages and seven calls from people wanting to know what kinds of recreational drugs I'm trying to unload before the weekend."

Demetra was confused, then it clicked: "Oh yeah. I forgot the words 'candy' and 'drugs' are interchangeable amongst your set."

Ava nodded. "Well, apparently, the regular guy in these parts is bone dry. Even Rourke called me, asking if I carried Spanish Fly."

"Tell me you messed with his head!" shrieked Demetra. Rourke had been the butt of their pranks and the subject of their ridicule for as long as they both could remember.

"Obvi!" replied Ava. "I told him I was holding a couple grams of gangster-crafted jarhyphenyl trip rocks from Leningrad."

"What's 'jarhyphenyl'?" asked Demetra.

"I made it up," answered Ava. "I said it gave the user passionate hallucinations with little to no comedown . . . our boy came over about an hour ago and gave me sixty bucks for a spare-button baggie full of Turbinado sugar."

Demetra laughed. "I thought Gabe dropped him off at the bus station with ferry fare and some lunch money, like, yesterday?"

"He did, and I just got it back. I guess Rourkie's been camping out!"

"But won't he know you ripped him off when the candy fails to get him high?"

"Well, he asked me if the drug was Chardonnay-soluble so I have to assume he was planning to use it on someone else," answered Ava.

"Eww, that is so bleak," said Demetra, beginning to dread her twenties. "So there never was any candy in here?"

"Never was. Unless you count Rourke's sugar."

"Devastating," she said, leaning on Ava's bedpost and thinking about Popeye sticks. "In other news, I think Gabriel's going to propose to Erica!"

Ava finally looked up at her little sister. "What makes you say that?"

"I heard mom and dad talking about how he asked for Grandma Betts's ring! I wonder how Arielle's going to like that . . ."

"What do you mean?" asked Ava, confused. "Arielle will be stoked for the party, and yet another chance to hog the dance floor."

"No way," said Demetra assuredly. "Kids my age aren't even holding hands yet, but I know a girl infatuated when I see one!" Ava argued that if Arielle really was into him, she'd have made a move on him long before Erica came along. "Arielle had been playing a slow hand until Erica swooped in and foiled it!" insisted

Demetra. "Just take one look into her true blue eyes whenever he walks into the room; she sparkles for him! Take note of the ear-to-ear smile she brandishes whenever she's spending time with him . . . I've yet to see anything else make her that happy."

Ava considered what her sister was saying and was beginning to see her point. "Now that you mention it," she concurred, "she really has been Gabe's pet since she got here. Wow," she said, staring off, "imagine how soul-crushing it must be for her to see him fall for someone else right in front of her!" They both paused, empathetically imagining Arielle's heartbreaking, pitiable position.

"Can't win 'em all," said Demetra softly and realistically. "I wonder if she'll stay if he marries Erica."

"I wonder," said Ava. "But do you think she has anywhere else to go anymore?"

Arielle woke up an hour later to the sound of something pinging her window. She sat up.

"Arielle! Come out here!" called Gabriel from out in the yard. It was raining, but the whole family was out there with him and they appeared to be waiting for her.

"Wake up, Abe Simpson, naptime is over!" called Erica. Another pebble pinged her window so she stood up and walked over.

"Careful, kids, you'll chip the glass!" said Lucia. It was beginning to come down hard out there, and the wind was picking up, blowing leaves and things around. Arielle stayed far enough away from her open windowpane that she didn't get splashed.

"Come out!" yelled Demetra. "We invented a new team sport and we need you to be referee!" Ava muttered something about dragging Arielle out and forcing her to face her water aversion head-on. She said it just loud enough that Arielle could hear her. Arielle gulped.

"You're going to love it, Arielle!" called Cliff. "What other game combines football and pugs? We're calling it Mud Dog Football!" The pugs ran loose around the 'court' they traced with their heels across the wet sand. Arielle peered out, wishing she could join them. Lucia, the only one close enough to see her face clearly, took a few steps towards Arielle's window to see that her skin looked oddly jaundiced. Concerned, she asked her, "Dear, what happened on your face?"

Suddenly remembering the copious amounts of self-tanning lotion she had applied just before falling asleep, Arielle rushed over to the mirror and gasped in horror as she discovered that her desired effect had not been achieved, and in fact the lotion had left her face streaked and blotched in an unnatural orange hue. Paired with her ultra-long flaming fingernails, she looked like a thing from the swamps of that fabled old 'hell' she'd once read about on a church billboard. She ran to the bathroom and splashed her face with water, but it didn't help. She dampened a facecloth and scrubbed her skin vigorously, and while it stained the towel, the streaks wouldn't budge. Even the palms of her hands were a deep, dark orange!

The family kept calling to her while she frantically searched through drawers and cupboards for a solution to her blunder. The pungent chemical smell of the lotion stung her nostrils while she pumiced, but to no avail. All the while, the family refused to let up, continually calling to her from outside.

"Arielle!" yelled Gabriel passionately. "Don't make us beg! Come play, it's a beautiful evening!" But Arielle, already unable to go out where it's wet, was now unable to go anywhere there might be people who'd see the result of her vanity. Staying low, she crept over and peeked out at them, praying they'd give up and leave her alone. No luck there.

"Good evening Pacific North-Westerners," said Erica in her best weather girl voice, "It's a beautiful day if you favor high winds and torrential downpour and by the look of that green sky, I would say that a hurricane is indeed fast-approaching."

"It sure is, Joyce," replied Gabriel, channeling the deep booming voice of an anchorman. "Big systems moving in and we are seeing waves cresting above the twenty-foot mark so we are advising all persons, without further delay, to get out to their nearest beach and enjoy this force of nature as it lashes over the Mud Dog arena." The pugs barked happily, excited by all the commotion. Olive sneezed out all the sand in her nose.

They all waited a few minutes for Arielle to break down and come out, but it seemed she had gone into hiding. "This is retarded," said Ava. "She has two minutes to get her little ass out here or I'm going inside."

"C'mon Arielle, please! We're about to lose Ava!" cried Gabriel, but still she didn't appear. "Fine; I'm coming in to get you!" he yelled as he started running towards the door.

Arielle heard that and panicked; Gabriel was the last person she wanted to see right then! So she searched the room for a quick place to hide and climbed inside the big wooden wardrobe. The hangers were still clanging together above her head when, not a moment later, he was standing in her doorway listening for her. She remained perfectly still, hoping to be invisible behind the fabric of a few dresses. He stepped inside. "Arielle where are you?"

The bedroom was seemingly empty. He knelt down to look under the bed, but she wasn't hiding there. He looked under the desk and behind the door, but saw her in none of those places. There was only one place left to check: the wardrobe.

As Gabriel took slow, quiet steps towards the wardrobe, Arielle began to quiver as she tried desperately to make her body as small and insignificant as possible. She could see him approaching through the cracks in the wood, tiptoeing closer and in any second, he would fling open the door. She prayed he wouldn't.

"Aha!" he said as she reached in to reveal the skinny, orangey creature inside who was hiding her face with blotchy, stained hands that sported ultralong fake nails. "Arielle?" he asked, confused and almost frightened. Her blue eyes peeked out at him from behind spread fingers and he started to laugh. "What did you do to yourself? Come out of there!" he demanded.

He offered her his hand, but she just shrunk herself into a smaller ball, wrapping her arms tightly around her knees. "Aww come on, Arielle. Come out and ref our game; no one will care that you look like a rabid Miami house hobbit!" Arielle shamefully fretted, wishing he would just leave her alone.

"What's the hold-up?" she heard a girl's voice ask just as Erica peeked her own head in. Even more embarrassed now, Arielle reached out her streaky, orange arm and pulled the wardrobe door tightly shut. Certain that Erica was about to start laughing at her too, she was shocked to hear Erica stepping up and taking over the situation, without a second's hesitation. "Run and tell the fam to start without us," she told Gabriel as she shooed him out and pulled the bedroom door shut.

She knelt down in front of the wardrobe. "You can come out, it's just us now," she said, but Arielle stayed put. Erica slowly pulled the wardrobe door open to find her crouched like a child in hiding. Erica giggled at the sight. As she giggled, Arielle's contempt for her grew. She, with her naturally bronzed epidermis that required no smelly lotion; she, with her easy laugh and way with words; she, who never had to trade her voice for a chance to get close to the boy they both wanted. Erica stood before her so effortlessly and it vexed Arielle that her feet didn't have to feel the sharp pain of pointy knives in every step. It took every ounce of restraint Arielle possessed not to jump out and violently attack her, and to scratch her pretty almond eyes out with those flaming orange nails.

"Okay, okay, no more making fun," said Erica, sensing Arielle's rage. She straightened the smile from her face and got down to business. "Is this what I think it is? A self-tanning blunder?" she asked knowingly. Arielle shrugged, then nodded. "Alright then, I have just the thing. Wait here."

Arielle sat perfectly still in the wardrobe for several minutes while Erica bustled around in the kitchen downstairs. When she finally came back, she was carrying an armload of various items and solutions from the kitchen.

"Alright you can climb out of there now," she said. Arielle wasn't sure why she was listening to her, but slowly and gingerly, she came out of hiding and followed her to the bathroom. Sitting down on the edge of the tub, Erica sprinkled baking soda onto a scrubbing brush wrapped in a damp facecloth. "This'll help to exfoliate and make the streaks less obvious," she said. The scrubbing scratched Arielle's delicate face and it hurt but she bore it, just like she'd bore every other pain that seemed to come part and parcel with life on land. When she was done scrubbing the face and arms, she applied lemon juice with cotton pads to help lighten her skin further. While Erica worked on her, Arielle wore a glum face. "Aww, don't feel too bad," said Erica, trying to lighten the mood. "I think every girl has screwed this up once. Mine was the winter of 2009."

Arielle did feel bad, but not so much about the discoloration of her skin anymore as the fact that Erica, the person she had been plotting against, was the one taking the time to help her out of an embarrassing situation. This was not the way she had planned it! Her plan was to emerge so tan and beautiful that she would outshine any olive-skinned hussy who crossed her path, not to suddenly need Erica's help, thereby indebting herself to her rival. No, this was not the way she had pictured her afternoon, and her disappointment was written all over her face. Her eyes seemed to ask, why are you being nice to me?

"It's funny how people always seem to want what they weren't meant to have, isn't it?" asked Erica as she took the lemon-soaked cotton to Arielle's eyebrows, being careful not to get citrus juice in her eyes. "Take me for example," she continued. "When I was a little kid, I used to tan so dark in the summer and I hated it. I wanted to look just like all the pretty fair-skinned blondes in my class, the ones that all the boys liked. "But once I learned to play the hand I was dealt, things began to really turn around for me!"

Arielle sat with her eyes closed while Erica swabbed her ears with lemon juice to take the drip stains off her lobes. She couldn't imagine anyone wanting pale white skin over sun-kissed gold.

"I say, own it!" said Erica with zest. "If you're pale, be Nicole Kidman pale and wear SPF 45 like you prefer it that way. Trust me,

Arielle, so much of what is appealing in a person is directly proportional to the value they themselves place on such attributes."

Outside in the yard, Mud Dog Football was well underway and the fun-loving shrieks and hollers of the new sport could be heard through the bathroom window. As usual, Arielle wished she could be out having fun in the rain with them but as usual, she was stuck inside, missing out. She watched as Erica glanced up from the lemony Q-Tips she swabbed her with to laugh at all the fun they were having, and, as Arielle noticed, the fun that Erica, too, was missing out on.

Arielle, with her irritated skin and dissipating hatred, began to realize that the mind-numbing jealousy she'd been feeling towards Erica had been blinding her to what was really going on. She realized as she was being gently buffed by Erica's kind hands that she had been engaged in a one-sided war against a girl who clearly didn't see it that way at all. Erica may have been her biggest rival in the most important contest of her life, but while she played against Erica, Erica played against no one and that was why she was winning. It became clear that to Erica, there was no contest, only love.

# twenty-nine

## Light of our Lives

The next day, while the afternoon sun was just over the hump, Erica and Arielle brought towels and a jug of iced tea to the beach to watch their boy surf. They were into the hottest days of summer now, when even in the chilly, North Pacific waters there were a precious few days when surfers could skip the wetsuit and take to the waves in bathers and board shorts. Erica wore a frilly marmalade-coloured bikini while Arielle wore a bucket hat, big sunglasses and an oversize long-sleeved nightie. Once again, Arielle found herself lying next to Erica feeling small and insignificant. While Erica soaked up the daylight like a ripening mango in the tropics, Arielle kept herself concealed, shy about her pale areas but now even more shy about her streaky ones.

Erica rolled onto her stomach to tan her back and suddenly her perfectly round, tight bottom was face-up and on display. Trying to draw her eyes away from it, Arielle noticed a dark brown imperfection on her shoulder that she hadn't ever noticed before. It kind of looked like a small slug or something but it appeared to be attached to the skin, and Arielle delighted in finally finding an imperfection on the seemingly flawless masterpiece that was Erica. While Erica lay face-down and unaware, Arielle leaned in really close to see what it was. Slowly, she stalked it, her pinching fingers at the ready to pluck it swiftly off her back the way a beak plucks a worm from the dirt . . .

"OWWW!" yelped Erica as she whipped her hand back to cover the now-sore birthmark. "What the eff?" she demanded.

Arielle looked confused. She didn't know it would hurt it to pinch it.

"It's my mole, okay?!" wailed Erica. "I've already gotten it checked; it's benign. So we definitely won't be needing anyone to PINCH it with their pointy acrylic talons, okay?" She smacked Arielle's hands away and rubbed the skin around the mole, half in pain, half laughing. Arielle smiled, looking a little embarrassed. Then she kissed her thumb and transferred the kiss to the mole.

"Thank you," said Erica sarcastically. But peculiarly enough, she felt no more throbbing and in fact it felt perfectly normal again.

"Thank you for that," she said, sounding surprised. Arielle smiled and lay back down, satisfied that the funny brown marking was permanent. Erica looked at her thoughtfully, as if chewing on something she wasn't sure she should say . . . then she just went for it. "I hope this isn't rude of me to ask," she began uncomfortably, "but have you always been a mute?"

Arielle's face darkened. Not in an angry way, but in a sad way that said she'd exhausted all her anger and all that was left was a deep, dull melancholy. She bitterly missed having a voice, for hers had had the power to enchant, and that if she still possessed it, its pretty notes would amplify her physical beauty in the eyes of the people the same way it always had for her under the sea. Ironic, she thought, that she had been her prettiest when there was no one around she cared to impress. She shook her head 'no.' No, you ignorant urchin, she thought, No, I've not always been *mute*.

"I didn't think so," said Erica, sounding relieved to have gotten that question out of the way. *How nice for you,* thought Arielle. She was learning sarcasm, even if she would only ever get to apply it within the confines of her inner monologue.

"I hope you don't mind, but there is something I've been wanting to talk to you about, or, . . . say . . . at you," started Erica awkwardly. Arielle's eyes were closed but she could still see Gabriel's wet body plunging in and out of the sea atop his smooth blue board. She could sense that Erica was about to start talking about something she wouldn't like to acknowledge so she kept her eyes closed and lay there motionless.

"I think I'm falling in love with Gabriel," said Erica. Arielle cringed. "I'm falling very quickly and very hard . . . it's crazy, really. It's all so new to me!" Erica smiled nervously but excitedly. Arielle kept perfectly still, pretending to be asleep, pretending she didn't hear any of that.

"I know you're awake, Arielle," said Erica with a nudge, ruining the charade just like she often ruined Arielle's plans. Slowly and grudgingly, Arielle sat up, removed her sunglasses, and glared into her enemy's eyes with a look that seemed to demand *'why are you telling me this?'*

Erica gathered her thoughts carefully, not wanting to say the wrong thing. "I know you haven't known the O'Faolains very long, but I can tell you adore them, and I know they all love you as if you were part of the family." She didn't want to lay it on too thick, but wanted to buffer her point nicely without appearing disingenuous. "You make them all very happy just being here, just being your quiet, mysterious and almost unreasonably talented self." Arielle smiled half-heartedly, for compliments, as sweet as they were for her ego, taunted her; her charms and talents felt worthless if they weren't helping her to win. Erica leaned forward and looked her in the eyes. "I know Gabriel loves you like family, but, well . . . there are times when I catch you looking at him in a way that makes me think that perhaps it all goes a bit deeper than that for you." Arielle shyly glanced away. She dug her toenails into the sand and fidgeted uncomfortably. "And I hope I'm not overstepping myself by saying this," Erica continued, "but there are times when, I don't know why, but I could swear that HE is the reason you came here . . . from whatever distant, unknowable place it is you came from." Arielle froze, and wondered what else she knew. "I can tell that you have a crush on him," Erica blurted.

Arielle lowered her eyes and shrunk into herself, helpless to stop Erica from saying more. "I understand if you think you love him but trust me, one day, you'll know what real love feels like, and you'll know that this is just a bit of infatuation!" said a chipper, hopeful-sounding Erica. Arielle was shocked that she was being told that by her, and wondered what on earth made her think she was qualified to make that judgment. He was not simply a crush! He was her love, he just didn't know it, and he might never see it because *she* was in their way.

"I like you a lot, Arielle," she said. "And I would just feel a lot better knowing that you and I have some kind of understanding. I know how much you mean to him, and how much he means to you. You mean a lot to me too now and I just want you to know that I love him and I didn't mean to take him, or anything, from you." Arielle was crestfallen. She watched Erica's lips move but refused to hear another word out of her mouth. She thought seriously for a moment about luring her to the water's edge, dragging her under, and drowning her. The idea made her sick, but so did the idea of losing out and dying herself so she entertained the fantasy. Of course she would have to go into the water with her, which would mean getting her legs wet. She'd have to wade in and pull her down, and she would probably see her tail but it would be okay because she'd lose consciousness soon enough anyway. There would be a few big bubbles, followed by a few smaller bubbles, until all the air was siphoned from her lungs and replaced with salty ocean. Then she would know what it was like. The water needn't even be very deep . . .

Arielle was disturbed by her own dark and murderous thoughts, and couldn't believe they were going on inside her own head. Impulsively, she stood up and ran away from Erica, frightened of what she might do if Erica insisted on continuing to call her exquisite love, simply a crush. She ran for the house and locked herself in the bathroom, sat down in the deep tub and covered her ears with her palms. She would not hear another word about it.

Erica, feeling bad for having upset her, stood up and was about to follow her in when she saw the man on both their minds approaching from the water.

"Polar bear hug!!" he shouted as he ran at her, ocean-cold body ready to tackle her down to her towel. He propped himself up on his elbows and brought his cold, wet lips to hers, and the frigid water from his board shorts dripped uncomfortably onto her hot skin. She let out a surprised screech as the first drops landed on her, but she couldn't object when he lowered his freezing, wet torso down onto her warm body and laid a three-second make-out on her like she'd never had before.

He pulled his lips from hers and rested his forehead on hers. "I'm really looking forward to our date tonight," he said. Water dripped from his hair to her face.

"Me too," she said, blinking the saltwater from her eyes. His touch made her chest pound so raucously, it was as if her heart grew a fist just to savagely bang it off her ribcage. There was no doubt about it; their bodies were on board with whatever their hearts and minds were planning.

# thirty

## Treasures

Erica stood waiting beside the garage, in a red dress she'd bought a year before but had been saving for the right occasion. It had even gone with her on her travels but had remained untouched in its garment bag, at the ready for a swanky soiree to pop up. She even had lipstick on to match - a deep and demure red - also an old purchase but also on its inaugural spin. She liked lipstick a lot and had dozens of shades ranging from pale nudes to almost purples but the truth was, none of them got very much wear, if any at all. She collected all color and manner of cosmetic, even though she habitually forwent them in favour of a more natural look. She had scores of tubes and palettes with hardly a swipe across them. To her, their value rested not in their utility but in the idea that they were her feminine indulgence, a weakness that was, she felt, every now and then deserving of a bit of frivolity.

As she stepped side to side, breaking in shoes that were also as yet unworn, moths and mosquitoes did their sputtering dance against the yellow bulb that hung from the garage wall. She smacked her lips and twirled her hair while she guessed where he might be taking her. Then she heard his footsteps behind her and turned to see him holding a bouquet of daisies for her. She accepted them, breathed them - then kissed him a very sweet thank-you. *Thank you. No, thank youuu.*

When Erica noticed the picnic basket Gabriel was carrying, it became clear he wasn't taking her anywhere with a Zagat rating. "You look ravishing," he said, "I've always loved you in red."

She'd waited her whole life for a boy to drop the word 'ravishing' on her. "Thanks," she replied, ruffling the dress in her fingers.

"And those shoes . . ." he continued, staring lustfully down at her ankles. "I think I feel a fetish awakening right now, but unfortunately you might have to rethink them for this particular evening."

"Well where are you taking me?" she asked as she stepped out of her hot shoes. "You said you made reservations so I only assumed . . ."

"The destination is a surprise," he said, "But we've had reservations at this spot for over a decade, and the hike over is a real treat."

Erica was caught completely off guard. The *HIKE*? She had been looking forward to an elegant evening but was down for whatever Gabriel had in mind so she swapped her sexy heels for an old pair of cowboy boots, took Gabriel's hand and gladly followed him into the dusk.

Unbeknown to them, Arielle had been present all the while, watching from the backseat of Gabriel's Jeep. As she hid beneath the car blanket, she enviously eyed the pretty daisies in Erica's hand. She was sure they would have driven to their date that night but when she saw them take off running down the moonlit beach, she climbed out and scurried sneakily along after them.

Erica didn't care if he was leading her to a swamp to dig for severed hands, she was just ecstatic to be alone with him. Half a mile down the beach, they ducked into a narrow bush path that led them towards the thick of a forest. It was dark in there but in swatches of moonlight, she was able to sneak glances into the basket. There was a baguette and that was promising for where there is bread there is always cheese and where there is cheese there is often wine. A glimmer of gold sticker caught her eye from deep inside. It looked like a champagne bottle. *Champagne! How nice!*

The deeper into the woods they ventured, the narrower the path became before it had them maneuvering around thick branches and barreling through spindly vines, catching spider webs in their faces. Arielle followed them closely, staying low and stepping lightly. She was almost more curious than Erica to learn what Gabriel was planning.

In the evening's humidity, Erica felt the hair she had so laboriously brushed and blow-dried pay homage to the wild, wiry underbrush that whipped their ankles as they dashed through. Gabriel held her hand tightly as he ran, and behind him, she floated, barely touching the ground. Drops of tree sap hit her hair and dress and falling pine needles and leaves adhered themselves. The time she spent bathing and primping suddenly seemed silly, for she should have known there'd be nothing ordinary about this date. Only during boring dates can any hairstyle maintain its integrity, and only after ordinary dates can a red dress escape without needing a dry cleaning.

Deeper down the path, Gabriel asked if she recognized anything, for they'd explored every inch of the forest as children.

"These woods are vaguely familiar, but I've still got no clue where you're taking me," she admitted, swatting bugs off her legs while looking up at the tall conifers. "Fun hike though!" she said cheerfully, wiping the sticky glow from her forehead.

"We're almost there," he said, stopping dead in his tracks and spinning back to face her. "Kiss me," he demanded softly, squeezing her hand as he pulled her in. She closed her eyes and leaned into him, pressing her lips to his and, opening her mouth just wide enough to taste his tongue, inhaled some of his sweet breath. To her, his breath was always sweet. She wondered if it really was, or if she was just physically incapable of perceiving anything about him as less than perfect, delicious, desirable. "We're almost there," he repeated once again before turning to lead her a little further. In a matter of seconds, their narrow path opened up into a bright, moon-lit clearing, and Gabriel set the basket down signaling to her that they'd arrived. Beneath their feet grew fluffy green moss that was soft as a mattress and covered the ground like a blanket. She kicked her boots off and stood in it, cooling her sweaty feet in the refreshing, dense mat. That feeling, combined with the damp, woodsy scent of the clearing jogged her memory in an unexpected way. Suddenly she remembered being in that exact same spot before, but couldn't remember when or why but was sure it would all come together soon enough. And while she and her date spread their picnic blanket and loosened the cage around the champagne cork, a sneaky, swift Arielle scaled the trunk of a maple tree to spy on them from high in its branches, concealed by a thick of red leaves.

Now watching from high above, she could see everything. While Gabriel unpacked their picnic, Erica ran her fingers through her hair trying to smooth out the tangles. Arielle watched her with seething envy as she made slight aesthetic improvements and in a quick decision to thwart her efforts, she grabbed an egg from the bird's nest on the branch next to her and whipped it hard down at Erica's head. As it descended upon her rival with expert precision, Arielle began to regret throwing it, and prayed that all that was inside was yolk and goo and not a partially-developed hatchling because that would have been morbid. She winced as it made contact.

"OWWW! MY GOD!" Erica howled as she ducked down to the blanket to take cover from whatever gross, gooey hard things were suddenly falling from the sky. Gabriel turned around in shock but once he got a good look at her, began to laugh hysterically. Arielle kept her eyes covered.

"An egg has fallen on my head, hasn't it?" Erica asked as she began to laugh. Once the initial shock wore off, she realized she wasn't really in any sort of pain. "Go figure," she said, "I spend five minutes in the woods, and already eggs are dropping on my head."

"I'd take it as a good omen!" said Gabriel cheerfully. "I bet that happens even less frequently than lightning strikes!"

Arielle finally peered out and was relieved to see that it was just yolk. She ceased being regretful and resumed being spiteful. Erica toweled off her yolky hair with a cloth napkin as Arielle snickered to herself up in the tree, for she was sure she'd managed to kill their mood . . .

Except that she definitely hadn't. The smashed egg did not stop Gabriel from pulling plates of fruits and cheeses out, and it certainly didn't slow him down from lighting a few tea candles and popping the champagne bottle. Having filled two plastic flutes with bubbly, he then toasted to their lifelong friendship.

"Erica, do you remember when we were little, like six or seven, and used to be obsessed with the idea that all the clocks would stop at Y2K and the world would come to a screeching halt?" She smiled – she did remember, and excitedly she recounted ideas they shared on how to re-invent things to be millennium proof. They laughed about how seriously they'd once bought into it, and about the preparations they'd made for the unlikely event of such an apocalypse.

"A time capsule?!" she asked him. "We made a time capsule together?"

"We sure did!" he replied. "And we filled it with things we feared might be scarce in a post-millennial wasteland."

Erica searched her memory for a moment before squealing with elation. Sometimes she squealed loudly and piercingly when she got overly excited or had a great idea. It was an involuntary reflex, for she never knew a squeal was on its way until it was halfway out and already deafening those nearby. It could have been somewhat embarrassing for her if the moments that typically inspired such squeals weren't always so overwhelmingly wonderful. She had forgotten all about that time capsule, but it sounded exactly like something they would have done. "We buried it for our future selves in case we survived the millennium, but if we didn't, then it was for future earthlings, right?!" He nodded. The whole concept was endlessly entertaining to them, for as fun as it was to make and bury the capsule all that time ago, being present for the unearthing several years later was a hundred times more magical, especially since they'd forgotten most of what they put inside. They sipped their champagne and tried to remember.

When the food was done and the bottle was almost empty, Gabriel pulled out a tattered old crayon-drawn map and a set of garden spades. The map showed an X drawn over the very tree they were sitting under. "The time capsule is here?" she asked him, laughing as she picked a blob of tree sap from her arm and flicked an insect from her hair.

"Shall we dig?" he asked. She nodded, downed her last bit of champagne, and they began.

Arielle watched with confusion, straining to see what they were digging for at the base of that tree. After about ten minutes of scooping the dirt around the thick, spindly roots, their spades finally touched upon something hard. Carefully, they excavated the earth around it until they could wiggle it free from its hole. "My Ninja Turtles lunch box!" he exclaimed excitedly as he brushed dirt away and began peeling at the tape with which they'd sealed it. Then he sat it down between them and they savored the anticipation before popping it open.

Erica brushed the dirt from her arms. "I can't believe we're doing this right now! It's like we're about to open a gift from a former version of ourselves . . . what a cool feeling!"

"It really is!" he replied, reaching down to pop open the plastic latch. Inside, sitting on top of everything and looking exactly the way they did when she put them in, were her prized Beanie Babies, a bull and a horse. "Tabasco and Whinny!" she squealed as she hugged them. "You guys look good as new!" She kissed their snouts then set them aside to rifle for more treasures.

Gabriel's prized baseball and Pokemon cards sat next to a wooden boomerang and a plastic slingshot. "I guess you thought you'd be doing some hunting!" she remarked.

"This thing could take down a bald eagle," he said, holding up his performance slingshot. "And this thing could behead a deer!" he said as he posed dangerously with his boomerang. Erica moved aside a VHS copy of *The Land Before Time* (a movie they had both loved since they were tiny) and found her favorite tube of glittery marshmallow Lip Smacker. She brought it to her nose and sniffed its glittery applicator. "Mmm, it still smells exactly the same!" She closed her eyes and inhaled its scent deeply, the way she always used to. But even though it smelled sweet and marshmallow-y as ever, she decided against putting it on. After all, it had been buried in the ground a long time.

Gabriel pulled out a baggie full of assorted lollipops and bubble gum. He pulled apart its zip-lock right under his nose and smiled blissfully as he inhaled the sugary medley of candy that had been stewing in there for so long. "Smells like a birthday party loot bag," he said. "Weren't those the days? Candy, all the time."

Erica took a sniff from the candy bag too. "Those were the days," she answered woefully. She didn't mean to be a downer, but it was sometimes difficult for her to reflect on the days of her youth without deeply missing both her parents. Gabriel could tell she was thinking of them because the same dreamy look seemed to cross her face whenever a happy memory left her full of longing. He wrapped his arms around her, and she rested her face on his strong chest in the musk of his skin and crisp scent of his deodorant. He was the closest thing to family she had left, and she treasured him. He wanted to be everything to her.

Then she glanced at the lunch box and noticed an envelope tucked beside a stack of Pogs and pictures. All it read was *E + G*. Now very curious, she carefully tore the end of it open to find a document hand-written in purple marker that said *CONTRACT* across the top. "Interesting . . ." she said as she began to read:

*CONTRACT*

*This contract is to ensure that Erica Emery + Gabriel O'Faolain, if neither are married by the time they're 21, shall agree to marry each other and have scores of neat kids who they'll raise to be nice people who are really good at sports, storytelling, and inventing cool stuff. Most importantly, both parties agree to fall in love and stay in love forever, even though Erica snores like a raging bull and Gabriel has the toes of an ogre.*

*Signed,*

*Erica Anne Emery     &     Gabriel Jacob O'Faolain*

*Spit sworn on: May 30, 1997*

Erica began to laugh nervously. It was all coming back to her like a barrage of old excitement - she remembered signing the contract and imagining what it would be like, years from then, when she and Gabriel would finally make good on it. They had written it up on a night just like this one, where summer celebrations abounded but, same as this night, they only wanted to hang out with each other. And while their families lit sparklers and roasted hot dogs on the fire, they had taken off together down long wooded trails to bury secret troves filled with their most exclusive hopes and promises. "We were crazy kids, weren't we?" she asked into his dear, dark eyes.

But she knew they weren't really crazy, just lucky, for they were and always had been like a pair of twin flames. "So I guess we're getting married this year!" she said with a laugh. "It appears that we're contractually bound!"

"I guess so," he replied, amused. "Now would that be the very worst thing?"

"No way!" she replied quickly, and kissed him on his stubbly cheek. "I'd marry you and this face of yours in a heartbeat." Thinking nothing more of it for the moment, she went back to digging through the capsule and pulled out a three-pack of Kinder eggs that looked surprisingly like they had retained their oviform. When she turned to show him, she saw him pull a little silver box out of the basket. She gasped. It looked like an antique, well-cared for and shiny, with delicate brass hinges and etched in a floral design. Undoubtedly, it held something old and important.

Erica didn't want to presume the box held a ring, because, she told herself, a box like that could carry a number of things. Like perhaps earrings, or maybe a Titanic-era brooch. It sure looked like a ring box though. But why would he have a ring box? She briefly considered that perhaps it held matches, or after-dinner mints.

But then he began presenting, the way men in movies always do, holding it up with both hands, fingers poised to pop it open. Erica held her breath as he cracked it at the hinge, allowing in just enough moonbeam that the stones inside caught the light and dazzled with prismatic glimmer. She asked herself if she was dreaming, but in doing so, acknowledged she wasn't. Nope, this is real life, and I am the luckiest bitch alive.

"Erica," he started as she stared amorously, glancing down at the ring in disbelief. "I've loved you since we were kids, and I've spent the last twelve years without you, looking for someone just like you. Now that you're back in my life, I can't imagine letting you go." Erica felt her head getting light as she sat perfectly still, afraid to move or do anything that might jinx her fairy tale moment. The ring was elegant and simple, with its modest teardrop diamond and a little emerald on either side. It was perfectly imperfect, for the diamond was riddled with inclusions and the emeralds looked mossy and showed dark veins throughout. But she loved it, and it was for her, more than any VVS stone would ever be. If it was from him, then it was exactly what she wanted.

"I know we're young," he continued softly, plucking the ring from its velvet casing and setting the box down. "But we can do anything together, Erica, we have the whole rest of our lives!" And without even waiting for her answer, he slipped it on her finger. A perfect fit. "So I guess what I'm asking is, how do you feel about being my very best friend and hanging with me 'til the end?"

Erica slowly began to unfreeze herself from the pose she'd been holding. Every word he spoke was like honey to her ears. "It's beautiful," she said, feeling tears well up in her eyes. "It's so beautiful, Gabe. I love it."

"It was my grandmother's," he said as he held her hand up to admire it on her. "I know it doesn't look like the rings most girls today expect, but believe me, this one's full of good luck! Every marriage that began with this ring has been strong, happy, and healthy, and has ended in matching burial plots, or, in the case of Betts and Old Pops, ashes sprinkled over the same lilac bush. That's all I really want, and I want it all with you. I want to keep you,

Erica." Gabriel looked at his fiancée with misty eyes. With egg yolk in her hair and bug bites on her arms, she was still the coolest thing he'd ever seen. "And by 'keep you'," he added, "I don't mean it in like a proprietary way, just in a way that means you'd be for me to hold." He smiled earnestly, just a boy asking a girl sincerely if she'd like to love him.

Erica swallowed the words he'd spoken like a gulp of sweetest nectar. "Gabriel," she started, still in disbelief, "I don't know what to say, except . . . yes! Yes, of course I'll marry you! You're the one; it can't be any other way!" She looked down at the ring on her finger, then planted a kiss on his lips. "I want to keep you, too," she whispered. She pulled away just far enough that she could look him in his eyes through the pale white light. "And when I say I want to keep you, you should know I mean it in a *very* proprietary way." She smiled and winked at him, her handsome newly betrothed. "You'll be the sweetest thing I'll ever own." Excitedly and with another ear-piercing squeal, she threw herself into his arms and they tumbled down across the blanket, all giddy and grateful and lapping up each other's adoration. Life was sweet and the moment was gorgeous; neither one had ever been so happy.

Arielle, still watching from above, felt dead inside. Her only wish and hope in life was dissipating more with their every kiss. It was over for her; the curtains were closing. She thought seriously for a moment about jumping from where she was perched, head-first straight down to the ground. But even though her fate was sealed anyway and a quick death would be far less painful, she couldn't bring herself to do it.

Suddenly feeling like a creepy voyeur watching from a tree as they made out, she climbed down quietly and left the two lovers to grope each other in peace. She was very sad, and felt very alone as she walked the soft path back out to the beach. All this time, she had hated Erica for coming in and taking what was hers when the truth of the matter all along was that Gabriel's heart had been Erica's since long before Arielle had ever laid eyes on him. It was a hard pill for the mermaid to swallow, for it left her with no options, no love, and nothing to do but wait until the day she'd silently slip away.


By the time the newly-engaged couple made it back to the house, the family was well into a game of Monopoly on the living room rug. Arielle was already effortlessly winning, the owner of all four railroads and with two hotels on each of her top-notch properties. This was much to the chagrin of Ava, who kept landing on them. It was a loud, boisterous foray into board-game real estate but when Erica and Gabriel walked in the front door holding hands, all fell silent and everyone looked up. After a few seconds of frozen stares, Gabriel made his announcement: "She said yes! We're getting married!" Everybody cheered and jumped up to hug them, and to admire how their Grandmother's sparkler looked on the next O'Faolain bride. The house was lit up with warm congratulations and everybody toasted to the future of their family. The only person in the room still sitting on the rug was Arielle.

In the midst of all their celebrating, Erica suddenly felt her joy hit a pause when she noticed Arielle on the floor pretending to be enthralled by the lint between her toes. Obviously, she was refusing to acknowledge their news.

"Arielle!" said Gabriel cheerily, excusing her avoidance. "Did you hear us? We're getting married! There's going to be a wedding!"

Arielle slowly let go of her toes and turned to stare at him from under lowered brows. Her blue eyes that normally held so much depth appeared hollow somehow. He in his ignorant naivety had thought she'd have been excited. He had no idea that his happiness and impending marriage to Erica would literally be the death of his little foundling.

Without taking her low, sad eyes off him, she rose up to her feet and took a step towards him. Although her heart seemed to weigh a ton, she still moved as lightly as ever to where he stood with his arm around his chosen love. So now it was over for her, and she had nothing to lose. Suddenly, she couldn't remember why she ever thought she had a chance with him in the first place.

She took another step towards them and her soles hurt once again as she tiptoed upon invisible points and serrations. As she moved towards them, her defenses felt weakened. Everything hurt. Bitterness built up inside her.

She took another step and thought about all the time she'd wasted trying to make him love her. He had stolen her heart just to give his own to someone else, and was too blind and too preoccupied to even notice.

As she moved closer, stepping faster towards them across the wide living room floor, she felt resentment flood her heart like a tide pool. *Why does he love Erica? Why is she so much better than me?* She thought about her life under the sea, and how she could have had her pick of any merman in the kingdom. Down there, she was the special one. Up in the dry world, she was cast aside for another. She shifted her gaze to Erica and her pretty, smooth visage and imagined smashing the giant pink conch from the coffee table into one of her plump, rosy cheekbones. She smiled eerily as she imagined retracting the conch only to bring it back to smash it through the bridge of her pretty button nose. Her eyes went from hollow to mercurial as she envisioned the bloody aesthetic ruin she'd inflict, if only she was braver. If her fury and bitterness had the powers of telekinesis, then the whole coast was about to go down in flames...

"Earth to Arielle!" she heard Demetra say excitedly, and it shook her out of her hostile daydream. "Did you hear him? There's going to be a wedding!" Arielle looked up at her Gabriel, then up at his Erica, whose face was still perfect. Then she glanced at the conch, still sitting untouched on the table.

With a sigh, she gave her newly engaged friends each an obligatory hug and a kiss, then ducked out of the way so the family could get back to excitedly discussing timelines and venues. Gabriel smelled his new fiancée's hair. Even with traces of egg in it, she smelled good. Really good. "We wish to be married as soon as possible!" he said, having agreed with Erica that a summer wedding was only appropriate, but neither wanted to wait until the following year.

"What's the rush?" asked Ava. "I'm sure you'll still be all googly-eyed about each other in a year's time." Gabriel and Erica smiled at each other adoringly. "Actually," he said, "we're thinking next week!"

Lucia was taken aback. "You're the first of my kids to wed!" she said. "I might need more than a week to plan it!"

"It's okay, Mom," assured Gabriel. "We don't need a huge wedding; we just want the important people there. And we want to have it on the Alexandria! I was planning to call Walt in the morning." The Walt he spoke of was a friend of his grandfather's, who lived in Prince Rupert and owned a small fleet of nice wooden ships. Most of them were used as charters for gambling cruises and sightseeing tours but there was one ship, the Alexandria, which stood apart from the rest. He had purchased the antique vessel in Malta back in the early nineties and had had her shipped back to his yard in pieces so he could rebuild her to her original glory. She was now all but completely restored, but with the addition of some modern conveniences like flushing toilets and an ocean GPS.

"He's on her finishing touches right now!" he said. "She'll be ready in just a few days!"

"And how do you know all this?" asked Cliff.

"I follow him on Twitter," Gabriel answered with a shrug.

"We'll need to book a caterer," added Lucia. "And someone to do the flowers!" But Erica explained how she had three aunts who owned a catering business, another aunt who built award-winning marzipan cakes, and an uncle who owned a floral shop. Also, she had a cousin who was a holy woman at a new-age spirituality commune in the Yukon.

"Well haven't you got a relative for all seasons," said Lucia, excitedly pulling out a stack of bridal magazines she had bought that afternoon. "So I guess the only base left to be covered is the matter of the dress you'll be donning on the big day!" But before Lucia could explain the significance of the pink, yellow, and purple sticky flags that poked out the sides of the pages, Erica informed her that she'd already chosen her dress.

"I'll be wearing my mother's," she said decisively, with a dreamy, nostalgic look in her eye. Lucia remembered the dress, for she'd attended the wedding back in '85 with Ava seven months fat in her tummy. "The butter cream lace?" she asked breathlessly, closing her eyes and remembering how pretty Erica's mother looked walking down the aisle.

"Yes, that's the one," Erica replied proudly. "I always dreamt of wearing it one day."

Gabriel covered his ears as they talked dresses. He had heard somewhere that it's bad luck to know anything about it, or something like that.

"I'm so excited, let's have this thing tomorrow!" said Lucia, grabbing a Niagara Falls souvenir plate off the sideboard and taking the family by surprise as she smashed it to the floor. "OPA!" she shouted, and kiss-kissed vivaciously her son and future daughter-in-law. Bubbling over with happiness, her husband grabbed her for a spin around the kitchen and together they smashed a few more plates for good measure. Arielle sat alone outside in the dark as inside, the family cheerily mapped out the day that would be her very last.

# thirty-one

## Deeds

*(the Lips of a Hobo)*

"Congratulations on your engagement," said Ava, poking her head inside her brother's bedroom door. Erica was still downstairs sipping champagne with the parents, and it was just the two siblings upstairs.

"Thanks, Aves," he said warmly. "Listen - I didn't mean to beat you to the punch. I know you're supposed to go first, being the eldest and all. Please know there is no shame in coming in second."

"If I ever get married at all," she said with a snort.

"Oh, you say that now. But one day, when you meet that perfect guy - "

Ava interrupted him. "Spare me, Gabe; I know all the trite clichés," she said, rolling her pretty dark eyes.

"I'm just saying, not all hope is lost." And while Gabriel put away a basket of clean laundry, Ava reached into her pocket and pulled a plastic-filtered cigarillo out and lit it. He hated when she did that in his room and was about to comment until she pulled a Cuban cigar out of the other pocket and handed it to him. He shrugged and smiled, gladly accepted, and sparked it in celebration.

"Brother Gabe, I'm about to tell you something I've never told anyone," said Ava, slowly exhaling the cherry-scented smoke. He braced himself, so sure she was about to admit she was a lesbian, finally. It wasn't that. "This is not something I'm proud of, but . . . I am a horrid bitch, straight through to my blackened core. I can pretend to be sweet and easygoing in front of a guy but never for long because the fact is I am neurotic, argumentative, and cold. I am cold as the Arctic Circle; I've been called Svalbard cold. And no one wants to marry Svalbard."

Gabriel's eyes smiled at that comment. "No arguments there! But that's the stuff we love you for," he said with a chuckle. "And there is a foot for every shoe. You might rip on people a lot and it might humiliate an individual deeply and irreparably from time to time but that doesn't make you a bad person. Doing bad things is what makes a person bad- you just call it like you see it, especially when doing so gives you the opportunity to be harsh and cold, that's all."

"It's more than that, Gabe. Not only am I incapable of genuine kindness, I am physically incapable of even saying anything nice. Even in instances where it could potentially benefit me. I can't even be nice for selfish reasons! It's all disses. Cold, mean scorn and scurrility. I've checked."

"Ava, maybe you should stop focusing your energy on the things you dislike about yourself and instead focus on being all the things you admire. And if you're looking for something nice to say right now, you can go ahead and tell me how sexbomb my new sneaks are!" he said, gesturing towards his fresh new footwear that still smelled like factory rubber. Gabriel loved new sneaker smell.

"Yeah, I was going to say, those are nice," Ava agreed.

". . . because you're trying to be a better person?" asked Gabriel.

"No, because they're pretty boss. I mean it; good choice," she answered.

"Thanks, Erica helped me pick them. But since we're beautifying our lives here, may I make one more suggestion?" She nodded. "For extra karmic credit, instead of coughing up cajolery, try executing a few random, anonymous acts of kindness." Gabriel smiled satisfyingly, as if he held the secret to all life's happiness in his hands.

"If it's nice things we're trying to do, what's the difference between doing it loud n' proud, and doing it in secret?"

"Well everyone knows anything truly selfless needs to be done in secret," he replied.

Ava thought about it for a second, trying to think of the last time she did something selfless for no rewards or praise or thanks. She thought long and hard, then came up with something. "I think I already kind of do that," she said hopefully. Then she explained how sometimes when she's walking through a downtown park smoking, she'll often flick her butt or joint roach while it's still reasonably smokeable.

"And who are you helping but the street sweepers you're giving job security to?" her brother asked.

"Obviously the hobos!" she replied. "I'll be like, I could take another few puffs and kill it, or I could flick it now and let a derelict have my 'resties!"

"People who flick their butts make this world a grosser place, you realize," he said, unimpressed.

Ava couldn't hold back her chortle. "You're looking at it all the wrong way!"

He chortled back, "Well then please enlighten me."

Ava grinned knowingly. "Just imagine the joy it would bring the down-and-out dero who chances upon it. Have you ever seen one, Gabe? Have you ever noticed their beady eyes as they sketchily yet diligently scan the ground? What do you think they're looking for?"

"Money?" he guessed.

"Money AND something to smoke!" she said. "They spend their days praying they'll find the sorts of pennies from heaven that I leave for them. And those guys'll put their lips to anything."

Gabriel made face. "This is way outta my league. I'm not exactly versed on what a hobo will or won't bring his lips to." He shuddered.

"Point is, while I can't really help them with everything else that's dingy in their lives, what I can do is leave the little surprises that make life to them worth living," she said with compassion.

"And what if a kid or a bird or a dog found it first and ate it? What then?" demanded Gabriel, crossing his arms and eyeing her inquisitively.

"It wouldn't happen," she said definitively. "No self-respecting wheedler lets a child or lesser species beat him to the payday!"

Gabriel sighed. "Well aren't you just the Princess Di of vagrants," he said ironically.

"I guess so," said Ava, nodding slowly, smiling and feeling a bit better about herself. Her eyes lit up in a way he hadn't seen them do in a long time; he was glad, but also unsure how much personal satisfaction she could honestly derive from the 'deeds' she'd been doing. In any event, he was happy for her.

"Good talk, bro! Congrats again on the engagement!" she said merrily, and with that, bouncily skipped out of his room, leaving him scratching his head.

# thirty-two

## The Run

---

Arielle had been asked to play ring-bearer at the wedding. She was told she'd be wearing orange.

It was during the night of the rehearsal dinner, over the loud, tangy meal prepared by Erica's formidable Greek aunts, in which all the wedding roles were assigned. Erica had asked her two best friends from camp, Jess and Juliana, to be her bridesmaids, and had asked Demetra to be the flower girl. Ava offered to be in charge of the punch bowl, and Arielle was asked to bear the rings.

Of course, she did not want this role. In fact, she wanted no part in the wedding at all. If given the choice, she'd have preferred to sit it out, watch everyone else set sail, and then lock herself in the bathroom so that when the time came, she could just evaporate into a tuft of salty froth, pitifully slipping off clean porcelain to slowly sink down the drain.

Her dress would be orange along with the bridesmaids and there would be flowers in her hair. No raincoats, no rain boots, so sorry. Orange shoes with an orange dress. Erica liked orange.

She didn't know why she agreed, or if she even actually agreed. When Erica giddily brought up the idea, she didn't nod but she didn't shake her head either, and so everyone present simply took her lack of response as a silent *'just pencil me right in'*. Now, she was obligated, and there would be no way around it.

So she was in, and she had the mass of orange silk and taffeta hanging in its clear dry cleaning bag on the back of her bedroom door to prove it. Tangerine Dream, as Erica called it. Sort of like Clementine Holiday, but zingier. It mocked her while she lay in bed wide awake. She didn't know why, but she detested the color orange. She loved yellow and she loved red, but there was something about the mix of the two colors that set her teeth on edge. She couldn't understand it, but she knew she hated it. And now, she hated it with a passion.

She sorely dreaded the next morning where she'd have to slip into the dress that had been chosen for her and pretend to be dazzled that the man of her dreams had found the woman of his dreams in someone else. It seemed almost poetic, she thought, that she should bear their rings; that she should guard the very adornments that signified her forthcoming death, and carry it to her beloved on a fluffy white pillow, no less.

After lying still for what felt like years, Arielle finally just got up and crept quietly out of the house so she could try and find a way to tire herself out. In the still evening air, it was as if even the wind was resting up for the big day that was about to begin in just a few short hours. The animals from the sea who came up to visit her could sense her melancholy, and so they respectfully kept their distance but watched her from afar.

She walked down the beach by herself, stepping far closer to the waves than she'd have ever dared in daylight and, even though she found herself surrounded by the magnificent surface world she had once so zealously coveted, she began to feel deeply and agonizingly alone.

She thought about her decisions and the foolish leap she had taken, just to get closer to a boy. She thought about how headstrong, stubborn, and defiant she had been. She had been a selfish girl to put her childish desires ahead of her people and the will of her father, the king. She hung her head down low; she felt like the worst princess ever.

In the stillness of this night, stars didn't even twinkle, they just glowed. No clouds passed between them and the Earth she stood upon and so all stood still, hung tight and beamed brightly. As she passed beneath them, she kept her face down, feeling undeserving of the splendor of basking in their light.

The deeper she journeyed down the road of regret, the more her face twisted into a crestfallen grimace. All the loathing, shame and pity she felt for herself began to weigh down on her, resting heavily and slothfully upon her wispy shoulders and neck. The tears behind her eyes that begged for release just circulated around her temples thumping, pressing, contracting. She longed to be free from it all, to just sink away into the cool sand, never to be seen again. Awash in her own despondent blue, she began wishing for an immediate, merciful ending so that she might retire to her state of eternal effervescence just one day sooner than scheduled.

Just as soon as the thought escaped her head, she felt the sharp pains she had gotten so used to stab through the toes, heels, and arches of her tender feet. In true heartbreaking fashion, the pain that shot through her feet served to remind her of how things can always get worse, especially when you already think you've arrived at rock bottom.

But then, something marvelous happened. Along with the sharp pains that plagued her came the reminder of the magnificent strength her feet and legs possessed. As she admired her little feet, the beautiful pair she traded her voice for, she recalled the rhythm and dance they'd shown her and the *ooohs* and *aaaahs* they'd earned her and finally understood why the sea witch had set their price so high.

She shook off her sorrow and began to leap upon her lovely feet. They were, after all, the one thing she got out of this deal that was totally hers to enjoy. They weren't like the boy she wanted whose attention required competition and whose approval she spent her days pining for. No, they were freely hers and they carried her lightly and gracefully, even when the rest of her body wanted to cave in and melt away. Sure they hurt to tread upon but she began to think of the pain as simply the heightened sensitivity that came along with their overdeveloped capacity for wonderment and grace. So she kicked her feet up high, tossed sand into the air with her twinkling, flicking toes and did cartwheels and flips along the shoreline. Then she stopped, noticed the awakening of the winds as they pushed through her loose, long hair, and began to chase them down the beach.

She ran, challenging the breeze, running as fast as her feet could carry her, leaping up and over the highest reaching waves like a bird taking to flight. The salmon that followed her from the water leapt and dove alongside the shore as she pushed the speed in her legs to the limit. She realized that while she had thoroughly tested the strength and beauty in her legs, she hadn't truly tested their speed until this moment. So, in a final tribute to their unreal dexterity, she took the legs that would be hers for just one more day and night, on a good, long run.

She ran until the contrast between bright moon and dark sky began to fade, then she turned around and ran back. She pushed herself so hard, running so fast on her bare little feet, leaping swiftly over the pieces of driftwood and rock that dotted the coastline.

When she finally returned to the point from where she'd begun, her sleepiness had finally caught up to her and exhaustion took over as she allowed herself to slump down into the sand and take the nap her body was begging for. It was the best warm, dry, wonderful sleep she had had, since she arrived.

She woke up to the sun's warm kisses upon her cheeks, the last morning kisses she would ever feel, at least in this life. She kept her eyes closed as the warmth penetrated through her lids and went deep into her, clearing out her guilt and regret, and making room for acceptance. A fire was lit inside her, telling her to enjoy this last day like it was a gift, the beauty of which made even clearer by the nature of its very near expiry. To her own surprise, she felt a smile creep over her face. It was sad to think about her own untimely ending, but the feeling of warmth on her chilly, sandy toes was enough to make her grateful for all the time she was given and had spent. She basked in it for a few precious moments, expressing gratitude to the universe for all the paradisiacal things she had been lucky enough to see in her short lifetime.

She stood up and shook the sand from her hair. Everyone would be rising soon, and they'd be wondering why she wasn't up and getting ready for the wedding. So she scampered inside to have one last bath before slipping into the orange dress.

thirty-three

## The Walking of the Aisle

At the hour of noon when the sun was high and hot, congregations of people clad in ties and cocktail dresses lined the O'Faolains' lawn and beach. They stood upon yards and yards of running carpet, an amenity Lucia had insisted on so that women's heels wouldn't aerate the lawn while they walked themselves down to the tender boats.

Cameras and camera phones were in everyone's hands as people shot rolls upon rolls of the marvelously refurbished relic. The Alexandria was riddled with richly carved accents but the most beautiful thing about her was her giant bow ornament, a pretty lady whose body charmingly ended in a fish's tail. The ship's proud white sails billowed with the stiff breeze as the seasoned vessel nudged at the waves, eager to set sail for the open water.

Once all were aboard, they took their seats on deck among the rows of white chairs that lined the shiny hardwood aisle. All around were huge flower arrangements in all colors. Arielle played the harp for everyone while they mingled and exchanged niceties, commented on the tasteful boat decor and on how last-minute yet utterly fabulous the wedding plans were turning out to be. Erica and Gabriel didn't expect that everyone could make it on such short notice, but there was not one invitation sent out that didn't net them an enthusiastic yes. Seated at her instrument, Arielle could see everyone as they poured in, full of smiles and all gawking at the talented little thing who could play the harp as angelically as she danced. And even though inside her heart she was mournful and almost numb, it pleased her to know that her efforts were helping to make Gabriel's big day extra lovely.

When she was given the signal to cut the harp and take her place among the wedding party, it struck her that she was simply a supernumerary in the production of her love's big day. His leading lady was already cast, but there was a nice, tertiary place for her among the extras. Indeed, hers was a modest role, but she had come that day to play her heart out and so she did.

Everyone went silent, and the string quartet began to play. Demetra came out first, sashaying and covering the aisle with a basket full of petals, followed by Arielle, swaying delicately with the rings on the pillow. Next came the bridesmaids, gliding in proud support of their dear friend, and looking forward to partying that night with the groomsmen, who were two of Gabriel's most dashing cousins. All the girls had flowers in their hair, and the breeze seemed to be having fun flicking them out.

When the whole party was in position at the front and the bride still had yet to emerge, everyone strained to look back through the curtains for any sign of her. The music kept playing, but still she didn't show . . .

Until out she came! She was positively glowing in her mother's dress, surrounded by all four of her short, portly aunts. With no brothers or close uncles to call upon, she had been expecting a solo aisle walk and had made peace with the idea long ago. It was her aunts who would not hear of it.

"You can't just give yourself away, where's the faith in that?" they asked as they tightened her corset and spritzed finishing spray on her hair before pinning in her veil. "You don't want people to think you don't have any family!"

They insisted that one of them should accompany her down the aisle and even though she resisted and told them she was fine walking alone, they all just kept on squabbling over who should have the honors. When go-time was upon them and they hadn't yet decided, they concluded that they should all share in the honor of walking her down, together. Erica was speechless. Their outfits didn't exactly go with her dress the way a handsome, middle-aged dad in a three-piece suit would have, if hers was still around.

But, crowded aisle or not, everyone was spellbound and gasped in amazement when Erica stepped out looking stunning in her mother's dress. Lucia and Cliff remembered the dress's original cut and couldn't believe how modern the off-the-shoulder lace looked after its frilly taffeta layers had been torn out and white ribbons had been added to lace up the back, making the dress fit her like a glove. She even wore white elbow gloves to add the perfect, elegant accent, and they served well to give the aunts something to grip with their long, colorful fingernails while they led her to the altar.

It wasn't how she'd always pictured it, gliding in her gown of white with four short European-born spinsters in tow. It wasn't ideal as far as aesthetics went, but the family support proved priceless and as each in turn took a seat in the front row and tearfully waved her hankie, Erica couldn't imagine a sweeter way to have been given away.

The ceremony was quick and lovely, non-denominational and concise. They chose not to hear any readings from bibles or subject their dear guests to any sort of rituals that require lots of standing up and sitting down. Their wedding was simply a celebration of love; twenty-five minutes of blessings and vows in front of their nearest and dearest, presided over by a woman in a lavender-colored robe. Also, there was a short performance art piece on 'Love as a Creative Life Force' performed by some of Gabriel's home-schooled cousins Saskatchewan. When the ceremony was over, everyone cheered and stood to follow the newly-weds to the dance floor as up-tempo beats were heard starting over the loudspeaker. Everyone was having the time of their life, and the only person who had the chance to get antsy and uptight was a six-month-old baby who was suddenly struck with a serious hankering for breast milk and a nap, in that order.

After a straight hour of spinning and grooving wildly surrounded by everyone they loved on Earth, the guests of honor took to the podium hand-in-hand and out of breath to say a few words to their people. As the ship they reveled upon sailed slowly along the coast, a myriad of fish followed them, swimming strangely close and unafraid as if they knew they were safe around a wedding ship, which carried no nets or lines. Gulls flew in circles above the boat but weren't dive-bombing the shallow-swimming fish like they normally would. No, it was a day off for everyone, for even they had come simply to enjoy the wedding and watch for glimpses of their princess, the fish who was now so famously out-of-water.

"Beloved family and honored guests," began Gabriel, "I just wanted to take a moment to thank you all for coming and joining us on this gorgeous, perfect day. I still can't believe we just got married!" The crowd cheered as the young married couple leaned in for a kiss, and then another. "We can't wait to party into the night with all of you but before things get outta hand, my beautiful bride has something to say to everyone here." Then he passed the mic to Erica and she took it in the hand that wasn't holding a champagne flute. Everyone fell into silent anticipation for what she was about to say.

Erica smiled huge for everyone there, for already they all felt like her extended family. "So far, this has been the greatest day of my life and it's only just begun!" she said. "Like my wonderful *husband* just said, thank you all for coming! And thanks especially to my astoundingly lovely new in-laws, for welcoming me in with open arms. I want you guys to know that literally every wish I've ever made in the last decade have all come true for me here today.

"Now, this next thing I have to say may come off a little harsh, but still, I feel it deserves the attention of every person here. The O'Faolains have sprung for an open bar this evening!" The crowd erupted into a cheer, and Erica paused to allow it before continuing. ". . .and I am certain that everyone here will drink to their hearts content and have a merry old time with us. Please, enjoy yourselves; that was the whole point of inviting all our favorite players.

"However, should any one of you choose to drink and then get behind a wheel of any kind tonight, be it that of a boat, auto, golf cart or float plane, then you had better pray that whatever 'accident' you get into kills you instantly because if it does not, I will come looking for you. And when I find you, I will kill you myself. With my bare hands. In this dress."

The crowd remained completely silent as they digested her violent yet understandable promise. Most everyone there already knew about her parents' tragic accident.

"There are taxi stubs with the valet at the harbor," she continued, "and there will be shuttles waiting when we dock to take you anywhere on the island, including all of the ferry docks and every hotel. Please, for the love of all things bright and wonderful about this life, please, I implore you all: make sure every bad decision made here tonight . . . is on the dance floor. Salut!" said the bride.

"Salut!" repeated everyone, and then the party re-commenced and they sailed out into the late afternoon. The wedding would go down in the history of their family as the prettiest Tofino had ever seen.

# thirty-four

## Setting Sail

---

After docking and saying what felt like a thousand good-nights and thank-yous, the last of the guests departed while the newlyweds, their wedding party and The Alexandria's crew pushed off to set sail for Kauai'i. As soon as they were back out on the water, they bid their best friends goodnight and excitedly retired to the master cabin to enjoy their first night as husband and wife.

Once back in their room, Erica locked the door behind them, dimmed the lights and lit the handful of candles she had brought in with her travel bag. She'd packed vanilla incense too, and some chocolates and some oils - everything had to be perfect when she made love to her husband for the first time. After all, she'd been dreaming about this moment since the moment he proposed.

Actually, the truth was, she'd been dreaming of this moment for far longer than that. Coincidentally, the very first moment she realized she liked boys was the same moment she realized she liked Gabriel. She still vividly remembered the day the ins and outs of intercourse were explained to her in her Sex Ed, and even though at the time it grossed her out, she remembered wondering how Gabriel's penis compared to the one being shown through the projector.

In this moment, standing in front of the only one she ever loved, she felt proud of herself for having had the restraint to hold out on giving herself to him until now. There had been so many times they could've but they didn't, because the wait was too sweet to squander and they knew they'd have the rest of their lives to succumb to it.


With the mood now nicely set, Erica stepped out of her dress to reveal a lacy white bustier. She had never really worn lingerie before, but then again, she'd never had someone she wanted to wear it for. But it was fun, and she felt like a vixen, uninhibited. She was ready now; she had never been so ready.

Gabriel's eyes widened at the sight of her, the pageantry of her sexy ensemble noted and appreciated. He stood in disbelief that it was all for him, like a kid discovering Santa got him everything on his list.

Following suit, he loosened his tie and unbuttoned his shirt 'til she could see the little black trail of hair that led down inside his boxers. This excited her now more than ever, because even though she'd seen it enough times before, she'd never seen it as his wife and with a delicious new sense of pride of ownership. Everything about him seemed more perfect now that he belonged to her.

He stepped closer, reached his arms around her, and pressed his fingertips into the small of her back until she gently fell forward into him. Her warm, lace-covered stomach pressed into his warm, bare stomach and she kissed him sweetly, dangling her arms around his neck and running her hands through his hair. Their kiss heated up, growing in passion as they held one another, letting the intensity of their love climb to new heights and swallow them. He reached his hands under her bum and picked her up by the thighs, squeezing her healthy muscles and flesh between his fingers. He was aroused by her health; his new wife was the very picture of it, and her body demonstrated its vitality with the damp warmth she pressed into his lap. He could feel her moisten more with every kiss, nibble, and nuzzle, this lusty, lovely partner of his. She was strong, and they would be strong together.

He held her up like a prize, leaning back and cradling her on his lap. He tasted her from her lips, to her neck, to her breasts. "Are you my new Missus?" he asked with a tone of disbelief, whispering in her ear as he brought her down on top of him.

"Closer than sharing last names!" she answered, gently pushing the crisp white shirt off his dark shoulders. She hugged him close, reaching under his arms to rub the back that daily surf sessions had made muscular and firm.

He smiled and took his bride by the back of her head to kiss her hard on the mouth. She closed her eyes and gave in to him, allowing all of her other senses to take over while she melted, overwhelmed with joy. Now that they were alone, there was no one else left in the world, and nowhere else in the universe either one would rather be.


The little mermaid lay alone in her bed, sleepy but awake, staring out to sea. She watched the moon and the trail of glitter it left upon the ripples, stretching from the edge of the horizon to the foot of her bed. She was afraid to fall asleep because she knew that once she closed her eyes, her time on earth would be up. So she kept them open, even though she was tired, and tried to hold onto every precious moment she had left.

Through her sad, blurry eyes, she noticed a formation swimming towards her, cutting through the glittery surface and headed straight for her window. When she sat up and squinted to see, she discovered it was all five of her sisters. She jumped up and ran out to the deck, climbing down the ladder to see them. It was so good to see their pretty white faces glimmering under the silver moon, but when she took the cold, wet hand of her eldest sister, she noticed right away that something was different. Then she looked around at all of them and saw that each one had had all of her beautiful hair chopped off.

"We sold our hair to the sea witch," said her sister. "In return, she gave us this dagger." The dagger she held was a thing of dark, intricate beauty, made of pure silver and with a handle of stacked ivory skulls. "You are to kill the human prince and cut out his heart," she said, passing the knife. ". . .and carry it, still beating, down to the sea witch. Only then will she give you back your beautiful tail so you can come back and live with us again."

The little mermaid held the dagger up to get a better look at it. Moonlight shone against the blade, and the pointed tip looked sharp enough to cut through hard stone as if it was warm butter.

She climbed back up the ladder, holding the dagger carefully in her hand and away from her body. She was afraid of it; it was indeed the last key to her salvation, yet it represented something monstrous and almost unfathomable. She stopped for a moment and looked back at her sisters. Her beautiful siren sisters loved her so fully, they had given up the gorgeous locks they loved so much just to bring her this dagger and a chance to live past the dawn. They thought it so easy; kill him and come back. He was just another human, after all. They would never understand how this would be the hardest trade she'd ever have to make.

# thirty-five

## Love, actually

All was quiet on the old ship. Everyone aboard was either sleeping soundly in their cabins, or passed out drunk from the festivities. In the still, calm darkness of the early morning, Arielle was sure she would not be seen. Creeping ever so lightly on her delicate feet and concealing the dagger among the folds of her nightgown, no one ever would have known that she carried the heaviest of burdens.

As she reached the grand wooden doors of the master suite, she stopped to listen before turning the knob. Nothing could be heard from inside except the slow, comfortable breathing of the sleeping newlyweds, and the bit of breeze that whistled in through the window and under the doors. Carefully, she pushed them open and stepped inside.

As soon as she entered and shut the door behind her, her nose and throat filled with the sweet and dewy scent of them. Her prince and his bride held each other in a warm, tangled embrace, the big canopy over their bed like a white cloud. How lovely he looked while he slept; how lovingly he held the one in his arms. As she crossed the room towards them, she couldn't take her eyes off his thick black eyelashes that fluttered so softly while he dreamt.

Watching him sleep, she wanted him more strongly than she'd ever wanted him before. In the daytime, he was tall and proud and everything a man should be but here in bed, asleep with his love as they lay clinging, his face conveyed a precious innocence she'd never noticed in him before. Even the day-old stubble that darkened his jaw seemed somehow childish, like he was just a boy in the body of a man, playing house with a girl for the very first time. With his bride at his side, his set appeared complete.

Arielle took little steps toward him until her toes were right under the bed's edge. She fixed her gaze down upon the man who didn't choose her, who never even once considered her in the running. For a second, she felt bitter jealousy poison her heart, and she welcomed it. After all, one would require sufficient hatred in order to muster up the rage it takes to cut a man's heart out.

The longer she stared, envious of the love they'd undoubtedly spent all night making, the more she cursed them both for leaving her out in the cold. Without taking her eyes off his face, she slowly began to raise the dagger over his heart.

She clutched the handle so tightly, her knuckles hurt. Her arms shook, and her wrists ached cold. She began to imagine what it would be like to hold his heart, finally. To dive back into the cool ocean with it pumping in her little hands. She wondered if he ever realized he'd been holding hers all along.

Suddenly, something took over her body. Without even thinking about it, her eyes shut, her knees buckled, and she threw the wretched instrument of death out the open window. As it hit the water, it turned the blue ocean around it a bloody shade of red, as if the dagger itself was bleeding in her love's place. He was safe, and her chance was gone. And now, her time was up.

As the dagger sunk out of view, a vibration of peace was restored to the room. In this moment of absolute clarity, Arielle realized there was no way that she or any desperate, terrified version of herself could have ever gone through with hurting Gabriel. It simply wouldn't have been possible; the love within her would have never agreed, for she knew that to live knowing she'd hurt one so wonderful would've been a fate far worse than death.

Now empty-handed and with no choice but to die, she looked down at him again. Blissfully asleep, he had no idea that his little foundling was about to leave his side forever. How terribly she missed him already.

Her lips began to quiver and she fell to her knees at his side. She whimpered without a sound, and wept without tears in the pathetically, unsatisfyingly dry cry that only mermaids know. As she wept, frustrated and sad, she kissed softly his hand that hung over the edge of the bed. Gently pressing her lips and rubbing her soft cheeks against the cluster of freckles that dotted his wrist, she silently sobbed some more, finding it unbearable to think that, just like on the day she saved him, the impending sunrise meant she'd have to part from him. Except this time, she'd never get to see him again. The idea of it was so devastating that it sucked the wind right out of her.

When she pulled away, she noticed there was a little drop of water sitting on his hand where her cheek had just been. Her eyes began to blur, as if they were filling up with moisture.

Investigating the wet peculiarity, she touched her finger to her lower lashes and then inspected what she found. *A tear! Could it be?* The feeling of release was merciful. The tear was so tiny and yet, looking down at the drop on her finger, she could imagine an entire wet universe within its blurry edges. It was such an incredible first that she wanted to save it, but then she remembered that where she was going, she could definitely not bring any keepsakes.

A few tears were followed by many and they began streaming down her face with increasing force. A floodgate had burst open, and there was no stopping the waters now. The tears came fast and strong, drenching her porcelain cheeks and reddening the whites of her blue eyes. She cried for her life that was over, and for all the pretty things she'd be leaving behind. She struggled to catch her breath as it all sank in, that she was leaving forever and never, ever coming back.

Then, all of a sudden, the tears ceased. All went quiet inside her head, and she felt a calm warmth roll over her body, expanding her from the chest out as she took long, slow breaths. In this moment of heightened senses and still-standing time, something assured her that there was nothing left to fear.

It was a peculiar feeling, for losing out on Gabriel's love had been the worst conceivable scenario from the start. But somehow, in this moment while she made peace with her ending, she couldn't ignore a feeling that the universe was unfolding exactly as it should, and everything, though presently it hurt, was all working out for the best. Warmth began to radiate from deep within her, and she found herself feeling glad for the two young lovers, and wishing beautiful things for their future.

She wiped her face dry and let out a deep sigh, peering misty-eyed out the window as the sun, still hidden behind the edge of the world, began to heat up the horizon. In just a few more moments, a new day would begin and it would be time for her body to become one with the whitecaps.

So, in the spirit of getting the hard part over with, she stood up and wiped her teary hands on the fabric of her nightgown. As she did so, she noticed that something strange was happening to the tips of her fingers. In addition to the water that was streaming through her eyes, her fingertips seemed to be disintegrating into tiny, wet bubbles. She observed them for a moment; as soon as they formed, they broke away from her body and floated out upon the air. Her ending was beginning, and that was all there was to know.

She turned and went for the door but when she reached for the handle, her hand fell right through it as more bubbles lifted away. She used her elbow to open it and as she stepped through, glanced down at her toes to see that small, foamy puddles surrounded them as well. The puddles evaporated almost as soon as she stepped past them. She was evaporating, too.

Realizing what was happening and knowing she hadn't much time, she started towards the back of the ship. She began to run, feeling herself become lighter as iridescent little bubbles dispersed into her wake. Tears fell from her eyes still, but now they did so in streaming globules of salty air that rolled down her cheeks to be licked away by the breeze. She was becoming sea foam.

When she reached the stern, she grabbed onto its white railing. Her fingers were now gone, but her palms remained. She lifted a foot to step up but fell forward, and tumbled right through the railing. She was tufts of shimmering opalescence, falling to the water in slow motion, witnessing the sun's rays break dawn one final time. As she breathed in her last breath of salty sea air, she thought of Gabriel's face.

As she hit the ocean water for the first time that summer, she expected to feel its beautiful, refreshing cold shoot through her. Instead, she felt a cozy tingling all over as her body disintegrated into a constellation of tiny air pockets, churning gently with the moving water. Waves rolled through her and twirled the last remaining bubbles from her nightgown, and she felt what it was to become one with the spritzing crest. Feeling her body recycle itself back into the will of the waters, she said a sweet goodbye to the short but extraordinary life she'd lived. And she closed her eyes, preparing to slip away for good.

But then, just as the last of her light was about to be extinguished, something gripped her in its warm, loving arms. She couldn't see what was holding her, but could feel it cradling her sweetly as it scooped her from the water, lifting her higher and higher. Soon, the waves she had just been rolling in were far beneath her and she was floating in the clouds.

"Who are you?" she asked as she looked all around her. She had her voice back, and it felt wonderful vibrating through her throat and chest again. She searched for a face in the clouds around her but saw no one. Then, she heard the most angelic voice, and knew without a doubt that she was being carried by the loving spirit of her mother.

As soon as she knew it, a beautiful, smiling face appeared before her. Diaphanous and otherworldly, her mother looked exactly like she'd always pictured, with the same flaxen hair and fair skin as her own, and the kind of deep blue eyes that seemed to peer straight into the core of her.

"My child, how I've been waiting to see you; I was prepared to wait three hundred years more!" Her face was so beautiful and beaming with joy, and she shone like a bright star. Arielle couldn't believe her eyes, and felt herself tear up again. She was so very happy to see her mother, but was ashamed of having failed, and for setting the whole plan out of order. "My beloved princess, why do you cry?" asked her mother. "There is nothing to fear anymore; we can rejoice now!" But the little mermaid just shook her head, remembering what the sea witch had told her. Since she hadn't found the love she'd set out to find, she'd have to give up her place among her family.

"Mother, there is no place for me in the heavens anymore. I am to remain as sea foam on the crests of the waves for all eternity." She cast her eyes down in disgrace, expecting her mother to just bring her back down to the water. Instead, her mother began to giggle until her laughter was so jubilant and delightful, it echoed out into the sky. "My dear daughter, you have not failed at finding love! You have found more love than most souls could even hope for." As they fell from her mother's rosy lips, the words sounded too good to be true. "Love comes to us in many ways, and takes many different forms," she explained. "You may not have found the exact love you were counting on, but rest assured that you *are* loved, and in ways that not even death could remove."

Arielle thought about what her mother was telling her. It was true, she had not found the romantic love she'd yearned for, but the more she thought about it, the more she realized that love truly had come to her from so many unexpected sources, from the beginning of her young life until the very end. She'd had the unconditional love of her family and people, and then when she ventured up on land, she'd found the love of a whole new family, and the kindness of so many souls. The more she examined this new definition of love, the more she realized it had been making her life sweeter every step of the way since long before she was even aware she was seeking it. Love was, and always had been, everything.

Arielle closed her eyes and let the natural high of such a great truth send ripples of joy through her ascending spirit. Looking down at the grand vessel below, she thought of Gabriel who'd be waking soon, and wanted to take one last look at him before she left forever. She asked her mother to wait for her, and then floated herself down towards the ship and through the top deck until she was hovering like an angel above his bed. She watched him quietly through the sheer canopy, still as deep in dreamland as he had been just a few moments before when she left him. Already, it felt to her like a lifetime had passed since then.

She drifted down until she was hovering right above him and gave her love a soft kiss on the brow. There had been so many things she had wanted to do to him, so many other ways in which she had wanted to kiss him. But now, while her spirit visited him this one last time, all there was to do was kiss him gently and unbeknown, the way she had done the first night when she had brought him to rest in the sand. She knew the memory of his face would live on in her dreams forever, and with that, she was finally ready to leave his side.

Then, just as she was about to leave, the little mermaid Arielle stopped to wish well upon her worthy adversary. She imagined how sweet Erica's dreams must have been as her head rested on the same pillow as Gabriel's. But this time, amazingly, she felt not even the tiniest twinge of jealousy, only gladness and gratitude. So she made a wish for the dewy young lovers, that they may never take for granted the enrapturing love they'd found. And then she kissed his bride on the forehead as well.

Just as she was about to float away, Erica stirred and yawned as if suddenly aware of her presence, but too sleepy to open her eyes. Arielle whispered in her ear, "Love him with all your soul," and set an intention for eternal happiness for the both of them. Erica's eyelashes fluttered softly, and she sleepily buried her face into her husband's shoulder.

"Forever I will," Erica whispered back, smiling and giggling softly in her half-dreaming state. And as Arielle looked upon the woman who had ultimately bested her, she knew that the words she spoke were genuine. So she kissed her once again and in a glimmer of light, disappeared through their canopy and into the dawn's pink skies. Just like that, she was gone from their lives forever.

Suddenly roused from her sleep, Erica sat up and looked around the room, adjusting to the morning light. She could've sworn she'd heard a girl's voice, but there was no one else in there except her snoozing sweetheart. Sleepily, she reached for her white silk robe and set her feet down off the bed. Groggily, she tiptoed towards the door, but the creak of the wooden floors woke her husband up. "Where are you going, beauty?" he asked as he sat up and rubbed his eyes.

"Where's Arielle?" she asked as she tied her robe.

"Sleeping," he answered curiously. But Erica looked somewhat worried, simply and intuitively shaking her head 'no.' Eyeing his new wife quizzically, Gabriel jumped up, pulled on a pair of pants followed her out. They were on a boat, after all, and there were only so many places their little friend could be hiding. But when they arrived at her door that was open just a crack, they saw that her bed and her room were empty.

The blankets were turned over but just as Erica had already somehow known, they hadn't been slept in. On her night table sat Gabriel's harmonica and on her pillow sat her priceless necklace, the only thing she'd come into their life wearing.

They searched all the rooms of the ship but she was nowhere to be found. The sunrise had already begun drying the dew off the decks, and they stood up on the top one, looking out to the glimmering waters. Then, just a few yards from the side of their grand vessel, she saw Arielle's nightie floating on the waves.

She gasped and leaned into her new husband. With heavy hearts, they both watched it drift away from the ship while they both came to understand that their little dancer was gone. As mysteriously and unexpectedly as she had come into their lives, she had now departed. They knew in their hearts that that was the last they'd ever see of her in this life. How terribly they already missed her.

The little mermaid blew them kisses as she floated up and up, in the arms and by the wings of her dear mother. Together, they sang songs of beauty, renewal, and the persistence of love. After all, it was love that had led a little mermaid to transcend her oceanic existence, and it was love that now carried her spirit up into the next realm. The little mermaid's soul would have an eternity to love, after all.

*the End.*

## Acknowledgements:

I have written a fresh version of my favourite old story for the new souls of my day to enjoy, that we may keep this gorgeous fairytale alive, as reflected through the eyes of this modern world.

Many people believed in me and supported me while I channeled and meditated upon the piece I was creating. To them I am eternally grateful, and it is with them in mind that I make this and any future contributions to the world's collective trove of works of imagination.

Elise M., my Phoenix, my designer, friend, and muse – thanks for sharing your vision and your talent to help me bring this piece from a scattered document into a beautiful book. Your encouragement saw me through the most discouraging of days. I am honoured to have created something with you.

Odette M., thanks for the time you took to read and edit this manuscript. Your keen eye was most helpful, and I am forever grateful.

Jessica H., thanks for being the dear friend who so thoroughly looked over my early draft. You were always wonderful like that.

My amazing mom & dad, Howie & Anh. Thanks for raising me in a safe and lovely realm of love where imagination and creativity are honoured. I am who I am because of you two!

Light, gratitude, and pretty thoughts for all.

Love,

*Leslie*

www.ingramcontent.com/pod-product-compliance
Lightning Source LLC
Chambersburg PA
CBHW070615260626

47161CB00007B/2445